A **JAKE PALMER** NOVEL

ASSASSIN'S MACE

RON McMANUS

Copyright © 2026 Ron McManus

All rights reserved.

No part of this publication in print or in electronic format may be reproduced, stored in a retrieval system, or transmitted in any form or by any means, electronic, mechanical, photocopying, recording, or otherwise without the prior written permission of the publisher.

NO AI/NO BOT. The author does not consent to any Artificial Intelligence (AI), generative AI, large language model, machine learning, chatbot, or other automated analysis, generative process, or replication program to reproduce, mimic, remix, summarize, or otherwise replicate any part of this creative work, via any means: print, graphic, sculpture, multimedia, audio, or other medium. We support the right of humans to control their artistic ability.

This is a work of fiction. Names, characters, organizations, places, events and incidents are either the products of the author's imagination or are used fictitiously. Any resemblance to actual persons, living or dead, or actual events is purely coincidental.

BAY BEACH
BOOKS

Published by Bay Beach Books
Design and distribution by Bublish

ISBN: 979-8-89989-124-3 (Paperback)
ISBN: 979-8-89989-123-6 (eBook)

To Robert Meade Armfield, a retired law enforcement officer,
as well as my friend and brother-in-law, who passed away
as I was finishing the final draft of this book.

ABBREVIATIONS AND ACRONYMS

AI: Artificial Intelligence

CIA: Central Intelligence Agency

DEFCON: Defense Readiness Condition

DGSE: General Directorate for External Security (France's foreign intelligence agency)

DoD: Department of Defense

EMTs: Emergency Medical Technicians

FSB: Federal Security Service (the Russian Federation's security agency)

GU: Main Intelligence Directorate (Russia's military intelligence agency, previously and still commonly called GRU)

ISI: Inter-Services Intelligence Agency (Pakistan's military intelligence service)

JSOC: Joint Special Operations Command

KIA: Killed in Action

MI6: Military Intelligence, Section 6 (the United Kingdom's secret intelligence service)

MIRV: Multiple Independently Targetable Reentry Vehicle

NOC: Nonofficial Cover

SCIF: Sensitive Compartmented Information Facility

SOCOM: Special Operations Command

SUPO: Finnish Security and Intelligence Service (Finland's national intelligence agency)

VPN: Virtual Private Network

Arctic Circle
SWEDEN
NORWAY
Oslo
Stockholm
DENMARK
Copenhagen
Baltic

Kola Peninsula
FINLAND
Helsinki
Gulf of Finland
Tallinn
ESTONIA
Saint Petersburg
RUSSIA
Moscow
LATVIA
Rīga
LITHUANIA
Vilnius
RUSSIA
Minsk

PROLOGUE

This novel is set against the backdrop of Russia's special military operation, which began on February 24, 2022, when President Vladimir Putin announced the operation to "demilitarize and denazify" Ukraine. At that time, Putin asserted that Russia had no plans to occupy the country.

Following Russia's invasion of Ukraine, Finland closed nine of its major border crossings on its 830-mile border with Russia. This restricted access to Russian tourists after many Russian men fled their country and traveled to Finland to escape conscription into the army. Finland's NATO membership was approved on April 4, 2023. In November 2023, all but the northernmost border crossings closed following a surge in asylum seekers, which Finland characterized as part of a "hybrid operation." Finland's prime minister stated, "Russia is enabling the instrumentalization of people and guiding them to the Finnish border in harsh winter conditions. Finland is determined to put an end to this phenomenon." In April 2024, Finland closed all border crossings indefinitely.

During this same period, a race was ongoing to develop and deploy next-generation hypersonic missiles. Unlike the current hypersonic missiles, which follow a predictable path to their target, these new missiles can maneuver, making them difficult to intercept and destroy. Russia and China possessed multiple iterations of hypersonic missiles, including MIRVs (multiple independently targetable reentry vehicles), while the US lagged two years behind. India, North Korea, Iran, France, and the UK were also making progress.

With the Russia-Ukraine war still ongoing in late September 2025, the leaders of Russia, China, and North Korea gathered in China for a military parade and a display of solidarity against the United States.

★ x ★

PART 1

1

NEAR THE PAKISTAN-IRANIAN BORDER
KHUZDĀR, PAKISTAN

The stealth US Army Black Hawk helicopter tore through the sky over the Kolāchi River, slicing through the narrow valley in the Pab mountain range like a predator on the hunt. Jake Palmer was strapped in tight, his arms crossed over his chest. Beside him sat Alona Green, also clad head-to-toe in full tactical gear; Palmer was armed with a Sig Sauer P226 9mm pistol and an H&K MP7 submachine gun, and Green with a Glock 19 9mm pistol and an MP5 submachine gun. This wasn't Palmer's show to command or to fight. That burden fell to their fellow passengers, eight US Joint Special Operations Command—known as JSOC—Army Delta Force operators, with their grips firm on their HK416 or M4A1 assault rifles, solid choices for the rough, brutal dance of close-quarters combat they anticipated.

Delta Force's primary objective was to capture or kill Al-Mansour. During and since the Afghan war, his network had carried out hundreds of attacks, including one on the US Embassy in Kabul, which later closed. Al-Mansour's reign of terror had no bounds. Palmer and Green were assigned to the operation to gather critical intelligence from the terrorist compound.

All this took Palmer back to his days as a Navy SEAL. The feeling was the same—the cold zip of adrenaline, the reassuring weight of his tactical gear—but missing was the distinctive, thunderous roar of an engine and the familiar whomp-whomp-whomp of rotors. No, this bird was stealth incarnate: shorter, with a five-blade rotor instead of four, and a much quieter engine. Everything had been engineered to minimize its acoustic signature and hide its presence on radar.

Palmer and Green were officers in JSOC's Task Force Orange, a ghostly entity that went by many other names—Intelligence Support Activity, the Activity, Gray Fox, and the Army of Northern Virginia. Its official mission was to harvest actionable intelligence for Tier 1 special operations units under JSOC's command, including the Army's Delta Force, the Air Force's Twenty-Fourth Special Tactics Squadron, and the Naval Special Warfare Development Group, or DEVGRU, better known as SEAL Team Six. However, when fate demanded it, Orange operators were also thrust into combat operations.

Before boarding the Black Hawk, Palmer had introduced himself and Green to the Deltas.

"A former SEAL, huh? Nice tan, surfer boy," quipped one of the Deltas as the others laughed.

"Good thing this op is on land. You guys can't swim. How's your golf game?" Palmer asked, knowing that the Army's Delta Force is headquartered in Fayetteville, North Carolina, with some members living in or near the golfing mecca of Pinehurst.

"Good enough to take a few skins from you," the Delta countered, using a golf term involving who wins or loses each hole.

Although fifteen to twenty years older than them, Palmer was a testament to relentless discipline, which had resulted in a body shaped by rigorous daily workouts and grueling runs. He stood tall and erect, a figure of authority and camaraderie, and could walk the walk and talk the talk with the best of them. He yearned for this fierce brotherhood he once knew, where the bonds transcended the professional and bound them together as a family forged in the crucible of combat.

They had flown southwest, skimming Pakistan's border with Iran toward their destination, Khuzdār, Pakistan, a town of around one hundred thousand—one of whom, Ibrahim Al-Mansour, was a designated global terrorist. As the leader of the Sunni Muslim separatist group Jaysh al-Adl, Al-Mansour operated within the rugged terrains of Iran's Sistan and Balochistan provinces and Pakistan's Baloch-majority areas in its Balochistan province. Always on the move and staying a step ahead, Al-Mansour occasionally sheltered in Khuzdār, where he had grown up.

Intel suggested that the town harbored Al-Mansour's loyalists—family and friends who were well armed and willing to die for him. That didn't guarantee their target would be there, too, however. Al-Mansour had survived because of his cunning and ruthless power. He frequently changed locations and operated under at least fifteen aliases and multiple birth dates. Despite the FBI's $10-million bounty on his head, Pakistan's government had long turned a blind eye, benefiting from his Sunni terrorist network to achieve its regional objectives. That was no longer the case. His recent attacks on Pakistani security forces had changed the game. Now Pakistan was willing to turn a blind eye not to Al-Mansour but to the United States, even clearing a path for their mission.

A tenacious CIA targeter in Islamabad, where Palmer and Green were based, had the unenviable task of pinpointing Al-Mansour's location, which he described as a whack-a-mole exercise. He had worked with Palmer and Green on assimilating intelligence regarding Al-Mansour from various sources since their assignment in Islamabad almost two years prior. One of his key sources was a Pakistani asset who monitored Al-Mansour's residence in Khuzdār. Just three days ago, this asset had confirmed that Al-Mansour had returned to his Khuzdār compound. He provided daily reports of his movements in Khuzdār and sent photos of him entering and leaving the compound. The targeting officer submitted a request and received approval to capture rather than kill Al-Mansour due to the value of the intel he could provide.

Previous requests had either been rejected by Pakistan or were delayed in the approval process for so long that by the time permission was granted, Al-Mansour had moved on. A debate had occurred regarding whether to use a drone strike or a missile attack on the building instead of sending in a team of special operators to capture Al-Mansour. In consultation with the president, the US Special Operations Command—SOCOM—concluded that capturing Al-Mansour was preferable to an air strike and deemed it worth the risk.

"We're approaching the landing zone in the foothills outside Khuzdār," the pilot said, speaking into the headsets of those aboard. "Prepare to disembark."

The bird touched down fifteen minutes later, at exactly 0300. The operation was scheduled to take ninety minutes, with extraction planned before sunrise.

Of the eight Delta Force operators, two remained with the helicopter's flight crew and deployed three small AI quadcopter surveillance and reconnaissance drones, each equipped with infrared sensors. The semiautonomous drones monitored any human or vehicle movement within a predefined area. When movement was detected, the drones autonomously zoomed in on the threat without human input. Two of the drones flew ahead of the team toward Al-Mansour's compound, disappearing into the clear moonless sky. Once there, the drones would hover, and the drone operator would provide live updates on the compound and surrounding area to the team. A third drone ascended straight up, where it would monitor movement within a one-mile radius of the Black Hawk.

Palmer and Green trailed behind the team of six as they moved away from the landing zone, situated approximately three miles from the compound. Palmer walked behind Green, slightly to her right, while the operator controlling the drones relayed that their path to the target was clear.

A howling wind whipped through the valley, stirring up sand as gritty as peppercorn. Khuzdār, perched at four thousand feet, saw little rain, and previous reconnaissance had revealed that the area surrounding the compound, on the southern edge of the town, offered scant cover for their approach.

They were within sight of the compound when the team leader, Army Master Sergeant Brown, raised a right-handed fist, a silent command to halt and remain quiet. He directed a red laser on a trip wire end to end, signaling them to step over it. Each complied and continued toward the compound's entrance.

Narrow balconies jutted out from the second and third floors, and an imposing eight-foot wall encircled the structure. The others were modest one- or two-story buildings, including those near the compound.

Palmer furrowed his brow at the sight. There was no guard on watch outside the gate. A man with such a substantial bounty on his head warranted constant vigilance. Had years of securing Al-Mansour's safety bred complacency in his security team, or were they chasing a red herring?

The six Deltas, Palmer, and Green closed in as they neared the gate, approaching swiftly. They were within fifty meters when a floodlight blinked on, probably triggered by a motion detector. A single guard holding a rifle stepped out onto a second floor balcony. Master Sergeant Brown held up his clenched fist and pointed to one of his teammates. The guard held his rifle firmly on his shoulder, aiming out as he scanned the area, the barrel following a trajectory that led directly to Task Force Orange.

Palmer, Green, and the rest of the team froze. Before the guard's aim reached them, the Delta Force operator whom Brown had pointed to took him out with a suppressed round and then shot out the floodlights. With the floodlights off and one man down, the team rushed the short distance to the entrance gate of the compound, where one of the operators compromised the lock.

Two Delta Force operators remained on watch, one just inside the gate and the other at the entrance to the building. The remaining four, with their night vision goggles activated, stood at the entrance, with Palmer and Green close behind them. The point operator tested the front door; it was unlocked. He pushed it open and stepped aside. The rusty hinges squeaked, and a burst of gunfire erupted from inside. So much for a quiet entry. One of the operators tossed a flash-bang grenade inside, closed the door, and moved to the side. The resulting explosion was thunderous, even outside the building. They entered a smoke-filled room. The men near the blast would have been deafened. If the tangos' gunfire hadn't jolted a good portion of Khuzdār out of their sleep, the flash-bang had.

Palmer and Green stayed near the entrance as the team cleared the first floor rooms. One by one, the Delta Force operators took out Al-Mansour's men with disciplined, accurate double-taps, using sound-suppressed rounds. One operator fired through the door as it was opening, even before another guard appeared. The Deltas cleared each room before moving up the stairs.

Palmer, who had participated in many clearing operations, yearned to be part of the team breaking down doors and clearing the building rather than relegated to a secondary role. However, in special forces operations, everyone had a specific job to perform, such as the two operators who remained behind to provide surveillance and communications around the compound as well as security for the Black Hawk and its crew. One of the operators on the second floor motioned for Palmer and Green to come up. They stepped over two bodies on the landing.

The four Deltas were on the stairs leading to the third floor when a solitary gunshot emanating from the top floor echoed through the building. Palmer watched as two Delta Force operators stormed the third and final story, shouting, "Clear!"

Palmer and Green were beckoned to the upstairs room moments later and were met at once with the harsh metallic smell of blood. Palmer stood by the body lying face up on the floor, a pistol nearby. Blood had pooled around the upper torso and was soaking into the rug. The top of his head had been blown away.

The body fit the description Palmer had been provided of Al-Mansour—a small man, five foot seven and 150 pounds. One of the operators took photos while another collected DNA samples. During the planning of the op, the team had decided that if they killed Al-Mansour, his body would be left where he had fallen.

The lead Delta Force operator told Palmer that Al-Mansour had died from a self-inflicted gunshot from the pistol. Palmer shook his head. Suicide was a flagrant contradiction of Islam, which taught "Kill not your own selves." But apparently Al-Mansour had concluded that, given the choice, he would rather die by his own hand than be captured or die at the hand of an enemy. His suicide notwithstanding, he would be treated within Islam as a martyr.

Green briefly cast her eyes down at the body as she walked toward a long table against the wall on one side of the bedroom. Palmer joined her. Green looked at him and said, "We've hit the jackpot."

On the table lay a laptop computer, flash drives, documents, and what was possibly Al-Mansour's cell phone. The cell phone and laptop were damaged; perhaps he had tried to destroy them and had run out of time. They had brought canvas bags with them, and with the help of one of the operators, they searched the room and gathered up everything that appeared the least bit useful. Before leaving, they checked each room for additional intelligence and grabbed anything they found, including the dead terrorists' cell phones, laptops, and devices.

Sergeant Brown's radio crackled, followed by the drone operator's voice: "Estimate twenty to thirty armed hostiles gathering two hundred meters from your location. Another group is breaching the wall on the south side of the compound."

"Roger that. Ready for exfil," the team leader said.

"ETA ten minutes," the drone operator replied.

The Delta Force operators, along with Palmer and Green, took defensive positions at the gate and the second floor windows of Al-Mansour's compound. A moment later, the incoming gunfire began. Initially, most of it was small arms fire, but soon rocket-propelled grenades were launched through the gate and over the wall, exploding near one of the windows where one of the operators had been picking off the men.

The hostiles spread out, using vehicles and buildings for cover.

One of the Deltas shouted, "Ma Deuce!" in warning, referring to an approaching .50-caliber machine gun mounted in the truck bed of a Toyota.

Palmer spotted its advance a second later. It peeled toward the entrance, firing as it approached, seemingly with no specific target in mind. Palmer and Green shifted behind the wall as a series of rounds struck nearby. Fragments ricocheted off Palmer's helmet. The .50-cal's large rounds slamming into the compound wall overwhelmed every other sound, including the Black Hawk, which seemed to appear out of nowhere. It hovered at about five hundred feet and began strafing the enemy positions with its twin M134 miniguns, each capable of firing two thousand to six thousand rounds a minute.

The Black Hawk's fire was on the Toyota before moving toward the other targets. An M261 explosive rocket with smoke came last. Using the smoke as cover, the Black Hawk set down at the compound entrance. The rotor downwash billowed sand and smoke away from it and toward the attackers. With the two drone operators providing covering fire, all were quickly aboard, and the bird lifted off.

—◈—

Two hours later, after disembarking at a US base in Karachi, Pakistan, about two hundred miles south of Khuzdār, Palmer shook Green's hand. "Well done, partner."

A nervous smile appeared as she replied, "Thanks. That was intense. I've never experienced anything quite like that."

"You never get accustomed to it, but with time, you learn how to do your job amid the chaos. Much of it comes from total confidence in your teammates doing their job and having your back."

Green nodded. "Well, the job isn't finished until the paperwork's done. We have a lot of intel to go through and communicate."

Palmer groaned. "Don't remind me."

The processing and analysis of the intelligence were best left to the experts. He greatly appreciated the people who did that work. He would stay for the initial overview of what they had and provide input if required, but he was no desk jockey. He didn't have the patience for it. Fortunately, much of it would fall on Dan Adams and his team of technical specialists, who reported to Green.

Palmer didn't ask Green if she was okay, just as he would never ask one of the Delta Force operators if they were okay. Green was as tough as they come. He knew she was all right.

—◈—

With assistance from other embassy-based intelligence officers and local translators fluent in Balochi, Pashto, and Sindhi, thousands of pieces of intelligence collected at Khuzdār were cataloged, reviewed, and shared. This included access to mobile phones, computers, and other devices. Most of the information focused on the separatist movement in Iran and on relations between Pakistan, Afghanistan, and Iran. Smaller amounts of intelligence related to the Russia-Ukraine war, Iran, the Houthi rebels, and the Pakistan-India conflict. Various US intelligence agencies, such as the Office of the Director of National Intelligence, the National Security Agency, the National Geospatial-Intelligence Agency, and the CIA, along with the five Department of Defense services (army, navy, air force, marines, coast guard, and space force), analyzed the data and integrated it into their threat assessment databases.

With fewer than one hundred days remaining on his two-year JSOC contract, Palmer had no other ops on the books. He was now, in military terms, a short-timer or a double-digit midget. He could cruise through the rest of his contract, and although he had no regrets, he was glad it was almost over. He could begin to focus his attention on his forthcoming nuptials with Fiona Collins and on establishing his contract business in Europe.

2

THE BOSCO CAFÉ
MOSCOW, RUSSIA

Dmitry Nikolaev Sokolov was in his late fifties and had honed his craft for nearly thirty years. He was at the peak of his game—and a deadly game it was. He carried the quiet confidence of someone who had spent decades solving impossible problems. His presence commanded respect in any room. Sokolov's once-thick brown hair was thinning and streaked with silver while his blue eyes still burned with the intensity of a man who had stared at the edge of innovation. He was at the pinnacle of Russian aerospace engineering—the mind behind the new generation of hypersonic missiles that had redefined modern warfare.

After a long day of meetings with Kremlin power brokers, Sokolov was ready to unwind. He had a few more meetings scheduled for the following day in Moscow, after which he would return to Saint Petersburg, where he lived and worked. Although it was a bit early for dinner, he asked his driver to take him to the Bosco Café in Red Square and wait for him.

Upon entering, the maître d' smiled and greeted Sokolov by name with a firm handshake, followed by a theatrical sweep of his arm and an upturned hand, directing him toward the bar. Though a frequent visitor to the restaurant, Sokolov paused to take in the lavish Italian interior and the striking views of Saint Basil's Cathedral, Lenin's Mausoleum, and the Kremlin. The magnificent Murano glass chandelier, designed by the Seguso family in Venice, set the tone, as did the faint aroma of coffee from the café's espresso maker. The bar was busier than usual, given the time of day. On his way, Sokolov nodded briefly and smiled at the pianist as the soft notes of Rachmaninoff's Concerto No. 2 played, providing a soothing backdrop to the hum of conversation.

Sokolov settled into his seat at the bar. The bartender, Grigory, already had Sokolov's favorite Mamont Siberian vodka in hand and poured it from its woolly mammoth tusk-shaped bottle into the shot glass he had set on the bar. "How are you this evening?"

"Very well, thank you. Only this vodka could improve my day, Grigory," Sokolov replied with a faint smile.

Sokolov downed his first two shots, as was the custom. The bartender lingered, poised to pour a third, when Sokolov felt a slight shove from his right. A young man wearing what Sokolov judged to be an off-the-rack department store suit had jostled between him and the patron next to him and was now leaning forward against the bar. "Stoli, please," the man said in accented Russian.

Sokolov shook his head. *Americans. They all drink Stolichnaya.*

The bartender glanced at Sokolov and rolled his eyes, then placed the Mamont bottle on the bar. He retrieved the Stolichnaya, poured a shot into a glass for the man, and waited as he drank it. Turning to Sokolov, he held up the Mamont bottle toward his shot glass in a silent question. Sokolov shook his head.

Grigory poured a second shot for the young man, who then promptly turned to Sokolov, raised his shot glass, and said, "*Za zdorovie." To your health.* He downed the shot and said, "Hello, I'm Patrick Howell."

"Dmitry. What brings you to Moscow, Mr. Howell?" Sokolov asked in Russian.

"I took a job at an international company that has offices here to improve my Russian language skills," Howell responded in Russian that sounded a little too enunciated and stilted to be native. It was still clear enough, though, Sokolov supposed.

"So it's a long-term role."

Howell laughed. "I've studied the language, but nothing compares to being immersed in it and the Russian culture. It's a wonderful opportunity."

"I don't see as many Americans in Russia as in the past."

"So I've discovered. Most moved out after the special military operation began," Howell replied.

Pointing at the bottle from which Grigory had poured Howell's drink, Sokolov said, "You shouldn't drink that swill. It's not even Russian. The anti-Russian owner officially rebranded it Stoli for sale outside of Russia because the Americans were boycotting it."

Sokolov turned to the bartender and held up two fingers. Grigory poured Mamont shots for both.

Sokolov offered a toast before they drank it.

Howell exhaled and looked at the shot glass. "That's amazing."

They continued talking for several minutes about Moscow, vodka, and the weather. After an initial negative impression, Sokolov had warmed up to the young American.

Howell glanced at his watch, his eyes now a little glassy. "Oh no. I'm sorry. Please excuse me. I'm meeting a colleague for dinner. The time has flown by. I'm going to be late if I don't leave now."

"You should have eaten here. It's the best in Moscow."

"I've heard that. A coworker said that it would be impossible to get a dinner reservation on short notice but that I should stop by for a drink. I'm glad I did. It's magnificent but way out of my price range."

"If I see you here again, I'll buy you a drink and treat you to dinner."

"That would be wonderful. Thank you." *You will see me again if I have anything to do with it*, Howell thought as he turned and walked away.

⁓

A couple of weeks later, Sokolov was again in Moscow for meetings and went to the Bosco Café. He was pleasantly surprised to spot Patrick Howell seated at the bar near where they had sat before. They shook hands and chatted briefly. Sokolov asked Howell to join him for dinner, to which he agreed, and soon they were seated at a table away from the bar, enjoying their wine while waiting for the main course.

Howell wiped his mouth with a napkin after savoring a bite of the blini with beluga caviar starter that Sokolov had ordered for them and said, "I haven't asked, but I assume you live in Moscow?"

"No. I live and work in Saint Petersburg," Sokolov said. "My work brings me here quite frequently."

"What business are you in?"

Sokolov paused. The American's candor took him by surprise. "I'm an aerospace engineer. I work on our missile development program," he replied, being cautious about what he told him. He had been involved in Russia's missile development for most of his career and was one of the most respected experts on new-generation hypersonic missiles in the world. He was the general director and chief designer at the Saint Petersburg Hypersonic System Research Institute, with overall responsibility for the development of Russia's missile armament, including its new-generation hypersonic missiles. The president of Russia, who was on a first-name basis with Sokolov, awarded him the Mikhail Kalashnikov Medal for excellence in innovation in the design, manufacturing, and commissioning of modern weapons and military equipment.

Howell sat back in his chair. "Wow. A rocket scientist. That's remarkable. I've read that Russia is leading the world in developing and deploying hypersonic missiles. You must be a busy man."

"Indeed, I am." Sokolov's defenses were up. He didn't like where this might be headed.

"This may be politically incorrect to ask, but I'm curious," Howell went on, taking a sip of his red wine. He seemed none the wiser to Sokolov's suspicions. "A lot of missiles were fired into Ukraine during the special military operation. It's a fact that countless lives were lost on both sides, including innocent civilians. What's your opinion of the war?"

Sokolov set his fork down on the plate and slid his chair back from the table. That was not a question to ask a Russian, particularly one who held a senior position in its government—and certainly not in a restaurant where someone might overhear the conversation.

"I'm not going to answer that. Instead, I'll ask you a question," Sokolov began, pinning Howell in place with his stare. Howell didn't flinch. "You said you worked at an international company. What is the name of that company, Mr. Howell?"

"I work at the US Embassy as a travel and entertainment coordinator."

Sokolov's brow furrowed, and he pressed his lips together. The response felt rehearsed. He leaned toward Howell and said in a whisper, "Travel and entertainment coordinator may be your cover job, but you're CIA, aren't you?"

Howell didn't respond. That was answer enough.

"Leave. Now."

Howell stood, reached into his shirt pocket, and handed Sokolov a business card. Sokolov shook his head and sat back in his chair. Howell placed the card on the table in front of Sokolov and tapped his index finger on a phone number. The rest of the card was blank. "Text that number if you ever want to continue our conversation."

Sokolov pointed his finger at Howell and said, in Russian, "*Ya bol'she ne khochu tebya videt.*" *I never want to see you again.*

He ripped the card in half and threw it on the floor.

After Howell left, Sokolov glanced at the two pieces of the card on the floor. If someone found them and remembered where he had sat, they might report the incident to the FSB—Russia's Federal Security Service and the successor to the KGB that disbanded in 1991. He picked up the pieces and put them in his jacket pocket. Sokolov was no politician, never one to court favor. He lived for the science, for the sheer thrill of bending physics to his will. But in Russia, even the brightest minds could not remain apolitical forever. He had seen colleagues disappear, projects classified beyond his reach, and whispers of internal power struggles that had little to do with science and everything to do with control.

He carried a weariness in him, an understanding that genius alone was insufficient to survive in his world. He knew too much, had built weapons that were too dangerous, and in the Kremlin's eyes, that made him either invaluable or expendable.

How could I have been so naive? Intelligence officers from numerous countries were always on the prowl for potential recruits as foreign agents. Russians were required to report any contact with an individual suspected of being a foreign intelligence officer. Should he report it the next morning? He'd suspected nothing at their initial meeting, and at the second, he questioned Howell, who admitted to working at the US Embassy. And Howell didn't deny he was CIA.

I'm not going to report it, Sokolov rationalized. However, he suspected that the FSB wouldn't have had the same interpretation of the requirement or of his failure to report his interactions with the American.

The next day, he returned home to Saint Petersburg and went straight to his study, where he took the two pieces of the card out of his jacket pocket and examined them. He taped them together, wrote Patrick Howell's name under the phone number, and hid the card.

★ 19 ★

3

RUSSIAN FEDERATION FEDERAL SECURITY SERVICE HEADQUARTERS MOSCOW, RUSSIA

Colonel Vladislav "Vlad" Maksimov, director of Russia's FSB counterintelligence group, massaged his forehead as he read through his team's monthly report. Appointed to the post after his predecessor was fired the previous year, his current priority was to monitor the Russian scientists and engineers working on hypersonic missile development. There were hundreds, if not thousands, of them.

After reading through the team's monthly report not once, but twice, and determining for certain it warranted escalation, he reluctantly entered the office of his boss, Colonel General Sergey Vasilyev of the FSB. Maksimov had the sense that this would be an uncomfortable encounter. Vasilyev, who reported directly to Russia's president, had overall responsibility for the FSB, including surveillance, border security, counterterrorism, and Maksimov's counterintelligence unit. Like Maksimov, he had also been on the job for a little over a year. That was when the president cleaned house and placed the former head under house arrest. His crime? The president reproached the FSB for the poor intel that preceded the invasion of Ukraine. The logistics of the initial operation had failed miserably. Even though Russia's foreign intelligence service and its military intelligence service had also been involved in providing the intel, the FSB took the brunt of the blame.

The meeting got off to a bad start when Vasilyev informed Maksimov that the president was dissatisfied with his team's arrest record. The hypersonic missile program was the president's pride and joy, and nothing would stop him from preserving the lead Russia had over the Americans. The president suspected that spies were providing the Americans with information about the missiles that could reduce or even eliminate Russia's two-year lead in developing them.

"I understand the importance of the hypersonic missile program; however, I respectfully disagree regarding our record." Moving closer to the desk and attempting to keep his voice and demeanor calm, Maksimov continued, "We have a watch list, and I meet with my senior staff to review it. The list includes hundreds of people. I've established surveillance of those at the top of the list domestically. Surveillance is doubled when they attend professional meetings outside the Russian Federation, although approval for foreign travel is rare. Over the past ten years, the FSB counterintelligence group has arrested over two hundred suspects, a quarter of whom were individuals spying for a foreign government, and the remaining were foreign intelligence service officers. The number of arrests has increased significantly under my watch."

Vasilyev moved around the desk and stood close to Maksimov. "I made the same point with the president and got nowhere," he said, tone clipped. Maksimov knew then that there would be no further debate on this topic. "He wants every scientist and engineer working on missile development to be interrogated and anyone who seems the least bit suspicious arrested. He is furious about the recent defections. He told me that if he hears of another one, he will once again make major leadership changes."

Maksimov hesitated before responding. Vasilyev was worried about his own job security, not that of others, which set them at odds. Maksimov's response could affect his own fate. He needed to be firm in his response, not argumentative, instead offering a solution that would satisfy Vasilyev and the president. "I—"

"This is not a request, Colonel Maksimov," Vasilyev interrupted. "This is a directive from the president and me. If you can't carry it out, we'll find someone who will."

"If he wants more arrests, he'll get them," Maksimov snapped, and Vasilyev's eyes widened just a fraction, indicating he'd stepped out of line. "That's easy enough if you don't care about the guilt or innocence of those arrested."

"Don't get smart with me," Vasilyev said sharply.

Maksimov calmed himself. "Arresting more scientists and engineers will result in fewer people working on the projects, especially the senior staff, who we'll prioritize and arrest first. To make arrests that are likely to hold up, we need to boost our surveillance and interrogation efforts. If the president is solely interested in numbers, we'll focus on lower-level staff who have a much smaller impact on development and production. If I'm ordered to target those already working with a foreign agent or in contact with a foreign intelligence officer, that's a different order." He hesitated. "Those men recently arrested for treason had published journal articles *after* state secrets review approval to do so. Either way, I'll need more resources."

"What type?" Vasilyev asked.

"The hypersonic missile program is massive and based at multiple facilities throughout the country. I'll need additional men for my counterintelligence team, specifically those trained in electronic surveillance. They'll plant listening devices in the homes and cars of high-level scientists and engineers and hack their phones. That approach would be more proactive than simply interrogating them, and it would increase the number of arrests. As for interrogations, we'll start at the top of the priority list now and work our way down as we receive additional resources. For those at the top of the list—the ones who would cause the most havoc if they defected or became spies—I want to put at least one or two men on them at home and whenever they are on the move. I'll work up the numbers and send them to you this afternoon."

Vasilyev's expression relaxed slightly. "You'd better be right, Colonel. I'll see to the transfer of electronic surveillance staff and qualified interrogators. Set up weekly status meetings with me." He paused, eyeing Vasilyev critically. "One more thing. If you identify someone in the process of defecting, don't let them leave Russia. If it's not possible to capture them, you have the president's permission to eliminate any potential defector and any foreign intelligence officer working with them. Use the FSB assassination team or Unit 29155, if necessary."

"I need Unit 29155 in on this now. After we begin interrogating, the word will get out, and the spies and their case officers will move quickly to organize defections to ensure their safety. The rats will run for the border. We must have 29155 in place."

Vasilyev put his hand on Maksimov's shoulder. "I'll notify the head of the FSB Border Service to increase their monitoring. I'll also assign someone from Unit 29155 to work with you. Those madmen will eliminate the traitors before they leave Russia or after. Borders make little difference to them."

"I don't want just anyone—I want Nikolai Ivanov." They both knew Ivanov was the most feared sniper in Unit 29155's stable. A feared Spetsnaz sniper, who still held the record for number of kills. He was known unofficially as an assassin's assassin.

Vasilyev scoffed. "That's impossible. He's booked up for months."

Maksimov folded his arms and locked his gaze on Vasilyev, allowing his silence to speak for him.

Vasilyev sighed, then shook his head. "Okay, I'll see what I can do."

The new recruits for Maksimov's counterintelligence team arrived shortly after he met with Vasilyev. Maksimov established the arrest criteria, the interrogation process, and the timeline for conducting them. His leadership team created a prioritized list of targets and met with Maksimov to review each one, highlighting potential vulnerabilities that could make them more likely to cooperate with the West. After a few minor adjustments, Maksimov approved their recommendations. Before interrogations began, the subjects' homes and cars were wired for audio and visual surveillance. This allowed them to gather intelligence before bringing the subjects in for questioning. A brief phone call with Vasilyev confirmed that Nikolai Ivanov would be transferred upon his return from an assignment in Kazakhstan.

With the enhanced process for interviewing key individuals involved in the hypersonic missile development program established, interviews could commence. Maksimov reviewed the interview schedule for the upcoming month and noted Dmitry Sokolov near the end. Although he didn't know Sokolov well, Maksimov was aware that he was pivotal to the ongoing expansion of the hypersonic missile program. Because he was divorced and had no children or living parents, he had nothing to lose by defecting—no family to leave behind and suffer the physical and financial consequences. Maksimov moved Sokolov up in priority.

4

ASTANA, KAZAKHSTAN

Only a few snipers had the stomach for the *mokrie dela*—or the so-called wet work—that Nikolai Ivanov possessed. A man of average height and looks, the thirty-six-year-old Ivanov attracted little attention from passersby on the street or while enjoying a beer at a bar. He lived in a small comfortable home just outside Vyshny Volochyok, an old merchant town halfway between Saint Petersburg and Moscow that provided him with the solitude he desired. On rare occasions, he drove four hours into Moscow for meetings. Otherwise, he worked from home or traveled to wherever his assignments took him. He enjoyed the company of women but had never married.

Ivanov had served in the Russian army's special operations group, Spetsnaz, where he qualified as a sniper with a long list of kills. The commander of Unit 29155 had contacted him and, following a brief discussion, offered him a position. Ivanov accepted it on the spot, knowing he had just become a full-time assassin.

He was informed that although he would continue to receive assignments from Unit 29155, his priorities would shift to assignments from Colonel Maksimov, the head of FSB counterintelligence. These assignments involved killing defectors who were either actively fleeing Russia or already had. The thought of killing defectors didn't bother Ivanov in the slightest. They deserved no less for the betrayal of Mother Russia. Besides, they knew the risks of such cowardice. He was told that this change would take effect after he completed his current assignment in Kazakhstan.

Ivanov traveled to Kazakhstan's capital city, Astana, for the assignment. Kazakhstan was the world's ninth largest country by land area, and Astana had a population of 1.4 million people. His target was Viktor Mikhailovich, who was scheduled to speak at Park Prezidentskiy Parkovka the following afternoon.

He woke up early the morning after his arrival and had a breakfast of blinis and honey, millet porridge, and fried eggs. After breakfast, he walked from his hotel to the park. It was located on the Ishim River and was one of the biggest parks in the city. A large crowd was expected to attend the speeches. Ironically, the park was the site of the Palace of Peace and Reconciliation.

Ivanov had already thoroughly researched the park's location, examining both the road and the satellite images available online. But still, they were poor substitutes for being there in person, where he could confirm that the spot he had chosen was ideal—close enough to see the speakers but far enough away to remain unseen if anyone looked his way. Security cameras might have been installed, so he walked the area alongside others strolling through the park. He wore a brimmed hat to hide his face. He made a few passes, each time looking from the stage to his selected vantage point. Satisfied that he had made a good choice, he returned to the hotel.

Back in his room, Ivanov packed his bag and set it, along with the case that held all the parts to his VSS Vintorez sniper rifle, by the door. To avoid detection by video surveillance at check-in, he made the reservation online using a false name and received an electronic key on his mobile phone. He wore gloves whenever he was in the room and took no shower or bath while there. He then wiped down every surface he had touched since arriving as well as some he had not. No one could ever place him in the room. The maid would have changed the linens by then. That was one of the reasons he stayed at five-star hotels. The staff thoroughly cleaned the room soon after a guest departed. Even if they determined he had stayed in the room, which was highly unlikely, there would be no DNA evidence or fingerprints indicating that he had ever been there.

He wiped the inside door handle, glanced back into the room for a final check, closed the door, and wiped the outside door handle. As he had done each time he had gone through the lobby, he wore a brimmed hat and kept his head down to avoid being identified by the security cameras in the lobby. Without stopping at the front desk, he got into the waiting car and rode to the location he had selected for the job: a vacant office building facing the stage.

Ivanov's Unit 29155 handler had gathered information about his target, Viktor Mikhailovich, and passed it along to Ivanov, who would memorize every detail to avoid leaving a paper trail or links to the information. Occasionally, he had to operate with minimal details. It was messy, and he didn't prefer to work that way; however, he followed orders. Ivanov's handler had informed him that the assassination must be in a public place with witnesses. The more cell phone videos and news footage, the better. Based on that, he elected to use his sniper rifle.

Ivanov had numerous ways to kill and a wide range of tools at his disposal. A sniper rifle was not his first choice, although he was an expert marksman. He preferred to be close to the victim, using a knife or garrote so that he could see and feel the death, talking to the victim as he or she understood death was inevitable. His least favorite was Novichok—a nerve agent developed by Russian scientists that stopped the heart and diaphragm muscles from functioning, resulting in fluids filling the lungs. The victim would die from heart failure or suffocation.

He regarded it as a coward's weapon. In addition, Novichok linked a death to Russia, as it was a Russian assassin's poison of choice.

Ivanov entered the vacant office building from the alley, wary of any vagrants who might be living inside. He climbed the stairs to the top floor, making his way to the office he had selected, which had a clear view over the trees to the park and stage. He opened the case containing the rifle parts and a sandbag sized to steady the rifle barrel. Examining and wiping down each component as he pieced it together, he assembled the rifle. He then cleaned each bullet with a cloth before loading it into the magazine, ensuring it was pristine and had none of his fingerprints on the brass, in case he left one behind—which he wouldn't.

Once assembled, he held out the rifle and examined it. The gun was identical to those used by the Kazakhstani security forces and was also a favorite among Spetsnaz operators. The VSS Vintorez was loaded with the same 9×39mm subsonic cartridges used by the Kazakhstan military as well as by other countries in the region. The rifle had an integral suppressor that hid the muzzle flash. He had other, more modern, sniper rifles, but this was his favorite. He opened the window and surveyed his view of the podium, content with his choice. He rested the rifle barrel on the sandbag positioned on the window ledge. The bag steadied the rifle by supporting its weight. He then removed the rifle, set it beside him, and waited.

By the time Mikhailovich and the other speakers took their places onstage, several hundred people had already gathered, forming a crowd. The podium lacked bulletproof shields protecting the speakers, and the distance was such that he was confident he could fire a single fatal shot. He relaxed as the crowd settled down during introductions. Ivanov placed his rifle on the sandbag and aimed at the speaker's head in the crosshairs of his scope, adjusting for the distance and the roughly five to eight kilometers per hour of left-to-right wind. He focused on his breathing, taking deep inhales and full exhales to slow his heart rate, and waited until Mikhailovich stepped to the podium and took the microphone from the holder. Even with the loudspeakers amplifying his voice, Ivanov was too far away to hear what he was saying—not that he was listening. The target was animated, walking back and forth across the stage, holding the microphone with his left hand and gesturing with his right. Ivanov tracked him through the scope as he moved. With his view limited to what he saw through the scope, all other distractions faded away.

After a few minutes, Mikhailovich stood still at the podium, head bowed as if checking his notes.

Ivanov exhaled slowly, squeezing the trigger as he did so, and fired the shot. The impact of the high-caliber round reduced Mikhailovich's head to a pink mist, his body thrown backward onto the stage. Blood sprayed those seated behind him. The crowd's collective gasp turned into screams. Two men, perhaps his bodyguards, rushed to him. Ivanov fired two more shots, killing both men. Everyone jumped off the stage and ran with the crowd. Ivanov's focus returned to the room. He closed the window and cleaned up his brass. *Three shots, three brasses.*

He disassembled the rifle and packed it in the case along with the sandbag. At the door, he stopped and looked around the room. Seeing nothing of concern, he wiped off the inside doorknob, closed the door, and wiped off the outside doorknob.

His driver was already waiting outside and popped open the trunk as soon as Ivanov appeared. In a smooth motion, Ivanov placed his gun case inside, shut the lid firmly, and got into the back seat. Neither of them said a word during the ride to the airport. The rifle would be smuggled back into Russia and delivered to his home the next day.

Some might say Ivanov was a paid serial killer, but wasn't that true of all assassins? He was killing for his beloved Russian Federation and getting paid for it. That seemed like a good deal. Occasionally, when weeks went by without an official assignment, he would allow himself to "practice" to keep himself sharp. He'd select a victim at random, following him or her for a few days, setting up the time and location of the kill, and carrying it out. He would be as diligent in the planning and execution of the kill as he would if it were one of his official professional assignments. As with any sport, practice made perfect.

Ivanov pictured his earlier shot, recalling the pink mist of blood, the force knocking the victim's lifeless body backward. With that, he fell sound asleep, a satisfied smile on his face, until the driver woke him at the airport.

5

MOSCOW, RUSSIA

Sokolov was having breakfast in his hotel suite in Moscow when TASS, the Russian News Agency, interrupted the program to broadcast breaking news. The newsreader said, "Three aerodynamic scientists at the Khristianovich Institute of Theoretical and Applied Mechanics in Siberia have reportedly been arrested . . ."

The fork slipped from Sokolov's hand and fell onto the plate, his attention fixed on the television. Those men had worked with him, and he considered each of them a friend. They were honorable men who, like him, had sacrificed much of their personal lives to advance Russia's missile program. He grabbed the remote and turned up the volume.

"The arrests," the newsreader went on, "are related to the scientists' presentations at professional meetings and their published works on Russia's next-generation hypersonic missiles . . ."

Sokolov stood, staring at the television and shaking his head in disbelief.

He didn't understand. Scientists and engineers, by their very nature, were collaborative. Sharing their nonclassified work at professional meetings and with colleagues abroad had never been seen as a crime. They also learned from what they shared. Their presentations and publications would have passed Russia's required reviews for state secrets just as his had in the past. Perhaps they had been arrested because the Kinzhal hypersonic missiles launched from jet aircraft in Ukraine had been shot down by the aging American Patriot missile system, embarrassing the Russian president, who had boasted to the world that the missiles were undefeatable.

A driver met Sokolov at his hotel and took him to a restricted site in Reutov, east of Moscow. The facility was the primary manufacturing location for the Russian Navy's Zircon hypersonic missile, which flew at speeds of Mach 8 and had a range of around 1,000 kilometers, or 621 miles. Testing was complete, and the missile was being deployed on the navy's eleven frigates and twenty-nine nuclear-powered submarines.

Sokolov was taken aback when he entered the conference room to deliver the lead presentation. The president's chief of staff, Alexi Volkov, had called him personally and asked him to speak, highlighting the issues on which the president wanted updates. He mentioned that a few others might also attend, but Sokolov hadn't expected to see all the top military leaders, the head of the Security Council, the director of the FSB, and other high-level presidential advisers. *Why are they here?*

The president sat at the head of the table with Volkov on his left and the head of the Security Council on his right. Remaining seated, he began. "The purpose of this meeting is to give me and the others I invited to attend assurance that the Zircon missile is truly invincible and that the aggressive production and deployment goals that I provided you will be met."

Sokolov stood. "I can assure you and the others that all Zircon missile production goals have been met, and it is ready for full deployment. With respect to invincibility, the enemy may intercept a small percentage, but the maneuverability of the missile makes it very difficult to defend against. The issues related to our earlier hypersonic missile, the Kinzhal, first used against the Ukrainians, have been addressed with the Zircon." Sokolov and others from his team responded to questions and concerns, giving the president confidence to deploy the missile.

Before adjourning, the president congratulated Sokolov on successfully testing and initially deploying the Oreshnik MIRV—multiple independently targeted reentry vehicle—missile. It had been used in Ukraine with a chilling effect. The Oreshnik, Russian for hazelnut tree, was the peak of Sokolov's career. The missile flew at Mach 10, or 4,700 miles per hour, and carried six submunitions—nuclear and nonnuclear warheads. Only the nonnuclear missiles had been tested and used in Ukraine.

Sokolov was finding it hard to resist his urge to ask about the arrests of his three colleagues and the negative impact this would have on the overall hypersonic missile program. Surely it was on the attendees' minds as well. But bringing it up would only inspire the president to go off on the same tirade he always did about traitors in their midst.

Ultimately, Sokolov didn't ask.

The president didn't discuss the arrests, and no one dared ask him to.

After the meeting, the facility director left to show the president and his team around the building. Sokolov stayed behind and used the empty conference room to catch up on a few things. He bent down to grab his laptop from his briefcase and noticed an envelope on the floor at the far end of the table, near where the president and Volkov had been seated.

Sokolov walked around the table, picked up the envelope, and returned to his seat. He held it in his hands and examined it. The envelope was void of a label or any writing and was secured by only a single clasp. The right thing to do was to phone Volkov. Perhaps the envelope contained information concerning the arrests of his three colleagues. Should he open it? He could say that he didn't know to whom the envelope belonged and had opened it to identify whose it was. What he really wanted to know was if it contained any information about the recent arrests.

Sokolov carefully unfastened the clasp, took out the papers inside, and fanned through them. It was his missile production data report he had sent to the president. He was nearing the bottom of the stack and about to put the papers back in the envelope when he noticed a separate document marked Top Secret. He studied the report, unconsciously taking deep breaths and shaking his head. He paid close attention to the pages marked with sticky notes. *What the hell is this?* In complete disbelief, he reread some sections to confirm that what he saw was real. *This explains why so many senior leaders had gathered here.*

Sokolov returned the papers to the envelope and set it beside him on the conference table. Using the secure landline phone in the conference room, he phoned Alexi Volkov, the president's chief of staff, and told him that he had found an envelope under the table near where he and the president had been sitting. Volkov said that they had not left the site and that he would be there in a few minutes.

Sokolov's hands were trembling. He could feel his heart beating in his chest. He fumbled his cell phone from his briefcase. *Why didn't I think of this before I called Volkov?* He extracted the top secret report from the envelope, took a photo of each page, placed them back in the envelope, and put his phone away.

Seconds later, Volkov entered without knocking. In his midfifties, his once-black hair had begun to recede and was streaked with gray. His expression was frozen in a permanent scowl. Sokolov had never known him to smile. The chief of staff wore his power like a second skin, neatly trimmed to maintain an air of precision. His face was lean, with high cheekbones and deep-set eyes that seemed to measure everything they saw. A faint scar along his jawline hinted at his unspoken past. His suits—always dark and impeccably tailored—exuded the quiet authority of someone who never needs to raise his voice to command a room.

Years of political maneuvering had given Volkov a composed stillness, a restraint in his movements that made him more intimidating than openly aggressive. When he spoke, his voice was calm and purposeful; each word was carefully selected for maximum effect. There was no need for theatrics. *True power doesn't have to shout.* He was a survivor who knew that loyalty was currency in the Kremlin, but fear was the smarter investment.

Volkov approached and, without saying a word, extended his hand. Sokolov passed him the envelope.

Volkov inspected both sides of the envelope, paying most attention to the clasp, before opening it. He pulled out the documents and flipped through them, much like Sokolov did. Nearing the end, his eyes widened. He barked out a question that sounded like an accusation: "Did you open this envelope?"

Sokolov tilted his head and held out both hands, palms up. "Of course not. I assumed it belonged to the president or you. I found it under the table where you both were sitting. I retrieved it and called you immediately."

Volkov studied him for a moment. Sokolov hoped it wasn't obvious how fast his heart was beating against his chest. Had he returned the documents to the envelope in the wrong order?

A few anxiety-inducing seconds passed before Volkov cleared his throat. "That was the right thing to do," he said stiffly. "The envelope was leaning against my briefcase. I grabbed my briefcase and left without it."

"Could happen to anyone," Sokolov reasoned, nodding his head.

"Let's keep this between ourselves."

"Of course."

Volkov turned without another word and left.

Only then did Sokolov breathe a deep sigh of relief. Volkov wouldn't tell the president about what had happened. If he did, the president would be furious. He couldn't think of any reason for Volkov to have had the document with him. Still, Sokolov worried. The distribution of a document like the one he had seen was highly restricted. Only the president's closest confidants and the highest military ranks involved in the operation's planning would've seen it. After the president and his entourage left the site, Sokolov opened his phone's photo app and reread the document.

⌇⌇

Sokolov took the Allegro high-speed train home to Saint Petersburg. The external clamor was silenced by his noise-canceling headphones as he listened to the soundtrack of his favorite opera, Verdi's *Aida*, which he had seen at the Mariinsky Theatre a few times.

He took a few low, deep breaths. Three aerospace scientists, who were colleagues and friends of his, had been arrested, and the top secret document he had seen in Moscow had shaken him to the core. Was he next on the FSB's interview list? Although he had done nothing wrong, that didn't mean he wouldn't be arrested, too. Would the president protect him? If he were arrested, the FSB would twist his words to fit their desired outcome. And what of the top secret document? How could that possibly be true? What had become of the Russia he loved?

Sokolov arrived home, tossed his keys on the table by the door, and could think only of one thing—the card he'd ripped up at dinner a few weeks ago. He marched to his office. *Where did I put it?* He stood at the door and scanned the room for anything that would remind him of where he had hidden it. On the second round of rifling through his desk drawers, he found it among some papers in a file folder in the bottom drawer.

Using an encrypted messaging app loaded on his phone, he typed a succinct message in English as fast as his one-fingered method would allow. He stared at the screen, vacillating between sending the message and deleting it. Concerned that he would change his mind if he waited a second longer, he hit send.

This is Dmitry. Haven't seen you since we had dinner at the Bosco Café. Let's get together soon and catch up.

Sokolov sat back in his desk chair and exhaled. The message would set in motion something that would forever change his life, if it did not result in his death. No matter the outcome, he knew one thing to be absolutely true: His Russian epithet from this point forward would be traitor.

6

UNITED STATES EMBASSY
MOSCOW, RUSSIA

Patrick Howell, CIA operations or case officer at Moscow station, pumped his fist in the air when he learned that Dmitry Sokolov had sent a message to the number he had given him. "Yes!" he said to himself, having quietly renounced all hope that Sokolov would reach out.

Indeed, he'd written off Sokolov. Moscow station's recruitment of Russian assets had been dismal over the past year. Too few CIA operations officers and increased FSB monitoring of embassy staff had taken their toll. Sokolov's recruitment would be a shining star in an otherwise crap year for Moscow station.

Restaurants and cafés were the field on which the game of asset recruitment was played. The higher the menu prices for food and drink, the more valuable the potential assets who frequented them. They were also the most difficult to recruit. Howell thought of it as analogous to fishing. Cast out and see if anything bites—a *dangle* in espionage terms—and if the fish aren't biting, you move on to another lake or stream. Some fish thrive in large open bodies of water while some prefer fast-flowing streams. Experience had taught him the difference.

Howell had studied the photographs and résumés of high-value individuals in the Russian government and recognized Sokolov the moment he saw him sitting at the Bosco Café bar in Red Square. The restaurant was a favorite of senior government and defense industry officials as well as the occasional oligarch. Howell had squeezed into a space beside Sokolov that was much too small and ordered a Stoli—a choice intended to solicit Sokolov's attention and perhaps spark conversation.

Lo and behold, it'd done just that. He'd then introduced himself to Sokolov, and they had a brief conversation. Two additional vodkas later, he'd left the restaurant, saying he had to meet a colleague. Recruiting someone such as Sokolov couldn't be rushed.

Over the next several weeks, Howell had made a point to occasionally stop by the bar, have a drink, and look for Sokolov, who lived in Saint Petersburg but who often traveled to Moscow for business. After doing this numerous times but failing to reconnect with the man, Howell was about to give up and move on to another location for potential recruits. Of course, it was then that Sokolov showed up.

They'd gotten along well. Perhaps that was where Howell had gotten it all wrong. He'd rushed into the discussion of politics and the Ukraine war—a rookie mistake. Leaving a card with Sokolov was an act of sheer desperation, which he didn't foresee paying off.

Even so, the next day Howell entered the contact into the agency database, as required. He needed to give Sokolov a cryptonym in the database. Howell had fished at every opportunity back when he was at Michigan State, and in fishing terms, a large fish, especially one that had put up a good fight, was a toad. Sokolov was a significant catch, so Howell was tempted to enter Sokolov's cryptonym name in the

CIA records as Toad but decided on Leapfrog instead, as Toad had a negative connotation. Besides, Leapfrog felt more appropriate, as he wanted Sokolov to jump sides and serve as a foreign agent, passing along valuable intelligence on hypersonic missiles to the US.

After receiving Sokolov's message, Howell updated the database and contacted CIA headquarters in Langley, Virginia, to describe Sokolov's text on a secure line. His contact at Langley inquired as to whether Sokolov was already providing information or serving as a paid agent, implying that the CIA might not have jurisdiction. Howell had shaken his head and said no. Before the end of the day, Langley confirmed that they were in discussions regarding the possible exfiltration of Sokolov to the US.

7

UNITED STATES EMBASSY
DIPLOMATIC ENCLAVE, ISLAMABAD, PAKISTAN

Jake Palmer pulled up his faded Philadelphia Eagles T-shirt and used it to wipe the sweat from his face. His five-mile run within the diplomatic enclave, which he'd begun in the dark, concluded in the predawn light of a cloudless Islamabad sky.

He placed his hands on a light post, stretched his hamstrings, and began his cooldown walk to the high-rise apartment building in the US Embassy complex he called home. This would be one of his final runs in Pakistan. Only days remained on his two-year contractual commitment with the US Joint Special Operations Command's Task Force Orange. His fiancée, Fiona Collins, was already sending him details about their wedding. Just days after leaving Islamabad, he would be standing with her before a vicar in the picturesque English village of Sevenoaks Weald in Kent, where she'd grown up.

Palmer's armband phone vibrated, snapping his thoughts back to the present. The name on the screen was ReyGun, Palmer's abbreviated phone name for Army Brigadier General Reynolds, the senior officer of the Joint Special Operations Command in Islamabad.

Palmer took the phone from his armband and tapped the screen, taking the call.

"Palmer," Reynolds said, sounding unusually curt. "Meet at my office at 0730."

"Roger that," Palmer said instinctively, though he was taken aback. He couldn't recall the last time Reynolds had contacted him directly. Normally, he asked his administrative assistant to reach out and make these sorts of appointments. "0730. I'll be there."

"See you then," Reynolds finished, and the call ended.

A couple of minutes later, Palmer's phone vibrated again. *Now what?* Badass lit up on the screen, which was his caller ID for Alona Green, his Task Force Orange partner. He had assigned it to her after an op a year ago during which she told him to shoot through her to kill a terrorist who was holding a gun to her head.

"An early morning meeting without warning or explanation," Green said as soon as he connected the call and before he could utter a word. "What the hell? This is unlike Reynolds. Something's up."

"He called me, too," Palmer informed her. "And I thought the same thing."

"Figured he'd call you first. Meet me downstairs. We'll walk over together."

"I'm almost back from my run. See you in twenty." He glanced at his watch. "Actually, make that twenty-five."

He sprinted the remaining half mile, giving him time for a quick shower and shave. He dressed and took the elevator to the lobby, where he found Green pacing near the door. He didn't even have to break stride after exiting the elevator; Green fell in step beside him.

"Seriously, you don't have a clue what this is about? Didn't you ask him?" Green said, matching his increased pace.

"No. Didn't you?" Receiving no response, he continued, "All right, if I were to guess, I'd say we're going somewhere. And we'll be leaving soon, otherwise I wouldn't have been invited to the party."

Green stopped in her tracks. Palmer took another step, stopped, and pivoted to face her.

She had a broad smile, her eyebrows raised. "This could be exciting."

Palmer shook his head. "No, Alona. This could be dangerous."

✦✦✦

When Palmer and Green arrived at Reynolds's office, he was on the phone. He waved his hand, signaling for them to come in. A mug of coffee and an untouched bran muffin sat on his desk. Reynolds listened more than he spoke to whoever was on the other end of the call, nodding and providing only short responses. "Yes, sir. They're in my office now. I'll keep you informed," he said, his voice raspy. He punched a button on his phone, ending the call.

Reynolds bit into the muffin and gulped the coffee to wash it down. "Never had our four-star call twice before breakfast regarding an operation."

Palmer nodded. The only four-star officer in their direct line was Vice Admiral John Welsch, commander of the Joint Special Operations Command, who was a four-star navy admiral. Palmer turned his head toward Green and mouthed, "Dangerous."

Before continuing, Reynolds ran his hands over his short graying hair and leaned forward. "Sorry for the early morning meeting, but he wanted to talk to me before he updated the secretary of defense and the president. I know you're curious as to why I called you here on such short notice."

Palmer looked toward the ceiling and shook his head. "Just spit it out, sir."

Reynolds cocked his head and leaned back. "Well then, here it is: Your selection for this assignment comes directly from Vice Admiral Welsch." He cleared his throat and took another sip of coffee. "You'll travel to Helsinki and then to Saint Petersburg under nonofficial cover. The fine details of this top secret operation have yet to be worked out. It will involve going into Russia and extracting a senior aerospace engineer, Dmitry Nikolaev Sokolov. Sokolov wants to defect and work with us on our hypersonic missile development program. This defection was unexpected and urgent, thus necessitating a lack of time for planning and preparation. Moscow-based British MI6 will assist in the operation, which will be run out of Saint Petersburg, where Sokolov lives and works. Your contact is Sania Reed, MI6's chief of Moscow station. Sokolov's only contact thus far has been Patrick Howell, a CIA case officer in Moscow. Howell has given him the cryptonym Leapfrog."

Several questions sprung to mind. Palmer went with the one at the top of his list. "Why isn't the CIA handling this? They always run exfiltration ops, especially those involving a high-profile asset like this engineer. Howell's already on the case."

"Sokolov presents a unique situation," Reynolds said with a sigh, as if he'd expected Palmer to ask this very question. "Howell never officially recruited him, and he never acted as one of our paid foreign assets. If he had, then the CIA would exfiltrate him. No question about it. But he's not. And he hasn't self-defected, like turning up at one of our embassies. So he's technically not a defector. Call it whatever you want—exfiltration, extraction, or defection—it's all semantics. Your assignment is to get him out of Russia and into US custody."

"Why were *we* chosen for the assignment?" Green asked.

Reynolds leaned forward and placed his elbows on the desk. "Admiral Welsch said it was your combined Task Force Orange experience, your track record, and the fact that you, Miss Green, are fluent in Ukrainian and speak passable Russian. Plus, you've worked together long enough that you often bicker like a married couple, which reduces suspicion. You'll travel together as husband and wife." Reynolds laughed. "Now get out of here. JSOC's ID cobbler is already working with Dan Adams to prepare your nonofficial cover documentation and backstop. I gave them a heads-up late yesterday after my initial call from Admiral Welsh, ahead of the final decision this morning. You depart for Helsinki on an air force executive jet tonight."

Palmer and Green didn't move, despite being dismissed.

Green cleared her throat. "But if he's such a high-value asset, why defect? He would be more useful as a paid agent. Once they defect, the flow of new information stops."

"Howell attempted to recruit Sokolov a while back and struck out. Something must have happened recently that lit a fire under Sokolov's tail. We can only speculate on his rationale or sense of urgency. Regardless, he's willing to work with us to accelerate our hypersonic missile program, and we damn well need him. A few years ago, someone in that five-sided squirrel cage in Arlington decided not to pursue this technology. Now the Pentagon is throwing money at defense contractors faster than they request it. Multiple programs are underway to develop the missiles and countermeasures against them. None of them has had any significant success. Even by the most optimistic estimates, we're two or three years behind Russia. Some say it's much longer than that. The enemy is rounding third and eyeing home plate while we're still looking for the ball in the outfield."

Palmer and Green had been keeping tabs on the hypersonic missile development in Russia, China, Iran, and North Korea for months. Russia had already deployed theirs onto their navy's ships. But years ago, the Pentagon concluded that hypersonic missiles were old technology that offered no real value over the country's existing hypersonic ballistic and cruise missiles already in use. The Pentagon was dead wrong. Ballistic missiles and cruise missiles were hypersonic but flew on a direct and predicable line to their target and therefore could be tracked and intercepted well in advance. In short, the advantage of the new generation of hypersonic missiles was that they were maneuverable. Maneuverability and their incredible speed made them almost impossible to track and defend against. Even if a US carrier strike group detected the missiles one hundred miles away traveling at six thousand miles per hour, it would have only one minute to prepare and respond.

Palmer said, "We understand that the Russian president is cracking down on defections of his key scientists and engineers working on the missile program. I suspect things will get dicey. What are our rules of engagement?"

"No doubt Sokolov will have FSB watchdogs all up his ass," Reynolds said, referring to Russia's Federal Security Service that had responsibility for surveillance, counterintelligence, counterterrorism, and border security. "Your usual rules of engagement apply. You must protect Sokolov. The FSB won't think twice about killing him rather than have him defect."

"And us along with him," Palmer added. "Last question: What are our exfil options?"

"This is high-priority shit. JSOC said all options are available to you. You'll make the decision once you're in Russia and have consulted with Reed and Howell."

⚊⚋⚊

Palmer and Green grabbed some coffee after leaving Reynolds's office and headed to see Dan Adams, the computer whiz kid who worked with Green. They found him glued to a bank of computer screens, his head snapping from one monitor to another.

They walked over and stood behind him. Palmer cleared his throat to get his attention. Adams swiveled his chair around and looked up at them.

"Have something to tell us, Adams?" Palmer asked, his arms crossed over his chest.

"Uh . . . uh, yes, sir. Have you met with Reynolds?"

"We have," Green said.

"Thank God. I've been working with the JSOC cobbler in the States on your NOC identities nonstop," Adams said, referring to the individual whose full-time job was creating nonofficial cover identities, documentation, and backstops for JSOC intelligence officers. "I'm sorry I didn't tell you. General Reynolds ordered me not to speak with either of you about it before you met with him."

Adams, one of the youngest members of the intelligence team in Islamabad, had been recruited by the University of California, Irvine, where he was on a full scholarship for playing on the varsity gaming team while pursuing his bachelor's and master's degrees in computer science. His present specialty was SIGINT, or signals intelligence, which was the collection of intelligence from communications and information systems. He would have never met the military's basic physical requirements. Still, the military had learned that the experience and expertise that recruits like Adams possessed were something the military could not teach them.

Adams continued, "You'll be traveling as Dennis Hall, a successful real estate salesman, and his wife, Lauren Hall, a university professor in computer science. You both live and work in Toronto. We've created backstops with phone numbers for the real estate company and the secondary school. If someone calls the numbers that are unique to your name and cover jobs, they will connect to a JSOC employee who will verify your identity and job titles."

Palmer nodded along, though he knew all of this. This wasn't his first rodeo, as it were. He allowed his eyes to glaze over while Adams went over the basics: If anyone were to pry for extra information, they would be easily stopped by various privacy protection laws and so forth. Palmer's concerns weren't prying eyes but extracting Sokolov from Russia undetected a short time after they arrived there.

Adams handed them their passports, visas, and an envelope. "The most difficult items were your passports, Russian visas, and credit cards. Canadian passports have a minimum of biometric data, only your photo, full name, date of birth, place of birth, and fingerprints. Don't take anything with you that confirms your real identity. Those credit cards are linked to a JSOC account under your names."

Palmer and Green shuffled through their passports and opened the envelopes.

"You've been busy," Green said to Adams.

"I was here all night. We also created bios for each of you," he said, handing them both a sheet of paper and an envelope. "Memorize the information on your paper and shred it before you leave the building tonight. The envelopes contain your pocket litter—a collection of show tickets, restaurant receipts, grocery store receipts, and anything else that could typically be found in someone's pocket, wallet, or purse. Because your cover identities are Canadian, some are from your home in Toronto, and a couple are from Helsinki, dated the day you arrive there."

"We're going to need weapons, secure cell phones, and a satellite phone," Palmer said, looking through what Adams had handed them. "I assume we'll get those in Saint Petersburg."

"Right. You'll be passing through immigration and passport control in Helsinki and again before entering Russia. It's best to go through both as clean as possible. MI6 will provide the hardware after you arrive in Saint Petersburg."

Palmer understood the implications of everything Adams had said. Their notional covers were limited to this short-term operation. Should they be caught, they would not withstand the intense scrutiny that a NOC would create for a US intelligence officer leading a long-term NOC life. If they were captured while attempting to get Sokolov out of the country, an experienced FSB interrogator would blow their covers within a few hours, if not sooner. After that, a quick trial for espionage, followed by a private execution, would be a blessing. More likely, however, after being put on public display, tortured, and tried, they would spend the rest of their lives in cold, filthy prisons: Palmer in the hellhole known as the Black Dolphin, named for the statue of a black dolphin at the main entrance, in Orenburg Oblast on the Russia-Kazakhstan border, and Green in the IK-14 women's prison located in Russia's Mordovia region.

8

UNITED STATES EMBASSY
DIPLOMATIC ENCLAVE, ISLAMABAD, PAKISTAN

Palmer left the meetings with Reynolds and Adams with more questions than answers. Entering Russia and extracting Sokolov from the country would be difficult. The only thing in their favor was the length of the operation—it would be a quick in-and-out visit, lasting two to three days at most.

On previous trips, he and Green had always traveled under official diplomatic cover, using their real identities, black diplomatic passports, and embassy cover jobs and titles. If there were a problem, they would have claimed diplomatic immunity. This was different. This was Russia, and they would be traveling under false identities. CIA field officers often lived under their NOC for years, keeping it separate from their real life and secret from their closest friends and family, even their spouse. Officers maintained cover jobs that explained their frequent foreign travel and long periods away from home. They became actors on the world stage. After years of living two lives, however, many found that the line between truth and fiction had become so blurred that they either left the agency or changed jobs.

Intelligence gathering in Islamabad had become routine. Palmer and Green monitored the ongoing conflict between India and Pakistan, although that had dialed back somewhat in the past year, except for the brouhaha created after India launched an unarmed hypersonic missile that inadvertently landed in Pakistan and after the Hindu nationalist government in India revoked the semiautonomous status of the Kashmir region, bringing it under New Delhi's direct control. Thousands of Kashmiri civilians and security forces had died.

Palmer and Green continued to work with Pakistani assets to gather information and provide intelligence to special operations forces in the Middle East and Africa. In addition to those duties, Green oversaw the collection and analysis of signal intelligence, or SIGINT, which involved gathering intelligence from communications between individuals and other means of electronic information transmission.

On a global scale, state actors in Russia and China were responsible for isolated cyberattacks on the US power grid and telecommunications. The US director of national intelligence believed these were tests to determine how easily the firewalls could be penetrated and in preparation for a future widespread attack on the country's infrastructure. Drone warfare, which had begun in the Russia-Ukraine war, had spread to the Houthi rebels in Yemen and elsewhere. Russia had launched ballistic missiles into space, which threatened US GPS and communications satellites. Russia, China, North Korea, and Iran had maneuverable hypersonic missiles that were nuclear-capable while the US and its allies were still in the development stage. The Chinese had conducted tests of their DF-26 missile against a mock-up of the US American cruisers and destroyers that escort aircraft carriers.

Though this mission held significant importance, he couldn't help but resent its timing. He was due to leave Islamabad and marry Fiona, and he'd grown excited about returning to civilian life. If this two- or three-day mission went as planned, he'd be fine—but what if it didn't?

He had already sold his Rittenhouse Square condominium in Philadelphia, including furnishings, and shipped his personal belongings to a storage facility near where Collins lived in Clapham, southwest London. Once they were married and settled in their new home, he would reestablish his business as an independent contractor in London, including work for the military, intelligence agencies, and the defense industry sector. Only one thing remained before he could begin that new life—this final operation, his last with his Orange partner, Alona Green. Green would leave Islamabad for a new assignment at a yet-to-be-determined location with a yet-to-be-assigned partner.

Despite all this, Palmer still felt a sense of uneasiness in his gut. It wasn't the operation, per se. As difficult as it might seem, he had been on navy special warfare missions that entailed far more dangerous locations and conditions than he had anticipated for this operation. Was it because for the first time in his life, someone he loved and who loved him would be waiting for him? What if his anxiety was not about the op at all? What if it was related to his impending marriage to Fiona? *Am I even good marriage material?* If anything, he was an independent soul doing what he wanted, when he wanted. Was he doing the right thing by Fiona? Palmer shook his head as if to remove those doubts from his mind.

9

JINNAH STREAM WITHIN THE DIPLOMATIC ENCLAVE
ISLAMABAD, PAKISTAN

Alona Green's mind was swirling like an out-of-control amusement park ride. She needed time, even if just a few minutes, to absorb everything and calm down from the exhilaration she was feeling. She was headed to Russia on a top secret mission with Jake Palmer, her ride or die. Did a more exciting operation even exist? She strongly doubted it.

Green exited the embassy and walked along Jinnah Stream, which flowed through the enclave to the south, into Rawal Lake at Lake View Park. It was a fitting name for the stream. In Islam, Jinnah, which translated to paradise garden, was the final home of the righteous and coexisted with the temporal world.

She sat on a bench overlooking the stream and the surrounding hills, which were gently sloped. The walkway along the stream was crowded, as usual. With forty-three embassies and high commissions in the enclave, work was nonstop. The doors never closed. Taking a walk by the stream offered a break from the tension of high-stress jobs. She closed her eyes and listened to the water rippling. A goose flying overhead honked, and someone in the distance laughed. Soon she was deep in thought about her past.

Going into Russia would be like returning home. Her father had been born in Ukraine when it was part of the Soviet Socialist Republic, but in his senior position in the KGB, and later after the breakup of the Soviet Union, the FSB, he spent most of his time in Russia and was fluent in the language.

For the first time, she felt her excitement ebb, replaced by fear. If caught, the FSB would determine she worked for a US special operations group and had entered the country with a false passport and visa. Given time, they would identify her as the daughter of a defector and treat her accordingly.

Over the years, her father's growing disappointment with the Communist Party had led to a significant shift in his perspective. A CIA case officer contacted him and convinced him to become a foreign agent, providing the US with information on the Russian security service's intelligence operations. Months later, a senior officer questioned Kolvalyova about his activities. He became nervous and knew that he had to get out. He and his wife had met his CIA case officer in the middle of the night and defected. The CIA then placed them in their covert security and resettlement program and moved them to Washington, DC, where they were given new identities, changing their surnames from Kolvalyova to Green. She was born in DC while her parents were living there. The CIA was responsible for their safety.

As a child, Green's father had told her that family security came with certain lifestyle restrictions due to his important job with the US government. In her early teens, she'd became more inquisitive and complained about not having social media accounts like her friends. Her father explained that their safety was of the utmost importance—and to ensure their safety, his employer prohibited any family member from having one. At the time, she wasn't old enough to digest what this might mean. Eventually, after receiving a cell phone, she promptly attempted to do whatever she wanted with it—only to discover that both her parents and the CIA closely monitored its use and tracked her location.

The night before she'd left for college, she was upstairs in her bedroom, packing her clothes, when she heard her parents arguing. She stormed downstairs and asked them what was going on. Her mother nudged her father in the side and said, "Go ahead. Tell her." Her father sighed and said they had something important to discuss before she left. What could it possibly be? Did one of them have cancer or a fatal disease of some kind?

With her mother sitting on the edge of the sofa, wringing her hands, her father told her the truth about how the CIA had helped them defect and that he had been working for the CIA for years. He'd also told her that the real reason for changing their names from Kolvalyova to Green was for their security; she'd always believed it was because they wanted a surname that sounded more American.

He told her that the CIA provided security for the family, and at MIT, she would have security, but if they did their job, she would never know they were there. After over twenty years, the type of security had been reduced. Much of it was now electronic or following them when they traveled out of the country. Their job was to keep her safe, not to monitor her academic and social life. She let the information and its implications sink in. They talked for hours, addressing all her concerns. She was in a state of shock, but for the first time, she understood why things had been the way they had—no social media, strict rules on phone usage, unreasonable curfews, the grilling of her friends, *especially* her boyfriends.

At MIT, she'd occasionally noticed people she thought might be following her. They dressed and acted like students but looked older.

Because there were post-graduate students and adult students on campus, she didn't give it much thought. Whatever her father had offered in terms of intel must have been of unthinkable value to justify affording for a covert security detail to follow her, and everyone else in her family for so long.

In her senior year at MIT, she told her father that the US Defense Intelligence Agency had recruited her to work for them as a contractor. Rather than supporting her as he always had, he told her not to do it, citing all the problems female intelligence officers faced. After she'd convinced him that she had already made her decision and that it wasn't up for discussion, he offered the sort of advice she'd never forget. In fact, even now, she still recalled it as clearly as if it were yesterday. *Everyone has secrets. People lie; trust no one. Beware, because someone is always watching you. And most importantly, because of the work you're considering and being my daughter, remember: Russia never forgets.*

Russia never forgets. Words that now had more significance than at any other time in her life. Sokolov had been involved in Russia's missile development for most of his career and was one of the world's most respected experts. This would be exciting, but Palmer was right—it *would* be dangerous. Couldn't the two coexist, excitement and fear? Wasn't that what riding a roller coaster was all about? It was frightening, but that was the point, and you were always eager to go again as soon as you got off.

There was another thing on her mind. This would be her last operation with Palmer. He would return to civilian life and marry Fiona Collins. Green was pleased for them on the one hand and sad to lose him as a partner on the other. There was none better than Jake Palmer. However, in her heart, Palmer was more than a work partner. The British nineteenth-century author Emily Dickinson had said it best: "The heart wants what it wants, or else it does not care."

Even though her relationship with Palmer had been business only, that hadn't prevented her feelings for him from growing stronger. Was she really in love with him, or was the quest for the unattainable driving her feelings? Could she deeply love someone who would never love her?

She supposed it didn't matter. She hadn't shared her true feelings with him and never would—not when working her dream job with JSOC's Task Force Orange. She wouldn't screw that up over a man, no matter who he was or how much she cared for him.

Well, Emily Dickenson, my heart could want whatever it damn well wants, but my intention is to never act on or tell him my true feelings.

Maybe his leaving was a blessing. He had never said or done anything that would be considered inappropriate, even if she'd invited it—like the time she'd gotten out of the water after swimming nude on a deserted North Carolina Outer Banks beach. She was certain he'd seen her, and yet he'd stayed on the beach towel and never commented on it. At the time, of course, he'd suspected she had murdered his friend. *Maybe that had dampened his desire.*

Green had never met Collins. Their only connection was through Palmer. He had never discussed Collins with her, and she was confident that the reverse was true—but Green *did* know that Collins at least was aware she existed thanks to the invitation Collins had sent her to attend their wedding in England. It'd come with a handwritten note on the invitation that read *"Looking forward to finally meeting you."*

Her initial reaction was that the invitation was a sweet gesture, and it would be wonderful to meet her as well. But then she reread the invitation and personal note a few times, envisioning exactly what she'd be getting herself into. *Hell no. Why would I do that to myself?* She scribbled a reply on the RSVP card, saying she was sorry that she could not attend because of a scheduling conflict at work and wished them a long and happy marriage.

Green drifted back from her thoughts as people strolled by. A quiet sigh escaped as she rose, the weight of unspoken feelings clinging to her as she made her way back to the embassy, her mind already turning toward the operation that lay ahead.

10

BRITISH EMBASSY, MOSCOW STATION
MOSCOW, RUSSIA

Sania Reed, the MI6 Moscow station chief, prepared her afternoon cup of tea and placed it on her desk. She had taken only a few sips when she received a video call from C, which was the unique moniker given to the chief of the British Secret Intelligence Service in London.

She shifted her seat, ran her fingers through her long hair, twisted it into a knot, cleared her throat, and accepted the call on her laptop.

"Hello, Miss Reed," C began before Sania had even said a word. "I'm afraid we have a situation."

"A situation, sir?"

"Dmitry Sokolov, a Russian aerospace engineer working on the hypersonic missile development program, wants to defect to the US."

Reed leaned closer to the computer screen. "Sokolov isn't just an aerospace engineer," she said with a scoff. "He's Russia's top hypersonic missile expert. He's the general director of the Hypersonic System Research Institute in Saint Petersburg."

C didn't react. Tone flat, he said, "Two American spec op intel officers from Islamabad are on the way to Saint Petersburg by way of Helsinki. We're going to help them."

"Islamabad? They're sending two *American* officers from Islamabad, and *we're* going to help them?"

"Right. Sounds like rubbish, doesn't it? Regardless, they require our assistance to pull this off. Patrick Howell, their Moscow-based CIA case officer, made the initial contact with Sokolov and is in communication with him now regarding the extraction from Russia. Howell will not be directly involved in this operation but will pass along the information he has. The US JSOC's special operations intelligence team has the lead. MI6 will assist, and you're it."

"Am I to work directly with the Americans?"

"Yes. Neither has ever set foot in Russia. Our hypersonic missile program will benefit from any information or assistance this defector provides to the Americans. I'll leave it up to you to determine how much involvement is required to ensure the op succeeds. Stay engaged from the time they arrive until they're out of the country with Sokolov. And don't do anything that would endanger your diplomatic cover status, like crossing the border with Sokolov."

"Understood, sir. How and when are they arriving?"

"They're flying to Helsinki on an air force executive jet tomorrow and then on the Allegro train to Saint Petersburg. They're traveling under nonofficial cover as Dennis and Lauren Hall, using false Canadian passports and Russian visas. The Americans are still working out the details."

"The FSB recently arrested three aerospace engineers who had presented their published papers on hypersonic missiles in the past, even though they had gone through all the approval hoops before doing so. Perhaps that's the root of Sokolov's sense of urgency," Sania noted, sipping her tea.

"Could be he's next on the list, or at least fears that he is. Aside from reading in your teammate, keep this quiet. The fewer who know about it, the better. I'll send you the Halls' contact information and that of their Islamabad techie, who should be in touch with yours. Our ambassador in Moscow requires plausible deniability. I'll give him a high-level heads-up without mentioning Sokolov's name and will keep him informed as needed. Stay safe."

With the call disconnected, Reed picked up her mug and walked to the window. From this vantage point, she could see the silhouette of the Kremlin in the distance, its red walls and towers punctuating the city's core with centuries of political authority. Her reflection in the bulletproof glass stared back at her—sharp cheekbones, dark hair twisted in a tight knot, and eyes that missed nothing.

The chief had left some wiggle room in the type of support she provided. If her role were for passive support and not as an active participant, she would be a footnote on the operation report—no points for her. And if the high-profile operation failed, the blowback would be swift and long-lasting. In the espionage business, second chances were a myth.

Many would consider this operation destined to fail, but she saw it as an opportunity to work with two US JSOC intelligence officers on a high-risk operation with a limited chance of success. This was the kind of operation capable of making or breaking one's career.

This was her game. *You survive it, or you vanish.* This mission wasn't just about her reputation; it was about her future. There was no soft landing in this business—not in Moscow. Not when the Kremlin still played the game like it was 1983 and everyone pretended the Cold War was over.

The Halls would soon be in Saint Petersburg. She would arrange for them to stay at the safe flat and meet with them soon after they arrived. Reed pulled herself away from the window and read in her techie, Dayton Hunnicutt.

Sania Reed was in her early forties and a rising star at MI6. Her posting in Moscow marked a crucial milestone in her career; few station chiefs were women. She'd been in her late twenties when MI6 had hired her—a Cambridge graduate with expertise in linguistics, political science, and international relations. She now had experience from several expatriate assignments, including a year at the British Consulate General in Ekaterinburg, Russia. Before going to Russia, she completed an introductory course in the Russian language and quickly became fluent. After Russia ordered the British to close Ekaterinburg, she moved to Moscow and was promoted to MI6's station chief there.

Her next post was likely to be a senior management role at MI6's Vauxhall Cross in London. However, her real goal was the MI6 liaison position in Washington, once held by the famous Sir Maurice Oldfield, the seventh director of MI6, and by the equally notorious Kim Philby, a double agent for the Soviet Union. The Washington posting would boost her chances of achieving her dream of becoming the first woman in MI6 to sign her correspondence with a C in green ink, continuing a tradition started by the first chief of the British Secret Intelligence Service, Captain Sir Mansfield Smith-Cumming, in 1909.

Reed found Hunnicutt reviewing intelligence reports on his desktop computer. She explained the situation to him and their role in the operation.

Hunnicutt nodded. "When are they arriving?"

"They're flying into Helsinki today and taking the Allegro train to Saint Petersburg. Hack into train passenger lists and verify which of today's trains Dennis and Lauren Hall are booked on. Also, find out everything you can about Sokolov, including the floor plans of his home, the car he drives, and the name of his dog, if he has one. I'll contact Howell at the US Embassy to see what he knows about Sokolov's defection and how we can reach him. I'll send you the contact info for the Halls' technical support. I should be in Saint Petersburg before they arrive, so I need to leave very early tomorrow morning. Also, have some gear delivered to the safe flat: Glocks, ammunition, a satellite phone, and an electronic bug detector."

"I'll arrange that with Boris." Hunnicutt shook his head slowly. "This sounds impossible on short notice: Locate Sokolov, rid him of his FSB security, and get him out of the country."

"These are the challenges that test us. If it were easy, MI6 wouldn't be involved."

Sania Reed returned to her office and called Howell, informing him that the team had been formed and that the Halls would arrive in Saint Petersburg today. She said he should travel to Saint Petersburg and remain there until they got Sokolov out of the country. Reed would contact him once the Americans arrived and schedule a call. She asked him to inform Sokolov and provide him with a secure phone.

11

SAINT PETERSBURG, RUSSIA

In the living room of his Saint Petersburg home, Dmitry Nikolaev Sokolov was growing more anxious about when he would leave Russia. A reporter on TASS nightly news was giving an update on the war with Ukraine. Sokolov had heard enough of what he knew were mostly lies. He turned down the sound and began to reflect on his decision to defect.

After reaching out to the number on Howell's card, the initial response had been quick. Howell had replied briefly, giving a different number to message and instructions for using an encrypted messaging app. He'd downloaded the app and messaged that he wanted to defect to the US immediately. Howell responded that he'd stay in touch but that organizing Sokolov's defection was complicated and would take a few days to complete. True to his word, Howell often made indirect references in their encrypted messages to finding a date and restaurant where they could meet for dinner—*dinner* being the code word for the date he would leave and *restaurant* the code word for where they would meet him.

Sokolov hadn't told Howell about the document he'd found left behind by the president's chief of staff, Volkov. He'd keep that information to himself for now, intending to use it as leverage if there was a problem with his defection. His anxiety had become overwhelming. He was sure it was only a matter of time before one or more FSB officers would burst into his office or home without warning and haul him away. At work, he looked up whenever someone walked by. The FSB followed him to and from work, making no attempt to disguise their surveillance. That had begun when the crackdown on defectors was initiated. At home, he kept the doors locked and his security system activated.

Sokolov heard something about engineers on the television. Believing it was an update on the arrests of his three colleagues, he picked up the remote and turned the volume up. A photograph of an engineer flashed on the screen. *My God. It's another one of my colleagues.*

The reporter went on to say that the arrests of scientists and engineers working on the missile programs had become an almost daily occurrence. Most were senior-level staff who the FSB believed the foreign intelligence agencies were targeting because, as spies, they could provide more valuable information on Russia's hypersonic missile program. He concluded by saying these spies were being recruited and groomed by foreign intelligence agencies, including America's CIA.

It had been only a few days, but Sokolov was now certain that time was running out. He'd have to find a way to leave Russia on his own if his defection wasn't underway in the next day or two. Maybe it would be easier that way.

12

SAINT PETERSBURG, RUSSIA

When Patrick Howell had texted Dmitry Sokolov that he'd heard from the team and they would be in place within the next day, he received an immediate reply saying he was relieved. Howell told him that he had a secure phone for Sokolov that he would need to use from this point on. They agreed to meet at a Lukoil petrol station near Sokolov's home. He'd instructed Sokolov to be at the station at seven o'clock after he left work. He should top off his tank, go inside to pay, and pick up some snack foods or cigarettes. Sokolov replied that he would be driving a silver Mercedes sedan and gave him the license number. Howell said he would wait in his car and go inside when he saw him filling up. When he went in to pay, Howell would brush past him and slip the secure phone into his coat pocket. They should not acknowledge each other.

Howell had driven the eight-hour trip from Moscow to Saint Petersburg multiple times. Due to the urgency, Howell instead took a shuttle flight to Saint Petersburg, rented a car at the airport, and drove to the Lukoil petrol station. Howell suspected that Sokolov's anxiety about the time it had taken to organize his exfiltration and get the team in place had been replaced by relief that it was now underway. What would now plague him would be the increasing anxiety concerning the risks involved in defecting.

Howell drummed his fingers on the steering wheel of his car. He was parked on a side street near the Lukoil station. Howell's team at the US Embassy in Moscow had set up the phone with a VPN and an encrypted messaging app. In addition, full disk encryption was enabled, and the location service was turned off. He told Sokolov to limit the use of his current personal phone, and, after receiving the new phone, he should delete the messaging app from his personal phone. Regardless of the encryption app that Sokolov had installed on his personal phone, it was much too vulnerable. Once the operation started, Sokolov would need to leave his personal phone turned on but use only the new secure phone for communications with the team.

Even then, Sokolov could use the new secure phone when he was in a place where he was sure no listening devices had been planted nearby and where no one could overhear him. That meant no calls from his home, car, or workplace.

Besides giving him the phone and connecting the team with Sokolov, Howell wouldn't have any official role in the defection unless the team asked for it. Sokolov was his recruit, and the CIA, including Howell, would be excluded from the operation. He understood the reasoning, but that did little to lessen his frustration.

Patrick Howell was a thirty-six-year-old graduate of Michigan State University with degrees in engineering and mathematics. He was a member of the MSU volleyball and swim teams and belonged to a social fraternity. He was a naval ROTC midshipman and was commissioned as a surface warfare officer upon graduation. A year after graduation, he applied to become an information warfare officer. He was accepted into and completed the Information Warfare Basic Course and the Naval Intelligence Officer Basic Course at the Special

Warfare Dam Neck Annex in Virginia Beach. The combined training lasted twenty-three weeks, during which he received his top secret/sensitive compartmented information clearance. His first assignment was aboard the USS *Harry S. Truman* (CVN-75), a nuclear-powered aircraft carrier based in Norfolk, Virginia.

During a subsequent foreign assignment in Naples, Italy, he completed his navy obligation and applied to the CIA. He was turned down due to a lack of sufficient fluency in a foreign language, although he spoke enough Italian to get by. Believing that Russia would be a challenging assignment and one that would propel his career, he studied Russian from a private instructor until he was fluent in the language. On his subsequent application, he was accepted. After rotating through departments at the CIA's headquarters at Langley in northern Virginia, and then assignments in Eastern Europe, he got the Moscow assignment of his dreams.

As a CIA case officer in the US Embassy in Moscow, his primary role was to recruit, maintain, and protect Russian agents who would provide intelligence on their work or on other classified information that would be useful to the US. His diplomatic cover job was as a travel and entertainment coordinator for senior embassy diplomats, including arranging transportation within Russia, a task that was handled by a senior administrator. Over the two years he had been in Moscow, Howell had spoken with numerous potential Russian agents. He was successful with several of them and was presently their handler. The rest were never seen again, because either the information they could provide was not of interest or they were wary of him and walked away as quickly as a potential customer hanging up on a telemarketer's cold call.

Some initial contacts were with individuals whom he had sought out and researched. However, most were selected at random. Howell was keenly aware that officers of Russia's Main Intelligence Directorate, the GRU, also frequented the same establishments, surveilling for American operatives or monitoring key Russians whom the West would want to recruit.

One night, he had struck up a conversation with a beautiful Russian woman named Natalia Petrova at a trendy nightclub. He had just gotten a vodka tonic when she'd bumped into him and spilled some of her drink on him. She apologized in Russian and began to wipe his jacket with a bar napkin. In Russian, he'd told her not to worry about it. She'd picked up on his English accent and switched to English. Her hair had been slicked back to highlight her face and eyes, which remained fixed on his while they talked. Her skirt was short for the time of the year, and her legs were long and athletic. She was as tall as he was—too tall for a gymnast or dancer, probably a former soccer goalie or volleyball player.

As they talked, Natalia edged closer to him. He could smell the soft, clean scent of her perfume. She was clearly out of his league, although her interest in him seemed genuine. When she asked him what he did for work, he said he was the travel coordinator at the US Embassy. She'd said she worked for the government as well. That had piqued his interest and alerted him to the possibility that she might have potential as an asset, depending on her role. They were on their third drink when she suggested they take their conversation somewhere quieter. That'd hit him like lightning striking a tree, breaking him out of the web Natalia had so skillfully spun. *She* was recruiting *him*. He'd promptly said that although that sounded wonderful, he had to leave; perhaps they could meet another time. He put his unfinished drink on the bar and left before she could pin him down for a date and time to meet again. There would be no other time—not when he didn't trust himself to resist her siren's call.

Howell glanced at his watch, his hand trembling. If Sokolov was a dangle, this was the first opportunity for the FSB to arrest him for participating in Sokolov's defection. Sometimes Russians contacted the embassy claiming they had sensitive information to share, but in reality, they were GRU dangles—bait to lure a CIA officer out in the open. If Sokolov was a dangle, the GRU would have wired him and collected evidence that the US was trying to recruit him as an agent. If that was the case, they would arrest Howell immediately, and he would likely never see the light of day again, despite his diplomatic immunity. It was also possible that they were after bigger targets and would wait for the team sent to assist in his defection from Russia. He didn't think this was the case, but those thoughts did, admittedly, keep him awake at night.

He glanced at his watch again.

Sokolov was fifteen minutes late.

Should I call or text? No. I'll wait a little longer. If he hasn't arrived by seven thirty, I'll call.

At seven twenty, the silver Mercedes pulled up to the pump, and Howell breathed a sigh of relief. Sokolov got out and began to fill his tank. Howell exited his car and went inside the station. A black Audi with tinted windows pulled in and stopped at the pumps across from Sokolov, but no one got out of the car. Sokolov, wearing a short dark-blue overcoat, came inside and walked toward the cooler containing water and soft drinks.

Howell approached him, a soft drink and a bag of chips in his left hand and the cell phone in his right. Without making eye contact or slowing down, he passed to the right of Sokolov, just close enough to slide the phone into his coat pocket.

Howell stopped by the cashier, paid for his purchase, and left. He waited in his car until Sokolov came out of the station and drove off. The Audi fell in behind Sokolov a few seconds later. Howell fell in behind the Audi, far enough back so as not to be perceived as following it.

13

TRAVELING FROM ISLAMABAD TO HELSINKI

Palmer and Green departed that evening after their meeting with General Reynolds. Commercial flights required at least one layover and took between fifteen and twenty hours from takeoff in Islamabad to landing in Helsinki. Due to the operation's importance, secrecy, and urgency, SOCOM diverted an air force Gulfstream C-37A to fly them to Helsinki. The jet is used for high-ranking military officers and VIPs; apart from the tail number, it had no identifying marks. The pilot and flight attendant were both in the air force and each had a high security clearance because of the passengers they would encounter on flights. Even with the detour around Russia, the flight was comfortably within the C-37A's range of seventy-five hundred miles. Palmer and Green were the only passengers. They sat across the narrow aisle from each other, about halfway back from the pilot's cabin. The interior was functional but not as kitted out or plush as a corporate jet.

Palmer flipped through the pages of his Canadian passport. Although the Canadian passports for Dennis and Lauren Hall had just been created, they appeared worn and had several false immigration stamps. Unlike the black US diplomatic passports they had been using, their nondiplomatic passports were navy blue, the same as issued to all Canadians. Their previous travels had been under official diplomatic cover, using their real identities and embassy cover jobs and titles. Not long after arriving in Islamabad, they'd flown to India-controlled Kashmir and were, upon arrival, pulled aside for secondary screening, including inspection of their bags, before being cleared for entry. If there had been an issue, they could have claimed diplomatic immunity by traveling with their real identities and embassy cover jobs.

But this was Russia, and they were traveling under false identities without diplomatic immunity—and the fake identities for Palmer and Green were very flimsy. Any seasoned Russian FSB interrogator could break them in less than an hour. They would be questioned separately and their answers compared. Sometimes suspects were tortured and questioned alone; other times they were questioned together. Palmer and Green memorized their aliases, addresses, details of how they first met, birth and anniversary dates, and their personal and work histories. The FSB would probe further, asking about their relatives' names, ages, and professions. They had started calling each other Lauren and Dennis. There could be no mistakes, no slipups. They spent hours taking turns acting as interrogators, firing questions back and forth at each other, and often repeating them to see if the answers were rehearsed or phrased differently. A single mistake could have deadly consequences. An hour after the jet took off, the only flight attendant offered Palmer and Green a drink and asked if they had eaten. Neither of them had. Green requested a chardonnay. Palmer asked if they had any Glenmorangie; they did not, but the flight attendant said they did have Macallan.

"That'll do."

They had finished their drinks and dinner when Green turned to Palmer and said, "I'm concerned about finding Sokolov, losing his tail, and getting the three of us out of the country."

"You should be," Palmer huffed. "Way too many variables and unknowns. All we have planned is getting into Russia. That's the easy part. Getting out with Sokolov? That's another matter entirely. I've been on two hostage rescues. Both required intensive training and planning before we left for the op, and we still encountered surprises. If we aren't careful, this could turn ugly."

Green stared out the window of the plane. She shifted in her seat and turned to face Palmer. "Does Fiona know about this operation?"

Palmer sighed. "Although I trust her with my life, we never discuss our work. I told her I'd be out of touch for a few days. She understands that means I'll go dark for a while."

"She's an intelligence analyst at MI6. Isn't there a chance she knows about our op?"

"I doubt it. Someone at her level wouldn't be copied on communications related to it. Even those who are aware of it won't know our real names. All comms about this operation will contain only Sokolov's cryptonym, Leapfrog, and our cover names." Palmer paused, then asked, "Ever been to Russia?"

Green bit her lip. "Never. And I have the oddest feeling about it. Before I was born, my father and mother fled the Soviet Union for the US in the middle of the night, accompanied by an American CIA operations officer. Now, all these years later, I'm the operations officer who will lead someone out of Russia to the US. Weird. Maybe I was born to do this. I know they're watching over me."

Palmer tapped his fingers on the armrest. "The Russians will not have forgotten that your father, a KGB officer, defected to the US. If they discover who you are—a JSOC Task Force Orange officer and the daughter of a KGB defector who worked for the CIA—they won't go easy on you."

Green uncrossed her legs, her gaze on Palmer. "The same goes for you—a former Navy SEAL who now works for a special warfare intelligence operations group. I suppose I may be on some Russian military intelligence agency watch list. But could they identify me through facial recognition? I doubt it. My father and mother have passed away, and my given name has always been Green. I must have relatives in Ukraine and Russia. I've considered taking a DNA test so that I can locate them."

"Why haven't you?"

Green took a moment to answer, crossing her arms in a hug before settling back into her seat, her gaze now out the window. "In our line of work, that would be another digital footprint in the metaverse—a huge, messy footprint that could easily backfire."

"True."

Green pulled out her passport and examined the photo. "I'm Lauren Hall, university professor, and you're my husband, Dennis Hall, a successful real estate salesman. Married eighteen years, no children, and apparently no social life. Neither of us is on any social media platform. Social media is another thing I avoid."

"Same here," Palmer said. "Navy SEALs have no social media presence, and those who are married are never mentioned by name or appear in photos that their family members post. Real friends keep up with you in person or on the phone, not through social media."

"Am I a real friend?" Green asked, her eyes fixed on his.

"You've saved my life."

"And you saved mine."

"Yes, I did," Palmer replied. "And both of those actions make you a friend in my eyes. Over the years, I've had a lot of close calls. The only two people who have done something that saved my life are you and Wade Jansen."

"Wade Jansen," Green said, shaking her head. "Your former SEAL teammate, right? You thought I'd murdered him."

"*Suspected* you might have murdered him," Palmer clarified. "And that was just because we were strangers back then. I'd just met you."

"The cold look in your eyes that day made me think you might kill me."

"I considered it, but look where we are now," he said with a laugh.

"Speaking of which, Fiona sent me an invitation to your wedding," Green said, carefully avoiding Palmer's eyes. That didn't go unnoticed by him. "I replied, saying I had a work conflict."

He wasn't aware of a work conflict but didn't press the point. He suspected that Green had feelings for him and that meeting Fiona and attending the wedding would be awkward and uncomfortable for her.

"I'm disappointed you're not coming. The two of you would hit it off, I'm sure."

Green chuckled. "We'd definitely have a lot to talk about."

Palmer held out his hand and twirled the worn wedding band Dan Adams had given him from what they called the Q-Locker—referring to Q from the Bond movies who managed all the gadgets. But there were no keys to bulletproof Aston Martins or shoe daggers in the Q-Locker. It mainly contained items used to disguise identity. The ring felt odd on his hand, not because of its actual texture but because of the implication that he was married to Green. It felt almost as if he were cheating on Fiona, which he was not. He saw Green looking at him as he fidgeted with his ring. She put her left hand beside his and looked at her diamond engagement ring and wedding band. Adams had told them to put them on immediately, because it was essential to get accustomed to wearing them. Fidgeting with them would be a quick tell for any Russian intelligence officer.

"Jake, there's something I need to tell you," Green said suddenly, the use of his first name taking him by surprise. "Just in case I don't make it back."

Palmer's eyes widened. He suspected she loved him, but would she really tell him something like that *now*—right before such a high-stakes mission? That didn't seem like her.

"We're going to make it back," he reassured her, "but I understand the desire and impulse to clear one's conscience before facing what we're about to do. My suggestion is to not bring up anything and to trust we'll get through—"

"I killed Aaliyah," Green blurted out, her voice lowered. "At least, I *think* I killed her."

Aaliyah was a Pakistan Inter-Services Intelligence officer who'd had a romantic relationship with a US intelligence officer in the Islamabad office for the sole purpose of compromising him and obtaining intelligence information—a honey trap, pure and simple. Palmer and Green found that the officer was passing sensitive information to her, including details about their work for Task Force Orange. The officer was wounded during a shootout at a safe house. While in the hospital, Aaliyah visited him and gave him a poison pill, convincing him to take it and end his life rather than face the humiliation of being convicted of spying for his own country and the torment of spending decades in prison.

Palmer cocked his head in disbelief. "You did what?"

Green glanced at the overhead and replied, "After we returned from London, I called and asked her to dinner. Dan drove me to the restaurant. We arrived early and saw Aaliyah get out of her car. While we were having dinner, Dan, who, aside from being a computer whiz, knows a hell of a lot about cars, did something to her vehicle's brakes. After dinner, I walked with her to her car, said good night, and she drove off. I might have kissed her and replied positively to her suggestion that we see each other again soon in a . . . more private setting."

Palmer rolled his eyes. "Of course you did."

"After Dan and I left the restaurant, we saw that a couple of cars had stopped and that people were looking downhill. Dan lowered his window and asked one of the onlookers what had happened. The man told him that a car went off the road and rolled a few times before stopping."

Palmer leaned back in his seat, staring straight ahead. "Aaliyah was an evil woman and deserved to die," he said plainly. "I considered taking her out myself."

"It was totally an off-the-books op. Besides Dan and me—and now you—no one knows about it. The problem is that I've never been able to find any information about Aaliyah or the wreck. It's as if it never happened. She disappeared."

Green proceeded to tell Palmer that the morning after the accident, a coworker who had also been at the restaurant was talking to another colleague in the break room and said he didn't see how anyone could have survived it. She never found any report of the incident in the newspapers or in any open-source intelligence information to support that she had died in the crash.

"A few days later, I called Aaliyah's mobile phone. The call went to voicemail, so I left a message saying I was following up on our dinner and wanted to know when we could get together again. After a few more days, I left another voicemail, expressing my concern that I hadn't heard from her and asking her to call. I pored over intelligence reports and created computer-generated alerts if her name or anything related to the crash—missing intelligence officers or her given name, Jasmine Abdolahzadeh—appeared on the web. *Nothing*." At this, she turned in her seat, eying Palmer directly. "Do you think Pakistani Inter-Services Intelligence was alerted and sent a cleanup team to sweep the scene? Or maybe Aaliyah survived the crash and called them to get to her? If they suspected I was responsible, wouldn't they send someone to apprehend or kill me?"

Palmer took it all in and shook his head almost imperceptibly. "Aaliyah compromised one of our intelligence officers, ruined his life, and, by giving him the poison, was responsible for his death. If she's not dead, you'll never find her—she'll eventually find you."

"I should've told you."

"Yes, you should have," he said softly, though he understood why she hadn't. "Like I said, she was an evil woman. If she's dead, that's no less than what she deserves. But you've risked your life by interfering with all of that, Alona."

Green perked up at his use of her first name. "I know. I'm sorry."

"And no matter how much you wanted to do it or how justified it may have been, you shouldn't have done it. It's called discipline, and it's our code." Palmer paused. "It's been almost two years since it happened. If the Pakistani intelligence had found out that you killed or even tried to kill her, you'd be dead by now. Have you talked to Adams about it?"

"Not since the day after it happened."

"Good. Let it go, Alona. It never happened. Not the dinner, not your unauthorized op. None of it. Never speak of this to anyone."

"I won't."

Aaliyah was one of the smartest and effective intelligence officers he had ever encountered. Her revenge—if she were alive—would be served ice-cold at a time and location that best suited her purpose.

Palmer moved his seat back as far as it would go and closed his eyes.

14

HELSINKI, FINLAND, AND SAINT PETERSBURG, RUSSIA

The air force executive jet landed in Helsinki early in the morning. Palmer, stiff from the long flight, stretched his legs and disembarked. The temperature was in the low fifties, a stark contrast from the summerlike weather he and Green had left in Islamabad.

Palmer had come prepared and slipped on a lightweight jacket. Arriving on an executive jet didn't exclude them from going through immigration and customs. They made slow progress in the long line of people snaking through the immigration process. Entry into Finland was the first of many challenges ahead. However, considering the totality of their mission, this was a simple low-risk test of their new identities.

With the forged Canadian passports in their hands, they approached the immigration stations. If Dan Adams and the JSOC cobbler had done their jobs, this would be a validation of Dennis and Lauren Hall. Palmer waited while Green did as those ahead of her had done, pressing her passport identification page onto a scanner and looking up at the screen. After a few seconds, the gate opened and she passed through. He did the same thing and went through as well.

On the surface, the process seemed less secure than handing a passport to an immigration officer, who looked you in the eye, gave you the once-over, compared you to your passport photo, and asked a couple of inane questions before stamping it. But it wasn't. The computer was checking their biometric data from the chip in the passport and comparing their faces with the photos on their passport using facial recognition software. It was a more accurate way to detect a difference in appearance or issues related to the data on the passport chip. If there were a problem, the computer would alert an immigration officer, who would take them aside for secondary screening.

SUPO, the Finnish Security and Intelligence Service, arranged for a driver to pick them up at Helsinki Airport and take them to Helsinki Central Station, a thirty-minute drive south. A case officer, who introduced himself as Johannes, met them in the arrivals hall. They followed him to his car, which had heavily tinted windows. Palmer and Green sat in the back.

Johannes reached over the seat and handed Palmer a card with his contact information. "SUPO is here if you need us. I'll be your primary contact. I don't know how or if you will be returning to Finland. If you do, I'll do all I can to facilitate your operation. Just know that Helsinki is full of Russian operatives."

"Yes, I expect so," Palmer said. "What with Russia's president drafting civilians into the military and forcing them to fight in Ukraine, that is. Many fled. You closed your borders to Russia over it."

Johannes nodded, face grim. "The FSB will be on your train to Saint Petersburg. Count on it."

Palmer leaned forward. "Are you in contact with Sania Reed? She's MI6 and will support us in Russia."

"We're coordinating with the US intelligence case officer, Patrick Howell, in Moscow, as well as with Sania Reed. We'll stay in touch with them and you until you're out of Russia with Leapfrog. Reed will contact you in Saint Petersburg. Once you board the train, I suggest turning off your phone and removing the SIM card. Reed will provide you with clean, secure phones. She doesn't want you picked up at Finland Station in Saint Petersburg. Too many eyes." He reached around and handed them a map of the Saint Petersburg metro. "I've highlighted the route she wants you to take. An MI6 driver named Boris will be waiting outside the metro. He's one of Reed's men. He'll have a small sign in the front window of his car with your cover surname on it. The sign will have a heart drawn instead of the letter *a* in Hall. He'll take you to an MI6 safe house. Reed will contact you there."

Getting from Helsinki to Saint Petersburg had been a prime concern in Palmer and Green's planning. They'd first considered the thirty-minute flight but ruled it out because airport immigration in Saint Petersburg would be thorough and would include facial recognition software. Traveling by ferry had its advantages, including the fact that it came with a seventy-two-hour Russian visa, but the one significant disadvantage was that the trip took up thirteen of those seventy-two hours. The fastest means of getting there with the least risk was by the Allegro train, which took just three and a half hours, and the immigration check would be conducted on board. Their travel plans had been communicated to the American case officer and the MI6 officer in Moscow.

Johannes pulled up to the drop-off at the Helsinki train station, Helsingin Päärautatieasema, an eye-catching architectural mix of art deco and art nouveau styles, featuring a clock tower and a 160-foot statue holding a globe-shaped lamp on each side of a massive arched entryway. Palmer retrieved their luggage from the trunk and Johannes said, "*Onnea*. Good luck," then drove off.

They had time for breakfast before making their way to the platform. The train was clean and modern in design, featuring cushioned seats with fold-out tables similar to those on an airplane. They had chosen the economy class, one class lower than business. Although they were not certain when they would return or even if they would return by train, they'd purchased round-trip tickets, which would have them arriving back in Helsinki a week later, thereby avoiding questions that a one-way ticket might elicit.

The Helsinki-Saint Petersburg rail route had existed since 1870 as part of Tsar Alexander II's development of the Russian railway network. The train pulled out on time and picked up speed once it was outside Helsinki, accelerating to 136 miles per hour. They stopped in Lahti, Kouvola, and Vainikkala—the last station before the Finland-Russia border. They had crossed the border and just pulled into Vyborg, the first stop in Russia, when Green nudged Palmer and nodded toward the window.

Palmer leaned over. Uniformed Russian immigration agents were boarding the train.

And now the fun begins.

Palmer and Green had, naturally, been trained on what to do and what not to do to avoid secondary screening at airports and train stations: avoid showing unusual nervousness or anxiety; don't switch lanes in the security line; speak the language of the country that issued your passport. Other triggers for security were the use of one-way tickets, unusual itineraries, and traveling without baggage. Wearing a baggy sweatsuit, as some do on overnight flights, would also catch the attention of security screening. Baggy clothing can hide forbidden items, and passengers wearing them are often referred to secondary screening.

After the train pulled away from the station, the immigration agents moved down the aisle, taking each passenger's passport and visa, examining them, and asking a couple of questions. Palmer had the aisle seat and handed his passport and visa to the agent. The stern-faced man glared back at him, as if Palmer had just insulted his mother. He then proceeded to very slowly examine the visa, the photo page, and the page on the passport where the entry into Finland was noted.

"Why are you visiting Russia?" he asked, his voice curt.

Palmer nodded toward Green. "We're visiting her family."

"Why did you not spend time in Helsinki before traveling to Russia?"

"We are eager to get to Saint Petersburg. Her grandmother is not well. We'll stay for a few days in Helsinki on the return trip."

The agent's gaze turned to Green, whom he had been eyeing as he moved down the aisle. Green handed him her passport and visa. She was wearing jeans and a sweater. Her hair was pulled back into a ponytail, and she wore no makeup. The agent looked at her and the photograph a couple of times. He flipped through her passport, checking the immigration stamps, and turned back to the first page, studying the picture and her name. The agent asked in English, "What is the purpose of your visit, Mrs. Hall?"

With her lips slightly upturned, she made direct eye contact with the agent. She betrayed no signs of insecurity or fear. "Sightseeing and visiting my relatives in Saint Petersburg."

"Mother and father?"

"Aunt, uncle, cousins, and grandmother," Green replied. "As my husband said, my grandmother is not doing well."

"Where do they live?"

"Somewhere in Saint Petersburg. One of my cousins is meeting us at the station and taking us to her home."

"How long are you staying?"

"We have booked the return in one week, but we may change our plans, depending on how our visit with my relatives goes."

"Do you speak Russian?"

"They speak English, and I speak a little Russian," Green said, speaking slowly in English-accented Russian.

The agent cringed, then handed the passport and visa back to Green. He said in English, "Your visas expire in two weeks. Make sure you are both out of the country by then, or you'll be arrested."

Their train arrived on time at Finland Station, or Finlyandsky Vokzal, in Saint Petersburg. Located on the north bank of the Neva River, it was one of four train stations in the city. The main concourse teemed with people rushing to and from the platforms, carrying their luggage and gathering around the ticketing areas, shops, and restaurants. The result was a cacophony of different languages and loud announcements in Russian and English. However, the Russian immigration officer on the train showed no outward sign of concern, and Palmer and Green blended in with the crowd in the main concourse.

Following the instructions Johannes had given them in Helsinki, Palmer and Green walked to the Ploshchad Lenina, or Lenin Square, metro within the train station. At the entrance was a large mosaic commemorating Lenin's speech to the workers in 1917. They purchased their metro tickets and proceeded down the center of the three escalators, two of which were descending and one of which was ascending. Because the arched concrete ceiling over the escalators seemed to echo and amplify the sound of everyone talking, they remained quiet. The trip from ground level to the platform took a few minutes, as it was deep underground. Built during the Cold War in the late 1950s, the metro was intended to serve as a bomb shelter in the event the US attacked Russia with nuclear weapons.

They waited on the platform until their train arrived. Announcements were made in Russian. Palmer whispered in Green's ear, asking if she understood them. She nodded. They got off at

Vyborgskaya, consulted the metro map—deliberately looking as if they were unsure they were at the right stop—and then reboarded just as the doors were closing. One man exited and headed toward the escalator, but no one else got off and back on as they had. This wasn't a foolproof move to detect that someone was following them. If it was an FSB team, those remaining on the train would have seen them jump back on as the doors were closing and recognize that it was a move to lose a tail.

Palmer and Green got off at the next stop, Lesnaya, or Forest Station. Two men in the carriage ahead also got off. They waited as the men exited the platform by the escalator without looking back at them. Seeing no one else, Palmer and Green boarded the next metro and took it to their final stop, named Ploshchad Muzhestva, or Courage Square. They exited the platform and took the long escalator ride up to the metro station's street level.

They walked along the parked taxis and cars, glancing at the windshields of the vehicles and the people standing outside, holding signs. Eventually, they spotted a small sign in the windshield of a white late model car with HALL written with a heart instead of an *a*.

The driver was leaning against the car, smoking a cigarette. He said his name, Boris, when they came toward him. Green and Boris spoke in Russian, as if they were family, and then got in. Once inside the vehicle, Boris spoke perfect English. Palmer recognized the Geordie accent, spoken in the northeast of England.

"I'm bringing you to the safe house. Well, it's not a house—it's more of a large flat. It'll take us about thirty minutes to get there, depending on the traffic. In the seat pocket behind me, you'll find an envelope. Inside are electronic entry key cards. They get you in the building and into flat 3A. I stocked the fridge and pantry with some bare necessities, although I don't expect you'll be there long. Your new secure phones are on the kitchen table, along with some instructions."

"When will we see Sania Reed?" Palmer asked, leaning forward toward Boris.

"She'll be in touch once I let her know you've arrived."

Boris double-parked close to the front door of a ten-story building that appeared newer than the nearby structures—a semi-recent addition squeezed into a relatively high-density residential area populated by a few restaurants, bars, and shops.

Boris said, "This is a safe area of Saint Petersburg—as safe as most, anyway."

"We have a lot of work to do in a short window of time," Palmer said, patting the driver's seat as he eyed Boris in the rearview mirror. "I doubt we'll be able to enjoy it."

Palmer grabbed the envelope and got out. Green was quick to follow. They took their suitcases into the building. Before going up, Palmer checked out the entry level, noting a hallway off the lobby that led to the rear emergency exit from the building. They rode up the slow, cramped elevator to the third floor and found 3A. Before going in, they located the emergency exit near the elevator. Palmer opened the door and saw carpeted steps up and down.

The apartment was spacious and decorated in a minimalistic Euro-modern style. Palmer closed the curtains in all the rooms. The larger of the two bedrooms had a king-size bed and an en suite bathroom. The other bedroom across the hall had two double beds. A fire exit was located off the larger bedroom.

"You take the big bedroom and bath. I'll take the smaller one," Palmer said.

"I'll not argue with you. Remember, if you come in at night to pee, don't disturb me; I sleep naked."

Palmer laughed and shook his head. "Keep a cover over you, just in case."

"Right, but if I get hot, it's coming off," she said, visibly enjoying the light banter.

They found two mobile phones on the kitchen table. Palmer knew these were the ones using a VPN and that had access to encrypted messaging services. Every security measure, he knew, would have been taken with these phones. Also on the counter were several tourist maps and brochures in English.

Green saw a kettle on the kitchen counter, a jar of instant coffee, and a container of tea bags. "I'm having a coffee. Would you like one?"

"Sure. Glad we got some sleep on the flight. We may not get any for the next couple of nights."

✦✦✦

Palmer and Green were settling into the flat when Palmer's new phone rang. He picked up and was relieved to hear the voice of a pert British woman whom he guessed to be in her late thirties or early forties say, "Good afternoon, Mr. Hall. This is Reed."

"Nice to make your acquaintance," Palmer said. "I'll put you on speaker."

"How's your safe house—or should I say safe flat?" Reed asked.

"All the conveniences of home with none of the expenses," he replied.

"Don't get too comfortable. You won't be spending much time there."

"The shorter, the better," Green said.

"I'll be staying at a nearby hotel we use whenever we visit Saint Petersburg on embassy business," Reed said. "That lessens the chance of compromising the flat. You must be starving. I'll swing by and get some takeaway on my way there. Less risky than meeting me for dinner somewhere. We left some presents for you under the sink. I'm almost finished with my surveillance detection route. I should be there in an hour or so." Reed described herself and what she would be wearing.

With that, she disconnected and ended the call.

Palmer opened the cabinet door and reached under the sink. It was empty except for a cardboard box. He took it out set it on the table.

Green was watching him. "What's that?"

He opened it without answering. Inside were three 9mm Glock 17 pistols, along with extra seventeen-round magazines, a satellite telephone, and an electronic scanner to detect cameras and listening devices. He passed Green one of the Glocks. The handguns were used by Russia's FSB and NATO forces. Palmer ejected the magazine and pulled back the slide to ensure that no round was in the chamber. The magazines were full. Palmer slammed one into his Glock with the butt of his hand. He assumed the third pistol was for Reed.

"Oh yeah. I feel better already," Palmer said as he examined the pistol closely.

Green took her weapon and inspected it as Palmer had. "Nice. What's the penalty if we get caught with these?"

Palmer turned his head toward her. "Only slightly less than actually using them."

15

SAINT PETERSBURG, RUSSIA

An hour later, a few sharp raps on the door echoed throughout the flat. Palmer, Glock in hand, asked, "Who is it?"

Reed replied, "It's me, Sania."

Palmer confirmed she was Sania Reed by taking a quick glance through the peephole in the door, then let her in.

Reed bustled inside, carrying paper bags filled with takeout, and eyed his pistol critically. "Do you normally greet guests this way?"

"Only in Russia," Palmer replied, grinning.

"One can't be too cautious here," Reed said with a nod, heading toward the kitchen. "I picked this up from Teremok."

Palmer knew enough about Russia to know she was referring to a Russian fast-food restaurant that contained an assortment of savory and sweet blinis. His mouth watered.

Reed stood about five feet ten inches tall, with a medium build, dark hair pulled back into a ponytail, and bright-blue eyes. She wore a gray jacket, navy blue pants, and sensible walking shoes. Reed set the bags on the kitchen table without taking her eyes off Palmer. She introduced herself and shook his hand firmly. Then she turned to Green and did the same.

During their introductions, Palmer and Green stuck to their NOC names—Dennis and Lauren Hall. This was a strategic choice. If things went sideways and Reed was pressed by the FSB for information, she wouldn't be able to give Palmer and Green up to Russian authorities even if she wanted to, because she never would've learned their true identities.

"Thank you for arranging for Boris to pick us up and for coordinating the transfers in Helsinki. We only just learned about this op," Palmer said, peeking into the bags. "There was barely time to pack and no time to plan."

"Same for me," Reed said. "The chief phoned me yesterday."

Green looked into the bags. Instead of reaching in, she asked Reed, "What do you know about Sokolov?"

"I know that he's Russia's top hypersonic missile expert and the general director of the Hypersonic System Research Institute in Saint Petersburg. Dmitry Sokolov could be one of the most significant defections from Russia the West has ever seen. After I learned MI6 would be involved, I contacted Patrick Howell. He said that Sokolov hasn't explained why he's defecting, only that his need is urgent."

"Is there a chance he's a dangle trying to draw us in?" Palmer inquired.

Reed nodded. "That's always a possibility with defections. This one is no different. Howell has exercised caution and discretion for precisely that reason. I don't know Sokolov's rationale for defecting, but I suspect his urgency is related to the recent FSB arrests of hypersonic missile scientists and engineers."

"We'll exercise some caution as well," Palmer added.

Palmer suspected that Reed—who seemed to be in her early forties and approaching the pinnacle of her career—was primed to move up the MI6 ladder. Her knowledge of FSB tactics and Russia would be vital to the op. But would she be overly cautious? Would she have their backs if push came to shove?

Reed continued, "Howell told Sokolov to carry on as usual while the team was formed and in place to get him out. Sokolov is at work during the day and at home at night. Howell has brush-passed a secure phone to Sokolov, complete with encryption."

They opened their phones and exchanged numbers, including Howell's and Sokolov's new secure phone numbers. Palmer set his phone on the table and said to Reed, "Let's talk with Howell first and then get Sokolov on the line. The CIA won't be involved in this op, but it'll be a useful transition for him to hand Sokolov off to us."

Reed opened the bags she had brought and emptied the contents on the table. "Howell said Sokolov is very impatient and getting anxious. We've conducted a brief nighttime drive-by of his house. It's in a posh development about forty-five minutes from here. FSB was parked front and back at night."

"How many?" Green asked, sorting through the food choices.

"One in each car, but they must take turns leaving to get something to eat and go to the loo. We've also observed that Sokolov leaves for work at 07:30. One of the FSB cars follows him when he does. His housekeeper comes in after he leaves and is gone before he returns with one of the cars tailing him. That's around 18:30. The second watchdog arrives a little later. We haven't monitored Sokolov or the FSB long enough to have any confidence in this schedule."

"Has the surveillance always been this intense for key scientists and engineers?" Green asked.

"Until recently, surveillance was random and relatively light unless someone left the country on holiday or a conference. The Russian president has become paranoid about defections and is cracking down on anyone suspected of working with the West, especially the hypersonic missile scientists and engineers. As a result, FSB surveillance of key personnel has intensified. Some have been arrested for treason recently, and one was given a lengthy prison sentence. We also suspect they've bugged the scientists' and engineers' houses and cars and placed trackers on their vehicles. If we go inside, be careful what you say, if you say anything at all."

"With two FSB officers watching his house, we believe the risk will be too great to meet him there," Palmer noted.

"I agree," Reed said.

Palmer and Green were well versed in their remit and had worked together long enough to develop a mutual trust and respect. He asked Reed, "What's your remit regarding working with us?"

"The chief said that MI6 was providing a supportive role. What that means is up to us to define. I'm here for whatever you need me for. It's your op." Glancing between them, she continued, "Look, I don't doubt your capabilities for this operation. If you weren't the full package, you wouldn't be here. However, from what I understand, neither of you has set foot in Russia before. If that's true, I believe I can add value to this operation."

Palmer could tell from the cut of Green's eyes toward Reed that the comment about this being their first time in Russia didn't sit well with her. Even though it was true, it must have been the tone of Reed's voice and the implication that they were fish out of water that Green found unexpectedly insulting.

Green responded in what Palmer believed was fluent Russian, although he could not understand a word she said.

Reed appeared surprised. She answered in Russian, albeit with what Palmer felt was a little less confidence in the language than Green.

Green responded in something that sounded different from Russian.

Reed cocked her head and responded in English, "Was that Ukrainian? I could only pick up a couple of words. I won't ask how you became fluent in those languages. It's best I don't know."

Palmer said, "I haven't a clue what either of you just said."

They all laughed.

Palmer continued, "You're correct. This is our first visit to Russia."

Reed took a breath and exhaled, perhaps sensing she may have offended them. "I've spent a lot of time in Russia and understand the people, the culture, and the GU and FSB mindsets. I also have a good sense of the geography in this part of Russia, which could be of use."

Green responded, "Your knowledge and experience will be invaluable."

"The more help we have, the better," Palmer said. "If you're an active participant, and we get into the shit—which is highly likely— what are your limitations, your rules of engagement?"

Reed hesitated before responding. "The chief said I must maintain my diplomatic immunity and my official diplomatic cover role."

Palmer had expected that reply, but he and Green needed to hear it for themselves. He interpreted it to mean that her orders were not to do anything that would threaten her position as MI6's Moscow station chief unless her life depended on it. She would, however, provide much-needed support in her knowledge of the geography and of the FSB. He had to push her to think bigger.

Palmer nodded. "Your primary role as station chief is intelligence gathering, carried out by developing relationships with potential sources and managing those relationships. Don't you also support MI6's overall role of defending the UK's national security? Aren't Russia and China at least two to three years ahead of the West in the development and deployment of maneuverable hypersonic missiles? And North Korea and Iran aren't too far behind them."

Green added, "Doesn't that pose a threat to the UK's national security? Won't Sokolov assist the US and the UK in closing that gap? Consider that one hypersonic missile could cause significant damage to an aircraft carrier, and if the flight deck were hit, it would put it out of commission. If that missile has a nuclear warhead, it will most likely sink it, along with thousands of sailors. Once the West has these missiles and the ability to detect and destroy them far enough in advance, the rule of mutually assured destruction takes effect, as it has with nuclear weapons for over seventy years."

Reed tugged at a loose thread on her sleeve and then clasped her hands. "I recently read a report that concluded that the theory of mutually assured destruction, which has existed since the Soviet Union developed its first nuclear weapon in 1949, is flawed."

"Flawed? How?" Palmer asked.

"The theory of mutually assured destruction relies on complete and perfect compliance, meaning no leader would ever initiate a nuclear strike out of perceived advantage, desperation, egotism, madness, or error—or, heaven forbid, an autonomous AI system bypasses the command-and-control system and launches an attack independently. If the theory of mutually assured destruction fails even once, the consequences would be catastrophic. People are imperfect, and autocrats who oversee some of the nuclear arsenals are even less reliable. The American Columbus-class submarine has the explosive power of eighteen thousand Hiroshima-size bombs, enough to end civilization as we know it—especially if launches lead to retaliation. Your President Carter once said that an all-out nuclear war would cause more death and destruction every second than in the entirety of World War II. Until there is verifiable nuclear disarmament, the world will remain at risk of destruction."

Palmer thought over what she had said. Her arguments were sound. "All we're concerned with is the weaponry currently available to the US, the UK, and our allies. We know that other countries can deliver nonnuclear and nuclear warheads with next-generation hypersonic missiles. We don't yet have the technology or the defenses against it. Look, we can't solve the world's problems. Our mission is to ensure that Sokolov is in the secure hands of the West. End of assignment. Pats on the back for us all."

Palmer waited for her response, knowing this op could make or break her chances for whatever she saw as her next MI6 role. She could go all in or stand on the sidelines. The safe and secure middle ground was a narrow one. Reed couldn't get involved in a shootout with the FSB because she was constrained by her specific role in gathering human intelligence, or HUMINT, under diplomatic cover. But she hadn't gotten to where she was in MI6 by playing it too safe. Big opportunities come to those who, on occasion, take calculated risks and succeed.

Reed crossed her legs. "You're right about MI6's larger role in national security. The op, if successful, will have a significant positive impact on US and UK national security as well as for that of our NATO allies. I'll do whatever is required to get Sokolov out of Russia and ultimately to the US. However, at some point, I'll have to leave it to you. I can't cross the Russian border with Sokolov. Those were my orders."

Green nodded. "Understood."

Looking at Green, Reed continued, "If we find ourselves in a difficult situation, one person must be in charge. That person will make the tough calls, if necessary. I won't assume which one of you that will be—"

"That's Dennis," Green interjected. "He's the lead. I'm his backup. If something happens to him, I'll take charge."

Palmer pretended to tip his imaginary hat to Green and said, "Agreed," then looked to Reed.

"I'm committed one hundred percent, within the limits I've described," Reed said. "And, Mr. Hall, you're in charge."

Palmer stood, walked to the refrigerator, and grabbed a bottle of water. "Our JSOC Orange guidance allows for adjustments to rules of engagement based on the mission and risks, but we use only the amount of force necessary to achieve our objectives. We should aim to avoid civilian casualties, if possible. For this operation, we'll define civilians as nonmilitary and non-Russian intelligence operatives. We'll treat FSB operatives the same as the military. They won't hesitate to take us out. Does that work for everyone?" Palmer asked, though his eyes remained fixed on Reed.

"I'm comfortable with that as it applies to the two of you," Reed replied, "but I personally can't get into a firefight with the Russians. My orders are clear about JSOC having the lead and about my role at MI6. We don't get into gunfights or get involved in car chases."

Palmer nodded. Intelligence officers, especially station chiefs like Reed, wouldn't get involved in a car chase or shootout on a public street, as portrayed in movies. That would mean losing the ability to do their job as recruiters and handlers of foreign assets. But Palmer had to wonder—would Reed override these orders if it meant protecting their lives? Or would she gamble with their lives in favor of maintaining her standing with M16?

"What about Howell's limitations?" Palmer asked, moving to a new topic. "I understand as CIA his hands are largely tied."

"That is correct. His hands are tied. He's not happy about that, but he understands the reason for it. His biggest contribution has been communicating with Sokolov regarding his defection; so far, he has kept him from making a solo run for the border. If we need him, Howell will jump at the chance."

"Howell has done his part to get us to this point. Job well done," Palmer said. "We need all the help we can get. Howell should be on standby in case we do. Let's include him on our initial call with Sokolov today. Lastly, there's the electronic side of the operation. We'll need someone to provide satellite and drone surveillance from the beginning, with access to US and UK special operations to facilitate exfiltration, if necessary. We'll use Dan Adams in Islamabad." Looking at Reed, he asked, "Do you have anyone in Moscow who can connect with Adams?"

"I'll speak with Dayton Hunnicutt, who works with me in Moscow. He can connect with Adams."

Green answered, "Dan is already on it. Give me Hunnicutt's contact information, and I'll have them connect."

Palmer picked up his bottle of water and took a long drink. "That settled, how do we get Sokolov out of his house and lose his FSB guards without alerting every police and intelligence agency in Russia? How would we even get into Sokolov's house, especially if the FSB has installed video surveillance in and around his home?"

Green examined the container of blinis and selected one. "We could distract one or both guards long enough to get him out. Or take advantage of that small window of opportunity after Sokolov returns from work. Only one FSB watcher will be on duty."

Reed replied, "We've had only a couple of days to monitor their schedule. To have complete confidence in that strategy would take more time than we've had, and I don't think Sokolov is willing to wait much longer."

Palmer picked a mushroom melt and took a bite. "Good point. Let's ask Sokolov to confirm his surveillance once we have him on the phone. Even if we get him out of the house, what's the exit strategy? How do we get him out of the country? Is it realistic to think we could catch the morning Allegro train and enjoy a smooth ride to Helsinki? Is it even the best way out of Russia? If the FSB realizes they've lost him, we'd have only a short time before alarms are raised. They would search all trains, planes, buses, and cars."

Reed nodded in agreement. "The earliest departure is at 06:15, an hour and fifteen minutes before he typically leaves for work. You'd reach the Russia-Finland border about an hour after that. If you exit at Vyborg in Russia or Vainikkala in Finland, passport control would be inside those stations. Crossing the border into Finland would not stop the FSB from coming after someone as valuable as Sokolov. If the train's not an option, we could drive toward the Finnish or Estonian border, taking the back roads. Depending on our route, the Estonian border is approximately two to three hours away. The direct route is on the E20, or the back roads. Driving to the Finnish border is about the same. That's a lot of time for the FSB to react."

"What if he called in and said that he's not feeling well and would be working from home that day?" Green asked.

"That might be a better choice," Reed said, "but we still have to get him out of his house, and the FSB would probably maintain their surveillance."

Palmer smiled and nodded. "I know a better way."

16

SAINT PETERSBURG, RUSSIA

Sania Reed called Patrick Howell on speakerphone and introduced him to the Halls—Palmer and Green. She clarified that the team consisted of Dennis Hall, Lauren Hall, and herself and that Howell was in Saint Petersburg to assist if requested.

Palmer added that Howell's only official role would be to transfer Sokolov to the team.

"I'm happy to make the transfer," said Howell. "I'm also willing and eager to help with anything you need. Just let me know."

Palmer chewed on that before responding. "The CIA isn't involved in this op, Howell. However, I have no problem with you being nearer the action, just in case. Sania?"

Reed looked at Palmer and Green, who were both nodding. "I concur."

"This may be a silly question, Howell," Palmer asked, "but do you have a safe house in Saint Petersburg?"

"Yes. That's where I'm staying."

They discussed options for freeing Sokolov from his FSB tails. With the FSB and the threat of their suspected video surveillance, there was no doubt in anyone's mind that getting him from his home would be difficult. They decided an easier plan would be for him to go to work and then leave from there. He could meet them somewhere, and then they would take the train with him to Helsinki. Green suggested that he feign illness and say he's going to see a doctor.

"If he's able to avoid mentioning which clinic he's going to, we could intercept him there," Reed said with a slight frown. "But I'm sure he has an FSB tracker on his car. They'll find out on their own if they discover he's left the facility—and which clinic he's gone to."

If they encountered problems, adjustments would need to be made. Howell and Reed confirmed that firearms and ammunition were prohibited on trains in Russia; however, there was no baggage check or metal detector in place before boarding a train, so it was arguably possible to bring the three pistols that Boris had delivered to the flat. Palmer decided they should take them to the station and then decide.

With everyone in agreement, Reed connected Sokolov to the call. Sokolov confirmed he was taking a walk outside the building and using earbuds so that he could listen and talk without risk of being monitored. Howell spoke first, saying that this was the team he would work with and introduced them, without stating who they worked for.

Palmer told Sokolov that he should go to work the next day and then claim he was sick and needed to go home and would visit a clinic on the way there. He would then drive to the clinic, where they would be waiting in two cars. Reed described their vehicles to him. Sokolov told them he would drive his Mercedes. They would leave the clinic, drive to the station, and catch the train to Helsinki.

Sokolov assured them that the FSB wouldn't follow him to the clinic because that was outside his usual routine. They typically followed him to work and then left, returning near the end of his workday. However, this plan would mean missing the early morning train. "We wouldn't reach Finland Station in Saint Petersburg until mid- to late morning. With luck, they wouldn't notice I was missing until the end of the day, when I usually leave for home. Although sometimes they check to confirm I'm still in the building." Sokolov provided them with the clinic's address where he would go. "What should I do with my personal phone and the one Howell gave me that I'm using now?"

"Leave your personal phone turned on at your home and bring the secure phone Howell gave you," Palmer replied.

⁓

After the call, Palmer and Green said they would stay in the flat until the last moment before the operation.

"I'll drive by the clinic after leaving to check if they have video surveillance cameras and, if so, where they're located," Reed said. "I'll come back with a proper meal for the three of us. It's safer than going out for dinner and risking the facial recognition security cameras identifying us and our location. I'll also have another car delivered to our underground parking deck, where I'll park after I return with dinner."

Palmer shook his head. There were so many moving parts—101 ways this could go wrong. However, it was a start, and as Howell had said, it was the simplest solution.

Palmer still had questions about Sokolov's urgency to defect. He wanted to look him in the eye and ask him point-blank for an answer, telling him that anything less than a valid reason would result in aborting the operation immediately. They were risking their lives for his extraction, after all.

The incentives behind becoming a foreign agent or spy could typically fall into one of four categories: money, ideology, coercion, or ego—otherwise referred to as MICE. Of all the incentives, coercion was often the strongest but was also the most negative factor.

Palmer tried to consider what would motivate Sokolov. *Coercion occurs when the recruiting officer has some information with which to threaten the person if they don't cooperate. Often, after convincing them to divulge some low-level classified information, they can use that as coercion. Recruited individuals remain valuable as foreign agents, passing classified information to their intelligence officer over the years. However, if they defect, the spigot of new information is turned off forever.*

Sokolov didn't need the money. He wasn't being coerced. Maybe he had a big ego. At his age, perhaps he was feeling unappreciated and pressured to perform. Palmer was certain it was ideology. Many Russians were opposed to the invasion of Ukraine—the drawn-out war that had resulted, the massive loss of life in Ukraine, and the Russian army and its mercenary Wagner Group. Opposing the war was most likely the motivator. But would that be enough for him to defect to the US on such an urgent basis? He didn't see it—not for someone in Sokolov's position. Maybe he was contemplating it, and something pushed him over the edge.

"Something has motivated him to defect immediately, and we need to know what that is," Palmer said.

Green stood and paced as she spoke. "He's seen what his weapons did to the Ukrainian people. Maybe he wants to leave the dark side and no longer wants to design and manufacture weapons of mass destruction that are more and more lethal than the previous ones and used against innocent civilians. My father left with my mother because he had become disenchanted with communism."

"That's possible," Palmer said, shaking his head. "But he would be doing the same thing for the US, speeding up our development of hypersonic missiles. The only difference is that the US would not be committing war crimes and killing innocent civilians. Maybe he's disillusioned with communism under the current regime. I need to hear that from him."

"I believe it's due to the fear that he might be arrested for treason, as some of his colleagues have been over the past few months," Reed added.

Green shook her head and exhaled. "Our orders are to get him out, not to interrogate him as to why he's fleeing Russia."

Palmer bit his tongue. She was right. Fear was a strong motivator. But to risk their lives for something like this, without gaining any clarity, was a tough pill to swallow.

"We could get a quick read on his rationale but not enough to satisfy anyone," Green went on. "He'll have plenty of interviews and lie detector tests, along with psychological testing and counseling, after he's in US custody and before he's cleared to work on our missile development programs. Part of that process will be to provide us with information on the Russian missile programs first. If anyone knows how to defend against them, it's him."

Palmer leaned back and interlocked his hands behind his head. Green was right. Their questioning would be superficial and insufficient to rule out that he was a dangle or to clear him to work with the military and its defense contractors. Their orders were clear: Get him out of the country.

Before Reed left for the clinic where they would meet Sokolov, and to pick up dinner for the three of them, she said, "We need a hearty meal and a good night's sleep. Depending on how tomorrow goes, it may be our last for a while."

17

FSB HEADQUARTERS AT BOLSHOY DOM
SAINT PETERSBURG, RUSSIA

Colonel Vladislav "Vlad" Maksimov, director of the Russian Federation's FSB counterintelligence, was working at the Bolshoy Dom building, FSB's Saint Petersburg headquarters at 4 Liteyny Avenue. Back in the days of the Soviet Union, the building, which was a block from the Neva River, had been the KGB's headquarters. Built in 1932 in the constructivist style, it was unofficially named and referred to as Bolshoy Dom, or Big House. For Saint Petersburg residents old enough to remember, it stood as a stark reminder of the KGB's reign of terror.

Maksimov leaned forward as he reviewed the daily FSB intelligence update on his desktop computer. Among the communication sections was one titled "Movement of Foreign Intelligence Operatives," which listed known or suspected intelligence operatives who'd been assigned to Russia and the reporting source. He pored over the listing, his eyes stopping on a notice that Jake Palmer and Alona Green, JSOC intelligence officers, had recently left Islamabad on a US Air Force executive plane. Transponder tracking data from the aircraft revealed their destination was Helsinki.

Maksimov wasn't particularly bothered by the information; Finland had joined NATO and was ramping up their base of intelligence operations because of the eight-hundred-mile border with Russia. As such, Finland's transition from a neutral country to a NATO country had resulted in both Finland and Russia increasing security along their shared border.

What had caught his attention, however, was that a Pakistani Inter-Services Intelligence officer was the cited source. Most of the listings were for information only. If no FSB files existed on these US officers, one would be created, and new information would be added to it as it was obtained. Why was an ISI officer reporting this? And why was the contact information for the reporting source included? It was like a plea for someone to call if the two were spotted in Russia. Perhaps out of curiosity more than concern, he called in his chief of staff, Andrei Fedorov, and asked him to initiate a search for Palmer and Green and to follow up with the reporting Pakistani intelligence officer.

Later that day, Andrei Fedorov entered Maksimov's office and reported that he had information on the two operatives and on the Pakistani intelligence officer who reported it. Jake Palmer and Alona Green were believed to have stopped a terrorist nuclear attack in London, and in doing so, killed a few Pakistani soldiers and a senior Pakistani naval officer.

"I remember that incident," Maksimov said. "Someone stole a nuclear device and had planned to detonate it in London. None of the individuals involved on either side were ever named."

"It is only speculation," Fedorov replied, unimpressed. "According to the ISI report, Palmer and Green are part of a secret US special warfare intelligence group—Task Force Orange—working out of Islamabad."

"Why should we be concerned?" Maksimov asked, leaning back in his chair.

"That depends on why they're in Helsinki."

"Probably training with Finland's NATO team or taking time off."

"But they flew on a military jet," Fedorov pointed out.

"They may have hopped a military flight going to Helsinki. Happens all the time."

"I checked flight and train databases to see if they had traveled from Helsinki to Russia or anywhere else. Nothing there. No flight or train record of Jake Palmer or Alona Green entering Russia exists. I need photographs of them to compare with facial recognition."

"If they enter Russia, they'll either travel under diplomatic cover using these names or under nonofficial cover using fake names," said Maksimov, sighing. "Did you speak with the officer?"

"I did. The officer is on the way here."

"Let's see what ISI has on these two."

Fedorov walked toward the office door, then turned before exiting. "One more thing, sir."

"What is it?"

"It was odd, but she said under no circumstances should we kill them before she arrives."

"What? Did you say *she* said?"

"Yes, the ISI officer is a woman. She goes by only a single name."

"Which is?"

"Aaliyah."

PART 2

18

ISLAMABAD, PAKISTAN

As Aaliyah bent to get into her car, a familiar searing pain shot through her leg. She stifled a groan and fell into the driver's seat, stretching out her leg, waiting for the pain to ease—haunted yet again by the memory of the night of her car accident.

She'd finished having dinner with Alona Green at a hilltop restaurant north of Islamabad and had been making progress toward convincing her to become a double agent. Green's lingering eye contact, attentiveness, and the softness of her voice during dinner led Aaliyah to believe Green was attracted to her, so she played that card and encouraged it. They had discussed plans to see each other again. Before they parted ways outside the restaurant, they kissed. That long and tender kiss was the last thing Aaliyah remembered. According to what she was told days later, her car went off the road in one of the curves and rolled over three times before stopping, leaving her more dead than alive. Investigators concluded that someone had tampered with the car's brakes.

Aaliyah's phone was lost in the crash. Once she was able, she had a trusted ISI officer bring her a replacement with the same number. She checked the phone and found voicemails from Green left a few days after the accident. She listened to them several times. Green's voicemail elicited two emotions in Aaliyah. One was a feeling of warmth when hearing the sincerity in Green's voice. The second was a feeling of anger.

Had Green participated, even indirectly, in her accident? Was Green simply keeping her distracted in the restaurant while someone else tampered with her car's brakes? If so, why? Was it because she'd given Martin Singleton, Green's fellow intelligence officer, a poison pill? Green would have understood that he would rather die than face the humiliation and shame that would soon follow. She had only given him the *option* of suicide. He'd been the one who decided to go through with it.

Her recovery had been tedious, filled with surgeries and long stretches of rehab, but she was determined to get back to work as soon as possible. Her surgically reconstructed face had mild scarring, which she concealed with her hairstyle and makeup. The sole positive was that the cosmetic surgeon had also made her look more than ten years younger.

Aaliyah would find Green, regardless of time or cost. Using ISI resources and her personal time to track and follow her, she wouldn't be deterred. Blood washes away blood. ISI supported her in taking her revenge, just not on Pakistani soil.

One morning, Aaliyah learned that Green and her JSOC partner, Jake Palmer, had boarded a small military jet. ISI tracked the plane to Helsinki using the aircraft's transponder data. She booked a seat on the first flight out of Islamabad to Helsinki with only one scheduled stop.

Pakistan maintained an Honorary Consulate General in Helsinki, with an office and a small staff, one of whom was Taimoor Abbas, an ISI intelligence officer who worked under diplomatic cover.

Pakistan's supervisory embassy for Finland was in Stockholm, Sweden. Aaliyah alerted Abbas to the military plane's departure and told him she would leave for the airport immediately and follow them. She sent him photos of Palmer and Green and told him they might be traveling under nonofficial cover with false names. They exchanged contact details and her flight schedule. Before she left for the airport, Aaliyah entered the information regarding Palmer and Green's travel to Helsinki into an intelligence reporting system, with instructions to contact her for further information.

⎯⎯~⎯⎯

As the plane taxied to the gate in Helsinki, Aaliyah checked her messages and spotted one from Andrei Fedorov in Russia's FSB. She'd follow up with him later, noting that he would work in their Saint Petersburg office until the end of the month. Another was a message from Abbas, saying he was waiting in the arrivals hall. He had attached a photo showing his face and what he was wearing. She replied, saying the plane had just landed, and she attached a photo of her face and upper body. Aaliyah wound her way through a long line at immigration and customs.

When she entered the arrivals hall, Aaliyah spotted Taimoor Abbas right away. She extended her hand to greet him, and Abbas shook it. They said little on their way to his car. After he drove off, Aaliyah asked, "Were you able to identify Palmer and Green?"

"Yes. Someone—probably a US Embassy intelligence officer— met them in the arrivals hall. One of my coworkers accompanied me. We followed them to short-term parking and from there to Helsinki Central Station. They were dropped off at the station entrance. With nowhere to park, my coworker got out and followed them in, texting me along the way. They boarded the high-speed Allegro train on platform nine and got off in Saint Petersburg, where someone was waiting to meet them. At that point, he lost them and took the next train back to Helsinki."

This was what Aaliyah had been yearning for. Now was her chance.

"I need to go to Saint Petersburg. I received a message from Andrei Fedorov at the FSB headquarters in Moscow regarding my entry in an intelligence database that tracks the movements of foreign intelligence officers. He wants to introduce me to his boss, Colonel Vladislav Maksimov," she said. "They're operating out of their Saint Petersburg office at Bolshoy Dom."

Abbas's eyebrows raised. "The FSB head of counterintelligence."

"Yes. I'm eager to meet with him."

Abbas grinned. "Impressive. You move fast, but you've got some catching up to do. You're running almost a day behind Palmer and Green."

"Thank you for your assistance. You've done me a great service. My best hope is to work with the FSB. When I do, I'm going to kill them."

"Inshallah," Abbas said with a slight bow.

19

SAINT PETERSBURG, RUSSIA

Sokolov left work and drove home, the same as any other day—but it was far from any other day.

If all went well, this would be the last night he would spend in his home and perhaps in Russia. Once inside, he went to his wine cellar and selected a 2009 Château Lafite Rothschild Bordeaux Pauillac. It was the most expensive bottle in his collection, which he'd been saving for a special occasion. He took care in removing the cork from the bottle. Using a two-pronged Ah-So opener to ensure the cork came out in one piece, he poured the contents into a Lalique decanter. He took the decanter and a glass into his sitting room and set them by his favorite chair, which overlooked his back garden.

He turned on his audio system and pulled up Act III of Verdi's *Aida*. A lover and patron of opera, and a season ticket holder at Saint Petersburg's Mariinsky Theatre, he knew the arias by heart. He sat and poured a glass of wine from the decanter, savoring each sip as he drank it slowly. As he reached the end of his second glass, the Ethiopian princess Aida sang the aria "O patria mia"—Oh, my country—a plangent lament for the homeland she would never see again. He wiped tears from the corners of his eyes as Aida left her home for the last time and looked back, singing repetitions of "*O patria mia, più ti rivedrò!*"—Oh, my country, I will never see you again!

After the aria finished, he turned the audio system off and thought about his reality. He cherished his homeland with its rich history, but the president had made it socially and politically unrecognizable from the Russia he'd come to know and love.

Howell had said he should leave his personal phone at home. What Howell didn't know, however, was that his phone contained photos of the document he intended to use as leverage with the Americans, as well as personal images, many of which were sentimental, such as those of his former wife. He didn't want to leave those behind. He proceeded to airdrop the pictures to the secure phone that Howell had given him and made a copy of the images on a USB flash drive. Once he did that, he deleted them from his personal phone. Fearing an FSB technician could still find the photos of the document, he reset the phone and installed and activated only the basic applications, including location services.

Sokolov considered what valuables or memorabilia he should take with him. The Americans had told him he would be traveling with a fake Russian passport and name and not to bring anything with him that would reveal his real identity.

He looked at the Rolex watch he was wearing. The president had bestowed it to him after the first successful test of a new-generation hypersonic missile. He loved this watch, but it was engraved with his name. He took it off and set it on the table by his chair. The house was full of artwork he had collected over the years. There were also numerous awards and commendations displayed on his office wall.

After he defected, or died trying, the FSB would break through the door and ransack his home. Many of his valuables would simply disappear. Although his ex-wife didn't know it, the house was still in both their names. The title would transfer to her after he defected unless the government declared the house a property of the state, which it probably would.

Aware that the FSB had probably bugged the house and installed cameras in many of the rooms, he feared they would take note of a memory tour of his home. Instead, Sokolov poured a final glass of wine from the decanter and looked no further. He would take nothing personal with him, except the clothes on his back.

Sokolov arrived at work the next morning at his usual time and entered his office. He reviewed his emails and had an early meeting with a coworker. At 09:15, he got up from his desk and went to the toilet. On his way back, he stopped by the desk of Natalya Orlova, who had been his assistant for over fifteen years. "Natalya, I'm feeling horrible, gastrointestinal issues, and I believe I have a fever." Sokolov reached up and pressed the palm of his hand to his forehead. "I must have caught COVID at the meeting in Moscow."

Orlova slid her chair back, distancing himself from Sokolov. "Sir, you should go home. Do you want me to have someone drive you?"

"I'm perfectly capable of driving myself. I'll phone my housekeeper and tell her to leave before I get home. Wouldn't want to infect the poor woman."

"You need to see a doctor."

"Yes. I'll swing by an outpatient clinic on the way home."

Sokolov returned to his office and phoned his housekeeper. He told her to leave and not return until he notified her it was safe. He shut down his computer and sat at his desk. He'd only been told of the plan the day before. He hadn't had enough time to properly worry about it. But now the reality that his defection was in motion was beginning to sink in. There was no going back. He pulled a tissue from the box on his desk and wiped sweat off his brow. Orlova was staring at him, visibly concerned. *My anxiety and nervousness are reinforcing the story that I'm not feeling well.*

Sokolov told her that he was going to bed when he got home and to hold all his calls. He wrote down the number of the secure phone that Howell had given him and instructed her to message him if anything urgent came up.

Sokolov exited the security gate at 09:40, glancing in his rearview mirror at the facility as he drove away. Regardless of the outcome of the day's events, he knew he would never see it again.

⸻ ❧ ⸻

Natalya Orlova raised her head from the computer screen. Two men walked by her without stopping to ask if Sokolov was available. They were dressed in the typical black attire of FSB officers, with jackets that had the FSB emblem on the back and their rank on a patch on their upper arms. Both were tall and muscular. One, the more senior of the two based on his officer rank, was gray at the temples; the other was younger, perhaps in his early thirties. They walked to Sokolov's closed office door, opened it, and went inside.

Orlova followed them into the office and asked, "May I assist you, gentlemen?"

"Where is Dmitry Sokolov?" The older of the two men glared at Orlova. "Where's your boss? We need to see him immediately."

"That's not possible. He looked terrible and thought he may have contracted COVID on a trip to Moscow. He was going to stop by a medical clinic for a COVID test and some medication before going home. What do you need to see him about? Maybe I can help you."

"How long ago did he leave?"

"You just missed him. No more than thirty minutes ago."

"Did he say which clinic?"

"No."

"Was he driving himself?"

"I believe so, but I'm not sure. Shall I call him and tell him you're looking for him? I'll tell him to wait at the clinic." Orlova despised the FSB and their arrogance and air of superiority but tried to stay calm and cooperative.

"Don't contact him. If he calls, do not tell him we were here. Do not tell him we were looking for him. Do not tell him anything. As far as he's concerned, this interaction never happened." The older man handed her a card with his contact information on it. "Call me immediately if you hear from him."

Orlova's eyes widened. "Of course."

As they walked away, she overheard them talking. "Let's go back to the car and check his vehicle tracker."

"We checked it before we set out this morning. How did we know he would leave?"

"If we can't find him, we'll have to phone the boss."

"We'll find him."

2 0

SAINT PETERSBURG, RUSSIA

Palmer and Green were ready to go when Reed arrived at the safe flat early the next morning.

"The traffic should be lighter this morning than when I drove to the clinic and back. Last night, it took me about thirty minutes each way. To avoid surveillance cameras, I didn't pull into the car park, but from the road, I saw that the clinic has video cameras at the front and rear entrances to the building. Based on that, I know where we should enter the car park and where we should park. Just follow me."

"Was the other car delivered here?" Palmer asked.

"Yes, and the driver dropped off the key fob at my hotel last night." Reed pulled it out of her coat pocket and handed it to Palmer.

They took the elevator to the underground parking level. Palmer used the fob to make the car horn blast and the lights flash so they could identify it. He watched Reed enter her car and followed her out of the underground parking area.

She pulled into a space at the clinic that she had confirmed was not surveilled by the two security cameras. Palmer parked one space over from her, leaving a space between their two cars for Sokolov to park. If FSB officers had planted a tracking device on Sokolov's vehicle, which they almost certainly had, they would see that his car was at the clinic.

Sokolov's Mercedes pulled into the clinic parking lot at 10:20. Palmer motioned him into the space between their vehicles and patted him down as soon as he stepped out. He found a cell phone in his jacket pocket.

Palmer held the phone out toward Sokolov and asked, "Is this the secure phone Patrick Howell gave you?"

"It is," Sokolov said with an avid nod. There was sweat on his upper lip. He appeared to be nervous, as he should be. That was a good sign. "I gave the number to my assistant and told her to message me if something urgent arose."

"I'll hold on to it for now. We're running late. Keep your time in the clinic to a minimum."

Sokolov handed Palmer the phone and his car keys and left for the clinic. Palmer walked around the car's exterior, checking the wheel wells and finding nothing. He moved inside the vehicle, eventually locating a tracker plugged into the vehicle's onboard diagnostics port under the dashboard on the steering column, which mechanics used to diagnose problems with the car. *Smart. The port also charged the tracker.* Palmer found an unlocked car nearby that also had a diagnostics port. He returned to Sokolov's car and removed the device, hurried back to the other car, inserted the device in that vehicle's diagnostics port, and shut the door. If the FSB noticed a slight blip, they probably wouldn't make anything of it. They would eventually locate the car, but valuable time would be gained for their escape.

The plan was for Sokolov to check in, stay awhile, and leave without saying anything. A few cars pulled in and parked while Sokolov was in the clinic. One was driven by a woman who appeared to be in her sixties and another by a young woman with a preschool child in tow. Others fit similar profiles, which Palmer ruled out as being FSB officers.

Ten minutes later, Sokolov returned from the clinic, got into the back seat of Palmer and Green's car, and lay down. Palmer nodded at Reed. She drove off with him following close behind. Reed knew the way to Finland Station, the same station where he and Green had arrived in Saint Petersburg. Palmer checked his rearview mirror frequently to determine whether anyone was following them. The handguns and ammunition were in the trunk.

Sokolov told them the drive to the station would take about thirty minutes, depending on the unpredictable Saint Petersburg traffic. Once they arrived, they would accompany him to the Allegro train scheduled to depart at twelve thirty. They would board the train, with Green sitting behind Sokolov and Palmer and Reed a few rows back. The plan was too simple, but as Howell had said, simple often worked best.

Palmer drove close behind Reed, who used a surveillance detection route after leaving the clinic to ensure they were not being followed. Because they were pressed for time, the route would be much shorter than a typical route to detect if they were being followed, which could take hours. It would add about fifteen to twenty minutes to their travel time to the station. They were cutting it close.

21

FSB HEADQUARTERS AT BOLSHOY DOM
SAINT PETERSBURG, RUSSIA

Lost in thought, Vladislav Maksimov stood in front of his office window and stared down at the river below until he heard a sharp rap on his office door. He turned his head and snapped at his chief of staff, Andrei Fedorov, "What is it?"

Fedorov replied, "Aaliyah is here to see you."

"Who?"

"The Pakistani ISI officer who filed a report about the two American intelligence officers who had traveled from Islamabad to Helsinki. She believes they may have entered Russia under false identities."

Maksimov tilted his head and squinted. "Why would she be so interested in this that she has traveled here from Islamabad?"

"I believe she has a score to settle with them, some sort of vendetta."

"I don't have time for this."

"Hear her out. She worked as a sparrow and lured an American intelligence officer into a romantic relationship and turned him into an asset, before poisoning him when his betrayal was discovered."

"Bold move," Maksimov said, only vaguely impressed. "Still not interested."

"She's very . . . attractive," Fedorov noted pointedly.

Maksimov sighed and stroked his chin. "Five minutes. That's all I've got."

"Yes, sir."

Fedorov returned with Aaliyah standing behind him. "I told her you have a busy schedule today and have only a few minutes to spare."

"That's what they all say," Aaliyah muttered under her breath.

"What was that?" Fedorov asked, believing he had misunderstood her disparaging retort.

"Nothing, just talking to myself. Must be the jet lag."

Fedorov introduced her to his boss and left, closing the door behind him.

Maksimov took her in from head to toe. *Damn, Fedorov was right.* "What are you doing in Russia?" Maksimov asked bluntly in English.

Responding in English, she said, "Pakistani ISI tracked Jake Palmer and Alona Green, American special operations intelligence officers based in Islamabad, as they flew on a military jet to Helsinki a couple of days ago."

"Two American intelligence officers? Helsinki is a beautiful place to visit. They're probably having a tryst."

"They didn't stay. One of our intelligence officers followed them from the Helsinki airport to the train station, where they took the fast train. The officer got on board and kept an eye on them. They disembarked here in Saint Petersburg. Our officer lost them after they got off the metro and then jumped back on just before the doors shut."

"Why do you need to find them?" he asked, cutting to the chase. He studied her. "Fedorov told me that you said not to kill them until you arrived. What sort of vendetta do you have against these two, Aaliyah?"

Her dark eyes were in gridlock with his—intense enough that he almost wanted to look away, but he wouldn't let himself. "One of them tried to kill me," she said simply. "Let me rephrase—one of them tried and thinks she successfully killed me."

"So it was the woman who tried to kill you? Well, that's your problem. What do you expect us to do about these Americans? Why didn't you kill them when they were in Pakistan? That would have been much easier and wouldn't involve us."

"ISI authorized me to kill them—just not in Pakistan."

Maksimov snorted, brows raised. "So you are going to shit in our house instead. Kill them here, cause an international incident, and let FSB take the blame. Is that right?"

"That's not my intention," Aaliyah said calmly. "My main purpose is to let you know why I'm here and to get your permission to find and kill them. I'll contact you when I learn why they are here."

"Russia is a massive country spanning across Europe and Asia. I can't spare the resources to assist you in finding two Americans who've done no wrong here. However, you're free to search for them. If you kill them, ISI will have some explaining to do. Our response to the American reaction to the deaths of two American intelligence officers would require an answer. That answer will be a Pakistani ISI officer killed them."

Maksimov pressed the intercom button on his phone. "Fedorov, Aaliyah will be leaving now."

He rose and walked her to the door, where Fedorov was waiting. "Pleasure to meet you, Aaliyah. Tell my chief of staff how to contact you. And keep him updated on your progress. You're welcome to stay until your visa expires." Maksimov shook her hand, which Aaliyah grasped with both hands and gently squeezed, her eyes locked on his.

"The pleasure has been all mine. Thank you for seeing me."

Maksimov returned to his desktop computer. *What a waste of time. However, Aaliyah would make an interesting dinner companion. She's beautiful and obviously very talented. Perhaps I'll have Fedorov schedule it.*

—◦◦◦—

Minutes after Aaliyah left, Andrei Fedorov again entered Maksimov's office, stopping halfway between the door and his desk.

Maksimov took a deep breath and exhaled. "Now what?" Maksimov asked, his voice raised.

Fedorov's face was pale. "Dmitry Sokolov has gone missing."

Maksimov sprang from his seat and slammed his fists on the desk so hard that the framed photo of him and the Russian president standing side by side fell onto the floor. "Sokolov is gone? How the *hell* did that happen?"

Fedorov, whose stance was straight and rigid, took a step backward.

Maksimov leaned forward, bracing both hands on his desk.

Fedorov cleared his throat. "Two of our men went to Sokolov's Saint Petersburg office today to take him in for interrogation regarding his publications and presentations at meetings. They discovered he had left work, complaining of COVID symptoms. He said he was going to a clinic to get checked out and go home."

"No one was following him?"

"It was out of his standard routine."

"How can you lose someone with a tracker on his car, video surveillance in his home, and location service on his phone?" Maksimov asked rhetorically, simmering with rage.

"We had all three, the same as anyone on our priority list of scientists and engineers working on the hypersonic missile program. They checked the car's tracking system before they left to go to the site. He had left his phone at home, and nothing on video surveillance alerted us to a problem. So they rechecked the tracker when he wasn't at his office. It showed that he was at a medical clinic. They were on the way there when the vehicle's tracker began moving. They caught up with it in a working-class area of Saint Petersburg a few miles from the clinic. The officers crashed through the door, and . . ."

"Well?" yelled Maksimov.

Fedorov cleared his throat again. "It was the home of an elderly couple. They had no connection to Sokolov. The man had taken his wife to the clinic for treatment of a urinary tract infection."

"Do I look like I give a shit what she had?" he asked, eyes bulging.

"No, sir. Of course not."

"How did a tracker get from Sokolov's car to their car?"

"Someone must have moved it."

"That was a rhetorical question!" Maksimov shouted, shaking his head. "Issue our rapid response alert for Dmitry Sokolov and possibly two Americans traveling with him. Have Border Security check for him at every border crossing out of Russia. Send them photos of Sokolov. Dispatch teams to train stations, airports, and bus depots. Double up at Finland Station—that's their fastest way out of Russia." He shook his finger at Fedorov. "If Sokolov gets out of Russia, there'll be hell to pay." A key part of Maksimov's plan to reduce the number of defectors was to capture them before they left the country. They had used the rapid response alert system twice before. It was successful both times.

"I'll get right on it," Fedorov said.

"Wait!"

"Sir?"

"Get that Pakistani woman back in here. Now!"

— ✧ —

Maksimov needed to inform Sergey Vasilyev, colonel general of the FSB, who would then be the one to notify the president. Both would be furious. Vasilyev had authorized additional resources to decrease the number of defections from Russia to the West. Now Russia's most crucial hypersonic missile engineer was on the run with his incredible knowledge of Russia's program—including, perhaps, any vulnerabilities they could use to defend against the missiles.

Maksimov called Unit 29155's Nikolai Ivanov.

"Dmitry Sokolov is attempting to flee the country. He was last seen in Piter," Maksimov said, using the locals' shortened name for Saint Petersburg. "He may be with two American intelligence officers—a man and a woman. When my FSB team locates them, I'll let you know."

Ivanov replied in a firm, confident voice, "I'll leave for Saint Petersburg today. I need to be closer to the Finnish border. That's where they'll head."

"I'm already in Piter today at our Bolshoy Dom . . . Hello?" There was no reply. Ivanov had already disconnected the call.

Maksimov looked at the phone and shook his head. Unit 29155 had its own intelligence organization and the technical staff to guide the assassins to their targets. Sokolov and the Americans had little chance of surviving, much less getting across the border.

Maksimov had just hung up the phone when Fedorov and Aaliyah entered. She approached and asked, "What can I do for you, sir?"

"One of our missile scientists is defecting. It's possible that Palmer and Green are assisting him. They will likely go to Finland Station and try to leave on the twelve thirty train to Finland. We've already alerted our team. I plan to join them. Would you like to go? You can identify them. The station is just across the river from here. We'll take one of our boats and be there in minutes."

Aaliyah's eyes lit up. "Thank you. Let's go."

2 2

SAINT PETERSBURG, RUSSIA

Palmer was following Reed, keeping one or two cars behind her, when he felt Sokolov's secure phone vibrate in his pocket. He handed the phone to Green and told Sokolov to give her the code to unlock it, which he did. Green entered the code and opened the encrypted messaging app.

She read the message out loud, in English: "'FSB came to see you after you left. Told them you were ill and had gone to a medical clinic to see if you had COVID, and then going home.'"

Green turned toward Palmer and then Sokolov. "That's Natalya, my assistant . . ."

Palmer raised his brows. "The one you gave your secure number?"

"Correct. I trust her with my life."

"Should I respond?" Green asked.

"Yes," Palmer replied, keeping his focus on Reed's car. "Tell her Sokolov tested positive."

Green banged out a quick reply. She read it aloud: "I've replied in Russian. How about this? 'Thank you. The doctor confirmed that I'm positive for COVID and gave me a prescription that should help with my symptoms. I'll work from home for a few days under quarantine.'"

Palmer and Sokolov nodded their agreement, and she sent the reply.

"Why would the FSB come to see you?" Palmer asked, knowing the most plausible reason was that he was being taken in for interrogation and possible arrest, much like his peers and colleagues.

"They are interrogating senior scientists and engineers who are working on the hypersonic missile program. Some have been arrested. The president knows me by name. I thought he would protect me. I was wrong. Those FSB officers didn't turn up unannounced for a friendly chat."

Palmer exhaled. "If you weren't worried until now, why are you defecting? The decision must have been difficult for you."

Sokolov, remaining out of sight in the back seat, responded, "Difficult is an understatement. Seeing how my missiles are being used in the war with Ukraine deeply disturbs me. They are precision weaponry, yet they are being used for indiscriminate destruction and death, with the sole intent of driving fear into the Ukrainians. Cities like Bakhmut were leveled, with no regard for civilian property or lives. The Wagner Group mercenaries and our military were killing and raping unarmed civilians. It disgusts me."

"Is that it?" Palmer asked dismissively. "You're surprised that the weapons you developed are being used to kill innocent civilians? Have you learned nothing from Russia's use of ballistic and cruise missiles in Syria? And you're shocked that your president would have the FSB arrest you as a traitor for your publications and presentations?"

"Why not stay in Russia and work with Howell and the US?" Green asked. "That would have provided an ongoing information stream to the US and NATO. As a defector, you've shut off that information stream while also putting a target on your back."

Sokolov was quiet for a moment. Palmer wondered if there was something he wasn't telling them—or something he was preparing to.

"I would've been arrested today for treason," he said flatly, "all because I shared *non*classified information related to my life's work, which had gone through the required secrets review process and been approved for publication and public review. As you might know, scientists and engineers in Russia are being punished for sharing their unclassified work. I would be imprisoned or monitored so closely that I couldn't function as one of your spies."

Sokolov turned to Green then and switched to speaking in Russian, his voice raised.

"What did he say?" Palmer asked, looking at Green.

Green laughed. "He said the US missile program is garbage, and we need his help. Oh, he also said that you're an asshole."

Sokolov smiled, stifling a laugh.

Palmer snapped back, "Who says you won't be spying on our program, failing or not?"

Green, her eyebrows raised, turned to Sokolov. "Our job is to get you out of Russia and take you to a safe location in a US- or NATO-controlled environment where you can complete your defection to the US. Once there, you'll be questioned about your motivation for leaving Russia and working with the US. They will confirm to their satisfaction that you are sincere in your desire to work with us and are not a double agent."

Palmer sighed, nodding his agreement. He had pushed the point once too often. "She's right. It's not our job to question your motivation. Our sole focus must be on getting you out of Russia."

"I'm not a border security expert," Sokolov said. "However, I'm eager to contribute what I can, because if the FSB captures us . . . Well, I don't have to spell that out to you. What are you, anyway? CIA?"

Green smiled. "It's best for you and us that you don't know."

—⁓—

As they approached the train station, traffic was almost at a standstill. They had been stuck in bumper-to-bumper traffic even before the station came into view.

The more people around, the better, thought Palmer. More people meant a lower chance of Sokolov or themselves being recognized by video surveillance, but this traffic and congestion could also cause them to miss the train.

When the station finally came into view, Palmer saw several police vehicles parked near the entrance and a heavy uniformed police presence outside. The others with them had to be FSB.

"What's happening?" asked Sokolov, still slumped out of sight in the back seat.

"Traffic is backed up on Ploshchad Lenina," Palmer replied without looking back, referring to the road circling Lenin Square, running between the square and the station. "There's an abnormal amount of congestion. Police and FSB are at the station. We'd be arrested before we even entered it. We need to rethink our plan. The simplest way of getting you out of the country—taking the Allegro train to Helsinki—is now out of the question. Our British colleague will be of some assistance, but we'll need your help identifying the best way out of Russia and into Estonia, Finland, Latvia, or Norway."

Sokolov rose enough to peek out the window and muttered something in Russian before saying, "Keep driving."

Palmer's phone rang. He took it from his shirt pocket. It was Reed.

"Traffic's usually busy at the station, but this is the worst I've seen," she said. "The police might be looking for your passenger."

"Are those FSB with the police?" Palmer asked to confirm his suspicion. "I'll put you on speaker."

"Most certainly," Reed confirmed.

Green said, "Sokolov received an encrypted message from his assistant on the phone that Howell gave him. Two FSB officers came to see him at the office not long after he left. Time to consider plan B and drive to Vyborg—the last Allegro train stop before the Finnish border."

Reed didn't miss a beat. "I'd think twice about that. Based on the intensity of the FSB response at the station already, I strongly suspect they'll be at Vyborg, too. Some cars are turning left ahead, driving away from the station. I'll do the same. We can't risk staying here. Follow my lead."

Palmer replied, "Roger that. Keep driving until we get to a place where we can talk. Remain on the phone."

Sokolov rose enough to peek tentatively out the window again. "Those men walking toward us are FSB officers, and there's a woman with them," he said, panicked.

Green saw them approaching the stalled traffic from their position nearer to the station and spoke to Reed on the speakerphone. "FSB officers approaching," she confirmed. "I don't think they're intending to direct traffic. Get us out of here. Take that turn, even if you do something illegal. Go!"

Reed drove within inches of the car in front of them and gave the horn a few short honks. The traffic moved forward just enough for her to make the turn. She pulled within inches of the rear of the vehicle ahead of them, creating space for Palmer to make the turn, too, even though the rear of his car was still in the travel lane of the road they had been on.

Palmer glanced in the rearview mirror at the man and the woman with him. The woman's attire caught his attention. "Damn it! Look behind us."

Green whipped her head around, first glancing at Palmer and then shifting her gaze to her side mirror. The woman, dressed in a typical Pakistani salwar kameez with a matching dupatta, was speaking to one of the men in a suit. "A Pakistani woman here . . . talking with FSB officers. That's strange."

"I'll say," Palmer responded.

The woman turned her head to speak to one of the officers, revealing her face. Palmer and Green, at once, realized this was bigger than they'd thought—and far more dangerous.

"It's Aaliyah," Green said with a shallow exhale.

"I was afraid of that," Palmer said.

"Who is Aaliyah?" Sokolov asked.

"She's a Pakistani ISI officer who's supposed to be dead," Palmer replied simply.

Sokolov stayed down. "What's she doing in Saint Petersburg, and why would she be looking for me?"

"She's not looking for you," Green said with a shake of her head. "She's looking for me."

Reed piped in over the phone's speaker. "And why would she be looking for you?"

"She believes I tried to kill her," Green replied.

Reed broke the ensuing silence. "Well, did you?"

"Yes."

23

SAINT PETERSBURG, RUSSIA

Palmer stayed just a few cars behind Reed. Once they cleared the traffic jam from the train station, Reed sped up. He'd seen no indication that they were being followed. However, their plan A was in the toilet, and they had not established a plan B.

Still on speakerphone, Reed said, "I'm going to run another surveillance detection route before I pull over."

Palmer replied, "Roger that. We'll watch our six."

Reed stayed off the major thoroughfares and used side streets, often going around the block and ending up on the same road. Three basic tests were part of any effective surveillance detection route: time, distance, and change of direction. *How long has someone been following you? How far have they followed you? And have they changed direction each time you have?*

Palmer stayed behind Reed. He had to smile after she went completely around a city block before proceeding on the road she had initially been traveling.

Palmer and Green watched the traffic behind them, although Green was mainly responsible for it. Both knew that an effective way to follow someone trying to spot a tail was to use two or three cars that frequently switch off from the vehicle or person being followed. Because the FSB would have had little time to plan a multiple-car strategy, Green doubted they were using that tactic. Green was tasked with describing the cars behind them, identifying each suspicious vehicle, and calling it out to Palmer. Running the detection route was easier within Saint Petersburg. It would be more difficult once outside the city center and on the highway. Palmer worked out that their overall direction was northwest, toward Finland.

Over the speakerphone, Reed said, "We're nearing City Mall at Udel'nyy Park. I'll find a spot to pull over and decide where we're going. I'm highly confident we're not being followed."

Before Palmer could comment, Reed turned abruptly into the City Mall shopping center. The store names were in Russian, but he recognized one only because of the large circular Burger King logo. He followed Reed until she parked. They needed a plan and had very little time to develop and execute it. As soon as he parked in the space beside her, Reed jumped out of her car and into the back seat of Palmer's, sitting across from Sokolov.

Sokolov sat upright. "Who the hell are you?"

"I'm the one assisting these two Americans getting you out of the country."

"Based on your accent, I'd say you're British, probably MI6," Sokolov surmised.

Reed didn't respond. "I know more about the borders of the neighboring NATO countries than they do, but you probably know more than the three of us combined."

Palmer twisted around and told Sokolov, "We're on the run. That wasn't our plan, but neither was the FSB showing up at your place of work this morning. That has complicated things. So here we are. The train stations and airports will be heavily guarded. Facial recognition cameras will be scanning for us, especially you. We can head to Finland, Estonia, Latvia, or even Norway. All are NATO countries. The more rural the area, the easier it will be to cross undetected."

Sokolov nodded in agreement. "Forget Norway. It's a long drive, and we would have to stop for gas and food multiple times. Norway's border with Russia is located at the north end of Finland and is a little less than one hundred twenty miles long. The Latvia-Russia border is about the same length as Norway's. It's also a long way to go undetected. I would eliminate that, too."

"For now, time is on our side," Palmer said. "We have a very narrow window while the FSB is catching up and deploying resources to capture or kill us. So which is it? Estonia or Finland?"

Sokolov hesitated with the other three looking at him. "If I were alone, I'd head to Finland."

"Of those two options, I agree with Finland," Reed said.

Green said, "Just curious, why would Finland be the better of the two?"

Sokolov exhaled. "Finland has closed most of the primary and provisional border crossings with Russia, not only because of the war with Ukraine but also because they fear Russia is trying to weaponize immigration so that, over time, Finland's population and political leanings would be altered. They are taking immigrants from as far away as Syria to the Finnish border. However, much of the eight-hundred-thirty-mile border with Finland is rural, with uninhabited forests and no security fences. Both countries use video, pressure sensors, and drones to monitor it."

"Why not Estonia?" Green asked.

Sokolov continued, "Estonia's border with Russia is about one hundred eighty miles and runs north and south. Much of the border is shaped by water. To the north is the Narva River, which forms seventy-six kilometers of the border and flows into the large Narva Reservoir, where the border runs along the Estonian side of the reservoir. The river and the Estonia-Russia border continue south of the reservoir, through Lake Peipus and then into the west side of Lake Pihkva before heading south inland."

"So lots of water," Green said.

"Yes, and bridges are funnel points, like the crossing at Narva, Estonia, and Ivangorod, Russia, where the border is on the bridge over the Narva River. A significant portion of the land border traverses rugged terrain. The southern border is relatively short and runs from the reservoir to Latvia, a considerable distance away. The northern part of Estonia borders the Gulf of Finland, which leads to the Baltic Sea. There, they have sea mines and anti-ship missiles to keep Russians away."

"You know a lot about the area," Palmer noted, meeting Sokolov's eyes in the rearview mirror.

"My wife and I spent a few holidays in Narva, Estonia," Sokolov said softly. "It's a mostly Russian-speaking, pro-Russian town."

"Sounds like Crimea," Green shot back. "If Estonia weren't a NATO member, your president would have invaded it just as he did Crimea."

Sokolov snickered mirthlessly. "Russia may have done it instead of, or in addition to, Crimea. Our president has become a power-hungry madman." His words were spoken slowly, conveying sorrow rather than anger. A grim understanding had replaced his admiration for the country's leader.

Reed twisted in her seat, her gaze turning to Palmer. "He's right. We'll need to stay off the highways as much as possible and cross the border in the rural areas away from official crossing points. Russia will be patrolling those areas, but not as much as the more populated spaces."

"I can give you another reason to stay off the major highways. If we continue along the E-18, we'll encounter toll booths," Sokolov added.

Reed hissed. "That's correct," she said. "Neither of our cars has a transponder, so we would have to pay at the booth, which the FSB monitors with cameras. Even if we had transponders, there's still a risk we would be caught on camera."

Sokolov replied, "We're managing time and risk. We could reach the Finnish border in about two hours from our current location. That means we'd be driving on the A-121 and either the E-18 to the south or 62 to the north, near Imatra. I suggest we drive northeast on the secondary roads, staying east of Lake Ladoga, which will take longer, but it's rural."

Palmer considered what he had said. "If we go the way you suggest, and it's in a thick forest or another inhospitable location, it will be tough. I have a satellite phone, and the technical support team can help guide us. We could also contact Johannes at SUPO, the Finnish Security and Intelligence Service. They'll need to pick us up once we've crossed the border or guide us out."

Looking out the windshield, Green said, "So where do we cross?"

Reed replied, "The FSB will assign the bulk of their resources near the Finnish border's main crossings even though they are closed. They'll most likely concentrate on the unfenced crossings. If they recognized us at Finland Station in Saint Petersburg, they'd have our car's make, model, and color, perhaps the tag number. We'd never have made it this far."

Sokolov said, "Farther north past Imatra, Finland, there are only a few secondary roads, and most don't come close to the border. We'd have to abandon the cars and make our way on foot. However, too far north along the border, and you'll be in Russia's Murmansk Oblast and the Kola Peninsula. Our nuclear Arctic fleet and nuclear weapon storage facilities are there as well as the Russian base for strategic nuclear forces. The few roads that go that far north are also the primary roads the military use to access those bases."

Palmer added, "Let's be optimistic. Once we're in Finland, we'll be okay. It's a NATO nation, and I assume that Finland's intelligence agency will welcome us into the country with open arms and a band playing. The trick is getting across the Russian border."

Sokolov nodded, lips pursed. "Remember, some border zones are up to four miles wide. I would go around Lake Lagoda and make our way to Vyartsilya. It's a small town of about three thousand residents and remains a major border crossing. We would have to go north or south of that to attempt to cross."

"I'd go between Imatra and Niirala," Reed offered. "And the possible temporary crossing at Parikkala."

Green, who had been quiet, added, "I'm liking Estonia more and more. I'm convinced that the FSB will focus on the Finnish border for the same reasons we are."

"We could also wait it out in Russia while we agree on our crossing point," Reed added with a shrug. "We have a safe house near Lake Lagoda, where we could hang out for several days. No one has used it recently, but it's kept stocked with supplies. They'll eventually assume we made it across and at the very least reduce the number of FSB and police devoted to finding us. Then we could head north to our crossing point."

Green smiled. "I like that, and I have a crazy idea to back it up. Adams and Hunnicutt could use AI to create a photo of Sokolov in Helsinki posing in front of the US Embassy, post it on social media, and leak it to the press. If the FSB believes he's already in Finland or even Estonia, they might stop looking for him. The trick would be creating a photo convincing enough that they believe it was true."

Everyone's head turned to her, faces expressing shock and awe.

Palmer said, "I like it, too."

"The next day," Green went on, "one could be created and posted of him in the US at a recognizable location, like the Lincoln Memorial."

Ultimately, it was Palmer's call to make. The Finnish border had its appeal, but so did Estonia's. There was also the option to hole up in a safe house for a few days. But hanging out in a safe house would give the Russians time to find them. Using an AI-generated image of Sokolov in Helsinki was a great idea; however, the Russians weren't stupid. The photos would only hold water briefly before the FSB found a way to identify them as fake.

"I've decided," Palmer announced. "It's Finland. The water crossings in Estonia are too dangerous. Let's notify Adams and Hunnicutt to proceed with an AI-generated photo of Sokolov, looking as if it were taken by someone who may have recognized him—a candid and not-so-obvious rendition of him entering the SUPO offices. Post it somewhere it will be seen by the FSB. Adams and Hunnicutt should notify Reynolds, who should contact JSOC as well as the chief of MI6. Meanwhile, we'll hide out at MI6's safe house or cabin for a few days, then decide how far north we'll go. With only a few roads that get close to the border, we won't have many options."

✦✦✦

Alexi Volkov was at war with himself. He couldn't decide which was worse: informing the president about the envelope and the possibility that Sokolov might have seen or even copied the top secret document that was inside it or not telling him at all and allowing everything to spiral even further out of control. What if they *did* catch Sokolov? He'd come forward about their conversation together, just days ago, regarding the envelope Volkov had left behind—and then there would be hell to pay.

One thing continued to haunt him: *If* Sokolov had indeed looked through contents of the envelope—and it seemed likely, given his defection only a few days later—then there was almost no chance he hadn't also thought to make a copy of the top secret document and perhaps use it as leverage for his defection. The document that shouldn't have been there . . .

The document outlining the plan to attack the US.

The president had given Volkov the top secret document to return to the secure facility. He'd inadvertently placed the missile data on top of it. After finishing a call, he'd stuffed the entire stack of papers into an envelope—a career-ending, if not life-ending, mistake.

But had Sokolov even opened the envelope? If he had, did he notice the document at the bottom of the stack? Sokolov claimed he hadn't opened the envelope. In this situation, Sokolov couldn't be trusted to tell the truth. Sokolov would have been shocked to find the document and would have been reluctant to admit he had seen it.

Perhaps Maksimov will put Ivanov on the case, Volkov thought hopefully. The mere idea gave him a rush of relief. The Unit 29155 assassin would kill Sokolov and the Americans, ending Russia's troubles as well as Volkov's in one fell swoop. But what if he wasn't killed and successfully defected to the US? What if the information had already been communicated to the US and its NATO allies?

Indeed, if that were the case, then telling the president wouldn't make any real difference. Would they cancel the attack altogether and claim it was a theoretical exercise? Either way, the president would still find out about the misplaced document—and he'd get to the bottom of who'd been responsible for it.

Would the president fire him or have him killed? He wouldn't put it past him. Volkov would have to be vigilant about where he went and what he ate and drank.

However, there might be a way out yet . . .

He could either help Sokolov defect or wait to see if Ivanov was assigned to the task of killing him. Being captured alive would be the worst-case scenario because Sokolov would break under torture and reveal the mistake Volkov had made. *What's one more missile scientist working with the West?*

Still, if the top secret operation occurred, it would most likely lead to a nuclear war.

24

FSB HEADQUARTERS AT BOLSHOY DOM
SAINT PETERSBURG, RUSSIA

Colonel Maksimov stayed at the Belmond Grand Hotel on Mikhaylovskaya Street in Saint Petersburg. The five-star hotel was only minutes from the Bolshoy Dom building, where he worked while in the city. Neither the FSB nor Aaliyah had confirmed if Palmer and Green were, indeed, the people Aaliyah had seen driving near the train station.

The car was lost in traffic before they could catch up with it. Maksimov invited Aaliyah to stay at the hotel at his expense. After that, she would be on her own in her search. That night, however, they'd had dinner together and gotten to know each other. She never made it to her room.

Maksimov awoke from a deep sleep the next morning after having had a big meal and too much vodka. He squinted, allowing the early morning sun that had lightened the room to awaken him. He yawned and stretched out his arms. His left hand touched something.

"Good morning, Vlad."

His eyes widened. *Aaliyah.* He rolled over and faced her.

"Last night was amazing," Aaliyah said in a soft, whispery voice.

"Yes, it was. But now I need to get to work. I have a traitor to catch."

"So early?" Aaliyah moved her hand under the sheet and between his legs. "Please stay a little longer."

Maksimov closed his eyes and sighed, enjoying the moment. "Oh hell, what's the rush?" he said, turning in the bed to face her. Aaliyah was one of the most beautiful women he'd ever seen, let alone been with. Her fair skin was soft to the touch, and her body was slim, although curvy in all the right places. And in bed, he knew of no equal.

After they made love, he phoned room service and had breakfast delivered. The waiter set the tray on the dining table in the suite. Maksimov and Aaliyah sat across from each other. Maksimov ate hurriedly.

Aaliyah poured herself another cup of coffee and reached over to top off his cup.

"No more for me," Maksimov said, placing his hand over the empty cup. "I'm late already."

"No need to apologize. You go to work. We shouldn't go in together, anyway."

"You're right. Take your time to freshen up after I leave. I'll have the hotel arrange a ride for you. Have security ring Andrei Fedorov when you arrive. He'll bring you up to my office."

⚊⚊⚯⚊⚊

Aaliyah took a hot shower, taking the time to get the overweight and out-of-shape Maksimov's scent off and out of her. He was married, not that she cared. He had succumbed to her wiles, as so many had before him. She felt good about getting back in the game, and Maksimov was the first man she had made love to since her accident. She was ready for more, but not from him. She had work to do.

She didn't doubt that Palmer and Green were helping Sokolov escape Russia. There were too many things adding up for it to all be a big coincidence. Besides, she didn't even care about Sokolov—the only thing she was interested in was exacting revenge against Alona Green. She had to see Green before Maksimov's assassin killed her or she was captured and imprisoned. Perhaps she could watch or participate in her torture and interrogation.

As much as Aaliyah hated Green for trying to kill her, she secretly felt sorry that things hadn't worked out. Their chemistry had been strong that night when they'd said goodbye with a kiss. She still remembered the scent of her perfume—My Way by Armani. Aaliyah had bought a bottle so she wouldn't forget. Green must have felt it, too. She'd called days after the accident, after all, trying to schedule the follow-up dinner they'd agreed to . . .

Why did Green try to kill her? The more she thought about it, the more it didn't seem likely that Green had wanted revenge for the role Aaliyah had played in Martin Singleton's suicide. If Green hated Aaliyah so much, she wouldn't have kissed her the way she had that night after dinner. That, or Green was an exceptional actor—to a sociopathic level.

Aaliyah called Farid Malik, a Pakistani ISI intelligence officer who worked under diplomatic cover at Pakistan's consulate in Saint Petersburg. They had met at Pakistan's embassy in Moscow soon after she arrived in Russia and before her initial meeting with Maksimov. Malik answered on the first ring.

"Palmer and Green are helping Sokolov defect. I'm sure of it," she reported. "Maksimov said the FSB has increased security at the Finland Station here in Saint Petersburg, and they'll try to cross the border north of Saint Petersburg, where it's much less secure."

"How will you know where to go?" Malik asked. "The border is over eight hundred miles long. That's about the distance from Islamabad to Karachi."

"I'll be at FSB's Saint Petersburg headquarters this morning. I'll get more information then about where they're headed. We'll never find them if we don't have their help."

"I'll stand by and be ready to leave whenever you like. The weapons we need are already in my car."

⚉

Maksimov paced across the office, shaking his head and breathing through his nose like a bull ready to charge at a matador's red cape. Twenty-two hours had passed since he'd learned that Sokolov was missing. He would stay at his command post at Bolshoy Dom until Sokolov was captured or killed; he didn't care which.

If Sokolov made his way out of Russia, everything Maksimov had done to decrease the number of defectors and spies working with the West would be for naught. He must stop him and the Americans who were enabling his escape. Now he was in the wind. All of FSB had been alerted, including border control.

Maksimov had assigned Unit 29155's Nikolai Ivanov with kill orders, whether within Russia or abroad. If Ivanov caught him inside Russia, he would shoot him and anyone with him, and Maksimov would reward him with a medal. Outside Russia, he would use a more discreet way to eliminate Sokolov.

Maksimov paused and looked out the window at the distant river, arms crossed. Why was Sokolov defecting? Had he been collaborating with the Americans all along? That would make sense. Or had Sokolov heard about the recent arrests of his colleagues and realized he might soon be questioned about his presentations and publications and possibly imprisoned? That was the only logical explanation—the stance he would likely take with Colonel General Vasilyev. *My program to prevent defections and catch spies has been so effective that the rats are coming out of hiding. I'm exposing the traitors.* He sat at his desk and checked the notices on his desktop computer. A recent one was highlighted as a priority. He opened it and saw a photograph of what appeared to be Sokolov entering the US Embassy's pre–World War II building on Kentmanni Street in Tallinn, Estonia. The photo had been taken from a distance and was a little out of focus. Maksimov zoomed in, which increased the image's graininess, but there was no doubt that it was Sokolov he was looking at.

"Fedorov!"

His chief of staff rushed in. Maksimov was staring at his computer. He walked over and stood next to him to get a closer look at his screen. It was an image of Sokolov in Tallinn.

With Maksimov still fixated on the picture, Fedorov said, "I know. I just saw it myself. The photo was picked up on social media and has gone viral. We should know something within a few hours. As expected, the US Embassy in Tallinn has responded with no comment to all inquiries. I'm having the image checked for authenticity. I was told that AI can't do hands well, often giving someone six fingers or distorting the hand. But he's not showing his hands. Early on, some apps were available to detect whether the image is fake, but it has become increasingly difficult."

"I don't care. How long will that take?" Maksimov asked, spinning his chair around to face Fedorov.

"A day or two. They'll give me updates on their progress."

Maksimov took a deep breath and called Vasilyev.

2 5

SAINT PETERSBURG, RUSSIA

Nikolai Ivanov studied the map of Russia's border with Finland, focusing on the area where he believed Dmitry Sokolov and the Americans would make their run. He had been underutilized since being assigned to FSB's Colonel Maksimov. This was his first job since his temporary transfer. The assignment intrigued him. It wasn't a straightforward assassination as he had done in Kazakhstan's capital city, Astana. This was a hunt-and-kill assignment. Like a hunter after his prey, he'd have to use all his skills to find Sokolov and the Americans. Killing them would be the easy part.

Maksimov had sent him the photo of Sokolov entering the US Embassy in Tallinn, Estonia. FSB would analyze the image to determine its authenticity, but Ivanov didn't need confirmation. Nobody in their right mind would attempt to cross the Russian border in Estonia illegally. They would cross Finland's border somewhere so remote and inhospitable that FSB border security patrols were rare or nonexistent. Those areas were monitored only by drones and motion sensors.

Ivanov knew where the weak points in the border were. Using data from FSB Border Service, he had pinpointed the most vulnerable locations for border crossing. He had used some himself to cross into Finland undetected. Some were in very harsh terrain, and depending on the time of year, anyone attempting to cross there would be more likely to die from exposure to the elements than by his hand.

Ivanov had access to a database of properties suspected to be US and UK safe houses, believing they might use one of them. He'd learned that the database sometimes identified properties that were not safe houses and probably missed ones that were. He searched for ones in Saint Petersburg and along the border near there but found nothing that piqued his interest.

2 6

MI6 SAFE HOUSE CABIN IN A FOREST
NORTH OF SAINT PETERSBURG, RUSSIA

Palmer and Reed pulled out of their parking spaces near the City Mall, north of the center of Saint Petersburg, and drove on city streets until they reached the 41K-064, which headed east toward Lake Ladoga. They had split up at this point to avoid detection. Reed drove the lead car with Green in the front passenger seat. Palmer drove the other car, with Sokolov staying low in the back seat, until they reached secondary roads.

Palmer and Green had their firearms under their seats and out of sight. They had begun the day with full gas tanks and could easily reach the MI6 safe house. The safest route was to drive around Lake Ladoga, avoiding motorways whenever possible. Sokolov, a fountain of information, explained that Finland had a landscape full of lakes, totaling 187,888, most of which were small, with over 600 islands within them. Lake Ladoga, however, was enormous, stretching over 136 miles long and 51 miles wide.

Only one motorway led north to Murmansk Oblast and the Kola Peninsula, the E105, which ran parallel to the border with Finland. The highway was the primary route for Russia's military vehicles to and from their bases and their nuclear storage facilities. The farther north one ventured, the more military vehicles would be on the road.

Gambling that the FSB had not yet fully distributed information about Sokolov's defection attempt to all FSB and border security personnel, and believing the FSB did not have information about the cars they were driving, they took the E105 around the southern part of the lake, which saved them hours. After that, the road led north, running somewhat parallel to Finland's border until they came to the safe house.

The rustic cabin blended into the quiet forest that surrounded it. Sokolov told them that the small structure near the cabin was probably a sauna. The only sounds were those created by nature: the wind blowing through the trees and the birds calling to one another. Once inside, Palmer lit the wood-burning stove. The heat it generated brought the entire cabin to a comfortable temperature. However, it also meant that smoke was coming out of the chimney, letting anyone passing near it know that someone was inside. They had no Wi-Fi, but they did have a weak telephone signal.

They had passed other cabins and cottages, all presumably unoccupied. This was a perfect getaway for anyone wanting to escape the hurried pace of Saint Petersburg, and it served as a great safe house if isolation was the goal. But this was no ordinary time. The FSB, one of the world's most effective and ruthless organizations, was hunting for them—and they would beeline straight for remote places like this. Their saving grace was most likely there were thousands of them.

The only window shades were in the two bedrooms. Reed found a few nonperishables and some wine and liquor in the cabinets. Although the risk was small, Palmer warned them to stay away from the windows, both at night and during the day. Palmer decided that they should stay only a couple of days because remaining longer would allow the FSB time to fully deploy in the search for them.

On their second day in the cabin, their last planned day, they huddled around a paper map of Finland that Reed had brought and identified their crossing point. Following further discussion of the options with the aid of the map, Palmer had elected to go north and take a secondary road on the River Kem. That road crossed the border near Tukhkala, Russia, and Alatalo, Finland. That would put them between the major heavily patrolled border crossings at Vartius and Kuusamo—just south of Finland's Lapland and near Finland's Hossa National Park. Palmer contacted Johannes at the Finnish Security and Intelligence Service and provided him with the coordinates of their planned crossing point as well as those of the cabin.

Before sunrise the next morning, they would leave and drive north on the primary E105 motorway, using the 86K-14 until it turned east and away from Finland at Porosozero, Russia. After that, they would use only narrow rural roads, travel as close to the border as possible, and then walk the remaining distance. Sokolov estimated the trip would take ten hours or longer. They would need to stop at least once to refuel the cars and purchase food and water.

A quick check of social media revealed that Hunnicutt and Adams had posted the AI-doctored photos of Sokolov in Estonia. Whatever impact that had on the FSB's search for him had already peaked. If the FSB had identified them as fake, they had not made that known to the public—and Palmer suspected that's precisely what they would do, as soon as they possibly could.

Although it was only four o'clock in the afternoon, Reed opened one of the several bottles of wine in the cabin's pantry. No one complained. They shared toasts, which helped lighten the mood.

Reed topped off her glass of wine. "Tomorrow, we'll drive as close as possible to the crossing point. At that time, I'll see you off and leave for Moscow."

"Are you sure you don't want to tag along?" Green asked.

"I'd love to, but duty calls." She paused. "I'm just following orders from C."

"We'll save the tearful goodbye for later then," Green joked.

"We have a tough day ahead tomorrow," Palmer added, sobering the group slightly. "I'm confident that this team is up to the task. Here's to good fortune and a safe passage into Finland."

Sokolov, who had been quiet, held up his glass. "Thanks to each of you, whatever your real names are. I understand the risks you're taking. If successful, this will be a bittersweet passage for me. I'm Russian through and through, and tomorrow I'll leave and never return. Except for the trauma of my wife leaving me, this is the most difficult thing I've ever done. However, I am committed to crossing the border with you and working for the US. Cheers, as you say in the West."

"Cheers," everyone said, raising their glasses.

Before their wineglasses had met their lips, the piercing blast of a gunshot rang out in the forest.

Immediately, Sokolov dropped to the floor like someone had shoved him. His wineglass shattered beside him. Then there was another gunshot, and Reed fell to the floor.

Palmer and Green dropped down of their own accord. His eyes met Green's eyes. "Stay down!"

One glance at Reed and Sokolov confirmed they were hit—but alive.

Palmer commando-crawled to the table where their pistols and extra magazines were located and brought them back. He handed Green and Reed theirs and kept one for himself. Green attended to Reed's injury while they laid on the floor. "The bullet grazed her back," Green reported. "She's bleeding, but the wound doesn't appear serious."

Sokolov was wincing in pain and holding his upper arm. Palmer checked out the wound, which was more serious than Reed's and would ultimately require medical care. The bullet had gone straight through his arm, at least, so there was no threat of needing to remove bullet fragments. "You'll be okay, but we need to stop the bleeding," he said, removing his belt to use as a tourniquet.

"What now?" Green asked.

"Firing single shots from a distance isn't the tactic an entire FSB team would use. We can't sit here and wait. He'll either try to finish us off or keep us here and call for FSB reinforcements. I need to go out there and find him."

"That's suicide," Green said rather bluntly.

"Suicide is sitting here and doing nothing," Palmer replied. "You get everyone to the wall near that window, if you can. That gives him no shot. Our only chance is for me to reach the shooter. Otherwise, he'll keep us pinned down in the cabin until reinforcements arrive. I'm going out the back window."

Palmer checked his pistol and crawled back to the table for extra clips. He slid a couple of them to Green. Looking to her, he said, "Give me five minutes, then fire two shots out the broken window. Do not stick your head up; raise the pistol and fire. It doesn't matter where you point it."

Palmer crawled to the bedroom opposite the side of the cabin from where the shots had come through. He raised the window and climbed out. The farther away the shooter was, the more the trees blocked his view and limited his vision. He figured he was five hundred yards away, maximum. He stood with his back against the house and slid along it near the corner. This wasn't a sniper. An FSB sniper would use a sound-suppressed rifle and would wait for a kill shot. *Snipers don't miss. Did the double pane window deflect the first bullet? The first bullet would have made only a hole in the glass, not shatter it.* Reed reacted and turned when Sokolov was hit, and the second shot grazed her back. If she had not turned, it would've hit her in the chest. The shooter would have seen through his scope that the bullets were not kill shots. He might consider rushing the house and using his backup weapons.

Palmer was in place when Green's shots echoed through the forest. Palmer sprinted to the sauna house and came to a stop. No sign of the shooter. Had he moved behind the tree, or did he have his view through the scope locked on the window and saw that the shots were unaimed? The shooter would know by the sound of Green's gunshot that it was a pistol. He might find it curious that someone would fire a gun with zero chance of hitting him.

Palmer needed to circle rather than move directly toward him. He scanned the ground between him and a tree about ten feet from the sauna, looking for any obstacle that he would either trip over or step on and make a sound the shooter would hear. He took a deep breath and made his move, quick and careful, glancing in the general direction of where he thought the shots had been fired. He saw nothing. If the shooter suspected they had moved against a wall, he might relocate and shoot through another window.

Palmer heard a faint snap, followed by another. The shooter was on the move.

He sprinted from tree to tree toward where he had heard the noise. The sounds were ahead of him and to his left. Peeking out from behind a tree, he caught his first glimpse of the gunman. He was wearing green camo and moving toward the cabin door with a determined tread. Palmer quick-stepped ahead, keeping the trees between him and the shooter, gripped his pistol with two hands, and swung from behind the tree. The shooter was twenty feet from the cabin, the rifle up and pressed against his shoulder. He shot out the window he had fired through previously and stepped quickly to stand with his back against the cabin near the window. He had something in his right hand—a grenade? A fail-safe against whatever he was hunting? He was preparing to pull the pin and toss it in.

Sensing it was his last chance, Palmer fired. His first shot hit the shooter in the back, causing him to fall to his knees and drop the device on the ground. It was indeed a grenade. He turned, looked at Palmer, and grimaced. He reached out for the grenade—which, thankfully, hadn't exploded, meaning it still had the pin in place.

Palmer fired twice into the man's chest before he could reach the grenade. The force of the bullets striking him knocked him onto his back. After a quick check to ensure he was dead, Palmer ran to the cabin and tried to open the door. It was locked. He knocked on it three times. "It's me. All clear!" No one answered, so he moved to the window. Standing with his back to the wall beside it, he shouted, "It's me. The shooter is down. All clear."

He waited a moment and peeked through the window. Green was standing with her 9mm pistol still in her hands but lowered in front of her. Shards of glass were scattered on the floor.

"I need to check something before I come in. Unlock the door," he said.

The door opened, and Green stepped out.

"Everyone okay inside?" he asked.

"Except for their original wounds, yes." Her gaze moved to the body. "I'll wait inside."

Palmer knelt beside the man, who looked to be in his late twenties or early thirties. He pressed the neck again to check for a pulse and confirmed there was none. Then he examined the rifle and scope. Neither appeared to be the kind a typical FSB sniper would use. They looked more like hunting gear. He rolled him onto his side, removed a small rucksack from his back, and unzipped it. Inside was ammunition, binoculars, water bottles, and a radio communicator. He then checked his pockets and found a wallet with his FSB ID card—Sergei Veronin. He also found a cell phone and a vehicle key fob in his coat pocket. Palmer touched the phone screen and held it up to the shooter's face; it unlocked.

Palmer stuffed the wallet, phone, and key fob in his pocket and threw the rucksack over his shoulder with the rifle. "He's an FSB officer. We need to leave. He probably heard about the search for Sokolov but ignored it because he was hunting. Then he stumbled on the cabin and saw Sokolov through his scope or binoculars and decided to take a shot at him. Literally."

Reed fidgeted with the bandage around her waist. "The FSB alert would have included photos of Sokolov. He was the one who was shot first."

Sokolov cleared his throat. "Right. It's Eurasian . . ." His voice tailed off.

"What?" Reed said.

Sokolov groaned. "It's Eurasian bear season."

Palmer nodded. "That explains his bolt-action rifle and scope. No sniper would ever use those. We must assume that he's alerted the FSB and that they're on the way here. Before we leave, let's check his phone."

Palmer went outside and again unlocked the phone using Face ID. Everything was in Russian. He went back inside and handed it to Reed. "Turn off the location finder and change the setting so it remains unlocked. After we leave, see if you can find anything useful on it."

Palmer handed Green the radio. "See if you can determine whether he alerted FSB about our location."

Green turned the radio over in her hand. "It's a P25 two-way digital radio with encryption. It's probably tuned to his FSB channel. We can use it to receive FSB communications about the search for us and let us know if they find the body. They might communicate information about roadblocks on the major roads. However, if they suspect the radio is lost or stolen, they'll either change the encryption key and we'll be locked out or they'll leave it on so they can track the radio's location and us along with it."

Palmer said, "Let's keep it for a while. Once we hear they found his body, we'll reconsider. What about Hunnicutt and Adams? Satellite surveillance and drones?"

"We can't fly drones in Russian airspace," Reed said, "and the UK depends on the US for SAR—synthetic aperture radar satellite capability. Those satellites work in all weather conditions, day and night, and can penetrate through foliage. Both the UK and Finland will have the technology in a couple of years. Russia has it now and is likely repositioning a satellite over the border, if it hasn't already. I've sent a request for a satellite reroute. Hunnicutt and Adams are pressing for it."

"She's right," Green said. "Even without infrared detectors, it could aid in security checks on the motorway and at our final crossing point. I'll ask Adams to connect with Hunnicutt and see if we can get a satellite surveillance of any kind in time to help us."

27

MI6 SAFE HOUSE CABIN IN A FOREST NORTH OF SAINT PETERSBURG, RUSSIA

After examining Sokolov's wound once again, Palmer looked in the cabinet and found a bottle of vodka. He then pulled a sheet off one of the beds and tore it into strips, wrapping Sokolov's shoulder and arm so that they were pinned against his chest. "This is going to hurt," Palmer said, and without giving Sokolov time to respond, he poured vodka over his own hands, rubbed them together, and then applied them over the wound. Sokolov said something in Russian, which Palmer assumed was a string of expletives because Green looked taken aback.

"Sorry about that. How are you feeling?" Palmer asked.

Sokolov responded, his brow contracted, "Like hell. How does it look?"

"I've seen worse. The main thing is to keep pressure on the wound. That will stop the bleeding. You're going to be fine. Can you make it to the car?"

"I believe so."

Palmer was concerned. Sokolov needed medical attention, which would not be available until after they crossed the border, which had to be in the next twelve to twenty-four hours at the most. Again, they were running out of time.

Alona Green went with Sania Reed to one of the bedrooms, bringing the vodka with her, and helped her take off her damaged and bloody blouse and bra.

"What do you think?" Reed asked, her voice trembling with apprehension.

"It's not too bad. There's not as much bleeding as I expected. The damage seems superficial and not deep enough to cause muscle or bone damage. Does it hurt?"

"It's more of a burning sensation," Reed said.

"I have some analgesics in my toiletries kit. Acetaminophen, also known as paracetamol in the UK, I believe. Sokolov will need some, too."

"When Sokolov fell, I immediately turned toward him, and then I was hit," Reed noted, her face going slightly pale. "If I hadn't turned . . ."

"Let's not go there." Green doused her hands and then Reed's wound with the vodka. Reed inhaled and gasped, her eyes full of tears. Green wrapped the remaining strips of the clean bedsheets around her upper torso.

"I have another blouse and bra in my small case on the bed," Reed said.

Green walked over to the bed and opened the case. Reed's clothes were folded and neatly arranged. She held up the bra and recognized the British brand Myla. "This is too nice to ruin if blood seeps through the bandages. It might also be too painful to wear if it rubs against the bandages and wound."

"Let's try it and see."

Green took it over to her, and she slipped it on without fastening it in the back. Reed's breasts were larger than hers and needed support. She understood why Reed would not want to go without one.

"What do you think?" Reed asked.

Green examined the bandaged wound. "If I fasten it looser than you normally wear it, I think it will be fine."

"Do it."

Green did her best to ensure the bra did not press too firmly against the bandages. "You're going to have a nice scar."

Reed flinched. "We all have scars; some are just more visible than others. Do you believe you're going to make it across the border?"

"I do. If Dennis Hall can't get us across, no one can. That man is amazing."

Reed turned her head to look at Green standing behind her. "He looks amazing." Changing the subject, she said, "Lauren, I want to go with you to Finland. There's just that one problem. C told me not to cross the border with Sokolov. It would negate my diplomatic immunity."

Green walked around to face her. "I can't tell you to disregard your instructions from the chief of MI6. If it were me, I'd do whatever would benefit the mission."

Reed was quiet for a moment. "I've never shot at anyone, much less wounded or killed them. I'm not sure I could do it if it comes to that."

"You might surprise yourself. Now let's go join the boys."

⸻ ⁓ ⸻

Reed had resumed working on Veronin's phone. Palmer asked, "Find anything?"

"A call was made to a Saint Petersburg number about the time the initial shooting occurred. I assume it was just before he took the shot, perhaps to report what he had seen and get authorization to fire. Either way, he was letting someone—probably the FSB—know he had spotted us."

"Any other texts about that time?"

"None."

Palmer walked over to her. If she were right and Veronin had called the FSB office, he would have given them the location of the cabin. They needed to leave now. "It'd be a big plus if you stayed with us until we reach our border crossing point. But if you need to leave for Moscow, we'll understand."

"I'm going with you," Reed quickly replied.

"I'm surprised," Palmer retorted. "You said you couldn't cross the border. Somewhere in our trek, we'll get to the point of no return. The Russians will be pursuing, and if you're with us and get caught, your diplomatic passport won't be worth five rubles."

Reed paused. "You're right. There will come a time when I realize I can't contribute anything more to the mission and need to head to Moscow. I'll let you and Lauren know when that happens. I can't risk jeopardizing the mission by waiting too long, getting arrested, and being interrogated."

The wounds were bandaged. Sokolov and Reed had each taken a hefty dose of paracetamol. Palmer and Green helped Sokolov into the car. Reed insisted she didn't require any assistance.

"Ready to go?" Green asked, looking at Palmer.

"I need to do one more thing," he said with a glance toward Veronin. Green nodded knowingly. "Load up. I'll be back in a moment."

Palmer walked fast to the cabin and stood beside Sergei Veronin's body, wondering what to do with it and if it was worth spending time on. He could leave it for the Eurasian bears. That would make for a good headline: Bear Eats Hunter. No. Veronin was wearing a wedding ring. He had a wife and possibly children waiting for him to return home. He had simply been doing his job. Palmer dragged Veronin's body into the cabin. He looked at it one last time and left, closing the door behind him. He returned to the car and placed the shooter's rifle and rucksack in the trunk. Sokolov was lying on the back seat.

They sped away from the cabin along a narrow, unpaved, single-lane road and drove until reaching an intersection with a paved two-lane road.

Palmer spotted a black four-door pickup parked off the road at the intersection—without anyone seated inside—and pulled in behind it. Green parked behind him. Palmer took Veronin's key fob from his pocket and hit the unlock button. The truck's lights flashed.

He jumped out and got in the truck. The vehicle's registration was in the dashboard compartment. It was a new Sollers ST6 pickup registered to Veronin. Palmer opened the console between the seats and found the officer's handgun inside. If Veronin called it in, he would have given them the approximate coordinates of the cabin and told them his vehicle was parked off the road. If the FSB were searching for him, they would notice the vehicle and follow the single-track road.

That meant one thing: *They needed to move the truck.*

Reed said she could drive the other car until they found a place to hide the truck.

Reed led their covert convoy, followed by Green and Sokolov. Palmer was behind them all in the truck. About ten miles down the road, Reed took a turn onto another single-track road and pulled over to the roadside. Palmer and Green followed Reed and pulled in behind her, and all three drivers got out of their vehicles.

"I've had a thought," Reed said. "If we don't get to the border soon, Sokolov may not make it. He's lost some blood. It's too far and we'll encounter some rugged terrain. Our cars are two-wheel drive sedans. I'm guessing the truck is four-wheel drive, so we can get farther into the forest with the truck before we start walking. We don't need three vehicles. It draws attention." She paused, eyeing them both pointedly before saying, "Let's ditch one of the two cars instead of the truck. The FSB won't be looking for this truck anywhere but where Veronin said it'd be parked. I believe it'll slip under their radar—at least until they find his body. Then they'll be looking for it."

Green looked to Palmer. "She makes a good point."

Palmer asked her, "If you're not crossing the border, how will you get back to Moscow?"

"I'll not lie. My back's killing me . . . When we get to the point where you have to start walking, I'll drive the truck back to where we left the car and take it to Moscow."

Palmer considered this for a moment. Reed wanted to stay with the team for as long as possible—and was an undeniable asset—but if the FSB apprehended them, and her, that would endanger her safety, her career, and the mission as a whole.

"No," he decided, saying the word softly. "You leave when we turn west toward the Finnish border. Sokolov knows as much about the area as you do, probably more. You need to return to Moscow. We can't afford the FSB grabbing you. And if you started walking with us, there would be no turning back."

Reed nodded, albeit reluctantly. "All right. Taking the agreed route will be longer than we initially anticipated, but it's worth it to cross the border much farther north. We should stay on the main north-south highway, the E105, as long as possible. We don't want to run out of petrol. Let's stop at a petrol station and fill up when we're getting low. I'll park the car I'm driving out of sight to the side. We'll top up the other car and the truck."

Green suggested, "Let's move Sokolov to the back seat of the truck now before we leave. He's less likely to be seen when we stop for gas."

"Let's do it," Palmer said. He and Green transferred Sokolov to the truck.

Palmer checked his phone. He looked to Green and Reed. "We still have cell service. Call if there's a problem."

2 8

CLAPHAM, GREATER LONDON, UNITED KINGDOM

Fiona Collins woke up before her phone on the nightstand alarm went off. Her bedroom was still dark. She tapped the screen on her phone. It was five o'clock. She fluffed up her pillow and tried to go back to sleep, but her thoughts and concerns wouldn't let her. The more she tried, the more she thought about Jake Palmer. She tapped her phone again. Only five minutes had passed.

Palmer had told her he would be out of communication for a few days and not to worry. This happened occasionally, and within a day or two, he would phone or text to say he had returned. She had stayed busy at work and maintained what she felt was a normal level of concern. No clandestine operation was without risk, and although she was confident that he could handle any situation he encountered, the longer he stayed out of contact, the more she worried about him.

The wedding date was approaching and her hen party was coming up soon. Carol Baxter, her closest friend at MI6 and her maid of honor, had planned everything; it would be a memorable evening out with the girls. She just hoped it wouldn't get out of hand, as some do, and be too memorable. With these thoughts swirling around in her head, she surrendered to the fact that she would not fall back asleep. She threw off the covers, ambled to the kitchen, and turned on the kettle to make a cup of tea.

In Fiona's role at MI6, she had access to all intelligence passed through her analysts' hands. She had remained true to her agreement with Palmer and had not searched for US operations that originated from Pakistan. She had seen an intelligence report that a designated global terrorist, Ibrahim Al-Mansour, the leader of a Sunni Muslim separatist group, Jaysh al-Adl, had been killed in a US Army Delta Force operation in Khuzdār, Pakistan. Several of his team and an undisclosed number of locals, who had responded to the gunfire and explosions and had joined the fight, were also killed. No US casualties were sustained. Delta Force was a part of the US Joint Special Operations Command. Palmer and Green were JSOC Task Force Orange. Had they been involved? She would have heard if he had been injured or killed. She cringed at the thought of either happening.

A thought came to her on her way to work on the tube. She had promised Jake that she would not try to find him, but she had *not* promised that she wouldn't try to find Alona Green, his Task Force Orange partner. The two were inseparable, which at times bothered her. When she arrived at work, she would run a search on Green and see what came up. She wasn't expecting much. If Palmer and Green were running an op, they could be traveling under nonofficial cover and using false identities.

Fiona had invited Green to the wedding, but she'd declined, citing a scheduling conflict. Fiona was disappointed she wouldn't be there. She and Green had never met or spoken before, so she'd been looking forward to meeting her.

Perhaps she would ask Carol out for a drink after work, under the pretense of discussing the hen party and the wedding. The wedding planning had taken a great deal of time. Jake had given her the names and contact information for some of his mates from the States, mostly former Navy SEAL teammates and other close friends. She had urged him to invite his father, stepmother, and brother. She had explained to him that in the UK, guests were typically invited to the wedding, reception, and party that followed while some were only invited to the reception and party. He'd said no to both, because he felt they probably wouldn't come.

—⁓—

When Fiona asked Carol Baxter to go out after work for a couple of drinks, Carol jumped at the chance, saying she had some things related to the wedding that she wanted to run by her. They left work and headed to their favorite after-work bar, located near their offices.

After they ordered wine, Baxter leaned close and said, "So what about the wedding do you want to talk about?"

"I'm worried about Jake," Fiona admitted rather stiffly.

"Afraid he'll do a runner and skip town?" Carol joked.

Fiona shook her head and smiled. "No. He's on an op, and I haven't heard from him since he called and said he was going dark. That was three or four days ago."

Carol sat back in her chair. "Is that unusual?"

"Not really. But I've got a bad feeling . . ."

"Because it's close to the wedding?"

"That's part of it. I've never attempted a search to find him or look for ongoing operations in or out of Pakistan, especially US JSOC ops. I mean, I've been tempted to, but he's strictly forbidden it."

"Yeah, I can see why. That wouldn't be a good thing for you to do."

"Have you seen anything unusual?" Fiona probed, and Carol looked reluctant to answer.

"I'm sure he's fine. Besides, whatever happens, you're powerless to do anything about it," she said with a sigh, but Fiona wasn't falling for it. "All right, well . . . it doesn't involve the US, but I was struck by what I recently saw regarding our MI6 station chief in Moscow."

"What about him?"

"Her, not him. Sania Reed. There's a high-value individual, cryptonym Leapfrog, in Russia who wants to defect to the US, and she's assisting."

"Assisting who?"

"The US."

"I'm confused. Why is she assisting the US on the defection of a Russian to the US?"

"I thought the same thing when I saw it," Baxter admitted, shaking her head. "The intel on this one is highly restricted and way above my pay grade. That's about all I know."

"Neither Jake nor Alona would be in Russia. They're based in Islamabad."

"Right. You're higher up than I am. See what you can find tomorrow." Baxter looked over her shoulder. "Where is that wine we ordered?"

⚬⚬⚬

Fiona shook the rain off her umbrella and entered MI6's Vauxhall Cross headquarters at five thirty the following morning. She aimed to arrive before the night shift ended and the first shift started. Unlike most workplaces, MI6 never closed. With operations underway around the globe, someone was always on-site.

The night shift ended and the first shift began at six o'clock, technically, but the hand off wasn't exact. The person leaving briefed the one arriving on what had happened during their shift and alerted them to any issues. Depending on what was going on, updating them could take half an hour or more.

Fiona's role wasn't tied to one of the three shifts, but she usually came in at eight o'clock or so and was home by six. This morning, her primary focus was to find out anything about Leapfrog's defection and why MI6 was involved in this American operation. Of greater importance, she wanted information about whether Jake and perhaps his work partner, Alona, were involved. She doubted that intelligence officers from Islamabad would be sent to Russia to facilitate a defection. He *had* told her he would be dark for two to three days, giving him plenty of time to be in the UK for their wedding, but she couldn't shake the feeling that something was wrong.

Several people were ahead of her in the security queue. Fiona tapped her foot impatiently. After a few minutes, she passed through and hurried to her office.

Fiona turned on the lights and set her purse on her desk. She logged on to her computer and reviewed emails and intelligence data received overnight for the next half hour. Nothing related to Leapfrog showed up. Next, she searched the restricted database for intelligence operations for MI6 Station Chief Sania Reed. Some background details on Reed popped up. Fiona pored over it. When she tried to locate information on her current activities, a notation appeared that read she was assisting the US in Operation Leapfrog. When she probed further, she received a restricted access warning.

Fiona sat back in her chair, looked at the ceiling, and exhaled. Restricted access was usually level-related or on a need-to-know basis only. She would speak to her boss when he came in. *What am I stressing about? There's no way Jake and Alona Green are involved in a Russian operation!*

RUSSIA, TRAVELING NORTH ON THE E105

Palmer drove the truck with Sokolov stretched out on the back seat. The E105 was a two-lane highway with a passing or turning lane near larger cities. Green was driving one of the cars, and Reed was driving the other. The FSB wouldn't start looking for a pickup truck until they found Veronin's body. After that, they would know the make, model, and color of the vehicle, and because there were very few pickups on the road in Russia, drone surveillance would easily spot them. Once they left the E105 and headed west on secondary roads, traffic would be lighter. So far, so good.

The three-vehicle motorcade made steady progress along the E105. Palmer experienced a few scares when military vehicles passed them and when another came close behind for about a mile before overtaking. As they traveled farther north, they encountered more military vehicles on the road.

Palmer asked Sokolov, "Is this unusual?"

"Is what unusual? I can't see anything. Do you want me to sit up?"

"No. Stay where you are. I'm seeing a lot of military vehicles," Palmer explained, gesturing with his hand. "Fortunately, none of them is paying us any attention."

"You're driving north toward the Kola Peninsula, one of Russia's most significant military hubs. This isn't just the main route for north-south travel to and from the peninsula; it's the *only* route," Sokolov replied from the back seat. He sounded winded, weak—and that concerned Palmer a bit. "The peninsula is rich in ores, minerals, and rare earth elements and hosts Russia's Northern Fleet and its nuclear submarines. The Kola is central to Russia's Arctic strategy. For example, we have forty icebreakers in the Arctic; you Americans have only two aging icebreakers that are often out of service. Can you even name the Arctic Circle countries?"

Palmer chuckled. "Geography isn't my forte. Let's see. Russia, Canada . . . Iceland, Norway, and maybe Alaska in the US."

"Nice try. Better than most Americans would do. You forgot Finland, Sweden, and Denmark via Greenland—eight countries in all, each of which is affected by climate change. The Arctic Ocean ice is melting, opening new sea lanes. Of those, Finland and Sweden have no land that lies within the Arctic Ocean, but they are located within the Arctic Circle. Russia accounts for approximately fifty percent of the Arctic Ocean coastline."

Palmer paused, realizing Sokolov hadn't answered his question earlier. "I understand we're driving close to a military base, but still, that doesn't fully explain all this activity. What's going on? Is this normal?" *What's he not telling me?* "I've worked on or near military bases most of my adult life. When there's this much activity, something has happened or is about to happen."

"I haven't a clue. I've been to the Kola Peninsula only once, in the summer many years ago. It's a different kind of cold in the winter months, most of it under a sunless sky. I fear this area will someday lead Russia down a dark path. The temptation of the vast resources of the seabed will become too great to resist." Sokolov groaned as he shifted in the back seat.

"And Russians aren't big into sharing," Palmer noted. "Reed's turning into a gas station. Stay down. I'm pulling up to the pump."

"Pay cash if you have it."

Palmer thought about that. He didn't have that many rubles. Should he use his Dennis Hall credit card? It would serve as a signal to those monitoring the operation, including MI6 and the Joint Special Operations Command. If somehow the FSB had linked their aliases, Dennis Hall and Lauren Hall, to Sokolov's disappearance, it could also be a red flag. He didn't want to go inside to pay, either.

Reed had parked out of sight beside the station. No one would notice or report her car until closing or early the next day. Palmer pulled in across from Green, who was getting out to use the gas pump. Reed hurried toward Palmer, her arms folded tightly over her chest. She was wearing a light jacket because it was colder than at the cabin, and the wind had picked up. It also concealed any blood on her blouse that might have seeped through the bandages. The station was busy, and as is typical at gas stations everywhere, most people were minding their own business, paying no attention to anyone else.

Reed whispered to Palmer as he was pumping gas into his car. "I'll go in and pay cash for both vehicles because English isn't spoken in this part of Russia. I'll let Lauren know that I'm riding with her. Follow us when we leave."

"Roger that," Palmer said.

Reed walked over to Green, who was replacing the gas nozzle in the pump, spoke to her, and went inside.

━⁓⁓⁓━

Reed left the station after paying and got in the car with Green, who drove around to the side of the Lukoil gas station, with its classic red signage and white lettering, where Reed had parked. Palmer followed and backed the truck next to Green's car so they could roll down the windows instead of standing outside and attracting attention. Palmer said, "We need to get off the E105. We've been lucky so far, but that won't last forever. The longer we're on this road, the greater the chance of getting caught or running into an FSB checkpoint."

Reed nodded. "I'd like for us to drive farther north, but I agree. I'll check my maps app." She keyed in some information, her movements stilted to accommodate her injury. "We're only a few miles from the intersection of the E105 and the 86K-3, a T-intersection. The 86K-3 will be on our left. It'll take us to the Finnish border. There's a small provincial crossing at App Inari on the Russian side and Karttimon on the Finnish side. Before you get to App Inari, you'll need to drive the truck into the forest until you can't go any farther and make your way to the border on foot."

Green's smile was cavalier. "Great. What's the downside?"

Sokolov sat up. "We don't want to drive too close to the App Inari border crossing before we get into the forest. We'll see and hear the drones when we get close to the border, and if we can see them, they can see us. Both the Finns and the Russians use them in remote areas to patrol their borders. They also use motion sensors, infrared sensors, and cameras."

"He's right," Reed said. "Pressure sensors are also used, and there's no way to determine where they might be."

"Sounds like a plan," Palmer said. *A loose plan but a plan.* "We'll follow in the truck and stay far enough behind so it doesn't appear we're together."

"How many pickup trucks have you seen since we began this adventure?" Sokolov asked, pausing for a moment. When Palmer couldn't answer, Sokolov scoffed. "Just as I thought—you can't recall seeing even a single one! Pickup trucks are rare in Russia, especially in urban areas. If the FSB determined the shooter was driving one, they'll be looking for it. This truck will stand out on the road like a sore thumb, even more so because it's new."

"Let's turn onto the 86K-3 and assess the traffic." Palmer looked at Green. "Lauren, you drive. I'll contact Finnish intelligence about the section of the border where we're planning to cross."

3 0

FSB HEADQUARTERS AT BOLSHOY DOM
SAINT PETERSBURG, RUSSIA

"An off-duty FSB officer hunting bear in the forest north of Saint Petersburg spotted Sokolov through his binoculars," Andrei Fedorov announced, rushing into Maksimov's office. "Two cars were parked outside an isolated cabin. He wanted to report the sighting and receive permission to shoot, which we gave him. He confirmed he had shot Sokolov and a woman with him."

Maksimov's wiry brows raised. "Are they dead? When did this happen?"

"A few hours ago. He didn't say whether they were alive or dead. Nothing has been heard from him since then, and he's not answering his radio," Fedorov said, and Maksimov groaned. "An FSB team is headed to the coordinates provided by the officer. I've messaged the coordinates to you. Should I call Ivanov and have him stand down?"

"No. I need proof that Sokolov is dead first. Send Ivanov the coordinates. And tell that FSB team leader to call me as soon as they arrive and assess the situation."

"Will do. Oh, and Aaliyah is waiting at the front desk."

"Bring her in. Don't mention this to her; I'll do it."

Ten minutes later, Aaliyah entered Maksimov's office and went straight to his desk, where he was seated, as if she'd done so a million times.

"Andrei said you had some news," she said, not wasting any time.

Maksimov stood and walked around the desk to her. "One of our FSB officers was hunting and stumbled onto a cabin in the forest north of here. Through his binoculars, he identified Sokolov and shot him and the woman with him. We don't know if they're dead or alive. We've heard nothing more. Communications are hit or miss in the forest. An FSB team is en route to the coordinates he sent. They'll let me know what they find."

The news hit her unexpectedly hard, and her legs weakened. The woman with Sokolov was shot—and according to everything she'd seen so far, that woman *had* to have been Green. Which meant right now, somewhere, Green could be dead or dying.

She pulled up a chair at the small conference table and sat down. Maksimov sat beside her.

"If she's still alive, don't let them kill her," she told him. "I need to see her first."

"I can't do that."

"Well, assuming it's Sokolov, the woman would be Alona Green. You didn't mention him seeing another man, but Jake Palmer would be with her. I'm sure of it. If Palmer's still alive and no one's heard anything since that communication, your FSB hunter is dead."

"Don't jump to conclusions, Aaliyah. All we know is that he shot Sokolov and a woman. No name or description of who was with him was provided."

"I must see the American before she dies!" Aaliyah nearly shouted.

"So you've said," Maksimov replied, voice calm. "An FSB team from Saint Petersburg is preparing to head to the cabin's location. I don't think Sokolov will try to cross the border there. Too closely guarded. Instead, I believe they will go farther north. But if two are wounded, they might try to cross at the closest point to them in order to receive medical care. This team might be the first one to catch up with them. I'll tell the leader to take you with them, or you can choose to go on your own. Fedorov will give you the coordinates."

Aaliyah considered the offer. "One of our embassy staff is on standby. He'll drive me. Thank you, Vlad. Will I see you later?" she asked, momentarily satisfied.

"Yes, whenever you return. I'll call you if I hear anything."

"What is your next move?" she asked, curious.

Maksimov sighed. "Now I have to inform my boss, Colonel General Sergey Vasilyev," he said, the expression on his face growing austere, "who will then, without a doubt, inform the president."

⁓

Andrei Fedorov had followed Maksimov's orders and relayed to Nikolai Ivanov that an off-duty FSB officer had shot Sokolov and a woman who was with him while on a hunting trip. There had been no contact since the report was made.

Was the officer attempting to apprehend them?

Were Sokolov and the woman dead? There were still so many unknowns.

The officer had not responded to radio communications since reporting the shooting. Fedorov sent Ivanov the coordinates for the cabin, which he then entered in the navigation app on his phone and checked the location. The cabin was in a remote part of the forest, relatively close to Finland's border, but it was not a place where anyone in their right mind would risk crossing. It was one of the most heavily guarded sections on the Russian and Finnish sides. Crossing there would be nearly impossible. His gut told him that they would go farther north but not as far as Lapland.

Ivanov could wait no longer. He grabbed his go bag and the firearms he suspected he would need, throwing them in the trunk of his car. He would drive from his home in Vyshny Volochyok toward Saint Petersburg. In the four hours it would take him to get there, Maksimov was likely to have more information from the cabin site.

This was going to be fun.

31

SAINT PETERSBURG, RUSSIA

Natalya Orlova, Dmitry Sokolov's assistant, looked at her desk phone and recognized the caller ID at once: Alexi Volkov, the president's chief of staff. She picked up on the third ring.

Before she could say anything, Volkov spoke. "Hello, Natalya. I called Dmitry's number knowing that you would pick up and not him, because your boss isn't there, is he?"

Her boss *wasn't* there. How did Volkov know that? *The FSB officers.* News travels fast. Bad news travels faster.

Again, before she could say anything, Volkov added, "Sokolov is defecting to the West."

"What? That cannot be true," she said, breathing into the phone's receiver.

His head was spinning so fast he could barely keep up with his own thoughts. Volkov's tone shifted from severe to desperate. "I need to speak with Dmitry at once. I have urgent and critically important information that could save his life. I've tried his personal phone; it went to voicemail. He probably has a secure phone with him. Give me the number where I can reach him."

"I wasn't aware that he was defecting. The last time I saw him, he said he was sick, possibly with COVID, and was going to stop by a clinic and then go home . . ."

Orlova clutched the phone, heart racing in her chest. If Sokolov were defecting, he was in grave danger, and she worried that giving Volkov a number to reach him at would compromise his safety even more than it already was. But if she didn't offer that number now, however, and the government found out it had been in his possession . . .

She'd be found culpable, an accessory to Sokolov's defection.

She swallowed hard. "He has a secure phone, but he keeps that number to himself."

"Listen carefully," Volkov instructed, his voice a rasp. "I'll share something with you, and you need to pass it along to Sokolov. You already know the situation: Sokolov is defecting. The president has learned that Sokolov and a woman with him were shot by an FSB officer who was hunting bear and stumbled upon a cabin north of Lake Ladoga where they were hiding. If Sokolov isn't already dead, his life depends on this. Tell him that Maksimov has sent an FSB team to the cabin to investigate. If Dmitry and those facilitating his defection are still there, they need to leave immediately. The FSB will be setting up roadblocks. If he has any questions, please have him call me at this number, or you can relay his message to me."

"Why are you doing this? You're the president's right-hand man."

"I have my reasons, Natalya. Believe me."

"For the record, sir, I don't know anything about him having a secure phone with him," she emphasized.

Orlova harbored a deep dislike and mistrust of Volkov. He was the worst of the worst. Was this a setup to trap Sokolov? First the FSB had barged into the office to see Sokolov, probably to take him in for interrogation. Now she was on a call with the president's chief of staff. If Volkov was serious, it could save Sokolov's life and get him out of the country. What choice did she have? None. She had to call Sokolov at the number he'd given her the morning he'd walked out.

★　180　★

3 2

FSB HEADQUARTERS AT BOLSHOY DOM
SAINT PETERSBURG, RUSSIA

Andrei Fedorov walked into Maksimov's office. "The FSB team leader is on the phone. They're at the cabin and have completed their preliminary assessment. He wants to give you a status report. Mind if I sit in so I can write it up and keep everyone who needs to know informed?"

Maksimov nodded, and Fedorov took a seat.

Maksimov accessed the call on speakerphone. "What have you found?"

"We have a male, dead from gunshot wounds. From the looks of things, he was killed outside the cabin and dragged inside."

"Why would someone move the body inside?" Maksimov asked.

"Either so no one would see it—which would be odd, as there was a lot of blood on the ground, a window was shot out, and there was more than enough to draw someone's attention—or someone didn't want to leave him for the bears to devour."

"Are they stupid? If a bear tore into the body, the evidence would be gone with it. You'd have seen the blood and bear tracks and concluded the bear had killed him."

"On our drive to the cabin, we saw one lumbering around. It was huge and would've made a quick meal of him."

"Anything else?"

"I was informed that Sergei Veronin was the one who called in the contact."

"Was it his body you found?"

"There wasn't an ID on the body to confirm it as being Veronin's. We suspect it was him, though. Who else would it be?"

"He said he was hunting. Any evidence of that?"

"We didn't find a hunting rifle or ammunition but those could've easily been taken, considering the body also didn't have a phone, his FSB radio, or his wallet."

"They probably have all of it, including his radio. We'll need to switch to another secure channel for our FSB comms," Maksimov said.

"Inside the cabin, two areas of blood are on the floor. That fits what was reported—that Veronin shot Sokolov and a woman. If they were dead, I'd expect to see drag marks on the floor or outside the cabin. I didn't. We found an almost empty bottle of vodka and part of a sheet, which were probably used for disinfecting the wounds and bandages. One area of blood was relatively small. The other was much larger, indicating a more serious wound. My preliminary assessment is that the dead man is Sergei Veronin and that we have at least two wounded runners."

"At least?"

"Yes. We found tire tracks from two passenger cars near the cabin. We haven't found Veronin's vehicle. Hunters usually park near the road and walk in, so I don't believe one set of the tracks were his. I suspect that someone else in that cabin decided to drive Veronin's vehicle. His keys are missing, along with everything else. I'll have someone check the make and model of the vehicle and will let you know."

"To drive away in three vehicles, there must be at least two others, possibly three . . ." Maksimov said, thinking out loud. He thudded a meaty fist against his desk. "Those bastards will pay for this! Find and kill them."

"We have drones in the air and roadblocks are being assembled north and south of here. We're done at the cabin and heading north. We'll find them, sir," the team leader added reassuringly.

"I'm going to concentrate our FSB resources north of the cabin. The farther north, the rougher the terrain, but the less secure the border. Sokolov knows that. If they go far north, they'll need gas and supplies. Check the petrol stations and see if anyone has seen them. Just to let you know, in case you run into him—Ivanov, the Unit 29155 assassin, is hunting for them, too."

"Ivanov?" the officer roared. "We'll steer well clear of him. He enjoys killing too much."

"Oh, a female Pakistani ISI officer is also searching for them." Maksimov chuckled, thinking about the night they'd spent together in the hotel. "I'd watch out for her as well."

"Pakistani ISI? What the hell is she looking for?"

"Revenge."

3 3

RUSSIA, NEAR THE BORDER WITH FINLAND

Since leaving the Lukoil station, Palmer with Sokolov in the truck, and Green with Reed in the car, they had made good progress and reached the 86K-3 turnoff, where there was very little traffic. By Palmer's calculation, about three to four hours remained before they would need to abandon the truck and trek the rest of the way on foot.

Palmer used his satellite phone to call Johannes at SUPO, the Finnish Security and Intelligence Service. "Johannes, Dennis Hall here. We're heading west toward the border near the provincial crossing at App Inari and Karttimon. ETA in about five or more hours, but it could be longer."

"Ah yes, Mr. Hall . . . I'm pleased to hear from you. I was getting concerned. You're just north of Finland's lake district. App Inari is the Russian border crossing on the 86K-3. On the Finnish side of the border, the crossing is Karttimon. The border lies between the two stations. Last time I checked, the Karttimon border station is closed but may be manned because the Russians keep sending immigrants to our crossings. That problem has been at the main crossings, not the small ones like Karttimon. However, the Russians may be manning the App Inari crossing station."

"We plan to get off the 86K-3 and into the forest before we get there. We won't be crossing near those stations."

"I'm looking at a map on my computer, and there aren't many options available. I see one location near the App Inari crossing, maybe two or three miles away. You'll see a lake on your right before reaching App Inari. As you approach the north end of the lake, you may need to backtrack after spotting it. There seems to be a small secondary road on your right, but I can't tell if it's an unpaved road or a walking trail that circles around the lake. Both Russia and Finland have drone coverage of the area. Leave your vehicles where the canopy is too thick for a drone to see through and out of sight of anyone, but they have infrared cameras to pick up heat signatures. And we can't rule out Russia's SAR—synthetic aperture radar—satellites that can see through the tree canopies. They would have to position them, and without knowing where you are crossing, that might not be a worry . . . Don't walk on the road or trail. Stay in the forest. The Utti Jaeger Regiment—our army special forces group—is on standby. Keep me updated on your precise crossing point and timing."

"I'll give you a more specific location when we arrive. I'm using a satellite phone. Can I call you on the number I just used?" Palmer asked.

"That'll work. That's my mobile phone number," he said. "Who else is crossing with you?"

"Lauren will be with us. By the way, Sokolov is wounded and will need medical attention. An FSB officer was hunting and stumbled upon us."

"Seriously?"

"Through-and-through on his arm. We've stopped the bleeding." With Sokolov in the back seat, Palmer held off conveying his concern about the wound reopening when they started walking. "We're with a

British diplomatic cover officer. She's going to bail on us once we start walking. She has a graze wound on her back."

"Damn," Johannes said. "What happened to the FSB officer?"

"Dead."

"Double damn. You'll have every FSB officer in Russia looking for you."

"I fear they've already found his body and are looking for us already."

"I'll call the Utti Jaeger Regiment. They know the border better than anyone. They can't *cross* the border, but you'll need help after you do. The Russians might cross into Finland, kill all of you, and take your bodies back to the Russian side. If they see the regiment, they'll stand down. Call me with updates."

Palmer concluded his call with Johannes and then contacted Reed, who put him on speakerphone so Green could hear while she was driving. He summarized his conversation with Johannes, including the information about the crossings, and then shifted gears to say, pointedly, "Sania, you need to head back to Moscow. Lauren can ride with Sokolov and me. It's totally your call."

He heard Reed sigh. "I've decided to stay until you have to take the truck off-road into the forest. It's not that much farther. Then I'll take the car and drive back to Moscow."

Palmer considered what she had said. "Roger that. It's your decision to make."

Palmer ended that call, another box now checked, leaving the biggest and most formidable ones of this op: leave the truck behind, then travel on foot across the border while evading pressure mines, drones, satellite footage, infrared cameras, and the inevitable presence of the FSB—not to mention making it into Finland safely with Sokolov, who was suffering from an untreated gunshot wound.

He'd been driving behind Green and Reed for only a few more miles when he saw the brake lights of Green's car as it skidded to a stop on the shoulder of the road.

Palmer pulled in behind them.

"What now?" Sokolov asked.

"Time for a powwow," Palmer said, getting out of the car.

Green and Reed were talking and shaking their heads when he approached them. A car whizzed by on the road beside them, and Palmer felt himself getting nervous. What was the purpose of stopping here and unnecessarily drawing attention to themselves?

"What's up? Reed ready to head to Moscow?" Palmer asked.

Green said in her rapid-fire style she used when stressed, "We heard on the FSB radio that an FSB team located the cabin. They found Veronin's body and know his name. By now, they'll not only have determined his truck's make, model, and color but also, based on tire tracks leaving the scene, know that there were two cars at the cabin."

Palmer's jaw tightened. "Veronin must have given them the cabin's coordinates."

"They announced that it was possible that 'the defector and his accomplices' had Veronin's FSB radio," Green said, glancing unconsciously at Sokolov sitting up in the truck. "Then they cut off. They likely have an OTAR—over-the-air rekeying—radio system. With those, they can lock out a specific lost or stolen radio. Hence why I didn't want to risk calling either of you to convey this information." She looked at Reed and Palmer, her expression serious but calm. "Now we're out of contact. Time to get rid of the radio."

Palmer looked back at the truck. "We left one of the cars at the station. Chances are they'll find it. It won't take a genius to determine this is the road we took. Lauren, turn off the radio and give it to me."

Green handed it to him. Palmer got out of the vehicle. He removed the battery and put the radio under the front tire of the truck so he would crush it when they left.

"Any aerial surveillance that follows this road will spot us before we can hide the truck and get to the border. If they block the road, we'll be trapped," he added.

"What should we do?" Reed said.

"Ditch the truck right now," Green replied. "It stands out and is easy to spot."

Reed bit her lip. "Or the three of you get in the truck and race for the border through the forest. I'll head home. If the Russians are manning the App Inari crossing, the border guard will come down this road searching for us. I can't afford to get trapped with no way out."

Palmer listened. Both were good ideas. "If we stay, we'd be cut off. There would be no plan B. No exit strategy. The Russian border guards must be aware of the trail that leads to the border. We'd need to go into the forest farther north to cross into Finland."

The faint ringing of a phone sounded from the pickup. Reed rushed over to the truck and answered Sokolov's secure phone.

Reed answered in Russian and put the caller on speaker. "I've asked her to speak English."

"I'm Natalya Orlova, Dmitry Sokolov's assistant. Is he with you?"

"Hold on." She muted the phone. "What should we do?"

"Let's let Sokolov talk with her on speaker," Palmer suggested. "He'll know if that's really his assistant and whether or not to trust her."

"Hold on, I'll put him on the line," Reed said.

They walked over to the truck and opened the back passenger door. Palmer held the phone and told Sokolov that someone claiming to be his assistant had something important to communicate. "Speak in English," Palmer said firmly.

Palmer unmuted the phone and held it close to Sokolov, who had sat up. "Speak in English," Sokolov said. "Natalya?"

"Sir. How are you? I heard you were wounded," the woman on the line said, clearly concerned.

"I'm fine. Nothing serious, I assure you."

"Alexi Volkov asked me to pass information to you. I told him I had no way to get in touch with you. He didn't believe me and wouldn't say why he wanted to help, but he didn't threaten to have me arrested, which is a mark in his favor. I think he may genuinely want to help you."

"That's most odd." Sokolov seemed to be thinking hard about something that Palmer wished he'd disclose with the group. Instead, he asked, "What did he say?"

"Maksimov is moving FSB and border security from the south to areas north of the cabin location. He has set up roadblocks on the major roads and is blocking off all roads leading to the Finnish border, although it will take time to complete. He's also put the Unit 29155 assassin Nikolai Ivanov on your tail."

"You're not telling me much we didn't already know or suspect," Sokolov said. "Why is Volkov doing this? He's the last person I'd expect to help me. It could be a trap."

"I asked him and he would only say that he had his reasons."

"Thank you, Natalya. For everything. Whether I'm successful or not, I'll miss you," Sokolov said, ending the call.

Palmer's gaze was on Reed's eyes. "You're right. They'll be blocking this road soon—time for you to leave. You've been a great help. We'll have Hunnicutt and Adams to update us on satellite images and SUPO to provide a final drone image at the point where we'll attempt to cross."

Reed met his eyes, nodding. "The size of the border zone varies. In some places, it's up to three to four kilometers on the Finnish side and almost eight or more on the Russian side. That's six miles or more at some crossing points. The Finns' electronic surveillance is concentrated in the southernmost two hundred kilometers, where motion detectors and drone surveillance are standard, and the Finnish Border Guard has irregular dog patrols."

Palmer gave her his satellite phone number, and Reed said, "I'll call you from my mobile when I'm safely out of this part of Russia."

"Good luck. We've got this." Green gently hugged her, careful not to touch her wound.

Palmer got back in the truck and ran over Veronin's FSB radio with the front and rear wheels as he, Green, and Sokolov drove away.

***

Sania Reed had mixed feelings about leaving Sokolov and the Americans, but she needed to follow orders. She reasoned that they were nearing the border and in contact with Johannes, so there wasn't much she could add to the operation at this point. Her job was done.

She approached a curve in the road that she remembered was just before the intersection with the E105. As she rounded the curve, she slammed on the brakes and stopped. Across the highway, two cars had pulled onto the shoulder. Four people—three men and a woman— were outside having an animated conversation. Two of the men were dressed like FSB officers. The other man was dressed in casual clothes and appeared to have a darker skin tone, similar to that of the woman.

Reed's chest tightened at the sight of her.

She looked like the Pakistani woman they had spotted at the train station in Helsinki—Aaliyah!

Reed was far enough away that her car wasn't obvious but close enough to see what was happening. One of the men pointed in the direction of the service station where they had fueled up and left one of their cars, which indicated that these men had to be FSB and that they'd found their abandoned vehicle. They were closer on their heels than she'd thought.

She shifted the car into reverse and let it slowly roll back around the curve at idle, keeping an eye on the four people. Once she could no longer see them, she stopped the car and put it in park. Reed slammed her fist on the car's dashboard. She had done the right thing by deciding to return to Moscow. Her orders from C had been crystal clear—assist the Americans in Sokolov's defection, but don't cross the border with them. She had done her job well and been wounded by an FSB officer in the process. No MI6 brownie points for that. They could cross the border without her. Nothing she could do would alter the outcome.

Now her options were clear. Turn onto the motorway and drive comfortably back to Moscow or Saint Petersburg. Or catch up with Sokolov and the Americans, warn them of what she had seen, and travel across the border with them—in which case she would be violating a direct order.

If she complied with her orders and returned to Moscow, and the team didn't make it, she couldn't be blamed for the failure. She would have done her job as instructed. She would, however, forever wonder if she could have changed the outcome. Their *lives* were at stake. This was bigger than a failed mission, more important than her professional track record.

If she turned back and the FSB chased and pulled her over, she could simply say she'd made a wrong turn. Perhaps they wouldn't suspect anyone coming from App Inari crossing, let alone a female driving a sedan. Unlikely. If they chased after her and pulled her over, she would show them her embassy identification. To her knowledge, they didn't suspect that anyone from the embassy or MI6 was involved with Sokolov's defection. And after checking in, the FSB officers would discover that she was the MI6 station chief.

Reed drummed her fingers on the steering wheel. Throughout her entire MI6 career, she had consistently followed orders and excelled at her job. She was not a rule breaker. She was the Moscow station chief and awaiting her next big assignment. A "good girl" wouldn't think twice about what to do next—she'd follow orders and continue onto the E105 and return to Moscow.

Reed sighed, gripping the steering wheel tighter. *Who's ever made a name for themselves by taking the easy way out? No one.*

She whipped the car around and sped back to join the team. She called Dennis Hall's satellite phone and told him what she had seen and that she was coming back. He said they would wait for her. *Hurry.*

34

FSB HEADQUARTERS AT BOLSHOY DOM
SAINT PETERSBURG, RUSSIA

Maksimov stared at the large digital display of the Russia-Finland border, hands on his hips, and smiled. Sokolov and one of the enablers were wounded. He was certain they were heading north, where the terrain was rugged and the border was less well monitored. The FSB team, the assassin Ivanov, and Aaliyah were searching for them. He had alerted FSB border security. Drone surveillance of the border had been strengthened. Roadblocks had been set up on the E105, forcing them onto secondary roads, and many of those roads ended long before the border, too far for two wounded people to walk.

Like a chess master on a massive board, he moved his pieces, aiming to encircle the opponent and leave them with no escape. *Checkmate.* To do this, he'd reallocated his FSB resources, focusing on the Saint Petersburg area and the northern Estonian border, which spanned from just south of the cabin all the way to Norway at the far north edge of the Russia-Finland border. Checkpoints were not yet active on the

E105. Still, his units were spread across hundreds of miles of border and thousands of square miles of land and lakes. It would take days to get them all into position. However, he was hedging his bets by concentrating on the middle section of the border. The southern border was too heavily guarded, and the northern border was too distant for easy travel without detection. The FSB units in the central part of the border could respond more quickly, some within hours, just as they had traveled to the cabin using the coordinates Veronin provided. The teams moving from the southern Estonian and Finnish borders would take longer to deploy.

Maksimov was a skilled chess player, and as much as he had studied the possible options that Sokolov would take, there was always, in chess terms, a *zwischenzug*, or as the Italians called it, intermezzo— an unexpected move that had dire consequences. But on the chess board he was playing, there would be no *zwischenzug*—not for him, at least. Only checkmate and death awaited his opponent. Russia would make a grand, unexpected move within a few days, shocking the world.

He would contact Aaliyah when their location was known. He owed her that. She wanted her revenge and wasn't someone who would show mercy. His FSB officers would tell him when they found Sokolov and his accomplices. As much as he wanted them dead, a trial and calling out the US for the operations in which an FSB officer was killed would be a more fitting end.

As for Ivanov, unless he was ordered to stand down, he would kill them regardless of where they were, even if it took months to do so.

3 5

ON THE 86K-3 NEAR THE RUSSIA-FINLAND BORDER

After speaking with Reed, Palmer pulled over and waited so she could catch up with them. Sokolov was lying in the back seat, and Green was in the front passenger seat. The forest was thick on both sides of the road. The trees weren't large, but they were packed so tightly that it would be difficult to get far enough off the road to hide their vehicles. Occasionally, they passed bare patches where they could pull into the forest to reach the border. He needed to get as close as possible to the border to minimize the walking. Sokolov appeared fine, but under stress, his blood pressure would become elevated and the wound might reopen.

Green monitored their progress on the satellite phone's GPS, although the battery was running low. Without it, they could still reach the border crossing, even though signs indicated that Finland's border at the Karttimon provisional crossing was closed. Still, the Russian App Inari border guards would be watching for them. And with the Finnish border closed, the Russian guards had little else to do.

Eventually, Reed caught up with them, and they drove off with her following at a distance. Palmer's respect for her had grown. She could have driven away, but she chose to stay with the team and to cross the border, going against the chief of MI6. Of course, if the FSB hadn't been at that intersection, she would have been well on her way to Moscow or Saint Petersburg, with no one the wiser that she had ever been involved. Now that she was involved, he would give her one of the 9mm handguns. He hoped she wouldn't need it.

After some time of driving in silence, Sokolov sat up. "If we're running out of ammo and the FSB is going to capture us . . . shoot me. If I'm arrested, I'll be imprisoned, tortured, and executed. I don't want to give them the satisfaction."

"We're going to make it. I'm confident of that," Palmer replied.

"You don't know these people. They make your CIA look like small-town sheriffs."

"How about I give you a gun and let you shoot yourself then?" Palmer negotiated. "I'm not going to do it for you."

Sokolov ignored him. "I have something you need to see in case we don't make it," he went on in a somber tone, his voice weak. "I was planning to use it as leverage if you didn't agree to help me defect, or if we did, give it to you after we were out of Russia."

Palmer bit his tongue. As arrogant as Sokolov was, he sensed that this wasn't going to be yet another bombastic tangent about Russia's superiority over America. In fact, Palmer had long suspected that Sokolov wasn't telling them everything—and this appeared to be the moment he finally would.

"Now is the time to tell us, if you're going to," he said neutrally, eyes focused on the road.

Sokolov extended his hand. "Give me my secure phone."

Palmer gave him the phone and waited while he searched for what he was looking for.

"It's in Russian," Sokolov said as he passed the phone back to the front seat—but instead of giving it to Palmer, he handed it to Green. "She can translate it."

Green scrolled through the pages of the Russian document on Sokolov's phone. Her jaw dropped. "Oh my God."

"What does it say?" Palmer asked.

"It's a top secret executive summary of a much larger document. The full document runs hundreds of pages in length. Russia, China, Iran, and North Korea are planning simultaneous attacks on the US. The opportunity to attack now presents itself because of the US and NATO's slow development of hypersonic missiles and their lack of defenses against them. These new-generation hypersonic missiles are Russia and China's *shashoujian,* or assassin's mace, giving them a huge strategic edge over the West. If the US and its allies had similar capabilities, the principle of mutually assured destruction would prevail."

"Give me the gist of the plan," Palmer said.

"Russia will target key military sites, including naval bases in Norfolk and San Diego, as well as army posts at Fort Bragg in North Carolina, Fort Stewart in Georgia, and Joint Base Lewis-McChord in Washington state, among many others. Brussels will also be a target. North Korea is expected to attack South Korea. Iran will strike Tel Aviv and American interests in the region. China plans to attack Taipei, Taiwan. The attacks will likely be preceded by large-scale cyberattacks on America's critical infrastructure, including the power grid and communication networks. Hypersonic missile strikes are also expected against each of the US's underway carrier strike groups. This follows China's extensive electronic simulations of hypersonic missile strikes and the US cruisers and destroyers' Aegis radar missile defense systems, which serve as a protective shield around the carriers. Carriers have limited weapons beyond the F-18s on their flight decks. The cruisers and destroyers that make up the strike group are there to protect the carriers," Green relayed, hands shaking. She looked to Palmer, who kept his eyes on the road. "What's to prevent a wide-scale nuclear counterattack?"

Green continued, "China will use lasers to destroy the DoD's key satellites for defense and communication. China, Russia, North Korea, and Iran would launch massive cyberattacks on infrastructure and defense weapon systems that would include the US, South Korea, Taiwan, and Israel. They recognize this will not be one hundred percent effective, but it will significantly reduce the counterattacks."

She took a moment before reading on. "The Russians have already positioned their fleet, including submarines, along the coastline of each major country that borders the Arctic Ocean and will claim the entire ocean as their own. They will place the countries under threat of launching hypersonic missiles with nuclear warheads at the capitals of each country at such a close range that defenses can't respond."

Palmer turned to Sokolov. "Is this a hypothetical plan?"

"I don't think so. This is a battle plan. I believe this is one of the reasons the president ordered an update on the status of missile manufacturing and testing before deployment on naval vessels. In addition, confirmation was sought that the issues observed with the Kinzhal hypersonic missile in Ukraine would not be a problem with the Zircon hypersonic missile. These will be indefensible. Remember the military traffic heading north on the E105?"

"I do," Palmer replied. "How did you come about it? I wouldn't think an aerospace engineer would be copied on this."

"I wasn't copied on it," Sokolov said with a light scoff. "Recently, I presented the status of our programs to the president. It was strange because I hadn't expected that his top military leaders and advisers would also attend. I assured him that we were ready to deploy the missiles. After the meeting ended, they left for a tour of the facility, and I stayed in the conference room to work. I saw an envelope on the floor near where the president and his chief of staff, Alexi Volkov, had sat and picked it up. Curious, I opened the envelope and found the document among some minor confidential papers. I quickly took photos of the pages and put the originals back in the envelope. Because the president's entourage was still on-site, I called Volkov, and he came immediately to retrieve it. He looked nervous and asked if I had opened it. I said no. I'm sure he didn't tell the president because I was certain he wasn't supposed to bring the top secret document with him, let alone misplace it and allow it to fall into the hands of anyone who came upon it and gave in to their sense of curiosity. Later, I read the document on my phone. It was numbered, and each recipient was assigned a specific number that would link the image I've shared with you now to his specific paperwork. Volkov wants me out of the country—or dead. That's why he has reached out and tried to help me."

"That does indeed explain why Volkov wants to help us. Call JSOC on the satellite phone," Palmer said, looking to Green. "Let's update them."

She turned the phone in her direction, her expression changing. "We can't. The battery is dead. Too much use."

Everyone looked at Palmer.

"We'll just have to get across the border and find a cell signal. Then we can talk to someone and send the photos of the document from Sokolov's secure phone. We need to talk to Reed." Palmer pulled over and stopped.

Reed, who had been keeping her distance, parked behind the truck. She hurried over and, seeing their expressions, asked, "What's going on?"

Green handed her Sokolov's phone. "Read this."

She quickly went through the pages on the photos app. "Bloody hell. This can't be true." She looked at Sokolov.

"I'm afraid it is," Sokolov said.

"What were you thinking?" Reed asked, looking at Sokolov and raising her voice. "Earlier, we could have called or radioed the information! Now we're in a situation where we can't."

"I thought we'd be across the border on the Allegro train after I left work. Once we crossed the border, I would've given it to you. Now I'm worried that I'm not going to make it," Sokolov told her, his face still on the gray side. He clutched his arm. "The three of you need to know about this."

"We've lost precious time. Millions of lives are in danger. This could trigger World War III and wipe out half the planet!" Reed's gaze shifted to Palmer. "We must tell someone," she said, her voice growing louder with each word. "Anyone!"

"How? Our satellite phone's battery is dead, and we don't have a charger," Green said, shaking her head. "And we have no cell signal. The cell phone will pick up networks once you're in or near Finland, but I can't lock onto them from here. The same is true for Sokolov's phone."

Sokolov said, "In this part of Russia, coverage is spotty, at best. Most of it is east of here near the E105. Very little of Finland is without mobile phone service, except for the far north in Lapland. We'll be fine once we are in or near Finland."

"I had a weak cell signal at the intersection with the E105. I'll drive back and phone C. He'll want to see the document." Reed looked at Palmer. "I'll need to take his phone with me."

Palmer shook his head. "No. There are downsides to that. From what we know, the four you saw at the intersection are already coming down this road headed our way. You'll get caught, they'll kill or arrest you and take the phone, and we won't be able to send it. When the FSB finds the document on the phone, they'll torture you on the spot for intel. Our best and only hope is to get across this border as quickly as possible. Even now, we're wasting precious time."

Reed, Green, and Sokolov exchanged glances.

Ultimately, they couldn't disagree with Palmer's logic.

3 6

ON THE 86K-3 NEAR THE APP INARI
BORDER CROSSING

Palmer was driving the pickup with Sokolov in the back. Green had gotten into the car with Reed, and they were now following Palmer. The main goal was to get rid of the car and get everyone into the truck, which was a four-wheel drive vehicle that could travel farther into the woods than the car. Driving the car into the lake was an option, or he could drive it into a dense cluster of trees to hide it. They kept going until they reached the lake Johannes had mentioned. Palmer turned right before arriving at the northern end of the lake, at one of the clearings like those seen before. The spot was out of sight from the road. This lake seemed like the better option if it was deep enough to sink the car so that it wouldn't be visible from above, either by someone or by drone surveillance.

They got out of their vehicles. Palmer found a branch he could wedge between the gas pedal and the seat at full speed. He tested it and saw that it was too long. He leaned it against a tree and slammed his foot into it, breaking it into two pieces. He checked the branch size twice with the car off, making sure it wouldn't pop out. It was possible that the impact with the water could cause the branch to come loose, and the car would stop before submerging. *Screw it.* The only foolproof solution was to drive it into the water himself. He tossed the branch aside and rolled down all the windows except the one on the driver's side. That would prevent the water from crashing into him. In theory, once it sank, he would have an easy escape out the passenger side window. The car would float with its momentum and then sink into the deep part. Palmer threw rocks into the lake. The plop of the rock indicated it was deep, several feet from the shoreline, but how deep? *Only one way to find out.* He stripped down to his skivvies.

Reed and Green looked at each other.

Palmer heard them whispering to each other and giggling. He took a running start and dived in, disappearing into the lake. One minute passed, then two. He came up gasping for air and swam ashore. "It's plenty deep and cold," he announced with a shiver.

Green hurried over and handed him a towel she'd grabbed from the cabin, just in case they needed it to clean and dress Sokolov's wound. Palmer dried his face and hands before heading back to the car. He backed it up to the far edge of the shoreline, putting about a hundred feet between the car and the water. He revved the engine several times. With the other three watching nervously, Palmer shifted into gear and slammed down the accelerator. The car lunged forward down the slight embankment and hit the water with a mighty splash. The impact triggered the airbag to deploy, which he had expected. The car floated briefly before sinking out of sight.

The water rushed through the open windows. Palmer took a deep breath before it went above his head and filled the car. He moved over to the passenger window. The car was still sinking. Using his hands to hold on to the sides of the open window, he pulled hard and exited the vehicle.

He swam with a near-perfect crawl stroke to the shore, where Green met him again with a smile and the towel. Reed accompanied her. Subdued applause and muted shouts of joy rang out from the three of them.

"That was amazing!" Reed said, her eyes scanning his torso.

Palmer dried off. "I need to get out of these wet skivvies before I put on my pants. Do you mind?" He made a motion with his hand, indicating they should turn around.

The women winked at each other and burst out laughing as they turned away.

After he dressed, they got into the five-passenger pickup with Palmer behind the wheel. The sun was setting. He continued until he saw the path that Johannes had mentioned and drove on it for only a short while. Using the setting sun for reference and his memory of the map, he headed around the lake in a westward direction.

Everyone was quiet until Green said, "You really are our ride or die."

He chuckled. "Better, I guess, than your ride *and* die."

Green gave a nervous laugh. "Yes. I suppose so."

"The forest isn't very thick here, and it'll be dark soon. I'll pull off the path here and get into the forest. I don't want a drone to pick us up on the trail." He dodged the trees and got out of sight of the road. The truck was striking tree roots and bouncing around.

"There it is," Reed said, pointing at a small lake on their right. "I remember this lake on the map. We need to park and start walking. We're probably five to ten miles from where we want to cross."

Palmer noticed occasional gaps in the tree canopy where a drone camera could see the truck. "Let's get a little deeper into the woods." He examined the path ahead and drove recklessly until he reached larger trees and couldn't go any farther.

Palmer got out of the truck and assisted Sokolov. Green and Reed came over to help unload what they needed for their trek to the border. Everything was going according to plan—they'd evaded the FSB this far and had officially discarded and concealed their other vehicle.

Now they just had to cross the border.

But just when he started to feel optimistic, Palmer heard a rustling in the forest. He froze—as did the others—as he pinpointed the sound's source. Two men slipped out of the darkness of the tree line. Both were wearing body armor or bulletproof vests. One of them, older and clearly in charge, cradled a rifle, which Palmer recognized as a Russian ShAK-12—a fully automatic gun built for urban slaughter and favored by the FSB. The other held a 9mm pistol and had the relaxed posture and confidence of someone who had used it many times before.

"Good evening," the older man called in English. His finger was on the trigger, and his rifle barrel swayed like a metronome, moving across the four of them. "Step forward, nice and slow."

Reed and Green moved beside Palmer and Sokolov.

Sokolov whispered, "FSB."

"Come closer, move out of the shadows. Please keep your hands where I can see them."

Reed and Green moved toward the two officers and nearer to Palmer and Sokolov.

"Well, look who we have here," the younger officer said. "Jake Palmer and Alona Green."

They neither flinched nor reacted to his identification of them.

Reed's jaw dropped, and she whispered to Palmer, "Jake Palmer and Alona Green?"

The FSB officer glared at Sokolov. "And Dmitry Sokolov. Going somewhere, Dmitry?"

Sokolov remained silent and stone-faced.

The man's attention shifted to Reed. "You look familiar? You are . . . ?"

"Sania Reed, British Embassy."

The man gave them a sour grin. "Of course, the Moscow station chief. You're lucky. The president will want to trade you for one or more Russians, who the British or Americans have unlawfully imprisoned, so I won't kill you. Anyway, enough small talk. You know what I like about the Finns? They *despise* small talk."

Palmer gave a dry smile. "That's a stereotype."

"It's only a stereotype if it's not true. Now put that pistol on the ground, Mr. Palmer. There are more of us on the way."

Palmer knelt slowly and laid down his weapon.

"My boss wants me to introduce you to someone before we arrest or kill you. I haven't made up my mind which." He turned his head slightly, not taking his eyes off them, and shouted, "You can come out now!"

Branches rustled behind the two men. A woman emerged from the woods. Her skin tone, posture, and the raw intensity in her eyes told Palmer everything he needed to know about who she was and what she was doing there.

Her eyes locked on Green. "Hello, Alona."

Green didn't blink. "Hello, Aaliyah. You're a long way from Islamabad."

Aaliyah stepped closer to Green, stopping about ten feet ahead of the FSB officers.

Palmer shifted closer to Green.

"Seeing you and Jake Palmer has made the long trip worthwhile," she said, not taking her eyes off Green for even a second.

"You look incredible, Aaliyah," Green said. "More beautiful than ever. I'm glad to see you're doing well. I called and left messages."

"It's amazing what a gifted plastic surgeon can do," Aaliyah said, her voice hardening. "But tell me, Alona—did you expect me to answer, or were you trying to find out if I was alive? The Inter-Services

Intelligence investigators concluded someone had tampered with my brakes. Would you know anything about that?"

Green answered, speaking with a soft affection, "I searched for you. Everywhere. I couldn't find anything. You'd gone dark. I feared you were dead."

"Feared or hoped? Just tell me," she said, her voice a rasp. "Did you do it?"

"No. I was with you during dinner and afterward, until you left," Green said.

"So it was Mr. Palmer then?"

Palmer raised an eyebrow. "Hell no. I can barely change a tire, let alone tamper with brakes."

Green's tone dropped, her voice less affectionate, more accusatory. "It was just business, Aaliyah. You crossed a line. You compromised our intelligence officer by entering a romantic relationship with him, ruining his life, and then giving him the pills he used to commit suicide."

Aaliyah's eyes narrowed. "More proof we're the same, Alona. We would've made a great team."

"You've said that before when trying to recruit me as a double agent."

"How is what I did so different from what you did, Alona? *You* played *me*. You faked your feelings, pretending you were willing to work with me and possibly develop a relationship. You attempted to kill me, which I suspect was done without authorization. You Americans love your moral high ground—but you're not standing on it! I thought we had a connection," she had, her voice surprisingly shaky. "All the while, you were plotting to kill me. I convinced Maksimov to let me talk to you before they killed you. He agreed. He also gave me the option to kill you myself." Aaliyah smiled. "I've decided to take that option."

"Why here? You could have easily killed me in Islamabad."

"ISI forbade it. I was told I could kill you, just not in Pakistan," Aaliyah said with a shrug.

The FSB officer with the rifle shouted, "That's enough! Finish it."

Green edged closer to Palmer. Reed, tense, stepped away.

"Let me kill her," Aaliyah said to the older FSB officer who was holding the rifle. "Then you can do whatever you want with the others."

She stepped toward them and held out her hand, demanding a firearm.

The FSB officer with the rifle nodded. He looked at the officer holding the 9mm pistol and motioned toward Aaliyah. "Give it to her. I've had enough of this."

The officer hesitated, then offered up his sidearm. Aaliyah took it with calm precision.

Both officers stepped back and watched. Their eyes were on Green. Aaliyah extended her arms, aiming the pistol directly at Green's chest.

Green's eyes were locked on Aaliyah. "Take care of yourself, Aaliyah. Russia is about to initiate an assault that will start World War III."

The officers glanced at each other, clearly out of the loop.

Aaliyah's hands were steady. Her posture never shifted. Her eyes never left Green.

Then she quickly pivoted, turning the gun on the two men beside and slightly behind her. Two shots rang out, deafening in the stillness, striking the officer with the ShAK-12 rifle in the head and neck. The second officer had barely turned before she'd put one round in his head.

With the gunshots still echoing through the forest, Aaliyah dropped the weapon on the ground.

"Goodbye, Alona. You're close to the border. They've spotted your truck with their drones. More units are on the way."

Aaliyah began walking away.

"Goodbye, Aaliyah. Will I see you again?"

Aaliyah stopped. "If you survive this, you will. Because next time, I might not be feeling so merciful."

A man stepped out from the shadows—Pakistani, by his appearance—and joined her. They disappeared into the forest without another word.

Alona approached Palmer, who held out his arms, expecting a hug. Instead, Green pushed him hard in the chest with both hands, and he stumbled backward.

"What the hell?" Palmer said, catching his balance.

"Why didn't you do some of your navy frogman shit?"

"She wasn't going to shoot you."

"How can you be so sure?"

Palmer shrugged. "Her eyes. That wasn't hate I saw. She may have come seeking revenge, but that changed when she saw you. Besides, I would have been shot the moment I made a move toward them."

Reed and Sokolov moved toward them. Reed's face was pale, her jaw tight. "Those were the same four I saw near the E105 intersection."

Palmer looked at them. "We need to get out of here and across the border. Grab your gear. We're leaving now."

37

RUSSIA, NEAR THE APP INARI BORDER CROSSING

Palmer wasn't going to be caught without a loaded firearm again. He picked up the pistol Aaliyah had used, then walked over to the two bodies and grabbed the FSB officer's Russian ShAK-12 rifle, along with their extra ammunition. Aaliyah had fooled the two FSB officers, costing them their lives. No officer or soldier in that situation should ever give up their firearm. He searched the bodies but found no radio; they had likely left it in their vehicle.

Palmer told Sokolov to rest, then headed back to Veronin's truck, which was parked about four hundred feet behind them. He lifted the solid tonneau cover from the bed, grabbed the guns, and picked up the rucksack with the extra ammo, slinging it over his shoulder. He returned to Green and Reed, handing each a 9mm pistol while keeping one for himself. He gave Veronin's bolt-action hunting rifle to Green.

Palmer looked to Sokolov and Reed and asked, "Which way to the border?"

Sokolov responded, "The App Inari crossing should be on the part of the border that extends out to the west, so the crossing should be almost directly south of our current location. We left the car at the northern end of the lake. If we go west, we should reach the border a few miles north of the crossing."

The glacial movement during the ice age had formed the bedrock and soil. The advancing ice had moved the soil into heaps, exposing the underlying granite rock and making rocky outcrops. The forest floor was overgrown with peat and other vegetation, often hiding the stones underneath. They were a couple of hundred miles south of the Arctic Circle and about four hundred miles north of Saint Petersburg. The ground would be covered with snow if it were later in the year. Large trees, mostly spruce, pine, and birch, towered above them in the darkness, forming a canopy that blocked the crescent moon's light. The still air amplified the quiet rhythm of unseen life, both animal and human. Everything was concealed and felt closer. Every sensation was sharp with a portent of danger.

Palmer led the way, with Green bringing up the rear. Reed walked between them alongside Sokolov. Protruding roots, marshy patches, and fallen limbs made footing treacherous, slowing their progress. They needed to cross before the sun set. Darkness would worsen each of the hazards.

The trees were tall but not wide, and they were close enough to one another that weaving through them slowed their progress. They could rarely walk in a straight line for more than a few steps. Sokolov warned them that wildlife, including wolves, elk, foxes, and bears, were abundant in the forest. Palmer wasn't too worried about that; they had enough firepower to defend themselves from feral predators. The only predator Palmer was concerned about was the FSB.

The trek to the border over the rugged terrain was exhausting for Sokolov. He had stumbled a couple of times and would have fallen if Reed hadn't been supporting him with his good arm. Sokolov was not obese, but like many, he had put on extra weight as he aged. Palmer guessed Sokolov was a little over two hundred pounds on his six-foot frame, with little or none of it being lean muscle mass, the result of a sedentary lifestyle. Palmer told them to stay close together, saying that slow was better than fast. Fast made more noise and caused mistakes.

After an hour, they stopped where the thick canopy overhead offered Sokolov a place to rest and catch his breath. Palmer looked at his watch. He figured they had three or more miles to go. He checked the makeshift bandage on Sokolov's arm and, much to his relief, found no signs of fresh bleeding. But even so, Sokolov was weak and out of shape. That, plus his gunshot wound, set him at a distinct and severe disadvantage that Palmer couldn't overlook—even if they were only three miles away.

Sokolov sat on a boulder. "I'm not going to make it. I don't know how much longer I can continue."

"You're going to cross the border even if we have to carry you," Palmer said. "We're almost there. Rest and we'll go again. As difficult as it is tonight, it would be more dangerous in the daylight."

They had a little water in the rucksack. Palmer passed around the bottles, which they drank while resting.

"Hear that?" Palmer asked Reed, who was close behind him.

"Drones," she replied. "Most certainly with infrared cameras."

"Yes, and perhaps thermal vision sensors to detect heat signatures."

Palmer had given Johannes the coordinates for the App Inari crossing, but they were going to cross the border northwest of that location. The Finnish special forces team would spread out, but without an update on their exact location, their actual crossing point could be up to a few miles from where they had anticipated they would be.

They resumed their laborious hike and came to a narrow unpaved road on which they could have moved along much faster. However, the FSB at the border would be aware of that and would likely check it in their search.

As they crossed the path, the opening gave a better view of the sky. Palmer checked their bearings. Without a compass, they relied on a paper map, instinct, and the North Star, which was difficult to spot through the canopy. He stood facing the star. Their direction would be to his left, westward. The sliver of a moon provided little in the way of light, which he considered a good thing. After walking another arduous fifteen minutes, Sokolov announced that he needed a brief rest. Palmer motioned for Reed and Green to come to him, away from Sokolov.

"I suspect you've come to the same conclusion I have. Assisting Sokolov's defection will make zero difference in US and NATO security if the planned assaults are carried out. The impact on the countries and the planet, however, will be unimaginable. Getting this document in the hands of the right people must be our highest priority."

Green and Reed nodded their agreement, his message loud and clear.

Reed crossed her arms over her chest. "At the pace we're going, it will take hours to get across the border, and when we do, SUPO and the spec ops team may not even be there."

"You're right," Green said to Palmer. "One of us needs to cross the border as soon as possible and transfer that document to the right people—but, to be clear, you're not suggesting we leave him behind, are you?"

"No. I'm suggesting I go ahead of you. I can reconnoiter the way to the border and the border crossing."

Reed added, "She's right. You're physically more capable and have vast experience with firearms, which you'll need if you encounter the FSB."

"I don't like splitting up," Palmer acknowledged, "but I can get across in a quarter of the time it'd take all four of us. I'll find SUPO and the special ops team, transfer the document, update them on your new crossing point coordinates, and then come back for you."

"Should we tell Sokolov you're going to check out the path to the border and determine whether we have a clear way to cross?" Green asked.

"I'm doing that plus getting to where I hope is a cell signal and disseminating this information."

They returned to Sokolov. Palmer explained their strategy to him. Sokolov hung his head and nodded. "You're giving up on me."

"No, we're not," Reed said just firmly enough for Sokolov to believe her. "The two of us will see this through with you. Palmer will return and guide us across, if needed. His surveillance of the route will assure you and us that we have a pathway to your freedom."

Palmer shook Sokolov's hand and hugged Reed.

"Good luck," Reed said.

"You, too." He hugged Green and reminded her, "You have one of the 9mm pistols and a box of ammunition as well as Veronin's bolt-action rifle and ammo. As I recall from Cape Charles, you're pretty adept at using a rifle."

"Damn straight, I am. I saved your ass with one that day." Green hugged him tightly. "Stay in one piece. You're getting married soon. She'll want you to have all your parts."

Palmer checked the firearms to ensure the safeties were on. The last thing he needed was to fall and end up shooting himself and letting the FSB know his location. He ran his hand through the strap of the fully automatic rifle he'd taken off the FSB guard and put it over his shoulder. He stuffed the 9mm handgun in his waistband. His pants and coat pockets were filled with additional magazines of ammo, in case he needed it.

Palmer had Sokolov's phone, including his unlock code, and the phone Reed had left for him in Saint Petersburg. He turned on Sokolov's phone and unlocked it with the passcode. There were no bars. The battery life indicator showed it was over 50 percent charged. He immediately turned it off to save the charge and to prevent someone from tracking it. He'd stand a greater chance of picking up cell service when he got closer to the border and out from under the forest canopy. He whispered farewell to the others and disappeared into the darkness.

38

RUSSIA, NEAR THE FINLAND BORDER

Palmer moved swiftly across the forest floor, cautious not to stumble on a moss-covered rock or the peat overlaying the ground. It would be catastrophic if he twisted his ankle—or worse, broke a bone, especially now that he was out here on his own.

Palmer treaded carefully, avoiding anything that might create noise. He was aware that as he approached the border, there would be pressure sensors and motion sensors, but he could do little to avoid them without slowing to a crawl. The FSB was already in pursuit. Of that he was certain. The terrain that slowed his and the others' progress was also slowing the FSB's progress, but Green and Reed were held back by Sokolov's failing condition. The silence of the forest amplified even the faintest noise, such as when he stepped on a dead twig. He moved at least twice as fast as he did when he was with Sokolov, however, so that was something.

Occasionally, he paused for a few seconds to listen for the sounds of the FSB, their dogs, or forest predators. Once, he thought he'd heard the distant snort of a bear, though he never saw one.

The hum of the drones grew louder than when he had heard them earlier. He took that as a sign he was headed in the right direction and getting closer to the border. Whether they were Russian or Finnish drones surveilling the border zone, he couldn't yet tell. With each passing drone, he glanced at his watch and marked their relative timing as they flew through the border zone.

Eventually, Palmer caught his first glimpse of the border zone through the trees. He checked his watch. It had taken him two hours. He estimated it would take Green, Reed, and Sokolov four hours, if not more, to cover the same ground. The longer they were in the woods, the greater the risk the FSB would catch up with them before they got to the border. If they had continued at the same pace, they were now about two hours away. Two hours was too slow. The FSB would be gaining ground on them. He began second-guessing his decision to race to the border.

He knelt behind a tree. Nearest to him was a large yellow sign with the image of a palm of a hand that read STOP and BORDER ZONE, NO ENTRY WITHOUT SPECIAL PERMIT in five languages, one of which was English. Beyond the signs was a red-and-green-striped post with the coat of arms of the Russian Federation at the top, designating the beginning of the Russian border zone. In the distance, he spotted the blue-and-white-striped post with Finland's coat of arms at the top. About the same distance between them was an unmarked white post denoting the actual border. The entire border zone was relatively narrow. This was a relief. Some border areas could be miles wide. It was also free of trees, as it had been clear-cut at some point and maintained to keep the vegetation down. Thankfully, he didn't have to negotiate high fencing or razor wire. Provided he somehow escaped the drones, it was a clear shot through the border zone and into Finland.

He waited at the edge of the forest, patiently observing the area, which was not an official crossing. Neither Russia nor Finland permitted border crossings unless they were done at an official crossing point. He was miles north of the provisional crossing of App Inari, Russia, and Karttimon, Finland. He was also between the international Finnish crossing points of Kuusamo to the north and Vartius to the south. He neither saw nor heard patrols with dogs. He scanned the area for motion detectors and cameras and found none. That didn't mean they weren't there.

As he'd neared the border, he noted the relative times of the drones passing and checked his watch. Based on that, he believed that the drone surveillance was on a regular schedule, but although he'd detected a slight difference in the sounds, he couldn't identify which they were. Now he waited for their next appearance and noted the one on the Russian side passed about every twenty minutes and the one on the Finnish side every fifteen minutes. This meant there was no time during which the border zone was not surveilled by one entity or the other.

His immediate concern was the Russian drones, which flew directly over his head or farther into the Russian side. The Finnish ones always flew directly over the Finnish border. The video coverage would include the complete border zone and some of the wooded area outside. Palmer stayed well into the woods and moved around trees to keep out of sight of the cameras and hopefully their infrared sensors as he approached, attempting to forge a plan. Even if he were detected by the sensors, it would take the FSB time to get to his location. Also, he surmised that the sensors often picked up illegal crossings, and they would be focused on looking for Sokolov and two or three others crossing with him. Perhaps the Russians would pay little attention to an individual man going across.

After observing two more cycles of the drones, he was confident he'd narrowed down their pattern and routes. He'd read intelligence reports that confirmed the Russians also used the Orlan-10 drone, which flew at three to five thousand feet aboveground. Because of their height and the wide angle of their zoomed-in camera, they covered a much larger area than the small drones he had observed. This was controversial because it blurred the line between border security and military surveillance.

Palmer would race across the border zone about ten minutes after a Russian drone flew overhead, about halfway through its cycle. That should be seven or eight minutes before the next one passed by. He looked at his watch and began counting down the minutes.

Three minutes . . . Two . . . One . . .

Palmer began a fast walk across the zone. Running would imply he was trying to escape. Walking too slow, and the next Russian drone would pick him up.

The Finnish drone flew by before he reached the blue and white Finland border post. He kept walking and went about half a mile into the forest on the Finnish side, just to be absolutely certain no one on the Russian side of the border could see him.

He hoped that Johannes and SUPO were monitoring the drone. He had probably triggered motion detectors and been picked up on video cameras in both countries.

Palmer turned on Sokolov's phone, checked for a signal, and smiled. It was a Finnish weak signal, called a one-two signal, but it was a signal. He called Johannes.

"Where's the Utti Jaeger team?" Palmer asked.

"They're waiting near our Karttimon crossing with App Inari."

"I'm a few miles north of that. I'll drop a pin." Palmer pulled up the map app and dropped a pin so that Johannes could pinpoint his exact location.

After a moment, Johannes said, "Got it. It will take the team a bit, but they're on the way. Are you alone?"

"I went ahead of the others to surveil our route and the border zone and get to a cell connection. Leapfrog is injured, which has slowed our progress. They should be at the border in about an hour—two at the most. I have some critical information to pass along. Long story short, we have evidence of an imminent Russia-China assault, which also includes North Korea and Iran, on the US and NATO allies. The assault will come in waves, starting with cyberattacks on communications and the power grid."

"*What?*" Johannes's voice was sharp. "When is this supposed to happen?"

"As soon as four days," Palmer replied. "By the time we found out, our radio battery was dead, and we had no cell signal in western Russia. We need to notify everyone about the planned assault."

"Is the intel reliable? How did you come about this information? What proof is there that this is not some hypothetical scenario?"

"That's for the president and others to decide once they have the document. Now that I have a cell connection, I'm forwarding the document to my senior contacts, the SOCOM commander and the chief of Secret Intelligence Services, MI6, which will be sent via my contact there, or at least those for whom I know their email addresses. The defection of our Russian friend is still underway. They should reach the border about the time your team gets here. I'll show you the document when you arrive."

In a very Finnish way of downplaying even the worst of news, Johannes concluded, "If this happens, it would be unpleasant for everyone."

39

NEAR THE RUSSIA-FINLAND BORDER

While waiting for the Finnish Utti Jaeger team to arrive at his position, Palmer found a rock to sit on and used Sokolov's secure cell to send a text message to General Reynolds in Islamabad: Leapfrog showed us the attached document yesterday. Lack of cell coverage delayed its sending. According to Leapfrog, this is neither a scenario nor an exercise. This is an actual planned assault, but we lack solid proof. An urgent notification is needed for the president, Joint Chiefs, and commander JSOC. Additionally, forwarding to my MI6 contact to get it to the chief urgently. Please confirm receipt of this message and the document.

Palmer attached the document photos and sent them off. *That will stir up a hornet's nest of activity.*

He then called Reed and Green but got no answer, so he sent a text to let them know they would see it as soon as they had a cell signal. I've sent the document to General Reynolds for distribution within the US, including the president, he typed out. I also sent it to my MI6 contact for distribution there. I was advised that the current mission is ongoing but is now considered secondary to a possible assault. Finns are on their way to my location.

Palmer couldn't remember the last time he'd felt this impatient and anxious. Three FSB officers were dead, and possibly more would die before Green, Reed, and Sokolov reached safety in Finland. He would wait for them. And if he heard gunfire from the Russian side, he would cross back over the border and move quickly toward where it was coming from.

An hour had gone by since he'd entered Finland. Where was the Utti Jaeger team? Should he call Johannes to see if they had an ETA? No, he decided to keep waiting.

An hour later, his phone vibrated. It was a text from Reynolds: Document received and distributed, as requested, to NATO, Israel, and South Korea. US moving DEFCON 2 with move to DEFCON 1 at first evidence of an attack. Back-channel comms with Russia and China regarding intentions and repercussions.

Palmer paused. He wasn't surprised to hear about DEFCON 2 being initiated, but the mere thought of DEFCON 1, which meant an immediate response to an attack, was difficult to wrap his mind around, despite all the evidence he'd seen already.

He continued reading: Any attack on US infrastructure, communications networks, or communications satellites will be considered the beginning of an assault, resulting in a swift and overwhelming response.

Palmer reread the text and shook his head. The world as everyone knew it could change within the next forty-eight hours. The warning signs were evident. He and Green had reviewed the intelligence and discussed it. They had read the Office of the Director of National Intelligence's annual threat assessment report. China and Russia were behind recent outages of cellular networks and sporadic issues with the US power grid. These cyberattacks had been large but short-lived. Russia had launched ballistic missiles into space that could disable US

GPS and defense satellites as well as commercial ones. Iran had been supplying drones to Russia and the Houthi rebels and was building a nuclear stockpile. North Korea had been conducting frequent tests of its hypersonic missile systems. All four countries possessed nuclear-armed hypersonic missile capabilities years ahead of the US missile and missile defense programs.

Intelligence was a process of assessing small pieces of information and ultimately determining more tactical or strategic conclusions. Nothing Palmer had seen had put the pieces of the Russia-China-North Korea-Iran alliance together and predicted that a coordinated attack would potentially occur. Perhaps it was so far out of the realm of possibility that it simply wasn't considered. Instead, intelligence on each country had been assessed separately. The rule of mutually assured destruction had kept the world safe since Nagasaki and Hiroshima in 1945 during World War II. No nuclear power country could use nuclear weapons against another because the retaliation would also result in the offending country's destruction. However, the strategic advantage those countries now had in new-generation hypersonic missiles and defense systems provided a window of opportunity for them.

Faint voices coming from the border zone broke Palmer from his thoughts.

He moved behind a large tree and confirmed that his phone and Sokolov's phone were on silent. The voices got louder; they were moving closer to him. He stuck his head out just enough to see two Russian guards with dogs walking along the Russian side of the border. The guards were shining their powerful flashlights into the forest on both sides of the zone.

Palmer was well hidden, a quarter mile into the forest. He noted that he was downwind and his scent wasn't likely to be picked up by the dogs. He remained still and controlled his breath. At one point, the dogs stopped and sniffed the ground. He felt his chest tighten with anxiety. He grabbed a handgun, slid off the safety, and prepared for the worst.

Had they picked up his scent from earlier when he'd crossed? The guards aimed their flashlights into the Finnish side of the border, illuminating the area very close to where he was hidden. They had every reason to come investigate this area, just to be sure . . .

But after a couple of tense minutes, the dogs lost the scent, and the guards continued walking, their voices fading away. How far would they go before turning around? He texted Green and Reed, warning them of the dog patrol and that they should keep quiet as they approached the border. God willing, they would have cell service and see the text before they got too close.

40

NEAR THE RUSSIA-FINLAND BORDER

The Russian border guards and their dogs passed by in the opposite direction two hours after he had first seen them. Palmer had moved farther into the forest to lower the chance that the dogs would catch his scent. Once again, the dogs stopped in the same area of the zone where he had crossed earlier. However, unlike before, the dogs started to follow the scent in his direction. They reached the border marker for Finland, and the guards engaged in an animated discussion about something.

If Green or Reed were with him, they could translate what they were saying. He assumed they were discussing entering Finland to find whoever the dogs had picked up. Palmer was lying prone on the ground with his rifle set to semiautomatic on his shoulder. If they came across the border and continued in his direction, he had a clear line of fire. His heart was pounding in his chest. He had shot and killed men, but never dogs, and hoped he wouldn't have to make that decision. He scoffed at his introspection. Strange that he was more concerned about killing the two dogs than about killing the two FSB border guards.

One of the guards began talking into a radio strapped near his shoulder. Palmer could overhear what he was saying—but again, it was all in Russian. The guard with the radio stopped talking and said something to the other guard. After a moment, he spoke into the radio again, and Palmer heard him say, "Nyet . . . Nyet," one of the few Russian words he knew. The guard was saying, "No . . . No."

The guard disconnected the radio call, said something to the other guard, and they left. Perhaps the guard had sought permission to allow the dogs to follow the scent they had picked up into Finland, which was denied. Palmer remained hidden until he could no longer hear them talking.

Where were Green, Reed, and Sokolov? By his calculation, they were long overdue. Now would be a good time to cross because the guards had left. And where were the Finns? They should have already arrived. Palmer felt a vibration from Sokolov's phone. He cleared his throat and said, "Hello."

"Jake?" came the familiar voice of Alona Green.

"Yes. Where are you?"

"We're approaching the border zone. We heard and saw the dog patrol and waited until they passed."

"Can you see the red and green Russian post?"

Green hesitated, then said, "Yes, I see it. It's about five hundred yards to our left."

"I'm in the forest ahead of that. Wait a few minutes after the next Russian drone goes by until you make your move. They fly by just over your position. I'll work my way down to where you are. When you pass the Finnish blue and white post on your left, you're in Finland. When you get to that post, you should see me. I'll be near the forest's edge."

"We're moving even slower than when you left. Leapfrog's condition has worsened. His wound might be infected. Are the Finns there?"

"Not yet. They should be here soon. Stay on the line."

"We heard faint voices behind us a while back, but nothing recently. I don't want to wait too long to cross, especially because it's daylight now."

"Use your judgment on how close they're getting to your location. I'll cover you when you cross. Move as fast as you can."

———

Palmer was racing to the spot where they would be crossing when he heard a series of gunshots ringing through the forest. They were coming from the Russian side of the border. The FSB was closing in on them. He had to go back.

He sprinted across the border zone back into Russia.

Using the still active phone once he was across the open zone, he said, "I'm coming to you, Alona. Fire two pistol shots so I can pinpoint your location." He heard the shots and zigzagged between trees in that direction until he saw them. They were pinned down behind a rocky outcrop. Green was firing an occasional shot with the rifle, probably to let them know they were armed.

"How many are there?" Palmer asked as he got to the safety of the rocks.

Green replied, "Maybe four or five. It's hard to tell. They stopped advancing when I returned fire."

The crack of bullets ricocheting off the rock was frequent. Palmer looked at Sokolov, who was pale and panting. "I'll stay and hold them off. You and Reed take Sokolov and get to the border zone. Then wait for me to help get Sokolov across the open span and into Finland."

Reed nodded. "It'll take two of us to get him across and one to provide covering fire."

"I don't like it," Green admitted but couldn't come up with a better plan.

"Remember our agreement. I'm in charge. I make the tough calls," Palmer reminded her, taking the weight of this choice and putting it on himself. "This is one of those tough calls. Stay behind the trees as much as possible. I'll provide covering fire from here and give you time to reach the edge of the border zone. Fire a single pistol shot when you're there and ready to cross. Then wait for me."

Palmer gave them a few minutes and crawled to a vantage point where he could see beyond the rocky outcropping. He spotted two FSB officers about a hundred yards away. They might have seen that Sokolov was wounded and with two women. The officers were already moving out from behind the cover of trees to open fire. They had absolutely no idea they were being zeroed in on. He needed to make sure his first shot counted for something or else he'd blow his cover.

Palmer aimed his rifle at one of the trees and waited until an officer appeared. He fired a single shot and saw him go down. *That should slow their advance.*

Palmer rolled to the other side of the outcrop, taking cover. This time, the wait was longer before another officer peeked out, exposing his head. Palmer fired. Two down, and maybe three or more to go. Reinforcements were likely on the way, including border guards who would stop Green, Reed, and Sokolov from crossing.

Then Palmer heard a single shot ahead of him. Green, Reed, and Sokolov were on the Russian side of the border zone, waiting for him. He moved carefully, trying not to give the FSB a clear shot. Bullets whizzed past him, some striking trees, causing an explosion of splintered wood and bark.

He didn't see Green and the others up ahead, but they had to be nearby. He heard Green shout that he was directly back and fifty yards from them. When he reached them, they were huddled together near a clearing behind another rocky outcrop. He slid in beside them.

Then he saw what they had already seen. Several of Finland's special forces soldiers were inside the border zone near the Finnish side. They stood with weapons aimed in the direction of the Russians. Disregarding the invisible lines on the ground, they advanced into the border zone toward Palmer and the others, daring the Russians to shoot them.

The Finns approached them and made a gap in their line for them to pass through. Palmer nodded to Green and Reed, indicating that they should go first. He grabbed Sokolov by the good shoulder and followed them.

The Finnish soldiers had stopped firing. Palmer glanced back at the Russians and realized they had stepped out into the open with their weapons lowered. They would be justified in shooting Sokolov, if not all of them—so what were they doing? Why surrender?

Palmer was within feet of Finland's border and struggling with Sokolov's weight. One of the Finnish soldiers came out to assist him. Together, they were making good progress toward the last of the border zone on the Finnish side. Palmer heard a familiar thump, softer than when a bullet hits a tree. His first thought was that he had been shot, but he didn't feel anything.

Then Sokolov slumped over and fell to the ground, pulling Palmer down with him. Both Green and Reed looked at Sokolov. Reed gasped. "Oh no!"

"Get down!" one of the Finnish operators shouted.

The front line of the Finnish soldiers was retreating while they fired in the direction the shot had come from.

Blood was dripping from Sokolov's upper back near his shoulder on his already wounded arm, suggesting he'd been shot—but Palmer hadn't heard a gunshot. Somebody had to be firing a weapon with a suppressor. Two Finnish soldiers ran out and carried Sokolov the remainder of the way across the border into Finland while the other Finnish soldiers provided covering fire. The two soldiers carried Sokolov to a secure location where the medic was waiting. He immediately went to work on Sokolov, who was alive but in serious condition.

Unlike the FSB bear hunter or the FSB officers Palmer had shot earlier, he suspected this shooter was a highly trained sniper using a rifle equipped with a sound suppressor. *That* was why the Russians had stopped firing—he'd told them to stand down and in doing so had lured Sokolov out of cover under a false sense of security.

Palmer, Green, and Reed, all now safely in Finland, stepped back from Sokolov, watching the medic work on him.

Sokolov briefly regained consciousness and said in a strained, weak voice, "*O patria mia, più ti rivedrò. O patria mia, più ti rivedrò.*"

Palmer looked at Green and said, "That's not Russian, is it?"

"Sounds Italian," Green said.

Palmer asked the medic, who was frantically working on Sokolov, "Is he going to make it?"

"He's already weak from the earlier wound and has been fighting an infection. Now this. It doesn't look good. I'll see if I can get the bullet out, but we need to medevac him."

Palmer turned his attention toward the direction from which the sniper's shot had come. The soldiers who had carried Sokolov began to retreat farther into the woods. Palmer did the same.

This shooter was a professional, likely a member of the FSB's Unit 29155 and possibly wearing a ghillie suit that camouflaged him almost completely. The Finnish lead operator motioned for Palmer to go back. Palmer shook his head. The operator nodded and gestured with his hand to the left of their position. He then pointed to his teammates individually, indicating they should move right or left.

A part of a dead tree limb was beside Palmer's feet. After a minute had passed, he picked it up. He waited a moment, held it out, and waved it slowly back and forth. A shot shattered the limb. Palmer nodded and shook his hand to shake off the sting. A sniper would shoot at whatever moves in a situation like the one they were in. The bullet had thrown the limb back and to his right. Palmer whistled softly. The team leader looked his way. Palmer moved his extended hand in a tomahawk motion in the area the shot had come from. The team leader nodded and indicated to his teammates that they should focus on that direction.

41

FINLAND, NEAR THE RUSSIA BORDER

Palmer understood this situation for what it was: a game of cat and mouse. The Finnish border drone—even if the Finnish soldiers could access it—would be of little use considering the number of people moving about. Also, the sniper was probably wearing a ghillie suit, the newer version of which blocked much of the body's heat signature picked up by drones.

The sniper wouldn't expose himself in the open border zone. He would remain in Russia and move along the border, staying hidden until the right moment, and then cross into Finland. Palmer and the Finns planned to create a semicircular trap with the border as the backstop.

Palmer suspected the sniper's goal was to pick them off one by one as they moved, forcing them to shift position to find him. He was situated at the far left of the four Finns. One of them had already been shot; the bullet had grazed his side.

The medic was still attending to Sokolov. Green and Reed had stayed with him and the medic, where they were safe from the sniper.

Palmer needed to move forward and left to form the end of the semicircle. If the sniper broke through or went around him, everyone would be exposed, including the medic, Green, and Reed. Palmer had once played football at the University of North Carolina as a defensive end. His role was to protect the edge and prevent the ball carrier from getting around him and into the open field. His task here was to stop the shooter from getting around and behind him.

Palmer picked up another limb and stuck it out from behind the tree. Nothing. He threw it in the direction he believed the sniper was and listened. Still nothing. Palmer looked at the team leader and shrugged. Had the sniper already gotten around them? How? Perhaps the mission was to kill them all and his strategy wasn't to move parallel to the border until he could cross—it was to move inland, circling back to the medic and the others. Palmer was confident that Green would be the lookout for the others, but she had never faced an opponent like this. If the sniper circled the rocky formation where the medic was working on Sokolov, they would be an easy target. The sniper could fire shots faster than they could evade them.

Palmer listened for any sign that the sniper was moving. He heard nothing. Surely the Finnish special operators had flash-bang grenades or real grenades. He whistled again and mimicked pulling the pin from a grenade and tossing it. The leader pointed back to where the medic was. Palmer was a bit surprised that they didn't have any on hand. What were they thinking? Then again, you don't expect to use a flash-bang or grenade against standard FSB operators in a border standoff. Palmer motioned that he was going back to where the others were. The leader nodded in acknowledgment.

Green was savvy. She and Reed might have taken cover. He texted Green: Returning to your location. Sniper may be headed your way. Take cover and don't shoot me.

Green texted a quick thumbs-up reply.

Palmer rapidly stepped from tree to tree. He could see the medic working on Sokolov. Green was close by with the butt of Veronin's rifle firmly against her shoulder and the 9mm pistol at the ready. Reed was crouched down near her, gripping her own 9mm pistol.

Snipers were patient, and this one would wait them out. Reinforcements may have been called along with the medevac. Sokolov and the medic would be the primary targets. Kill the medic, and Sokolov would die—or kill the medic and then put a round in Sokolov's head. Sooner or later, someone would get careless. Palmer needed to flush the sniper out of hiding. He needed those grenades.

He texted Green again: I have you in sight. Grenades or flash-bangs near you? Ask the medic.

He saw Green turn to talk to the medic, look around, and text, See u. Grenades and FBs.

Palmer texted, On the way. Cover me.

About fifty yards separated Palmer from the others. He was impatient. That impatience could sabotage his decision-making or galvanize him to make a bold move others would hesitate over for too long, missing their chance.

The sniper could hit a moving target, but it would be a tough shot, especially if he were fully zeroed in on his scope, which he probably was. Also, the sniper had to contend with trees in his line of fire. Without another thought, Palmer put his rifle on full-auto and blind-fired a short burst in the general direction of where he thought the sniper might be, then sprinted toward Green. Return fire cracked by Palmer and thudded into the trees, but he made it. The shots had given him another read on the sniper's probable location.

"Where are they?" he asked Green.

"There," she said, pointing at their rucksack with the ammo and some bags of equipment the special operators had brought.

The large outcrop that they were behind blocked the sniper's view of them. But now that Palmer was no longer a concern, the sniper could move faster. They soon would be exposed.

He turned to Green. "Cover me."

Green fired shots toward the woods on the other side of the outcrop. A couple of sniper bullets missed Palmer and ricocheted off the rock.

Palmer ran to the rucksack and grabbed it, along with a couple of the other bags. From their weight, he felt sure they were the ones he needed. He rushed back, dropped down beside the others, and unzipped the heaviest bag. *Bingo.* The flash-bangs, stun grenades, and live grenades were easy to distinguish. The flash-bangs were cylindrical and marked while the other grenades were rounded.

He took a flash-bang and pulled the pin. "Fire in the hole!"

The medic, Green, and Reed put their hands over their ears.

Palmer threw a flash-bang in the sniper's general direction, covering his ears as soon as it left his hand. The noise was deafening. Palmer sensed movement near the explosive sound. There was some motion to the right of where he had thrown it. He picked up a live grenade, pulled the pin, and threw it in the same direction. The explosion was loud but not as loud as the flash-bang. He watched for movement and saw none.

Palmer readied a full magazine to use if he emptied the half-full magazine of his rifle with another fully automatic burst. He considered his next move. Stay and protect Sokolov, Green, Reed, and the medic, or go after the sniper? Where were the members of the special forces team? Had the sniper doubled back and taken them out?

The sniper's goal was clear: to kill Sokolov and those helping him defect from Russia. He had shot Sokolov once but probably knew he hadn't killed him. The special forces team was there to prevent that because they were protecting Sokolov.

The medic crawled over to them. "I've stopped the bleeding, changed the dressing on that shoulder wound, and administered an antibacterial and an analgesic for pain. He won't survive if he doesn't get to a hospital. I've called in a medevac. It's en route, but we must get Sokolov to the landing zone. We passed it on the way in. It's about three kilometers from here. The bird could land in the border zone, but that isn't safe and would create an even bigger diplomatic problem than we already have."

"Can't they lower a stretcher here and haul him up?" Reed asked.

"Yes, but it's dangerous. The sniper could shoot the stretcher or into the open door as the stretcher is being lowered and raised. He might even figure it's worth it to fire at the helicopter's pilot and down the aircraft altogether if that's what it takes to get the job done."

Palmer added, "You'll need more than one stretcher. At least one of your teammates is wounded."

Green asked, "Who is this sniper? He's operating in Finland?"

The medic replied, "I believe he's FSB Unit 29155. He'll kill us all or follow us to Helsinki if we don't stop him."

Palmer had no choice. He had to stay with them. Time was on the sniper's side.

42

FINLAND, NEAR THE RUSSIAN BORDER

Palmer reevaluated the situation. The sniper wouldn't come from the opposite side of the outcrop they were hiding behind. Instead, he would circle around. A better plan would be to head into the trees behind them and look for signs of movement on their right or left flanks. He explained his strategy to Green, Reed, and the medic. Green and Reed would stay with Sokolov while he left to search for the sniper.

"That's a good tactical strategy," Green reasoned. "He'll likely fire a few rounds off the outcrop, drawing our attention in that direction, then flank us from behind, where he'd have an unobstructed line of fire."

Palmer's gaze turned to Green. "I'm going to find him."

Green's jaw was set, her eyes narrowed. "Yeah. Don't go to sleep out there."

"I'm wide awake. Did this all the time in the SEALs."

Green shook her head. "I'm sure you did, but you're not the young buck you once were."

Reed's brow was furrowed and her lips pursed. This was not her wheelhouse.

Green glanced at her. "You ready, Reed?"

"I'm ready. No going back now," she added, more to herself than anyone else.

"We can do this," Green reiterated firmly.

The medic interrupted their conversation. "Sokolov will be out for a while, but I need to stay nearby. We've got this." He gave Palmer a stern look and added, "You kill that bastard."

***

Palmer crouched low and moved toward a cluster of small trees far enough out that the sniper would need to pass by him to get a shot at Sokolov. The sky was mostly cloudy. His chances of seeing the sniper were lower if the clouds were thick.

How many of the Finnish operators were alive? Would they remain where they were or reposition to where Sokolov and the others were?

His duty was to protect the others, including Sokolov. But of those, Green was special to him.

***

Green watched as Palmer disappeared among the trees. She was worried about being exposed behind the outcrop. Would they have been safer in the woods? A more pressing concern troubled her. Would Jake make it back alive? He was up against a pro, sent by the FSB to ensure Sokolov wasn't successful in defecting—the diplomatic blowback from an op that had turned deadly. The Russian president wouldn't be concerned. What could the US do? Impose more sanctions? If the Russians and their allies launched a nuclear war with the US and

NATO, the op and the small group involved would be a mere speck of flotsam or jetsam in the ocean, a footnote in a future tome about World War III—if anyone was still around to write about it.

Reed looked at the pistol in her hand and closed her eyes for a moment. She was exhausted and beginning to smell herself. She longed for a shower and a hot meal after this was over and she was safe in Helsinki. Her grand plan to support the operation without getting too involved and not crossing the border with Sokolov was officially dead in the water. She could have made the turn on the E105 and gone back to Saint Petersburg or Moscow. Maybe she should have. In the past few days, she had seen Russian FSB officers killed, crossed into Finland with Sokolov, and watched him get shot twice and possibly die. The chances for rescue or reinforcements were slim. Gone were her dreams of being the MI6 liaison in Washington and the first female chief of the British Secret Intelligence Service. She'd be lucky if her next assignment was station chief in some insignificant country where nothing of consequence was happening.

Jake Palmer and Alona Green were an impressive duo. *Dennis and Lauren Hall. Ha.*

She'd recognized who they were the moment Aaliyah said their names. Palmer was a legend in the navy special warfare and intelligence services. Having worked with him, she could see why. He was a handsome physical specimen who showed no fear in the face of adversity.

Green was a no-nonsense intelligence officer who relished the danger that came with the job. She was highly trained and experienced with firearms. She spoke Russian and Ukrainian. Putting it all together, she could see why the chief had selected her for the op. However, the op had gone pear-shaped, or as the Americans would say, fubar.

Now, no matter how she felt about it, she was stuck smack in the middle of this ominous situation with Green and the medic. The medic was stationed between her and Green, scanning the tree line with his rifle. Green also had her rifle at the ready. At least *they* looked competent using a firearm. The one Reed held in her hands felt utterly foreign, like trying to write with her left hand.

Palmer was out there . . . somewhere.

And on top of it all, she still hadn't been able to wrap her head around the real possibility of a nuclear weapons attack as widespread as the document described. They'd heard nothing since Palmer sent the document to JSOC and the MI6 chief.

Without taking her eyes off the forest, Green said to Reed, "You okay?"

"Not really. I'm not comfortable handling weapons or being in a Russian sniper's line of fire. It's nerve-racking. Early in my training as a diplomatic cover officer, I learned to use various types of firearms and became fairly proficient with them. Since then, I've never had to use one. It's been years."

Green cocked her head. "Your instincts will take over," she said, though Reed had to disagree.

"I was certain Aaliyah was going to kill you," Reed said, her gaze locked on the forest. "I was so sure of it that I'd closed my eyes. When the two gunshots rang out, I thought *you* were dead. I opened them, and you were standing, and the two FSB officers were on the ground."

"After she'd casually shot those two FSB officers, I just knew she was going to kill me next. I kept waiting for Jake to do something to save me. He told me that the look in her eyes betrayed her."

Reed laughed. "I saw you shove him. I had to laugh. Well . . . here's to him and killing the sniper."

"Roger that. We've been a team for two years and have a lot of confidence in each other. His contract's up soon. JSOC will assign me a new partner at a different location shortly after we return to Islamabad."

"Not to sound like your shrink, but how do you feel about that?" Reed asked. "I sense some chemistry between the two of you."

"If you've seen any chemistry, it's all one-sided," Green said, her voice soft. "Some days I feel like I'm about to spontaneously combust, like when he took his clothes off and jumped in the lake. I think about him more than I should, but I respect what we have as a team. If anything were to happen between us, we could no longer work together. Maybe it's good that he's leaving JSOC and getting married."

"That man is certainly easy on the eyes. Let's face it, Alona. Our jobs don't lend themselves to a happy, healthy relationship or marriage. The travel, demands, and missions are tough on a spouse. I'm living proof of that."

"Were you married?"

"Yes, and happily so for a while. Then my work-life balance became heavily weighted to the job. That's when I realized that I loved my job more than I loved being married—the excitement, visibility, and travel. I was and, I suppose, still am, an adrenaline junkie. I'm getting transferred soon, if my career and I survive this op."

"Where to?"

"Washington, I hope. Maybe that would improve my chances of finding someone. The relationship prospects in Russia are nonexistent. I can't recall the last time I had a date, if that's what it's still called."

⁓

Palmer stayed low to the ground, minimizing his body movements. The sniper was somewhere out there. Snipers were trained in the art of camouflage, and this one wore a ghillie suit designed to mimic the local vegetation. Spotting him would be difficult in daylight and almost impossible at night.

The sniper needed to get closer and around him to have any shot at Sokolov and the others. Staying where he was had gotten him nowhere.

Palmer had situated himself in what he considered the ideal spot to see him when he repositioned. The air was still. Palmer listened for any movement and imagined the sniper was doing the same thing.

Palmer's eyes were getting heavy. He had last slept at the cabin near Saint Petersburg. He felt himself nod off twice and shook his head to wake up. Nocturnal animals move about at night, and in this part of Finland, just south of Lapland, there were a lot of them. A wolf had already come within twenty feet of him, stopped, and sniffed the air before moving on. He had seen a few small animals moving about, too.

The Finnish operators were somewhere out there, so he couldn't shoot at just any sound. On the other hand, they might mistake him for a sniper. He heard movement to his right and shifted his eyes in that direction. He slowly moved the butt of his rifle to his shoulder, lowered himself to his stomach, and waited. A flying insect, probably a mosquito, buzzed around his ear. He didn't swat at the pest for fear of giving away his position. It was like trying not to scratch a persistent itch. The sun would be rising soon. The sniper would want to conclude his hunt before the predawn hour. Palmer tried to calculate when that would be. This close to the Arctic Circle, the timing was much different than he was accustomed to in Islamabad. Once the sniper fired his shots, he would have to escape, allowing time to work his way back to the border and get across the border zone and into Russia before the predawn light.

Palmer had to do something to draw out the sniper. He felt around and found a rock about the size of a baseball. Snipers won't fire at something they can't see, but it might make him move. Still lying on the ground while looking straight out and holding the rifle steady with his left hand, he flipped the rock over his head and to his left, where it landed approximately fifty feet away. He saw a sudden, slight movement ahead of him. He wanted to shoot where he'd seen the movement—but if he fired and missed him or just wounded him, his muzzle flash would spotlight his location and the sniper would have him pinned down. And what if it was just an animal reacting to the thrown rock?

Three bullets cracked as they flew by a tree near him.

The sound suppressor on the sniper's rifle also prevented muzzle flash, another advantage the sniper had over him. Now the sniper knew his location, and he was the only thing between the sniper and those the sniper wanted to kill.

Reed and Green's concerns over Sokolov's injuries were increasing, despite the medic's reassurances that his condition was serious but stable. They hadn't heard from Palmer since he'd left to find the sniper and serve as their backstop.

Green and Reed heard the distant sound of rotors from the helicopter and turned to the medic, who, on his comms link, was speaking Finnish. He noted the worry in their eyes and said, "It's the medevac with one of my teammates on board. A larger helicopter with reinforcements is behind them but will have to land a little farther out. I told them that there was an American friendly and a Russian sniper between them and us. They'll wait until I give them the okay before setting out."

"Any comms from your teammates?" Reed asked.

"None. They may be waiting until dawn before coming in."

Green shook her head. The medic was first and foremost a special forces operator, but he had to stay with Sokolov. Reed and Sokolov would be safe with him. Her gaze turned to the medic and then to Reed. "I'm going to find Palmer. We can't remain in this stalemate forever. It'll be daylight soon."

"That's not a good idea," Reed said.

"I'm not waiting any longer," Green snapped back.

Reed grabbed her by the arm. "Listen. Sokolov's defection is your and Palmer's op. Not mine. You stay with him. My role is to assist, and that's what I'll do."

Green took one hand from her rifle to brush back a few strands of hair from her face. Her eyes flickered between a dying defector and the distant trees where Palmer was caught in a stalemate with a sniper's ruthless determination to kill them all. Reed had made a valid point. She and Palmer were responsible for Sokolov, not Reed. This was their op. Reed was in a supporting role. "You're right. You need to do this."

"I can and I will," Reed said more to herself than to Green.

She recalled one of her favorite Churchill quotes: *Fear is a reaction. Courage is a decision.*

⁓

Palmer noticed the sky seemed a little brighter. Sunrise would be slow coming but it couldn't be more than an hour away. Palmer heard the unmistakable sound of an approaching helicopter. The sniper would have heard it, too, and would know he had to either complete his mission or abort and leave. It was time to move.

Palmer checked his cover from left to right. A couple of trees to his right offered more protection than if he went to his left. He took a deep breath, stood, and moved quickly to the first tree. The next was several feet away. He paused, took three large leaps, and stood sideways behind the tree.

A bullet cracked by him. Another thudded into the tree.

Both shots were from a sound-suppressed weapon. The sniper was probably wearing night vision goggles. This confirmed that he knew where Palmer was and was waiting patiently for him.

After two moves to his right, Palmer had a couple of trees for protection in front of him, so he moved forward and slightly left.

A bullet hit the tree beside him.

He sighed, pinned down. It was then that he heard a sound to his left—leaves rustling. He strained to see what it was. Had the sniper moved that quickly? Was it an animal? He glimpsed a figure behind a tree and tried to identify who it was. *Reed?* She was about fifty feet away, holding her pistol and looking in his direction. Palmer pointed to where he believed the sniper was. Reed nodded.

Palmer ran his fingers through his hair. *Why Reed?* Of the three of them, excluding Sokolov, she had the least experience with a gun. Then it hit him. This was their operation. Green needed to protect Sokolov. He pointed at the sniper with his index finger out and his thumb up, mimicking a pistol. He wanted her to distract the sniper while he moved several trees in his direction.

Reed nodded. Palmer held up his hand with his fingers spread wide. Then he made a fist. She nodded again as he counted on his fingers and thumb: one, two, three, four, five.

As he reached five, she fired in the direction of the sniper while keeping her body behind the tree, then pulled her hand back. The sniper returned fire, with two shots hitting the tree behind her. In the seconds the sniper was distracted, Palmer sprinted toward him about twenty feet and stood sideways behind the cover of a large pine.

Palmer gave Reed a thumbs-up, then signaled for her to stay put with his palm facing her.

He glanced around the tree, toward the sniper. He strained his eyes to see in the dark. After a few scans, he finally spotted him. The sniper was to his left about fifty feet away. He was on the ground behind a shrub, dressed in a ghillie suit, with his rifle aimed directly at Reed.

He must think I moved—that the person behind that tree is me, not Reed . . .

The sniper clearly didn't realize there were two of them now.

Palmer searched for Reed, struggling to make out her features in the dark. When he found her, she was looking at him. He again signaled her to stay there. She nodded.

Perhaps the sniper was so distracted by her shot that his scope was zeroed on where he had seen the muzzle flash from her pistol. That would've narrowed his field of view significantly. It was entirely possible that the sniper hadn't seen Palmer move at all.

Palmer inserted his pistol in his belt and raised his rifle. He moved slowly, avoiding any sense of motion the sniper could detect. He flipped the rifle action to semiautomatic, aimed, and fired two shots. At fifty feet, he was certain he had hit him with at least one of the two. The sniper would now know he had two pursuers. Palmer restrained his desire to peek around the tree. The sniper would have total focus on it.

Palmer's gaze moved in Reed's direction. She was shaking her head. Again, he held out his palm facing her to indicate that she should hold where she was. He pointed at his chest and then toward the sniper.

She pointed in his direction and shouted, "Sniper!"

Palmer turned, saw the sniper, still in the ghillie suit, standing fewer than five feet away. Before Palmer could react, the sniper lunged forward and struck him in the forehead with the butt of his rifle, knocking him to the ground. Palmer dropped his weapon. The sniper kicked it away, out of Palmer's reach.

Palmer lay there, blinking, hoping it would help him see clearly again. The sniper was going in and out of focus, speaking Russian in a stern voice and pausing long enough to spit on him. It was a strangely emotional reaction. Most snipers fulfilled their duty, packed their things, and left the scene.

Palmer wanted to grab his rifle, but he couldn't move. The sniper stopped talking and pointed the barrel of his rifle toward Palmer's face.

In Palmer's last conscious action, he grabbed the end of the barrel with both hands, moved it away from him, and pulled. The sniper wasn't expecting his move and temporarily lost his balance. As the sniper regained his footing, he stepped back and shouted something in Russian.

Palmer closed his eyes. *This is it. I'm going to die in Finland at the hands of a Russian sniper. I'm never going to get married. I'll have let Green down, and—*

He heard a gun fire.

But he didn't feel anything.

He opened his eyes and saw the sniper stumble back, his eyes widening with understanding. It was at that moment that Palmer realized the gunshot he'd just heard wasn't suppressed. The sniper caught his balance and raised his rifle again, but his movement was slow. Palmer was trying to sit up when he heard another shot, then another.

—∿∿—

Palmer regained consciousness, entirely unsure of how long he'd been out. He could've been unconscious for days or five minutes; it was impossible to say.

His vision was blurry. Someone was slapping him. *I must fight back.* Using all the energy he could muster, he pushed his back off the ground and shoved the figure in front of him. He reached for the pistol in his belt.

"It's me! It's me, Jake!" she said, calling him by his real name, now that she knew it.

A female voice. He blinked and tried to focus on the fuzzy figure kneeling over him. He reached out to grab the person and then realized it was Sania Reed.

"Jake! Jake?" Reed said in a concerned voice. "Are you okay?"

"I'm alive," Palmer said, feeling his forehead where the sniper had hit him with the rifle butt. His hand felt wet. He looked at it and saw blood.

"You don't look okay. When I first saw you, I thought you were dead."

"What happened?"

"I saw the sniper hit you with his rifle. I approached slowly at first so I wouldn't draw his attention, fearing for my life. He was cursing loudly in Russian. I saw him raise the rifle. I stopped, fired a shot. He didn't go down, so fired again and again." She turned and looked down at the bloodied body lying on the ground beside Palmer. Her hands trembling, she said, "I think I . . ." *Killed him.*

She didn't need to finish her sentence.

Palmer glanced at the sniper. He was definitely dead.

Knowing this, Palmer took his time and stood. Still feeling a bit unsteady, he took the pistol from Reed. She would soon realize that, for the first time, she had taken a life. He had been through it, and he had seen new teammates face it, too. You never forget the first one. Your teammates might support or even congratulate you, but eventually the weight of your actions sinks in—and if you were a good person, you'd second-guess yourself.

Reed, he knew, was a good person.

"Sania, you saved my life. Another half second, and I would have been dead," Palmer said, now sitting upright with his arms wrapped around his knees. He knew that it was more important to reframe the situation, to look at it objectively. Yes, she'd killed that man, but if she hadn't, he would've killed Palmer, her, and everyone else.

They heard someone or something rushing through the forest, yelling, "Jake! Jake!"

It was Green.

Green ran up to them, holding Veronin's rifle. She took one look at Palmer's bloody face, dropped to the ground, and hugged him tight.

"Sania's the one you need to hug. She saved my life," he said.

Green stood up. "What? Once again, a woman saved your life. What would you do without us?"

Palmer mustered a faint laugh.

"This is the sniper, I'm guessing?" Green asked, eyeing the Russian's body.

Palmer heard others approaching. Two Finnish special forces operators appeared, one of whom introduced himself as Henrik Koskinen, leader of this Utti Jaeger team.

Palmer introduced him to Green and Reed.

Koskinen looked at Palmer's head. "What happened to you?" Koskinen said, kneeling to examine the body. "I don't recognize him. I thought he might be Nikolai Ivanov—Russia's Unit 29155's top sniper and assassin."

"He hit me in the head with the butt of his rifle. I may have wounded him earlier, but it was Ms. Reed who shot and killed him a second before he was going to kill me."

"He's not Ivanov," Koskinen confirmed. "If it were him, he wouldn't have hit you with the butt of his rifle. He would have shot you as soon as he saw you. Although Ivanov has been known to torture his victims and draw out their deaths. I've heard he loves the knife."

Koskinen stepped forward and faced Reed, extending his hand. "Allow me to shake your hand, Ms. Reed." Reed reached out her hand, and Koskinen shook it firmly.

"The chief is going to be furious," she said. "Against his orders, I crossed into Finland with a Russian defector, and now I've killed a Russian sniper. My career is ruined."

Palmer smiled. "Only those of us present, and a precious few senior authorities, will ever know about this. The Russian president will never reference it. If he did, he would have to explain why one of his snipers was in Finland."

As if snapping back to reality, Koskinen said, "We need to move out. *Now*. We'll take you lot and Sokolov to Helsinki." He turned to Palmer and Green. "Russia and its allies are about to start World War III."

Palmer replied, "He needs medical care. The three of us can't leave his side. He's a high-value defector."

"In that case, we'll all ride on our NH90, including the wounded. Sokolov can be treated at our base and be assessed for more intensive care. If required, we'll decide where to take him."

Out of respect for the deceased sniper, two Utti Jaeger operators carried the body to the border and placed it in the neutral zone between the two borders, where the Russians could find it. Two others carried Sokolov on a stretcher to the NH90 helicopter; the rest walked ahead, including the two men wounded by the sniper. Reed waved off the need for immediate medical attention for her back wound, claiming that Sokolov and the Utti Jaeger soldiers were the priority and that her injury was minor by comparison. Green insisted she have it examined, and Reed, who was in no state to argue, agreed.

Koskinen moved close to Palmer. He pointed to Palmer's head and told the medic, "That also needs attention."

One of the medics worked on Palmer's head wound while they waited until the men who had carried the body to the border zone returned. Koskinen explained that Finland's helicopter battalion's twenty large NH90s had replaced the ten Mi-8s they had used for years. "These birds are vast improvements over the ones that they replaced."

Once the wounded had been treated and the men returned from the border zone, they all boarded the helicopter.

43

FINLAND, NEAR THE FINLAND-RUSSIA BORDER

Palmer and Green were strapped in the NH90 on opposites sides of the medic. Koskinen was sitting opposite them, with Reed across from them. Now that everyone was present, the medic gave them a quick update before they lifted off, repeating some of what he'd already told Palmer, Green, and Reed. "I've done the basics on Sokolov. I cleaned and dressed the wounds and gave him an antibiotic for the initial wound that is infected. The only good news is that he has no major organ injuries. On the other hand, he's lost a lot of blood, has a low-grade fever, and is dehydrated. I gave him three units of blood, saline, and an intravenous antibiotic to treat the infection. His condition is serious but manageable. At this stage, he needs some rest and time to heal."

Palmer let the medic's words sink in. "We need to get him to a hospital, but that would be much less secure than your HQ. If we brought him to the US Embassy, could he be treated there?"

Koskinen countered, "First, the US Embassy doesn't have a heliport. And second, I doubt they have a surgeon or the facility to treat him. We could escort him to a hospital by car and provide security until he's discharged."

Palmer added, "That would attract more attention. Where do your team members go when they're seriously wounded?"

"The more serious injuries and wounds have been treated at Tampere Hospital, a three-hour drive northwest of our headquarters in Kouvola, where we're based. However, the closest one to our base is Kymenlaakso, less than an hour's drive."

"What do you recommend?" Green asked.

"Tampere is a university hospital. The red tape for a Russian who requires surgery would be problematic. I recommend Kymenlaakso."

Palmer nodded. "I agree. Johannes said that Helsinki is full of Russian FSB officers, and traveling by car to the embassy would put him and anyone with him at great risk. Kymenlaakso seems like the better option of the two. We need your team to provide transportation and security for us until Sokolov leaves Finland."

"It's possible; however, the timing is problematic. You're aware that Russia and its allies are about to attack our countries?" Koskinen asked rhetorically.

"I'm the one who sent the document that Sokolov gave us," Palmer noted with a scoff. "I need an update on our exfil and a follow-up on next steps. That will influence our decision."

"Of course," Koskinen confirmed. "Meanwhile, I'll check in with my boss. The Russian president is furious with Finland and Sweden for joining NATO, but this seems like an over-the-top response," Koskinen said. "A plan this complex didn't develop overnight. Those four countries—five, if you include Belarus—have been working on it for a long time. To our knowledge, they've never met together, but some have had one-on-one meetings over the past year."

Palmer leaned forward in his seat to respond to Koskinen. "The reality is that Russia and China have a small strategic window of opportunity to use their new-generation hypersonic missiles against the US and its allies. Call them the axis of evil, the unholy alliance, the alliance of autocrats, or whatever you like; their combined advantage in hypersonic missile technology and cyber warfare, together with their nuclear capabilities, is concerning. If the attacks happen, the resulting nuclear apocalypse could be over within hours."

Palmer continued, "Russia used its war with Ukraine for live-fire testing of its missiles. They also learned about the effectiveness of the defenses against them. In 1947, with the realization of the damage and death the atomic bombs had caused to Nagasaki and Hiroshima in August 1945, Albert Einstein said, 'I know not with what weapons World War III would be fought, but World War IV will be fought with sticks and stones.' Even Einstein couldn't have envisioned the capabilities of these weapons and the vast dependence we have on computer systems and AI. We now have a clear view of what that might look like. World War III will be fought with nuclear weapons delivered by maneuverable hypersonic missiles and stealth fighter-bombers. They will be preceded by intense cyberattacks on critical infrastructure, including communication systems, which will throw the populace into panic and dysfunction. After the attack and counterattacks, little will remain. The world as we know it will cease to exist. That, my friend, is what we're looking at if we don't stop it."

Koskinen replied, "Sokolov's now a minor player, a footnote to history. His only use would be to verify how he got his hands on the document and perhaps advise us on any vulnerabilities of Russia's missiles."

Palmer nodded his agreement and added with conviction, "However, until I hear otherwise from JSOC, our mission has not changed."

Koskinen rubbed his temple and shook his head. "The Russian president wanted Sokolov dead. But he knows that Sokolov is insignificant now. Why worry about what he might reveal about Russia's missile development program? It would take months or years for Sokolov to have an impact, long after the events that transpire over the next few days or weeks have concluded. No. He would rather show him, in real time, the destructive and unstoppable impact of his weaponry."

★ 252 ★

44

UTTI JAEGER REGIMENT BASE, FINLAND

When they arrived at the Utti Jaeger base, Sokolov and Reed were taken to the clinic. Palmer refused to do a concussion protocol, saying he had endured worse hits playing football. Koskinen insisted, so he went. Koskinen pointed out the barracks to Green, where she could freshen up, get some sleep, and grab some food at the cafeteria. But Green said she was going with Sokolov.

Palmer completed the protocol and was told to rest for the next few days. He was heading to the barracks when Sokolov's secure phone, which he had kept since Saint Petersburg, buzzed. He pulled it from his pocket and glanced at the screen. He'd just received a text from General Reynolds: You're about to get a call from Vice Admiral John Welsch, commander JSOC.

Palmer knew Welsch was a former Navy SEAL, but he'd never met or spoken with him. In the time it had taken him to read the text, the phone rang.

"Jake Palmer?" Welsch said as soon as Palmer picked up the call.

"Yes, sir."

"This is Vice Admiral John Welsch. Are you somewhere where we can talk?"

"Yes, sir, Admiral Welsch."

"I spoke with General Reynolds and told him I would communicate with you directly. No need for a middleman in situations like this. He gave me your secure number. First, well done to you and Green on the Sokolov exfil. He remains important to us because he will expedite our development and potentially reveal vulnerabilities in Russia's hypersonic missiles. That said, I have another assignment for you both."

Before Palmer could respond, Welsch pressed on. "We've just learned that Alexi Volkov, the chief of staff to the Russian president, wants to defect and hand over Russia's full plan for the attack."

"Alexi Volkov?"

"Affirmative. Volkov contacted our embassy in Moscow and was transferred to Howell. Langley approved Howell's involvement in the exfil. The director of national intelligence is as giddy as a high school girl who just got kissed by the quarterback. You and Green will be in charge of the operation. Howell's role is to get him out of Russia and into Finland. They'll be on the Allegro train from Moscow to Helsinki, arriving tomorrow morning at the first station in Finland. He's a powerful and well-known man. No one in their right mind is going to stop him." Welsch provided Palmer with the information regarding Volkov that Howell had passed on, including Volkov's rationale for defecting, which was his dissatisfaction with the president and where he's taking Russia.

"What's happening concerning the earlier document that Sokolov gave us?" Palmer asked.

"There's been nonstop diplomatic pressure from the US and our NATO allies. The Russian president claims it was a theoretical exercise. We don't believe him. Regardless, the element of surprise has been taken away, and we're prepared to retaliate at the first sign of attack.

We need the complete document that Volkov has so that we can fully comprehend their thinking. Where are you now?"

"Sokolov, Green, Reed—our MI6 team member—and I are at the Utti Jaeger base, about two hours from Helsinki. Their team was crucial in helping us across the border into Finland. The wounded are being treated here. That includes Sokolov, whose condition is serious but stable. He requires additional medical care. With Volkov on the way, we need to get both of them to a US facility. We were considering the US Embassy in Helsinki."

"The embassy would be a transitory move and less secure than what I have in mind. The Baltic Sea's too shallow for our carriers. However, the USS *Kearsarge* Amphibious Ready Group is in the Baltic Sea participating in a NATO exercise. Once you have Volkov, we'll fly you and everyone else out on one of its MV-22 Ospreys."

The vertical takeoff and landing Osprey had been around since the late 1980s and was ideal for amphibious assaults and mission support of Marine Corps detachments aboard the USS *Kearsarge.*

Admiral Welsch continued, "The *Kearsarge* has an onboard hospital staffed and ready, second only to the navy's hospital ships. I'll speak with the group commander."

"This base is home to Finland's helicopter battalion and perfect for the Osprey. Henrik Koskinen, leader of the Utti Jaeger team we've worked with, is concerned that the priority will be preparing for a probable assault by Russia, which will limit what he can do."

"Don't worry. I'll clear it with the Finns."

"Outstanding. In addition to Green and me, we have a Brit, Sania Reed, the Moscow station chief, with us. She has a minor flesh wound, which has been treated. Should she come along?"

"Affirmative. She's part of the team and will need to be debriefed on the *Kearsarge,* as will you and Green. You mentioned her earlier. MI6's involvement was to assist while you were in Russia. What's she doing in Finland?"

"Shit happens, sir."
"Roger that, Palmer. Remember, front sight focus."
"Aye, aye, Admiral."

★

45

UTTI JAEGER REGIMENT BASE, FINLAND

Palmer found Green having lunch in the cafeteria. He grabbed a coffee and pulled up a chair across from where she was seated. "Ah, I needed this," he said, raising his coffee for her to view. "Whatever you're eating looks good. I'm starving."

Green used her spoon to point at her bowl. "I'm not sure what the Finns call it. It's a salmon and potato soup. I passed on the reindeer."

"I'll be right back." Palmer returned with a steaming hot bowl of stew, some bread, and what appeared to be a cinnamon roll.

Green looked at Palmer and set her spoon down. "You're acting weird. What's up? Wait a minute. You've checked in with JSOC, haven't you?"

He took a spoonful of the stew, swallowed, then said, "Actually, Admiral Welsch checked in with me on Sokolov's phone. I was going to update you after I ate."

Green pointed her spoon at him aggressively. "And I'll tell you what you told Reynolds when he was stalling before telling us we were going to Russia—*just spit it out.*"

Palmer hesitated a moment and exhaled, gauging how Green might react. He looked around the cafeteria to ensure no one was close enough to overhear their conversation. "Alexi Volkov, the Russian president's chief of staff, is defecting. Welsch has ordered us to bring him in."

Green eyes widened, and she shook her head. She turned away and looked up at the ceiling before glancing back at Palmer as if he had lost his mind. "That's a freaking suicide mission."

Palmer agreed that it would be risky but tried to ease her concern. "No. This will be more straightforward. Volkov contacted the US Embassy in Moscow and was transferred to Howell. Long story short, Howell is leaving Moscow with Volkov on the high-speed Allegro train tomorrow morning. They won't be traveling together, but they will be on the same train, possibly in the same car. The plan is for us to meet them at Vainikkala, the first train station in Finland, and take custody of Volkov."

Green leaned back in her chair. "What's Reed's role?"

"She'll need to check in with the MI6 chief to discuss that."

"What's his rationale for defecting? You thought Sokolov might be a dangle. Volkov?"

Palmer rested his elbows on the table and lowered his voice. "The Russians have denied any intention to attack the US or its allies, saying any plans were merely theoretical scenarios. Welch said that according to Volkov's account to Howell, it was clear to the Russians that someone had leaked the summary document. The documents were numbered and shared with a select group of individuals who were aware of the plans. Each person was required to read the document in a secure facility for sensitive information. When the document was shown to the Russians, they saw the security number and realized we had the president's copy. The president had given it to Volkov to return it to their equivalent of a SCIF, a sensitive compartmented information facility, but Volkov had accidentally taken it in an envelope with other information he brought to the meeting, where Sokolov was presenting. To make things worse, he forgot that envelope, leaving it there after the presentation ended. Sokolov later found it on the floor and contacted Volkov before they left the site."

Green's jaw dropped. "Does he know Sokolov took pictures of the document inside the envelope?"

"He suspects it," Palmer confirmed. "He'll know for certain shortly, though, I'm sure."

"Well, that aligns with what Sokolov told us."

"Yes. Volkov has an electronic copy of the complete document with him, including the details of the attacks. The Russian president doesn't tolerate mistakes of any kind, and this was one for which Volkov would be fired, if not imprisoned or executed. According to Volkov, this isn't just about fleeing for his life and avoiding the consequences of his own actions—he's trying to stop World War III."

Green laughed. "Yeah, sure. He's trying to save himself. If all he wants is to stop it, why not quit farting around and send an electronic copy to Howell for distribution? Or assassinate the president."

"He's using the document as leverage to escape Russia, just as Sokolov was prepared to do with the summary. The director of national intelligence is excited about the potential of having Volkov at his disposal."

"I suppose he is. He'd be a wealth of knowledge about the inner workings of the Kremlin."

"JSOC directed us to contact Howell and move forward. This should be easier than getting Sokolov out because no one would suspect that Volkov would defect. And no one will stop him and dare to question him if he's recognized. As the president's chief of staff, he's an extremely powerful man in his own right."

"Of course Howell's eager to help." Green took a bite of her soup. "Does the CIA know about any of this? Has he talked with them? We need to bring Reed in on this and see what she can commit to."

"Yes to all of that."

Someone called out Palmer's name. He turned to see who it was. It was Reed, walking quickly toward him. He noticed at once that she wasn't smiling.

Reed started talking as she approached the table. "I called in to update C and try to explain my way out of why I'm in Finland with Leapfrog. After he calmed down, I told him that I had killed a Russian sniper in Finland. He was furious!" she said, visibly flustered. "I removed the receiver from my ear and let him vent. Then he told me about Alexi Volkov. Have you heard about this?"

Green responded before Palmer could. "We just heard about it from JSOC. We're trying to wrap our minds around it. Howell's involved. Did C provide you with instructions about your role?"

Reed replied, "He did. He said Volkov doesn't need Howell to be his nursemaid. He could buy a ticket to the station, but Howell's involvement wasn't his call. He told me to provide whatever help I could and gave me a direct order not to kill another FSB officer."

Green giggled.

"That's not funny," Reed said, though she looked tempted to laugh.

"It sort of is," Green replied with a friendly smile, and Reed sighed, finally sitting down at the table.

The three of them sat in silence, allowing the weight of the task, as well as its risks and implications, to settle in. Palmer broke the silence. "I'll suggest to Koskinen that he go with Alona and me to Vainikkala to meet the train. Reed, you'll stay here with Sokolov. I'll bring this up with Koskinen and see if he can allocate Utti Jaeger's resources for the mission. However, for something this significant, he'll likely need approval from the regimental commander. When we return, Welsch is arranging for an Osprey to fly the three of us, along with Sokolov and Volkov, to the USS *Kearsarge*. It's currently in the Baltic, participating in a NATO exercise."

"What kind of ship is that?" Green asked. "And why do we need the Uttis?"

"An amphibious assault ship. It resembles a small aircraft carrier but is limited to fixed-wing aircraft and helicopters. This should be straightforward, but I'm not taking any chances; it could snafu on us in a heartbeat."

Reed countered, "If the attacks are imminent, does it make any difference that we have the full document?"

"JSOC believes it does. They want to understand Russia's line of thinking and identify our vulnerabilities. If we can learn the details of their plan a day or even hours ahead, we can prevent or halt it now," Palmer reasoned. "He also said we should use Volkov's code name, Tempest, in verbal or written communications."

⎯⎯⎯✦⎯⎯⎯

Palmer left the cafeteria and found Henrik Koskinen speaking with a couple of his men. When they finished, Koskinen came over and sat beside him.

"News travels fast, Mr. Palmer."

"Indeed it does."

"The commander, US Joint Special Operations Command, has been through the chain of command and spoken with my boss, Colonel Antti Virtanen, who has directed my team to assist you in bringing in Alexi Volkov, the Russian president's chief of staff, who is defecting."

Palmer smiled. "I'm glad we'll be collaborating on this operation. I hesitate to predict it will go smoothly, because that hasn't been the case since this mission started."

"He's also received approval for an Osprey from the USS *Kearsarge* in the Baltic to fly to our base and extract your team, including Sokolov, code name Leapfrog, and Volkov, code name Tempest."

Palmer ran through assignments with Koskinen. They agreed that Reed would remain on base with Sokolov. He, Green, Koskinen, and a few Utti Jaeger soldiers would drive to Vainikkala using their operations command center van and two armored SUVs. To allow for unforeseen problems en route, they would leave the base at 0600 the next day to get to Vainikkala two hours before the train's arrival.

❧

Palmer returned to the cafeteria. Green and Reed were still there, having finished their meal. He sat with them and told them what he and Koskinen had agreed to.

They stayed and talked while Palmer ate another bowl of stew. Tomorrow would be a long day, and they hadn't slept properly since leaving the cabin. After Palmer finished eating, they headed to the barracks to get some rest.

He collapsed onto the bed in his skivvies. For the first time since leaving Islamabad, it hit him—he might not make it to the UK for his wedding. He hadn't spoken with Fiona in days and wished he could break their agreement not to communicate while he was on a mission. She was probably getting worried about him. Considering her MI6 role, perhaps she, too, was overwhelmed with work related to the potential global assault that Russia and its allies had planned. If all went well, they would return to the base with Volkov, spend tomorrow night on the USS *Kearsarge*, and he would soon be waiting for her to walk down the aisle at the historic Kent village church in Sevenoaks Weald.

46

VAINIKKALA, FINLAND

Palmer and Green stood outside the Vainikkala railway station, silently looking down the track to the southwest, where the Allegro train from Vyborg, Russia, would soon arrive.

Dark clouds hung overhead and a cold rain dripped from the platform roof.

Howell had sent a cryptic message to Sokolov's secure phone, which Palmer still had. It read, Enjoying the Allegro first-class ride. See you soon.

Without commenting, he showed it to Green.

Vainikkala would be an unremarkable Finnish village if not for its railway station, which was situated a little over one kilometer from the Russia-Finland border. The station served as the key transit point for trains and vehicles traveling between the two countries, making it a focal point for Finnish immigration and customs officials. Yet the station was smaller than some commuter stations Palmer had seen in the northeast US. Most of the village's four hundred residents were employed by the railway company or by Finland's border services.

The hour-and-a-half drive east from the Utti Jaeger base to Vainikkala Station had been uneventful. Admiral Welsch's call to the Finns had paid off. Koskinen had brought eight of his elite team with him, two in a command center van and four with Palmer and him in two Patria 6×6 armored modular vehicles.

Koskinen emerged from the station, where he and his uniformed Utti Jaeger teammates had been staying out of sight inside, and approached Palmer and Green with an update. "The station manager said the train from Vyborg will arrive soon. You should come inside. Every FSB officer in Russia probably has your photo by now, and I can guarantee that a few of them are on the train looking for defectors. It will tip them off if they spot us, and they'll move on Volkov."

Palmer checked his watch and glanced at Koskinen. "We're in Finland. They have no jurisdiction here."

Koskinen cocked his head and looked at Palmer. "That didn't stop them from trying to kill Sokolov after he crossed into Finland, and it won't stop them now. They won't hesitate to act if they suspect the Russian president's chief of staff is defecting. Sokolov was a big catch, but Volkov? He's huge. His defection will expose details of the planned attacks and provide enough intelligence to keep the analysts busy for years. The implications are far-reaching and international, none more serious than the damage it will do to Russia. If the Kremlin knew he was defecting, they'd rather fire missiles and destroy the train and kill everyone on it rather than let him cross into the West."

Palmer's expression tightened. "Do the FSB officers get off the train here?"

"Some might stay and catch the next train back to Russia. Others will continue on to Helsinki. Think of them like air marshals—they blend in with the passengers, invisible until they're needed. Finnish border checks happen between Kouvola and Vainikkala while Russian border controls are done between Vyborg and Saint Petersburg. For anyone getting off here, like Volkov, the Finnish passport and customs checks are done inside the station. The Russians will have already checked Volkov's passport and know who he is. Not sure what excuse Volkov gave them for traveling to Finland, and who knows whether they thought it wise to alert the FSB on board. Most will recognize him anyway, and the FSB officers will watch him. When Volkov prepares to depart the train, I suspect they'll try to stop him and question why he's getting off in Vainikkala, if they haven't already."

Palmer grinned. "Maybe he told them it was none of their freakin' business what he was doing. From what I've heard, Volkov's a nasty piece of work and certainly not the type to be intimidated. I doubt the average FSB grunt would be bold or stupid enough to prevent him from disembarking."

Koskinen shrugged. "Maybe, but I've warned the station master and the passport and customs officials in the station that we're here to meet a senior Russian official. They'll keep anyone from entering the station until we get Volkov out the back. First-class passengers will disembark first. My men will stay hidden unless things go sideways. And leave the shooting to us. I don't want another international incident. We already have a big problem with a British intelligence officer killing a Russian sniper inside Finland."

Green smirked. "No witnesses to that one—at least none who'll testify to it happening."

Palmer nodded. "Yes, but there will be plenty here, and everyone will have a smartphone to video it."

47

ABOARD THE ALLEGRO TRAIN
VYBORG, RUSSIA

Two FSB officers aboard the Moscow to Helsinki Allegro train stood toward the back of the first-class car, whispering to each other while glancing at a man sitting near the front. The man they were staring at was none other than Alexi Volkov. He'd boarded in Moscow, and they'd paid him little attention, fully expecting him to get off in Saint Petersburg, but he didn't. Now they were at the Vyborg Station, the last stop before crossing the Finnish border, and facing a very real conundrum.

"We need to stop him now, before this train crosses the border," the junior of the two officers said in a whisper, eyeing Volkov.

"That's the president's chief of staff you're talking about," his colleague said harshly. "He'll have us drawn and quartered for questioning his fealty."

"He's defecting. I'd bet my life on it."

"You're betting *both* our lives on it. I'd call the president's office, but it's not like I have his contact information at my disposal. Damned if we do, damned if we don't. If we take him off the train and interrupt something he's authorized to be doing, we're screwed. If he defects in Finland, we're also screwed."

"Call Maksimov."

The senior agent exhaled. "Right."

He had Maksimov's number on his phone but had never called it. After several rings, the call went to voicemail. He left a whispered message, stating their situation and asking that he return the call right away.

An announcement came over the car's speakers: "The train is leaving the station in five minutes. Our next stop is Vainikkala, Finland."

The junior officer looked his superior in the face. "I'm going to confront him now and see how he reacts."

"Stop. We'll both go."

The two marched the short distance to Volkov's seat. The senior officer said, "Sir. We're sorry to disturb you. We're FSB officers. May I confirm that you have authorization to leave Russia?"

Volkov turned his head, his brow contracted, and his eyes narrowed in obvious rage. "Do you have any idea who I am?"

The senior officer, now regretting his decision to confront Volkov, replied, "Yes, you're Alexi Volkov, the president's chief of staff. We're just doing our job, sir."

Volkov reached into his jacket pocket and handed them a folded letter-size paper.

The senior officer read it. He looked to the junior officer beside him. "The document, signed by the president, authorizes his travel into Finland."

"Is that his actual signature?"

"I'm no handwriting expert, but it appears so."

Volkov overheard them and glared. "Are you satisfied? What are your names?"

"We're sorry, sir," the senior officer said. "We won't bother you again."

They walked to the back of the car. The junior officer whispered, "Volkov could have prepared that document and put it in front of the president to sign along with other mundane documents, or he forged the signature. We can't let him off the train until we hear from Maksimov. There'll be repercussions, but no one can blame us for doing our jobs."

"Oh yes they can, and they *will*."

"Screw it. We'll be heroes or villains, cheered or executed."

PART 3

48

VAINIKKALA, FINLAND, RAIL STATION

A horn blared in the distance, signaling the train's arrival. Palmer and Koskinen stepped into the station and stood by the window. Koskinen had shown Palmer photos of Volkov on the ride from Utti so he'd know who to look for. The Allegro train came to a stop at the platform. The sky had turned a solid gray, and rain pounded the station's roof, driven sideways by harsh gusts of wind. Thunder rumbled in the distance.

The first-class car doors swung open, and a handful of passengers stepped out, their heads bent low to shield themselves from the wind-driven rain as they made their way briskly into the station.

"I don't see Volkov," Palmer said.

"No. And I don't see anyone who looks like an American intelligence officer."

The phone in Palmer's pocket buzzed. "Text from Howell." Palmer read it aloud: "'Code red. Tell them not to let the train leave the station.'"

Before Koskinen could respond, Palmer hurried the short distance toward the first-class car with Green right behind him. He looked back once to see Koskinen exiting the station.

Howell stepped onto the gangway between the cars and met Palmer and Green. "They've got Volkov. They won't let him off the train until they verify his authorization to leave Russia. He showed them an official document, but they're demanding confirmation."

"Who's holding him?" Palmer asked.

"Two men. They approached him in Vyborg. I heard them say they were FSB officers."

Palmer chambered a round, tucked the pistol into the small of his back, and entered the car. Green did the same and slid her gun into her jacket pocket. The car was arranged with about fifteen rows of single seats on one side of the aisle and two seats on the other. The car was empty except for two large men with Volkov standing several rows from the entrance. The officers had blocked Volkov's exit and were shouting at him in Russian.

Howell followed Palmer and Green and paused just inside the door. Howell said, in English, "They think his papers are forged. Volkov's threatening both with arrest."

Palmer clenched his fist and said to Green and Howell, "This is about to go sideways."

Koskinen entered the car.

The sight of the uniformed and armed Finnish soldier startled the two Russian men. Their eyes widened. One quickly grabbed Volkov, pulling him forward as a human shield. The other drew a gun from a shoulder holster and pressed it against Volkov's head. Neither said a word. Volkov seemed unfazed and fearless, his eyes sharp and jaw tight.

"What's going on here?" Koskinen demanded in Russian as he pushed past Howell and Green. He slowly stepped forward and held out his hands, palms down, to de-escalate the situation. "Let's remain calm." Pointing at Volkov, he said, "This man is in Finland on official government business and under the protection of the Finnish government. We're here to escort him to his destination. If you have a problem with that, address it through the proper channels."

Green quietly translated for Palmer.

Palmer heard movement outside the car—two of Koskinen's soldiers entered. Koskinen turned and told them to wait on the gangway. The FSB officers were likely to kill Volkov before allowing him to leave with the Finnish soldiers.

Koskinen said, "Everyone, please calm down, and put that gun away. Now!"

The senior officer returned his pistol to his shoulder holster but kept Volkov firmly in his grasp. "We're waiting for a call to confirm that he's authorized to leave Russia."

"Why didn't you take him off the train before it crossed into Finland?" Koskinen asked.

"If he were anyone else, we would have pulled him off much sooner."

Volkov took a step away from the men, only for one of them to grab him by his coat collar and yank him back.

—⁂—

Andrei Fedorov, Maksimov's chief of staff, waited until his boss's meeting with two of his direct reports had begun before leaving to take a cigarette and coffee break. The meeting was scheduled for an hour, but he suspected it would likely go longer, as he'd seen Maksimov take out the vodka.

Chatting with one of his coworkers while on break, Fedorov glanced at his watch, apologized, and strolled back to his desk. The flashing light on the desk phone caught his attention. He picked up the receiver and listened to the message. "Oh no." He played the message again, confirming what he'd heard the first time was correct and not some terrible hallucination. He ran over to Maksimov's office and threw open the door. "Excuse me, sir, but—"

"Are you blind? I'm in a meeting!"

The two staff members shifted in their chairs and looked at Fedorov with questioning eyes.

"Well, what's so important?" Maksimov shouted.

"An FSB officer on the Moscow to Helsinki Allegro train called. Alexi Volkov is on their train and about to enter Finland."

Maksimov stood, bracing his hands on his desk. "Well, what else did he say?"

"After your meeting began, I left my desk for a coffee break. The officer had left a message saying they were about to leave Vyborg, the last stop before the border. When the officer questioned him, Volkov showed him and another FSB officer an authorization letter signed by the president. They want confirmation that the authorization is valid. They might be in Vainikkala by now."

Fedorov knew by the look on Maksimov's face that he had not seen or heard anything about Volkov leaving the country. Because of Volkov's senior position, the FSB would have been notified if he had been issued a travel authorization.

"Get that officer on the phone. Now!"

Fedorov picked up Maksimov's desk phone, his hand shaking as he held the note. He misdialed, hung up, and then tried again. Maksimov jerked the handset and paper from him and dialed the number himself.

⸺∾⸺

Inside the first-class car, a phone rang. Everyone looked in the direction of the sound. With his eyes focused on Koskinen and his hands extended and palms out in front of him, the senior FSB officer said, "It's mine. I need to see who it is."

Koskinen responded, "Okay, but no sudden movements!"

The FSB officer slid his hand to his pocket, but not so slowly as to risk the caller hanging up. He glanced at the screen. "This is the call I've been waiting for. I must answer it."

Koskinen nodded his approval. "Put it on speaker."

The officer tapped the accept button and switched it to speaker. A man's voice said, "This is Colonel Vladislav Maksimov. Who's this?"

Koskinen recognized the name. He was Russia's head of FSB counterintelligence.

As soon as Maksimov's name was mentioned, Volkov shoved the officer who had been holding him with both hands and sprinted toward the exit, pushing Koskinen aside. The junior FSB officer sprang after him. Palmer stepped in, blocking his path, and punched him square in the face. The officer fell like a massive tree in the forest, his head slamming against the hard floor with a resounding thud.

The other FSB officer jumped onto one of the seats, took out his weapon, and fired over the others at Volkov, who was almost at the exit.

Palmer snatched his pistol from the small of his back and fired at the officer.

The two shots rang out in quick succession. Their deafening reports in such a confined space echoed off the walls of the car. Everyone turned toward the exit door. Volkov was standing there, his head hanging low.

The sound of the gunfire was so loud that Maksimov pulled the handset from his ear and yelled furiously into it in Russian, "Who the *hell* fired those shots? What happened?"

A cacophony of shouting ensued, so loud he couldn't understand what was being said. After a few more attempts, it became clear that the phone had likely been dropped on the floor, disregarded. Whatever was going on was more important than speaking with him—

Which was bad. *Very* bad.

Maksimov hung up, pointed at the two men he'd been meeting with, and shouted, "Get out!"

He then pointed at Fedorov, who stood motionlessly beside his desk. "I'll deal with you later!" he said. "Go to your desk."

After Fedorov left, Maksimov sat in his chair. His first thought was to call the president; instead, he reached for the phone and called his boss, Sergey Vasilyev, colonel general of the FSB, who reported directly to the president.

Vasilyev answered on the first ring. Maksimov told him about Volkov and the gunshots.

Vasilyev said he knew nothing about Volkov leaving the country, so he couldn't say whether or not the president had signed an authorization for him to do so.

"You don't know who the shots were directed at," he said, confirming what he'd heard.

"That is correct," Maksimov replied. "The shots were fired in quick succession. I don't know who fired them or if anyone was hit."

"We don't know if Volkov is alive, dead, or wounded. Until we have proof, we'll assume he's alive. After I talk with the president, I'll call you. Meanwhile, get someone to the Vainikkala station who can locate Volkov and find out what happened as well as whether he's dead or alive. If he's alive and I learn that the president didn't authorize his travel, I want him dead. Do you understand me?" Vasilyev hung up before Maksimov could answer.

49

VAINIKKALA, FINLAND

Palmer and Koskinen hurried to Howell's side and knelt beside him. The bullet meant for Volkov had hit him in his upper chest. Green knelt down and helped turn Howell over, her hands immediately masked in the red of his blood, feeling for a pulse on his wrist and neck and checking his breathing.

But it was clear from the sight of him that he was dead.

She looked up at Palmer and shook her head. The wound was not survivable. He'd died the instant the bullet hit him. Howell had seen the FSB officer draw his weapon and had stepped in front of Volkov at the last moment, saving his life.

Within minutes, four police cars and two ambulances arrived at the station. The thunderstorm had just passed, only to be replaced by the chaos of sirens and the rush of uniformed first responders. Everyone at the station watched the scene unfold, some recording it on their phones. Green and the Finnish soldiers escorted Volkov inside. Koskinen talked with a few police officers and the ambulance driver inside the train car. He gave them a brief report of what had happened, emphasizing the sensitivity of the incident. He translated what he had said to Palmer, who had remained by Howell.

An EMT examined Howell and confirmed what they already suspected by a slow shake of his head.

Another EMT in the train car examined the FSB officer who Palmer had shot and confirmed that he was also dead. He moved on to the other officer, whom Palmer had punched and knocked out. That officer had regained consciousness and was sitting up on the floor of the train car, holding his head. His nose was bleeding, there was blood on the back of his head, and he'd gone white with shock.

The deceased FSB officer was placed on a gurney and transported to one of the ambulances, where he would be taken to the local medical examiner. The officer Palmer had knocked out was taken to the ambulance, treated, and turned over to the Finnish police. He was handcuffed and led away.

Palmer placed his hand on Koskinen's shoulder and said solemnly, "Howell's body goes with us. I'm not leaving him behind. He's a fallen CIA officer, killed in the line of duty. His remains must be treated with the utmost respect."

"Agreed." Koskinen walked over to the EMTs, spoke with them, and nodded to Palmer.

***

Palmer and Koskinen joined Green and Volkov inside the station, where he underwent a quick immigration and customs check. Koskinen's soldiers waited outside. Palmer kept Volkov within arm's reach. After he cleared, they closely surrounded him and escorted him into the Utti Jaeger team's command center van. A row of computer screens covered one entire side of the vehicle.

Palmer said, "Where's the document?"

Volkov replied in English, his voice cracking, "Guarantee me you won't take it and leave me here."

Palmer took a deep breath, his jaw clenched tight. "We just lost one of our intelligence officers, who saved your life. We killed one Russian FSB officer and injured another. I guarantee that if you don't give me the damn document, I'll personally put you on the next train to Russia."

Looking to Koskinen, Volkov asked, "Once you have it, what's to keep you from arresting me?"

Koskinen responded, "Arresting you would create a public relations nightmare. You're defecting to the US and as such have the full protection of Finland and ultimately the United States once you're at an American location."

Palmer added, "If all you wanted was for us to have the document, you could have emailed it to us. You didn't get off the train with any luggage and didn't tell us that it was on the train, so I assume you have a digital copy with you. There's no going back, Volkov. You'll never see Russia again, and at this point, that's a good thing. As a friend reminded me recently, *Russia never forgets*. Need I remind you of Yevgeny Prigozhin, the mercenary, oligarch, and leader of the Wagner Group? He stopped his group's march to Moscow, and your president made nice with him. Months later, he died in a suspicious plane crash. I'm sure you know the background to that unfortunate mishap."

Volkov sighed. "You're not telling me anything I don't already know. I'm not confident I'll even make it to wherever you're taking me, much less to the US. The president will do everything in his power to prevent it—and he has a *lot* of power." He took off his jacket and handed it to Palmer. "The document is on a USB drive in the lining, in the back."

Palmer handed it to Koskinen, who patted the back of the jacket. "Got it." He took a knife from his belt and cut it open. The USB drive was inside. Koskinen inserted it into a port on the computer panel as Palmer and Volkov watched.

The drive contained only one file. Koskinen ran it through security protocols to scan for viruses, malware, and other threats. The file was clean. He opened it. The document was in Russian. Koskinen used AI to translate it into English. Even though it was too lengthy to read in full, Green and Palmer scanned the document with Koskinen looking over their shoulders, their eyes catching fragments here and there.

Palmer took his eyes off the screen and slowly shook his head. "My God," he said, turning to face Volkov. His voice cracked in disbelief. "Is this real?"

"Yes."

Koskinen replied, "We must send this by secure transmission immediately."

Palmer gave Koskinen the email address for Admiral Welsch. "Send the original document and its translation to Admiral Welsch, US JSOC commander, for distribution. He'll review it with the US president, who will authorize the distribution, including to our NATO allies and non-NATO partner countries."

Then Palmer turned to Volkov. "When will the plan be initiated?"

"Soon. The president has kept the precise timing to himself. He's had private conversations with the heads of China, North Korea, and Iran. Only the most senior Kremlin and defense officials who worked on the plan know when this begins. They've been having private meetings in our secure facility for months. Ground-level forces are preparing, but they've been told it's a multicountry exercise."

Palmer nodded. "When we were driving north on the motorway in Russia, a large convoy of military vehicles was headed in the same direction. Although the FSB was searching for us, none of them paid us any attention."

Koskinen looked at his watch. "Russia has a massive military presence on the Kola Peninsula, including nuclear missiles and a torpedo submarine base. We must leave for our base now. It's an hour-and-a-half drive if we don't encounter any problems. I want to cut that to one hour. We'll distribute it while we're riding."

"Any updates from Reed on Sokolov?" Palmer asked.

"No. I'll text her," Green said, typing out the message and then reading it aloud: "'Leaving now. Status on Leapfrog's condition? Can he travel?'"

Reed was quick to reply, and Green shared her response: "'Yes, after receiving IV fluids and a blood transfusion. Awaiting the doctor's release. Tempest?'"

Green looked to Palmer and replied, speaking out loud as she wrote: "'Tempest in our custody. Underway soon. Will advise ETA. Howell KIA.'"

5 0

SAINT PETERSBURG, RUSSIA

For the next few hours, Maksimov's phone kept ringing. As soon as he finished one call, Fedorov already had two more on hold waiting for him.

Earlier, the body of an FSB officer named Veronin was found in a cottage near Saint Petersburg. The FSB border patrol spotted a body during drone surveillance of the border zone between Russia and Finland near App Inari. The body belonged to an FSB officer, believed to be a sniper. Based on evidence at the scene, including several footprints, authorities suspected the officer was killed in Finland and then moved there after death. Expanding their search on the Russian side of the border, they found the bodies of two FSB officers in the forest miles from the border. Both had been shot at close range. They were looking for Sokolov and had recently been assigned to escort the Pakistani ISI officer Aaliyah. No weapons were found at the scene, and Aaliyah was not located. There was also a report that two FSB officers had been shot and killed trying to stop Sokolov from crossing the border.

Maksimov lowered his forehead into his hands. Where was Aaliyah? Where were Palmer and Green? Had she and the Pakistani ISI officer with her been killed? So many unanswered questions.

Maksimov's thoughts were interrupted by his chief of staff, Andrei Fedorov, who was carrying a laptop. He placed it on the desk and opened it. "You'll want to see this."

Maksimov sat beside him and leaned close to the screen. Fedorov opened a social media post and played a video at Vainikkala station showing Finnish soldiers and a woman escorting Volkov out of the train car. Others showed two body bags being carried from the train and a man, who appeared to be an FSB officer with a bloody face, being led away with the soldiers at gunpoint.

Maksimov's phone rang again. It was Vasilyev. *He's seen the videos.*

"The president is furious. Now not only is the summary plan for the assaults compromised, but the entire plan, which Volkov has, will also be compromised. He justifiably feared for his life and fled with the complete plan, probably as an insurance policy to get into Finland and then to the US. The president wants him dead as well as Sokolov; even though the damage may be done, he wants to send a strong message. Traitors will be found and killed. He said he would fire missiles at the location, regardless of who was with him. If we confirm he's on a helicopter or plane, he'll order it shot down. This is our highest priority. Find and kill Volkov and Sokolov and everyone with them."

"Yes, sir. Based on the information from the field, I believe that both will make an initial stop at Finland's Utti Jaeger base and from there be transferred to a US facility, perhaps the US Embassy in Helsinki."

The body count was piling up. *Where's that damn Ivanov?*

NEAR LAPPEENRANTA, FINLAND

As the soldiers prepared to load Howell's body into one of the armored modular vehicles, Palmer stepped out of the command vehicle beneath the gray brooding sky and stood at attention. He raised his right hand to his brow in a silent salute, holding it until the body was inside. Koskinen and the Finnish soldiers nearby mirrored his actions with the same precision, respect, and solemnity.

Standing between Palmer and Koskinen, Green put her hand over her heart. Soon, his mother, father, and relatives would learn that he had given his life for his country. A star commemorating Howell's death would be added to the Memorial Wall in the lobby of the CIA headquarters in Langley.

No one spoke as Palmer and the others climbed back inside. Palmer glanced at Volkov, who had remained in the vehicle. He sat silently with his head down as the three-vehicle caravan rumbled away from the station. They turned onto Rikkiläntie Road, where they drove a short distance before turning onto Route 387. They had traveled to Vainikkala in the dark. It was now approaching noon. The command center van had no windows except for the windshield, through which Palmer got an occasional view of the countryside.

Leaving Vainikkala, the landscape stretched into a vast rural expanse, punctuated by small sleepy villages. In the back of the van, a soldier hunched over a control panel, his eyes darting across screens, on high alert for anything that might thwart their mission, monitoring for any traffic or other issues that could slow or impede their progress. They had turned onto Route 6 at Lappeenranta, the largest town they had come to. Koskinen said they would stay on Route 6 the remainder of the way to the Utti Jaeger base. The soldier manning the bank of screens barked something in Finnish to Koskinen. He snapped his head up and said to Palmer, "Possible incoming missiles from Russia. He's alerted our base and the other vehicles."

"Damn it!" Palmer spat.

Koskinen snatched up the communicator, his voice rising, rapid and sharp in his native tongue, as he shouted to his fellow passengers and those in the other vehicles, "Possible incoming missiles! Retrieve your weapons! Get out and take cover! Move, move, move!"

They had to get outside the blast radius. The soldiers grabbed their weapons. One of them handed Palmer and Green identical Finnish SCAR rifles, used by Finnish special forces, and 9mm pistols, along with some extra ammo.

Everyone sprinted away from their vehicles. Shelter was scarce. Palmer grabbed Volkov and ran away from the vehicles, with Green not far behind. They looked skyward and saw explosions in the air. The Finnish surface-to-air missile defense system intercepted some of the incoming missiles, but it wouldn't eliminate them all. Palmer pushed Volkov to the ground and told him to cover his ears. Palmer hoped that the missiles were zeroed in on the vehicles. Otherwise, they were all toast.

They were fewer than fifty yards away and lying prone on the ground when the first missile slipped through the defense system. The impact shook the ground like an earthquake. Another hit seconds later.

Palmer didn't see it because his head was down, but he felt the ground shake again. Dirt, metal, and miscellaneous debris rained down from the sky. Everyone stayed down until it stopped and the air cleared.

Palmer had been near explosions of all types when he was a SEAL and, as a result, had tinnitus in both ears, but nothing he'd ever heard before sounded quite as loud as those hypersonic missiles hitting so close to his position. He removed his hands from his ears, but still, the ringing seemed to have doubled or tripled in volume.

Koskinen said something to him. Palmer shook his head and pointed to his ears.

Koskinen ordered everyone to get up and move farther from the vehicles. They were brushing the debris from their clothes when they heard more explosions in the air as the Finnish missile defense system attempted to eradicate another incoming missile attack.

Koskinen shouted, "Get down!"

The words were barely out of his mouth when the third missile struck, this one closer to their position.

They stayed prone for a few more minutes after impact before standing again. One of the armored modular vehicles and the command center van weren't just destroyed—they were obliterated. There was no evidence they had ever been there at all. The other armored vehicles had been damaged and were probably undrivable. It hit Palmer that one of the damaged vehicles held Howell's body.

Palmer moved next to Koskinen and whispered, "Are you thinking what I'm thinking?"

"The FSB wants to verify that Volkov is dead and eliminate him if he isn't . . ."

"Exactly. They probably timed the missile strike with their ETA to this location."

Koskinen said, "If you're right, they'll arrive soon. They'll expect only a few, if any, to have survived the missile attack. We need to spread out." He pointed at Volkov. "What about him?"

"He's all mine," Palmer said with a smile.

"I'll call for backup. We're on Highway 6, just past Lappeenranta. We're only thirty minutes out from the base."

Koskinen made the call, speaking rapid Finnish, and hung up. "News travels fast. They had picked up on the missile strikes and were loading up to deploy. They're about sixty clicks out. One of our helicopters will lift off soon and arrive here before them. They'll provide air support, which may be sufficient, and also transport the initial reinforcements."

Volkov stood up, brushing the dirt off himself as he looked at the debris field where the vehicles had been and slowly shook his head. The blasts had showered debris across a wide area.

Koskinen shouted in Finnish that everyone should spread out and take cover until the reinforcements arrived, which he translated into English for Palmer. Then he called the base again and reported that everyone had survived, although a couple of minor injuries were caused by falling debris. They would later learn that Finnish defense forces inland and US and NATO ships in the Baltic Sea had all fired defensive missiles at the Russian hypersonic missile assault.

Minutes later, one of Koskinen's men, watching the road through his binoculars, shouted that four SUVs were rapidly approaching from the southwest while police cars were coming from Lappeenranta in the northeast. Just as he spoke, the sound of sirens blaring filled the air.

"This has all the makings of a goat rodeo," Palmer said to Green with a strong sense of urgency. "We're getting Volkov the hell out of here."

Koskinen overheard and nodded in agreement. "They're probably FSB. My men and I will spread out and hold them off until the cavalry arrives. Take Volkov and get out of sight behind our line of defense."

"Copy that."

"Go while you have the chance. We've got this. They're probably your typical FSB officers, not Spetsnaz." He pointed to the north.

"Lappeenranta Airport is on the other side of the berm. Once you get over the berm, there's another two-lane road, followed by an access road and several outbuildings, some used to store heavy equipment."

"Is there a fence between the road and the buildings?"

"Surprisingly not. Or there's the forest to the south. Take your pick. Grab a couple of weapons. We have a surplus."

Palmer and Green took their rifles, pistols, and extra ammunition. Palmer had seen a small plane land at the airport as they were running from the van and before the missiles struck. Air traffic control in the tower would have seen the explosions and shut down the airport. The airport wouldn't be that busy for such a small town, but there would be plenty of buildings in which to hide from the FSB. The other choice, in the opposite direction, was the forest. He looked at Volkov. "Let's get out of here before the bullets start flying."

Volkov replied, "*Da!*"

5 2

LAPPEENRANTA AIRPORT, FINLAND

Palmer had grown weary of hiding behind trees and ruled out the forest as an option. He led Volkov and Green to the top of the berm, where they could view the area. At the base of the berm was the two-lane road that Koskinen had mentioned on the outer edge of the airport. The commuter airport was small, with a short runway. Security was lacking. The only barrier was a chain-link fence that could be easily scaled. Some commercial businesses were located along the road in close proximity to the runway. There was no barrier to getting to those. Palmer scanned the surrounding area, which appeared deserted. The workers must have evacuated moments after the missile strikes. Closest to them was a construction boom lift rental business and an airport warehouse that stored snowplows.

Confident that the Utti Jaeger soldiers would hold off the FSB, they made their way there to hide until the helicopter and reinforcements arrived. For the moment, they were safe. Volkov was curled up in his tailored suit against the wall of the building, looking exhausted and scared. He hadn't spoken a word since they'd left the van.

Palmer walked over and stood above Volkov.

Volkov raised his head. "Who are you? I saw what you did in the train car. You knocked out one of the FSB officers with a single punch and shot and killed the one who had shot at me. With those skills, I'm guessing you're both CIA."

Green stood watch by the entrance, looking for anyone who might have seen them and come to investigate. She was close enough to hear Palmer's conversation with Volkov.

"As far as you're concerned, my name is Dennis Hall, and that's Lauren Hall, and my job is of no concern to you," Palmer replied curtly. "All that matters is that I'm the only one who can get you out of here alive. For the chief of staff to the president of the Russian Federation, you've been quiet—too quiet. I have a question, and I'm looking for a truthful answer. If I don't get one, I swear I'll kill you here and claim a stray bullet hit you."

Volkov didn't blink. "What do you want to know?"

"Why is someone who works at the highest level of the Kremlin defecting? You're the head of the presidential executive office. You know every powerful person in Russia. You're a powerful person in your own right. Why defect?"

"Mr. Hall, my position had become more of a curse than a privilege. The more you witness pure evil, the easier it is to dismiss it as acceptable and right. We were told we were going to 'denazify' Ukraine. We threatened them with nuclear missiles. We forbade them from attacking inside Russia while we sent in troops to do terrible things to civilians. We launched missiles and drones in Ukraine without regard for the innocent lives that would be lost. There have been over one million Russian casualties, including an estimated two hundred fifty thousand killed. North Korean soldiers were sent to help, but they were inexperienced in war and, as a result, most of them died. They may have looked like soldiers, but none had ever seen a battlefield. My position provided a window through which I could see the truth. I'd finally had enough."

"We've seen the summary document and the full top secret document. Your president has claimed they're both planning documents for how Russia and its allies could coordinate and potentially conduct a devastating attack on the US and its selected allies. He knows we have the summary document and have Sokolov. He's probably been informed by now that we also have you."

"Are you planning to ask me a question, Mr. Hall, or merely recite the obvious?" Volkov inquired.

"Are these scenario documents outlining what *could* happen, or are they an actual battle plan that will be initiated?"

Volkov took a moment to consider his response. "Everything I know about the president and the documents tells me they are just as you say—a plan. He wants his allies' buy-in if the plan becomes a reality now or in the future. Face it, Mr. Hall. Russia, China, Iran, and even North Korea have every technological advantage in the weapons with which such a war would be fought."

"For now, at least, that is true. You hold a strategic and tactical advantage. The time to act is now, rather than waiting a year or two when the US and its allies will have developed and deployed comparable or superior weapons and defenses. What's stopping your president from acting now?"

"There is the realization that pushing the button to start this would result in an earth-altering reality. It could last for years, even if limited to conventional weapons. And it would likely rapidly escalate to nuclear, in which case . . . well, you know."

"A nuclear apocalypse," Palmer filled in.

"Precisely, and not even Russia wants that."

"When we were driving north on the E105, the closer we got to the Kola Peninsula, the more military traffic we saw, all headed north," Palmer commented. "Surely something's up."

Volkov crossed his arms around his knees and took a deep breath but said nothing.

Palmer bent over, his face inches from Volkov's, and with deadly calm said, "Answer my question."

"Well, I suppose if I'm going to be a traitor, I may as well go all in. The plans are real, but they are a distraction that draws attention away from what is really occurring."

"A decoy?" Palmer asked.

"Yes," he said. "You've seen enough of the plan to know. What do *you* think its focus is?"

Palmer collected his thoughts, unsure whether he was interested in playing this game.

Eventually, he decided to bite. "For Iran to destroy Israel. For the Chinese to take over Taiwan. For North Korea to destroy South Korea. And for Russia to attack the US."

"*Bingo*, as you Americans say. However, Russia could never conquer and control a nation as big and powerful as the US with such a large globally disbursed military. And a country where a third of the population owns one or more guns. We haven't even managed to do it in Ukraine. Hell, we couldn't even do it in Afghanistan," Volkov said, shaking his head. "The goal would be to damage your carrier operations and critical infrastructure and to disrupt your government. All the while, we would take command over something the US believes is strategically important now but even more so in the future."

Palmer put both hands on his head and suddenly remembered one of his earlier conversations with Sokolov. "The Arctic! It's the Arctic, isn't it? Russia controls fifty percent of the Arctic coastline, but your president wants it *all*."

He could tell by the look on Volkov's face that he was right.

Volkov nodded. "It's simple. Invade Greenland and seize it from Denmark. Would the Danes want to fight Russia over Greenland? Would NATO care? Would Europe care? Invade and take over Grimsey

Island, which is Iceland's only claim to being an Arctic country—and voilà. Iceland is no longer within the Arctic Circle. Again, who cares? Then we block access for Norway, Sweden, and Finland. All that remains is Canada and a small northern part of Alaska. The US has no icebreaker fleet, and Canada wouldn't put up much resistance. The objective is to overwhelm the Arctic countries and claim it all: the shipping lanes, oil, and rare earth minerals."

"When does this begin?"

"It already has. You saw the military vehicles traveling up the Kola Peninsula."

"If this is true, what's your rationale for defecting?" Palmer felt for his phone, remembering that he had left it in the now destroyed control van, but he still had Sokolov's. "We've got to go back."

Their conversation was interrupted by the sound of distant small arms fire.

"Too late, Mr. Hall."

53

LAPPEENRANTA AIRPORT, FINLAND

Volkov was right—it was too late to turn back. The air was already filled with the staccato of automatic gunfire as the Finnish special forces clashed with what Palmer assumed was the FSB. Palmer's eyes met Volkov's anxious gaze. "You wait here. I'll see if I can determine how things are going."

"Don't leave me here without a weapon!" Volkov said, his voice trembling slightly.

Palmer ignored him, grabbed his rifle, and stepped outside. Green was still standing sentry just outside the door. "I'm going to see what's going on," he told her. "Don't let him move. I'll be right back."

"Got it. Don't do anything reckless."

Palmer allowed himself a brief rueful smile. "Why does everyone tell me that?"

Palmer crossed the road and peered through the trees between the berm and the highway, observing the relative positions of the two combatant groups. There was no clear shot through the trees. He could circle around and surprise the FSB officers, but that would take valuable time.

Peering through the dense trees lining the berm and the highway, he was limited in what he could discern about the relative positions of the opposing forces. The local police and emergency vehicles from Lappeenranta had arrived. The police appeared to be preparing to move out and join the fight. In Finland, a small nation with limited resources, all security authorities support one another.

Palmer heard more automatic weapons firing and witnessed the ongoing confrontation between the uniformed Utti Jaeger soldiers and the other men. The EMTs had to wait until the battle was over and it was safe to move forward.

Returning to Green and Volkov, Palmer saw several fully extended telescopic boom lifts standing like metal sentinels and ran to them. The lifts were extended to prevent anyone from getting to the controls in the basket. Palmer's eyes narrowed as he examined the lift controls on the ground section. No keys were in sight. He could try bypassing the lock, but that would waste valuable time.

He glanced at the building. The keys would be inside. He noted the number on the boom lift closest to him and hurried over. The door was unlocked and creaked open easily, with only a slight push.

Not seeing anyone, Palmer entered and called out, "Is anyone here?"

There was no reply.

Moving slowly, his eyes landed on the board behind the desk, where numerous keys hung from rusty hooks. He chose the one that matched the boom's number and hurried out.

Inserting the key, he started the boom lift and lowered the basket. He climbed inside and located the controls for the boom—a series of toggle switches, each with a small diagram indicating its function. Two joysticks offered additional control options. He couldn't get it to work until he noticed a pedal on the basket floor. He pressed it, and the controls activated. He tested the toggles until he found the ones that controlled up-and-down motion as well as side-to-side movement. He raised it to the maximum height. From his elevated position, he had a clear view over the berm and the trees and could see the FSB officers in position approximately five hundred yards away. One of the FSB officers had pinned down a couple of the Finns.

Every rifle has its character, and every marksman must adjust their sights to account for distance, wind direction and velocity, and changing weather conditions. He recalled what Welsch always said: *front sight focus.* It was a SEAL training term referring to a marksman focusing on the front sight of the weapon rather than on the target. Focusing on the target results in the front sight being out of focus. However, Admiral Welsch's advice resonated on a deeper level. He wasn't talking about shooting tactics; he was speaking metaphorically, reminding him to not lose sight of the most crucial goals and objectives aligned with his mission.

Palmer took aim, inhaled a deep breath to calm his racing heart, and exhaled slowly as he squeezed the trigger. The shot was a bit off to the left. The shooter looked in Palmer's direction, spotted him, and swung the barrel of his rifle around to face him, but Palmer took his time, adjusted his aim, and fired again. This time, his target went down.

The Finns were outnumbered, but despite that, Palmer was confident they would prevail. Additional reinforcements from the Utti Jaeger Regiment would arrive soon. They only needed to hold off the FSB fighters until the helicopter came to provide air support and reinforcements.

Palmer resisted the urge to leave Green with Volkov in the warehouse while he joined the battle. He'd had some experience with hostage rescue from his days as a SEAL team member that had taught him the top priority was always to protect the hostage. Although Volkov wasn't a hostage, most of the same rules applied. As much as he wanted to join the fray, leaving Volkov would be a mistake.

Something caught his eye as he prepared to lower the boom lift. Two vehicles he hadn't noticed earlier had pulled off the road several hundred feet behind the police and EMTs. Four men in civilian clothes had emerged from the cars, two from each vehicle. It didn't appear that they had seen him, but he waited, not wanting to draw attention to the lift or himself. He guessed they were probably FSB, but he had to be cautious. They could also be allies. Still, it made sense that the call for the FSB officers to intercept the Utti Jaeger vehicles and eliminate Volkov had brought Russians from both directions. Looking carefully, he saw the men hurriedly removing weapons from the car trunks. They were watching the emergency responders, and their weapons were automatic rifles and pistols. All of them appeared to be Russian.

One man caught Palmer's attention—he was the last to exit the car. He had a long gun with an attached sound suppressor, likely a sniper rifle.

Ivanov.

He was the first to leave the group, walking quickly toward the airport without talking to anyone, and the others followed a few minutes later. The police and EMTs were focused on the gunfight and didn't seem to notice the cars behind them. Now that the men had left, they'd only see two illegally parked cars, which wouldn't matter much amid the chaos unfolding. Palmer was drawn to the gunfight, but he knew he had to protect Volkov. He needed to talk to Green and devise a plan.

54

LAPPEENRANTA AIRPORT, FINLAND

The three FSB officers hurried to grab their rifles and pistols from the trunk of their cars. A passenger in the vehicle, Nikolai Ivanov, waited until they finished, stepped forward, and opened the case containing his rifle. He took it out, inspected it, and then attached a suppressor. He had several rifles and chose them based on weather conditions and range. He preferred his VSS Vintorez for most assignments, but for this one, he'd brought his SVD—*snayperskaya vintovka Dragunova*—for the Dragunov sniper rifle, due to its greater effective range and the semiautomatic firing he expected to need. Hearing the gunfire, he realized he had just entered an ongoing battle, confirming his choice of the SVD. Afterward, he slammed the trunk lid shut and stormed off, saying something to the man who had driven the car in which he was a passenger.

Initially, Ivanov's priority was Sokolov, but it later shifted to Volkov. His handler was adjusting the priorities as the locations continued to change.

Ivanov observed the battlefield. This was not the kind of work in which he excelled. That took meticulous effort and involved identifying and locating the target, planning the time and method of the kill, and executing it. There was a time and place for snipers who worked amid the chaos within an active combat zone. He had done it in the past with Spetsnaz, but that wasn't his style now. In Unit 29155, he had perfected a different approach. His assignments were well planned and executed, leaving no evidence behind, and thus there would be no blowback on Russia.

He had caught a ride with three FSB officers, their chests pumped out and their guns loaded. The presence of the FSB, Finnish soldiers, and American intelligence complicated things, which increased the risk of his mission—kill Volkov. To make matters worse, Russian missiles had been fired at the armored Finnish convoy, attracting the attention of local law enforcement.

Yet here he was, near Lappeenranta, amid a gunfight between the Finnish Utti Jaeger special forces and the FSB. The Utti Jaeger were wise enough to keep Volkov far away from them. The Americans would have pulled him out of harm's way during the battle. He stood silently, surveying the scene. He quickly dismissed the forest across the road. His eyes settled on the buildings near the airport, where there were plenty of places to hide until the gunfire stopped.

He saw the boom lifts, their baskets extended, resembling a herd of mechanical giraffes. Staying hidden among the trees, he screwed the sound suppressor onto his rifle, inserted a magazine, and drew his 9mm pistol from its holster, resting it by his right shoulder.

While walking around and out of sight of the police and EMTs, he heard the unmistakable sound of an approaching helicopter. *This should be interesting.*

The thunder of rotors grew louder as it got closer, spraying an incredibly high rate of fire at the FSB positions. The three people he was with likely hadn't gotten into position. The helicopter hovered low to the ground while several soldiers fast-roped down. *Game over.*

Additional reinforcements were probably on the way. With the battle over, it would be safe for the Americans and Volkov to return to where the Finnish soldiers had gathered. If he was correct, they would be hiding in one of the buildings at the airport and would have to cross over the berm and onto the road to rejoin the soldiers. He would be waiting for them.

Lying on his stomach on the berm, he watched the police cars drive off toward the Finnish soldiers, with the ambulances close behind. The police officers' primary role would be traffic control, keeping curious onlookers away from the area. Traffic would need to be rerouted. The missiles had damaged the road, and debris had to be removed before it could be repaired.

Ivanov shifted his attention to the outbuildings. Going door-to-door to find Volkov and his enablers would be time-consuming and dangerous. If he were correct in thinking they were hiding in one of the outbuildings, they would come out soon now that the battle was over. One of the two Americans would exit their hideout to confirm it was safe. Probably the man—Palmer. Ivanov grinned. He would take him out with a silenced round or two. When he didn't return, the American woman and Volkov would follow shortly thereafter. Theirs would be the same fate.

Things were shaping up.

55

LAPPEENRANTA AIRPORT, FINLAND

Green stood just inside the front door—the building's only exit—rifle in hand, where she could monitor what was happening outside and safeguard Volkov inside. She had seen Palmer raise the lift boom and take a couple of shots. He was now lowering it.

Green told Volkov in Russian, "This is a helluva situation you've put us in."

Looking slightly surprised, Volkov responded, "You speak Russian."

"We're going to get you out of here and to the US," she replied, ignoring his remark.

"I wish I had your confidence," he said, sighing. "By now, every FSB officer in Finland and Russia is searching for me. Those missiles illustrate the extremes to which they will go to kill me—firing missiles at Finnish soldiers in Finland, a NATO country. That crosses many lines in the sand. Where's Mr. Hall?"

"He'll be back soon," Green replied, glancing at Volkov while keeping her attention directed outside. "I overheard what you said regarding the Arctic strategy."

"I assume you're American, too. CIA?"

"Not even close."

"Your president claimed Greenland should be a part of the US, and everyone laughed except for Greenland and Denmark. He recognized that the sparsely populated island is important to the Arctic strategy. He may not acknowledge that climate change is real. Still, he understands that the Arctic passage is vital, both commercially and militarily, and the ice is melting, rapidly opening those lanes. That's why he's also said that Canada should become the fifty-first state."

"You know, some people believe that the KGB recruited our president in 1987. Compromised him in a honey trap."

Volkov laughed. "That's ridiculous."

Green remained stone-faced. "Wasn't the Russian president in the KGB then?"

"Yes. He left to enter politics."

⸺〰⸺

Palmer returned and motioned for Green to come outside. Lowering his voice, he updated her on what he had observed, including the arrival of the four Russians behind the local police and EMTs. "One was a sniper, who I believe is Nikolai Ivanov."

"He'll see the same thing you did—the boom lifts," she replied. "He'll beeline straight for the lifts and set up there. It's the perfect high ground for a sniper. Should you go into the office and take the keys? Or at least rearrange them?" Green asked.

"No," Palmer said with a shrug. "Snipers don't want to be trapped in a place with only one way in and out. I had a great perspective from there, but I also felt very exposed. If he goes up on the lift, I'll take him out before he gets to the top. If he's here to kill Volkov, he'll know he'd be somewhere safe, away from the firefight."

"How about the other three?" Green asked. "Will they be searching for us?"

"I don't think so. They were headed into the fight, and from what I saw, the Utti Jaeger soldiers are holding their own. We're safe here—at least for now."

While they talked, they heard the thunderous approach of a helicopter and looked up.

The Utti Jaeger helicopter flew low overhead, assessing the terrain and the ongoing gun battle while communicating with Koskinen. The soldier manning the minigun sprayed the area where the Russians were and then hovered over a clearing behind the Utti Jaeger line. Reinforcements fast-roped down, and the helicopter flew off in seconds. It ascended and circled back, firing its miniguns, killing or scattering the remaining Russians.

The gunfire persisted for only a short while after the helicopter's onslaught before tapering off until it was silent once again.

Speaking to Green, he said, "I need to talk with Koskinen." Palmer looked at Sokolov's secure phone. The battery was running low.

Palmer connected the call. Koskinen answered.

"I've put you on speaker," Palmer notified him. "We're hiding in a warehouse where the boom lifts are located at the airport."

"I can see them. Wait there. We'll come to you."

"Will do. You have a SITREP for us?" Palmer said, asking for a situation report.

"None killed. Two with gunshot wounds who are being treated. The Russians have either fled or are dead. We have more reinforcements driving here from the base. They're minutes away."

"Great news. While the battle was still waging, I saw two cars drive up and stop far behind where the local police and EMTs were parked. Four men got out. Three of them took rifles from the trunks and headed in the direction of the gunfire. A fourth set out on his own armed with a pistol and a sniper rifle."

Volkov, who had overheard Palmer's conversation, stood and asked, "What did he look like?"

"Male, average height and weight. He was too far away to get much more than that. Why?" Palmer stepped over to Volkov so that Koskinen could hear what he had to say.

Volkov said, "I bet it's Ivanov."

Green perked up. "I've seen intelligence reports. He was a legendary sniper with Spetsnaz before transferring to Unit 29155. Why are you so sure it's him?"

Palmer moved nearer to Volkov, holding the phone close to him so that Koskinen could hear his reply.

Volkov added, "He recently moved from Unit 29155 to the FSB under Maksimov's direction to kill defectors who have evaded the FSB. If the president wants me dead—and he does, because I'm deserting to the West—that's who Maksimov would unleash. Ivanov will track down his victim, no matter how many borders are crossed. Given enough time, he'll find his target. I'm not surprised he walked away from the others; he's a loner. Don't be fooled into labeling him a sniper. He's an assassin. He'll use any means necessary to eliminate his target, including his sniper rifle, a pistol, a knife, a garrote, and Novichok."

"Did you hear that?" Palmer asked.

"Yes," Koskinen replied. "If Ivanov is out there, you should stay inside. We'll come to you."

"What's your ETA to our location?"

"Not soon, I'm afraid. The local police and EMTs are here. We're showing them where the bodies are. I'd guess an hour."

"Roger that. Call before you head out."

Palmer disconnected.

Looking increasingly anxious, Green said, "I have a bad feeling. We need to get on that helicopter and get out of here."

"It may be a while. We're safe here. Let me do a little recon. Those three FSB officers and Ivanov may still be out there. I'll confirm it's safe for Koskinen and his team to come here."

★

5 6

LAPPEENRANTA AIRPORT, FINLAND

Palmer inched out the door and along the warehouse wall. The police cars and ambulances had left, probably to redirect traffic and provide aid to the wounded. There was no trace of the three FSB officers or Ivanov, but the two cars they had arrived in were still there.

Palmer needed to think like Ivanov. *What would a sniper do?*

Ivanov's mission was to kill Volkov. He would set up where he believed Volkov would be. That would not be with Koskinen and the Utti Jaeger soldiers or in the forest. Ivanov would conclude, just as Palmer had, that the safest place for Volkov would be in one of the several businesses and warehouses adjacent to the airport. Ivanov wouldn't have the time or the motivation to start searching them all. Clearing empty buildings was best left to a team of Spetsnaz operators. As he'd told Green already, the boom lifts weren't likely to be a viable option. They had the elevation, but with only one way in and one way out, they were too risky to set up in. Besides, as Palmer had found out himself, the boom lift baskets were open and would expose him. To top it off, raising and lowering the baskets was a slow process. Instead,

Ivanov would want to find a slightly elevated position, set up there, and wait until Volkov came out of whichever building he was hiding in. The berm would be an option, except it wasn't tall enough.

Where would he set up? The best view would be from the top of one of the warehouses or another building. He would wait there until Volkov came out of hiding. Patience was a sniper's stock-in-trade. Although he wouldn't have long to wait now that the helicopter and additional soldiers had arrived, it was time for Volkov to return, board the helicopter, and fly to a secure location. Then, if Ivanov killed Volkov or decided this wasn't the time or place to do so, he could either vanish into the forest or return to the cars and drive off.

If Ivanov spotted Palmer, he would expect him to head toward where Volkov was hiding. Ivanov would watch him until he confirmed which building Volkov was in and wait until they came out.

Palmer headed in the opposite direction from the soldiers toward the two parked cars, carefully moving from one sheltered space to the next. He was betting the FSB officers had likely left the keys in the cars. If one or both drivers had the keys with them and were killed or wounded, the others might be unable to escape. Their late-model vehicles would be equipped with smart keys—also called keyless ignition systems—allowing him to start the car without wasting time searching for them.

Palmer made his way toward the cars, hearing only the breeze rustling through the reeds on the berm and the crunch of gravel beneath his feet. The day had started with a rainy predawn departure from the Utti Jaeger base. Then the rain had stopped, and the sky had partially cleared. The sun was now dipping low in the sky. In this situation, a sniper would position himself west of the suspected target, placing the setting sun behind him and in the target's eyes. With that in mind,

Palmer climbed over the berm and, staying low, moved east toward the cars, using the berm's height as cover.

A red laser dot streaked across the ground on his right, just feet away from him. He dropped and waited. Had he imagined it, or had Ivanov scanned the area with his rifle? He waited for a few minutes, and when he didn't see it again, he proceeded. A macabre thought entered his mind: Ivanov's shot would be fatal to his center mass or head. One moment, he'd be alive; the next, he'd be dead with no pain or suffering and no awareness of being shot. More than his death, he couldn't bear the thought of Fiona receiving the news of his demise.

Palmer looked over the berm. The cars were just a few hundred feet away. He marked the spot ahead where he needed to go before rushing over the berm to them. When he reached it, he flipped his phone into selfie mode and, using it like a mirror, held it up above the berm's top. Nothing. No Ivanov. No FSB. He took a deep breath and sprinted toward the closest car—not the one he had seen the sniper exit.

The passenger's side door had been left slightly ajar. Apparently, they'd been in a hurry. Perhaps they hadn't closed it completely when they left. When he opened the driver's side door and got in, he smelled gunpowder and the metallic scent of blood. He turned to look in the rear seats and faced a man, his left side wet with blood. He was holding a 9mm pistol mere inches from Palmer's head.

"Give me reason I not kill you," the man said in broken English with a thick Russian accent.

The man's hand was trembling, his eyes only half-open.

"You've been shot and, by the looks of it, have lost a lot of blood. No one on this side of the Russian border is coming to treat that wound. Your friends, if they're not dead, won't do it. They'll either put a bullet in your head or push you onto the ground and leave you to die."

"You Palmer?"

"I am."

"I have orders . . . kill you."

"Hand me the gun, and I'll take you to get medical care," Palmer negotiated, "or you can shoot me dead right here and die right along with me. Your choice."

"You kill me like you kill my comrades."

"The ambulances that were parked ahead of you have gone to treat those who, like you, have been wounded. They're right over the hill." The man was growing weaker and was on the verge of losing consciousness. "Are you FSB?"

"Yes."

"Man, I don't want to see you die. Please give me the gun." The Russian's finger was loose on the trigger. He was struggling to hold the pistol up and keep from passing out.

When he didn't answer, Palmer slowly reached out, grasped the weapon, and took it from him. The Russian had offered no resistance. He just looked at Palmer with a blank stare and slowly set back in the seat. Out of sheer desperation, Palmer pressed the button that would only start the ignition if the car's smart key were inside the vehicle.

To his relief, the car started.

Palmer put it into gear and sped to pick up Green and Volkov on Lentokentäntie—the access road to the businesses along the airport. Afterward, he would drive to the EMTs to get medical care for the FSB officer and connect with Koskinen. Ivanov was out there somewhere, and a car driving in a straight line posed little challenge for a sniper of his caliber. Palmer swerved slightly back and forth to avoid giving him any predictable timing or pattern.

The warehouse where Green and Volkov were waiting was in sight when the first bullet struck the windshield, tearing through the front passenger seat.

Ivanov.

Palmer continued his evasive driving, doing everything he could to throw Ivanov's aim off. After a quick mental calculation of the bullet's trajectory, based on the holes in the windshield and seat, he deduced

Ivanov was on top of one of the warehouses. Picking up Green and Volkov would be a mistake, just as continuing toward the warehouse would be. He needed to stop. He decided to wait for one more shot. He didn't have to wait long. The bullet pierced the windshield, prompting Palmer to swerve off the road and slide sideways onto the berm. When the car came to a halt, it leaned on the side of the berm opposite the airport, tilted slightly to the left with the driver's side down. Because of the car's angle on the berm, Ivanov's line of fire would be disturbed. He would want to confirm that Palmer was dead.

"Stay down. I need to lure him in," Palmer said, turning to see his passenger. The officer was slumped back on the seat, his head tilted to the side. He had a chest wound that Palmer hadn't seen earlier. Ivanov's shot had finished him off. *Damn.*

He had to move quickly. Using most of his strength, he pulled the officer's body through the gap between the front seats. Then he opened the driver's side door and placed the officer in the seat, leaning against the steering wheel. Ivanov would be there soon and would have seen photos of Palmer and Green, but the car's tinted windows made it hard to see inside. He might approach the vehicle and fire a couple of shots at the body first. Still, he would want to report that he had killed one of his targets. Palmer guessed that he would come closer to confirm the body's identity. *Where should I wait for the assassin?*

Palmer had his pistol and rifle. He grabbed the rifle and took the 9mm pistol from his belt. Staying low, he slipped out of the car and quietly closed the door. Ivanov would approach the vehicle from the other side. The only shots fired from the rifle were those he'd discharged from the boom lift. Taking a deep breath, Palmer walked down the berm and into the woods beside it, where he hid behind a few trees.

Several minutes later, a man with a rifle appeared at the top of the berm near the car. The man stopped, raised his rifle, and fired shots into both the front and rear seats. Palmer couldn't be sure it was a sniper rifle the man was using—but either way, it wasn't silenced. That wasn't Ivanov. The man slung the gun over his shoulder and took a pistol from a concealed holster. When he reached the car, he used his left hand to open the front passenger door, keeping the pistol in his right hand. He looked inside, paused, and then walked around to the rear of the car and stopped.

Palmer could move quickly and either shoot him or bide his time. Snipers often have a spotter nearby or working with them to find their target. But was the shooter Ivanov or one of the other three men in the cars? The one who had returned to the car and was now dead was one of the three. This was most likely the second, perhaps the one who had been in the car with Ivanov.

In a battlefield situation, having spotters can provide extra security and help find the target. Right. Their job wasn't to join the battle. It was to find Volkov while the Utti Jaeger soldiers were in an ongoing gunfight. Palmer peeked out from behind the tree. The man's gaze was fixed back toward the airport, giving Palmer a chance. He decided to take it. He stepped away from the tree and raised his rifle.

"Nyet!" someone shouted. "Put down gun!"

57

LAPPEENRANTA AIRPORT, FINLAND

Palmer recognized the man. He knew, somehow, that it was Ivanov. With two men now pointing their weapons at him, he had no choice but to comply. Palmer lowered his rifle and set it on the ground, then asked, "Do you speak English?"

"A little. Kick rifle closer."

Palmer gave the rifle a half-hearted kick that moved it only two feet nearer to the Russian.

"Who is in car?" Ivanov asked.

"One of your officers. He was wounded. I was taking him to the ambulance so the EMTs could work on him," Palmer said, toying with the truth. He pointed at the other Russian and said, "He shot him through the windshield. Now he's dead."

Ivanov seemed entirely unaffected by this news. He moved closer to Palmer. "Where is Volkov?"

"Who?"

In a move too quick for Palmer to react, Ivanov struck Palmer in the stomach with the butt of the rifle. Palmer pitched forward, struggling to catch his breath.

"*Alexi Volkov.* Chief of staff to our president. You killed an FSB officer and helped Volkov defect."

Which FSB officer was Ivanov referring to? Palmer had lost count. "You just killed a wounded FSB officer yourself. Let's call it even and walk away. Besides, an FSB officer shot and killed an American diplomat who was there to negotiate the situation."

"Diplomat, my ass. Probably CIA operative working under diplomatic cover. I ask one more time. Where's Volkov?"

Palmer weighed his options, of which he had very few. One thing was certain: He wasn't going down without a fight. Ivanov, a former Spetsnaz operator, would be a formidable opponent. However, he appeared thick around the middle—still dangerous behind the scope but maybe not the physical specimen he once was. Had he lost his edge?

With Ivanov's arrival, the FSB officer at the car had relaxed his demeanor but remained a threat, especially with the handgun pointed in his direction.

Palmer edged closer to Ivanov. "Volkov is with the Utti Jaeger soldiers. My partner took him there after the gunfight ended." Before Ivanov could poke holes in his claims, he added, "You're Ivanov."

The sniper smiled. "No matter who I am. You are on my hit list and will be dead soon. I give you choice. Quick bullet to head or slow, painful death?"

Palmer glanced behind him. The FSB officer seemed to be waiting for Palmer's response to Ivanov's question.

"Let's go slow and painful." At least with that option, he had a little more time.

Without taking his eyes off Palmer, Ivanov walked over to the FSB officer and set his rifle on the ground beside him. He then smiled and drew a blade, its edge gleaming in the dusk. "I was hoping you would say that," Ivanov muttered as he began stepping into a slow, deliberate circle in a counterclockwise direction.

Palmer wasn't a knife guy but knew Ivanov's by its reputation—it was a Karatel. Russian Spetsnaz and FSB favored the Karatel, which was Russian for punisher, for close work. He had learned and practiced knife fighting when he was a Navy SEAL, but that was many years ago, and he had never actually been in a real knife fight. He recalled rule number one: Stabs are more deadly than cuts.

Palmer took an athletic stance—his feet planted wider than shoulder-width apart, knees bent, arms spread, hands up protecting his face and centerline, and his torso leaning forward. He kept Ivanov in front of him, never taking his eyes off the man. He shuffled, waiting.

As they circled, Palmer caught a glimpse of the FSB officer, who was gripping his pistol like a coiled spring, ready to shoot him if he gained any advantage. Palmer needed an edge, anything to distract them.

Ivanov lunged fast.

Palmer twisted aside, dodging Ivanov's first strike. The second came quicker—he batted it away. The next move was faster still and sliced across his forearm. Ivanov's second move had set up the third. Blood, warm against the cool air, flowed down Palmer's arm and dripped onto the ground.

Blood loss was a ticking clock. One way or the other, this had to end soon. He recalled his SEAL instructor saying that a cut on the arm can reduce your chances of surviving the fight to zero.

Palmer retreated a step, chest heaving. Now he recognized the tell of another strike—just the flick of Ivanov's gaze that betrayed the angle. Palmer backed up. Ivanov reset his stance—left foot forward, weight ready to spring toward him.

Then a crack split the air, echoing off the nearby buildings. Palmer flinched.

Something thudded behind him.

Ivanov's eyes widened. He'd seen what Palmer had only heard: someone had taken out his FSB backup. This was his chance. Palmer didn't hesitate. He surged forward, closing the gap between them in a heartbeat. His wounded arm deflected Ivanov's knife hand skyward just enough to get by. He drove a shoulder into Ivanov's chest, grinding him back with the force of a linebacker who had broken through the line to sack the quarterback. The impact rattled Ivanov, who fell against the car.

Ivanov recovered and shoved hard off the vehicle. His knife whipped through the air, flashing silver.

Palmer arched, stomach hollowed, but the Karatel still reached far enough to slash open his jacket and once again scored flesh.

They grappled in close quarters, both breathing hard, until Palmer clamped onto Ivanov's right wrist and pushed the knife away, but only an inch or two. Ivanov retaliated by seizing Palmer's injured left arm, fingers crushing into the wound, and squeezing tightly in an attempt to break Palmer's powerful grip.

White-hot pain shot through Palmer, blurring his vision. He staggered but hung on, slowly bending Ivanov's wrist back. Ivanov locked onto Palmer's free hand, their grips now slick with blood. The added pressure made the blood from Palmer's cut gush faster. He was running out of options.

Palmer's lips twisted into a smile. Ivanov's brow furrowed in confusion.

"You snipers," Palmer growled. "All eye, no muscle. You've gone soft."

Ivanov twisted his body, snarling, trying to rip free. Palmer was relentless, the Karatel's tip creeping closer to Ivanov's chest. Ivanov's grin was feral. He bucked forward, driving a knee into Palmer's groin.

Palmer doubled over but managed to maintain his balance. His hands were slipping away, releasing his grip on Ivanov and the knife.

Ivanov snarled, "You are a dead man!"

Palmer knew his time was running out. Every move he made now would be weaker than the last, so he had to make each one count. With all the strength he had left, he launched himself in a surge of rage and delivered a fierce uppercut to Ivanov's jaw. The crack was unmistakable. Ivanov crumpled and fell to the ground, knife still clenched in his fist, refusing to yield.

Palmer jumped on him and grabbed the hand that clutched the knife. The sniper wouldn't let go of the blade. Palmer slammed Ivanov's wrist repeatedly against a rock. Once. Twice. A third time. Bones cracked, then finally, the knife fell to the ground. Palmer lunged for the weapon and pressed the blade to Ivanov's throat. Ivanov bucked beneath him, but the fight was gone. His eyes filled with hatred.

"Do it," Ivanov spat, blood dripping from his lips. "Finish it."

Palmer held the knife steady, every nerve in his body demanding that he drive it home. He heard boots thundering behind him. Glancing back, he saw Koskinen and two of his operators rushing in, weapons trained. Palmer bent forward, hands on knees, and threw the knife to the side.

Ivanov lay still, breathing heavily. The left side of his jaw hung lower than the right, cheek already swelling. With his eyes fixed on Palmer, he growled something in Russian.

"Take him," Palmer rasped. He rose to his feet, clutching his bleeding arm, while one of Koskinen's men shackled Ivanov as he lay on the ground, his chest heaving. The Russian glared at Palmer, eyes promising vengeance, even as the soldier and Koskinen stood over him.

Palmer leaned against the car, one arm bleeding and some blood seeping through his jacket from his upper abdomen. The other soldier, who was a medic, immediately tended to Palmer's wounds and applied compression bandages before turning to Ivanov. Afterward, the two soldiers left with the sniper.

Koskinen looked at Palmer and shook his head. "You'll need to have those wounds examined and stitched up as soon as you're aboard the *Kearsarge*."

⸎

Bandaged and weak after days without enough sleep or proper meals, as well as too much action, Palmer took Koskinen to the warehouse where Green and Volkov were hiding.

Green saw Palmer and rushed over to hug him but stopped short when she saw the bandages and his bloodied clothes. She seemed to hold back a scream. "It took all my strength to resist tying Volkov up and leaving to find you. I heard gunshots!" she said, eyes sharp. "Then I remembered what you said. Protect Volkov at all costs. What happened?"

"A brief encounter with Ivanov and his knife."

"Ivanov!" Volkov exclaimed. He looked impressed. "And you survived?"

"Just barely." Palmer nodded toward Koskinen. "Our friend here showed up with two of his soldiers. One of them shot the FSB officer who was there to ensure that Ivanov won."

Volkov's eyes widened. "You've captured Russia's top assassin. Where is he now?"

Koskinen answered. "We treated his wounds and then took him into custody. Our reinforcements have arrived. They'll go back to the base with Ivanov. A helicopter will be here soon and will take us there." He then looked to Palmer. "We've recovered Howell's body. It'll be transported back to base. It was pretty banged up from the missile strike, but the family will at least have some closure."

⸎

A short time later, a Finnish helicopter swooped in at the edge of the runway near them. Koskinen, Palmer, Green, and Volkov boarded for the short flight to the Utti Jaeger base. They landed swiftly, the hum of the rotors fading as they were met by two Finnish soldiers who ushered them toward a waiting US Marine Corps V-22 Osprey.

Before they left, Koskinen gave Palmer a firm handshake. "It's been a pleasure, Mr. Palmer. I hope our paths cross again, but if they don't, fair winds and following seas, my friend."

Palmer pulled him in for a man hug and, with a couple of claps on his back, he replied, "It's been an honor to work with you and your incredible team. Let's keep in touch."

As they approached the Osprey, Green turned to Palmer, mouthing, "What the hell?" Pointing at the aircraft, she said, "An Osprey?"

"No need to worry. They've worked out the kinks," Palmer replied. "It'll be a safe, interesting, possibly even exciting experience."

"Worry? No," Green said. "This is going to be awesome."

The Osprey was a stark contrast to the stealthy Black Hawk. They boarded up the loading ramp at the rear of the plane. Thinly cushioned fold-down seats lined each side of the aircraft from fore to aft. Sania Reed and Dmitry Sokolov were already aboard, seated near the front on the starboard side. Two medics from the ship accompanied them. Howell's body was secured for the flight. Four US Marines sat across from them, their expressions stern. One stood up, his tone serious as he outlined the plane's safety features, each word punctuated by the reality of their mission. He handed out self-inflating life jackets that fastened securely around their heads and necks, serving as a chilling reminder of the risk of a Russian missile attack over the Gulf of Finland and the Baltic Sea that they would traverse. He then distributed helmets with snug noise suppressors to muffle the sounds of the aircraft.

The aircraft lifted off with its props in a vertical position, performing a helicopter-like takeoff. The plane's loading ramp remained open during the short flight to the USS *Kearsarge* (LHD 3), an amphibious assault ship. At the very least, it brought in fresh air, providing a welcome relief from the smell of sweat and JP-5 fuel. As it rose, the props shifted from a vertical to a horizontal position. Their helmets didn't entirely drown out the noise of the rotors and engines. When the plane neared the *Kearsarge*, the pilot switched the hybrid's props from horizontal back to vertical, allowing the aircraft to land like a helicopter on the flight deck.

A USS *Kearsarge* medical team met the Osprey and transported Howell's body to the hospital bay for transfer to a mortuary unit and ultimately to the US. A medic, who was with Sokolov, told Palmer that he needed to go with him for an examination of his head wound. He told the medic that he would come later.

Palmer, Green, Reed, and Volkov followed a navy lieutenant commander to the senior officer's wardroom, where food and drinks had been prepared for them. Minutes after their arrival, the ship's captain entered with three men dressed in civilian clothes. Two of the men took Alexi Volkov away, presumably for initial questioning.

Reed looked to the captain and whispered, "CIA?"

"Naval intelligence. CIA will get its opportunity soon enough." The captain paused, then said, "You've put this ship and the entire assault group, including our participating NATO partners, in the spotlight. The implications are both good and bad. We're at DEFCON 2, and this ship, as well as the others in this amphibious group, are at general quarters. Our orders are to provide you with medical care and to transport you and your two defectors to your destinations. Russia is searching for and may attempt to kill Sokolov and Volkov and anyone with them rather than have them defect to the US."

A well-rested Palmer wouldn't say what he was about to or, at least, would have been more diplomatic. He took a moment, then responded on behalf of the team. "Captain, with all due respect, this is a joint effort of JSOC Task Force Orange, MI6, and the Finnish Utti Jaeger special forces operation. We've been under attack for several days. We've killed several Russian FSB officers and lost one of our CIA officers in the process. Three of us have been wounded. We've survived a Russian missile attack and captured Russia's most feared assassin. We successfully extracted two high-value defectors under high-risk conditions. Sokolov is perhaps the most significant missile scientist and engineer to defect to the US since Wernher von Braun surrendered to the US Army in 1945. And to top it off, we turned over Russian plans outlining an attack on the US. If you have any questions about the priority of our mission, which you are now part of, I suggest speaking with the SOCOM commander or the president, sir."

The captain leaned back in his seat, furrowed his brow, and pressed his lips together.

Seeking support, he shifted his gaze to the navy intelligence officer, who said, "Captain, although not widely known, Palmer and Green are the two operatives who prevented the terrorist nuclear attack in London a while back and who now work for Task Force Orange."

"Captain," Reed chimed in, "Mr. Palmer is correct. Sokolov and Volkov represent perhaps the most significant defections in recent history. And the two documents he's referring to may prevent World War III and a nuclear holocaust."

Palmer added, "Volkov, the Russian president's chief of staff, has suggested the attack is a ruse for Russia to launch an all-out attempt to capture control of the Arctic."

The intelligence officer was visibly taken aback. "Is that true?"

"Yes. I suggest you press him on it during your initial interview," Palmer advised. "At this point, he is very cooperative. In our effort to cross into Finland, we witnessed the troops and equipment heading to the Kola Peninsula."

The captain, whose physical demeanor indicated that he now understood the gravity of the situation, said, "I want you to know that you have my full support and that of our entire NATO joint operation. Two US destroyers are joining the group and will provide additional protection. We can assist in getting you back to wherever you like."

"Perhaps London," Reed suggested. "I need to make a call to confirm that. By now, I'm persona non grata in Moscow."

Green said, "Islamabad for me."

Palmer added, "London. I'm getting married in"—he glanced at his watch—"fewer than forty-eight hours. How about Sokolov and Volkov?"

The captain looked at Palmer. "That will be decided soon. They're in US hands now, so your operation has been completed. You'll need those wounds examined and stitched up. I can't let you leave the ship like you are. One of my staff members will take you to our medical department. Meanwhile, I'll communicate with the brass and confirm where they want all of you taken, including Sokolov and Volkov. Your next stop will be Ramstein Air Base or perhaps SOCEUR—Special Operations Command Europe—in Stuttgart, both in Germany. You'll be safe there, and they can take custody of your defectors and sort out your travel."

5 8

WHITE HOUSE SITUATION ROOM
WASHINGTON, DC

The president of the Usnited States sat in the Situation Room at the White House, with the nuclear suitcase resting dutifully beside him, as he met with the Russian president by way of video call.

He issued a stern warning, telling him that the US was at DEFCON 2 and that any attack on the US power grid or communication satellites would be considered as much an act of war as a bomb strike, leading to an immediate response by the US. Any Russian military or proxy military actions against the US, including on US bases worldwide, would be regarded as acts of war, and the full might of the US and its NATO allies would be deployed. He reminded him that each of the US's fourteen stealth Ohio-class nuclear submarines carried twenty-four Trident missiles, each capable of holding up to twelve MIRVs—multiple independent reentry vehicles—with a yield of one hundred kilotons.

The Russian president leaned back and laughed.

He agreed the documents were part of a hypothetical plan that could be modified or initiated at any time, and he smirked when he said that if the US didn't have similar plans for such an attack—or a response to one—then they were either negligent, incompetent, or both.

He moved closer to the camera, his face filling much of the screen. "Our nuclear and nonnuclear offensive and defensive capabilities are far superior to those of the US and your NATO allies. Our new-generation hypersonic missiles cannot be reliably shot down by your air defenses."

The president of the United States said nothing.

At the end of the video call, the Russian president said, "You have two Russians: Dmitry Sokolov and Alexi Volkov. I want them returned to us immediately."

Now it was the US president's turn to laugh. "We have two defectors who fled your country and are now out of Russia. We're not returning them. They are under the full protection of the United States."

The Russian president, clearly angry, said, "I hold you accountable for the death of several of my FSB officers, some within Russia, and for the kidnapping of Sokolov and Volkov. You'll take responsibility for what happens to them and everyone with them."

With that, he disconnected the call.

The US president also spoke with the leaders of China, North Korea, and Iran. Each acknowledged they had seen Russia's plan but denied any intention to attack the US or any other NATO country. He assured them that the moment Russia, China, South Korea, or Iran blinked an eye, the US would launch a counterattack. Although the element of surprise was gone, the president realized that didn't guarantee anything, but he wanted them to be aware that the Ohio-class nuclear subs were in position and ready to strike.

Diplomats used back-channel communications to nip the global assault in the bud, although almost all lower-level staff to whom they spoke said they hadn't seen the plan. The joint special operations commander had sent the plan to the US president and his cabinet for onward distribution to all NATO countries and NATO affiliates. The US military was at DEFCON 2. The American fleet, with ships in range of China, North Korea, Iran, and Russia, was prepared to launch a counterattack at the first sign of a missile launch or a major cyberattack against any of those countries. The response was swift, with the heads of the NATO nations expressing their outrage and stating they were prepared to launch immediate counterattacks.

The country's missile defense systems and armed forces remained on high alert. The summary document on the joint assault was sufficient to move to DEFCON 2 and for electricity providers to take steps to protect the power grid.

After days of intense discussions and negotiations, Russia backed down, stating it was all an exercise to build a response to an attack on any of them. With them, Iran, North Korea, and China also caved.

The US president also warned Russia that any attempt to take full control of the Arctic Sea would face a rapid and severe response. The Russian president reassured everyone that their Arctic strategy was focused on maintaining regional stability and promoting cooperation with other Arctic nations. However, despite Russia's ongoing war with Ukraine, he held a high-profile meeting and rejected any "delays in Arctic projects due to sanctions or external pressure" and called for "maximum acceleration" of Russia's economic and military efforts in the Arctic region.

59

RAMSTEIN AIR BASE, GERMANY

Green didn't want to delay Palmer's departure, but she needed to talk to him before he left. They were sitting in an office while an airman arranged their travel, and she knew she'd waited until the very last moment to have this conversation. It couldn't wait any longer.

"Jake, this may be the last time I see you," she began.

"I doubt that, Alona. Besides, I'll be a civilian and doing contract work in Europe and probably elsewhere. I'll have more flexibility over when and where I go."

"No. You'll be married and have much *less* flexibility."

Palmer laughed. "We've been through too much to part ways and never see or talk with each other again."

"Be sure to call me then," she told him. "It'd be awkward for me to call you—you're soon to be a married man. Your wife might be jealous."

"Fiona's not like that."

"Every woman is like that."

Palmer placed his hand on her shoulder. "I'll stay in touch. I promise. Let me know where you're assigned and who your new partner is. I hear things are heating up between India and Pakistan over Kashmir once again. Where do you want to go?"

The question was one Green hadn't given much thought to, and it caught her off guard. "I don't know. Islamabad is considered a hardship post, but I've enjoyed my time there."

Palmer nodded, agreeing. "Islamabad is also a career-boosting opportunity because of the tempo and level of importance, particularly concerning the India-Pakistan dynamic and the number of terrorist organizations operating within the region. You'd be perfect for Ukraine or Russia, but I doubt they'll risk posting you in either. Ruling those out, I'd probably assign you to one of the Five or Nine Eyes nations, and from those, I'd go with France or Germany."

"Why France or Germany?"

"France has a strong diplomatic and intelligence presence. Their equivalent of the CIA, the Directorate General for External Security, or DGSE, is highly respected, and France is a leading center for counterterrorism. Besides, who doesn't want to live in Paris? Germany is a key NATO ally and a hub for European operations, as well as Russian and Eastern Bloc activity, not to mention its world-renowned beer. Stuttgart, Germany, is the headquarters for the US Special Operations Command Europe. It's a personal preference, because wherever you're assigned, you'll do great."

Green considered his suggestions, envisioning herself in these new exciting places and warming to the idea. "Paris would be wonderful," she said. "However, if Germany is a center for Russian and Eastern Bloc activity, that would be more aligned with my profile."

The administrator called Palmer's name. "I've got to go. I'm on a very tight timeline."

They embraced and kissed each other on the cheek, promising once more to stay in touch. Her heart believed him, but her mind doubted he would follow through. He had spent very little time with Fiona over the past two years. They were getting married, and she was happy for them. But how would they hold up in the long run? He never seemed like the settling-down type, much less the marriage type.

⚬⚬

Jake Palmer checked his watch, desperation gnawing at him as he begged for time to slow down. Instead, it was slipping away faster than he could bear. Someone suggested that he call the bride-to-be and ask her to delay the wedding until later that night. He had laughed and replied, "I called her earlier today and told her I would be there on time, and I will."

He was holding a clothes bag over his arm. Inside was a rented tuxedo that was a size too small. The base commander had called in a favor, promising that Palmer would ship the tuxedo back afterward.

The young airman responsible for scheduling the flights kept suggesting commercial airline options for Heathrow and Gatwick, the two main airports in London. Flying from Frankfurt, Germany, to London Heathrow or Gatwick wouldn't get him to the wedding on time. The airman, his voice tense and posture ramrod straight, said, "I'm sorry, sir. None of these options will get you there in time. I even considered military flights. Even if you arrived at Heathrow or Gatwick on time and the traffic was surprisingly light, you still wouldn't make it. What do you suggest?"

There was no need for Palmer to take out his frustration on the airman; he was just doing his job.

During Palmer's visits to London over the past couple of years, he and Collins had spent time in and around her home in Clapham, a part of Greater London, and in the county of Kent, where she was raised in Sevenoaks Weald. He remembered that they had driven past a small commuter airport, which Collins had said was a Royal Air Force base during World War II. It was about twenty miles and a thirty-minute drive to Sevenoaks Weald.

"Try Biggin Hill Airport in the south London borough of Bromley."

The airman scratched his head. "That's a new one on me, sir. Give me a minute." He typed some information into his computer. "Got it." He continued to type away, shake his head, and type more. Fifteen minutes later, which included him making a few calls, the airman announced, "Sorry that took so long. I looked at commercial flights. There are three to five nonstops per day. Either the timing of the flight was off or they were fully booked. However, I got approval to put you on an Air Force C-21A—a Learjet model 35 we use to fly VIPs around."

"When can we leave?"

"Forty-five minutes soon enough?" the airman asked with a grin. "I'll drive you over to the pickup point here. Someone will meet you at Biggin Hill and take you to the church."

60

SEVENOAKS WEALD, KENT, ENGLAND

The US Air Force C-21A executive jet had seven passenger seats, but Jake Palmer was the only one on board. He sat at the front of the plane. The pilot introduced himself. "Buckle up, Palmer," he said with a grin. "We've already got clearance. The flight will take approximately one hour and fifteen minutes once we're airborne."

After just a few minutes, they began taxiing.

As soon as they reached cruising altitude, Palmer changed into the tuxedo.

The flight was uneventful, and they landed at Biggin Hill on time. Inside the terminal, Palmer presented his Dennis Hall passport—the only one he had with him—to the immigration officer, who accepted it and waved for the next person to come forward. Customs was streamlined, as he didn't have any luggage. The driver that the airman had arranged was waiting for him, and they quickly set out for the short distance to the church in Sevenoaks Weald, a small village in Kent. He and Collins had made this trip a couple of times. His driver followed the same route they had taken through Westerham, a charming town just north of Chartwell, which had been Sir Winston Churchill's home for over forty years. He and Collins had visited it on one of their trips.

Palmer urged the driver to go faster. He glanced at his watch; it was going to be close.

His wedding to Fiona Isabella Collins was scheduled to commence at 2:00 p.m. That had seemed early to him, but according to Collins, most wedding ceremonies in the UK took place between 1:00 and 3:00 p.m. He had promised her that he would be there, come hell or high water. It was 1:20 p.m. The GPS on the dashboard showed they were thirty-four minutes from the church. If they ran into a traffic problem, they'd be screwed. At 1:55 p.m., the driver skidded to a halt in front of the church.

"Good luck, sir, and best wishes!" he said as Palmer thanked him and leaped out of the vehicle before it'd come to a full stop.

Now for the scary part of this entire adventure—getting married.

He stood at the door, took a deep breath, and ran his fingers through his hair. *Well, from here I walk into the unknown.*

He opened the door. Nearly everyone sitting in the pews turned to look at him. He didn't see Fiona but noticed the bridesmaids and groomsmen. It wasn't part of the protocol, but he walked down the aisle toward the waiting vicar and wedding party. Along the way, he heard whispers from the guests. The only familiar faces at the front were Carol Baker, Fiona's coworker and maid of honor, standing to his left of center, and Jim DuPont, his FBI friend, standing to the right. Carol smiled and winked. Palmer reached the altar, took his place at the center, and faced the rear of the church sanctuary, where Fiona would soon appear.

DuPont leaned toward him and whispered, "Perfect timing."

Palmer whispered back, "You've no idea."

Palmer's heart slowed, and his shoulders relaxed. He'd made it to the church on time. Now he was finally able to enjoy himself.

He let it sink in that he'd be seeing Fiona in minutes. This was their wedding day.

The church was bathed in a gentle light, and a delicate floral scent filled the air. The organist played softly. The guests were murmuring quietly, awaiting Collins's walk down the aisle. He noticed a few of his former SEAL teammates sitting together near the front, their faces wreathed in wide smiles as they whispered to one another. Palmer looked to the back of the church, where the shadows deepened and where the light coming through the stained-glass windows barely reached. In the farthest pew sat a middle-aged man with short hair, wearing sunglasses. A scar carved down his cheek gleamed in the dim light. *Who is this man? Why is he here?* He leaned toward DuPont and whispered, "Back row, scarred face, sunglasses."

"Spotted him already."

The organ music swelled as the vestibule doors at the back of the church opened, and a silence fell over the guests as they rose to face the rear of the church. Palmer looked away from the stranger and caught his first glimpse of his beautiful bride. She looked radiant, and for a few heartbeats, it felt like the world had narrowed to just the two of them. Their eyes locked.

Collins began her walk down the aisle. All eyes were on her as she slowly approached him. Palmer's heart swelled with joy. Her gown fit her to perfection and was a glorious blend of formal and sexy. She was the most beautiful woman he'd ever seen.

His eyes darted to the stranger, who was now watching Collins.

Halfway down the aisle, the music stopped, and so did Fiona. Palmer and the guests took a collaborative inhale of breath. The song then changed to a catchy pop tune with a dance beat. Fiona did a twirl and began dancing down the aisle toward him. The attendees, all standing, clapped in time to the beat and swayed to the music. Palmer's smile turned to a laugh. The vicar took it in stride. He had probably approved the music in advance. When she reached the altar, the music and laughter quietened. She looked up at Palmer with sparkling eyes, and the ceremony began.

The rest was a blur. Vows, rings, and finally cheers when the vicar said, "I now pronounce you husband and wife!" Looking at Palmer, he said, "You may kiss the bride."

All the while, his mind was still in that shadowed corner, trapped between love and dread.

They kissed and turned to walk back down the aisle.

Palmer looked one more time. The pew was empty.

The wedding reception was held in the church hall, where Fiona first asked Palmer about his head injury. He said a doctor had examined it and assured her not to worry. She understood not to press further about what caused it, but that didn't change the look of concern on her face. He planned to wait until he undressed that night to explain the bandages on his arm and chest.

She introduced Palmer to more people than he could ever remember, including her boss, the chief of MI6. Palmer briefly spoke with the chief in coded language about the operation, and after pointing to his injury, he mentioned Reed, whom he credited with saving his life. The chief, pressed for time, left the reception after a quick congratulations to Fiona.

After cutting the cake, Palmer said quietly to Fiona, "I saw a man sitting alone in the back row of the church. He had a scar on his face and wore sunglasses. He's not at the reception. Do you know him?"

Fiona looked puzzled. "No. Should I be concerned?"

That was an excellent question, one that he was also asking himself. Why was he there? Who was he? Was he a threat to either of them? How could anyone have known Palmer was getting married, let alone where and when the ceremony was being held? Because nothing untoward had happened, he assumed it was a warning of some kind.

"Not yet," he replied. He saw the wedding gifts on a table and said, "Are we opening those now?"

"No, we'll take them home to open after our honeymoon. I want to note who gave each gift to us so that I can write thank-you cards."

Almost everyone had left. Palmer, DuPont, and Baxter were taking the wedding gifts from the church hall to the waiting limousine that would bring them to their home in Clapham. Fiona held one up and said, "This one's beautifully wrapped."

"Who's it from?" Baxter asked, walking over to take a look.

"It doesn't say. There's a gold tag that reads 'Best wishes, Jake and Fiona. Open immediately. Perishable.'"

Palmer overheard her and rushed forward, grabbing Fiona's hand as she was about to open it. "Put it down. Carefully."

"Why?"

"*Now*," Palmer replied, his voice leaving no room for argument.

Fiona set the gift on the table in a slow, deliberate motion.

Palmer called DuPont over to join Fiona and Baxter and said, "I saw a suspicious man sitting alone at the back of the church. He had a scar on his face. No one I've asked can identify him, and now there's a gift that doesn't reveal who it's from and includes instructions to open it immediately. Maybe my time on this final mission is making me overly alert and hypervigilant, but to me, this is a red flag. We need to call the police bomb squad."

"Don't you think you're overreacting?" Fiona said.

Palmer wondered the same thing. *Was* he overreacting? Was it a combination of the past few days and seeing the stranger in the church? "I might be," he said honestly.

DuPont examined the box and concluded, "I'm no explosives expert, but I'd err on the side of caution and call the police bomb squad."

Fiona called the police, stating that she worked at MI6 and had a suspicious package at the church. The person she was speaking with told them to leave the church and wait outside; the police would be there soon. She found the vicar and explained what had happened. Within minutes, the police arrived, ensured no one was still inside the church, and cordoned off the area. The bomb squad arrived right behind them.

Palmer told a member of the bomb squad, now wearing heavy armor, where the gift package was located and described it, along with the gift tag on it. After about twenty minutes, he returned with a protective case carrying a containment tube.

"Explosive. Military grade," he explained. "I've put it in the tube. We'll take care of it. I've scanned the other packages. They're okay. It's safe to take them away."

Fiona looked at Palmer in disbelief. She showed one of the investigators a list of attendees on her phone and messaged him a copy. Palmer described the scar-faced man who had sat at the back of the church during the ceremony, who had left before the wedding was over, and who was not present at the reception. The investigator also spoke with the vicar, who provided him with his contact information.

After the police left, the limousine chauffeur drove them to their home in Clapham, where they unloaded the gifts. Collins was already packed for their honeymoon and had laid out some of Palmer's clothes, along with a few pieces she had bought for him. When they arrived, he took a shower and toweled off, having explained the bandages on his arm and chest beforehand. Fiona was waiting for him, wearing only a lace camisole. They slipped into bed and made love, their first time as man and wife.

The next morning, they relocated to the Milestone Hotel in London, where she had reserved a suite. Two days later, they departed for their honeymoon in Barcelona and checked into the One Barcelona, a five-star hotel situated near the city's famous Golden Mile.

On their first night there, the concierge made a dinner reservation for them at Botafumeiro for seven o'clock. He mentioned that it was one of the few restaurants that was open all day, as most establishments typically began serving dinner much later in the evening. Securing a reservation at any time could be challenging, but he assured them that due to the hotel's reputation, he had never encountered any issues.

They entered and followed the maître d through a narrow passageway, with the bar on their left and two-person tables against the wall on their right. The walls in the passageway were decorated with photographs of movie stars, sports celebrities, and politicians who had dined there. It then expanded into a large two-level area. The restaurant was bigger than it appeared from the street, and it was bustling with activity. Overall, it was a stunning Spanish eatery.

They ordered a salad to start and split the seafood paella with lobster.

"I can't believe we're married," Fiona said as they continued to enjoy the bottle of Spanish red wine the sommelier had recommended. "It will take me a while to become accustomed to being called Mrs. Fiona Collins Palmer."

"There were times during the past few days when I wasn't sure I'd make it," Palmer blurted out. He'd said it with a little too much honesty.

Collins paused, holding her glass of wine. "To the wedding?"

"At all," he said bluntly. "It was touch and go."

Fiona reached across the table and grasped his hand. "You served your country once again, and for that, you should be proud. However, I'm excited that you've finished your two-year commitment and can now start your contract business in London, and we can begin our life together." She sat back in her chair, her voice unwavering when she said, "I worried about you constantly while you were gone."

"I'm ready for a change, too. I spoke with your chief at the reception. He wants to meet with me to discuss some opportunities for MI6 contract work."

"Nothing dangerous, Jake," she said. "I'm serious."

"I'll see what he says and talk with you about it before I commit to anything."

This didn't seem to assuage her, but she didn't appear interested in discussing it.

"We haven't heard anything from the police regarding the bomb," she said, changing the subject.

"When we get home, I'll follow up with them to see if they have any new information about the bomb or Scarface. I doubt they found any fingerprints on the device."

"I worry he'll try again. Maybe he was after the MI6 chief." Fiona paused. "Have you heard from Alona?"

"She's meeting with General Reynolds in Islamabad. He'll tell her where she'll be assigned and who her new partner will be."

"I was a little jealous of the two of you working together," she admitted, sipping her wine. "I hate that she knows more about you than I do. Where you're going, if you're safe, what you've been through—all of that is a mystery to me."

"I assure you that our relationship is strictly business. I told her we'd stay in touch. Alona said you wouldn't like her calling me . . . or us, so I promised I'd be the one to contact her."

Fiona reached across the table and grasped his hand. "That's silly. I love you and trust you. I'd love to meet her one day. Maybe she can visit us."

It wasn't so much what Fiona had said but how she'd said it. Palmer remembered Green's words: *All women are that way.* Perhaps she was right.

The night air was fresh and cool, so they decided to walk back to the hotel. Palmer said, "I keep thinking about the man at the church, who most likely planted the gift bomb. If you had opened that present, we'd be dead. The police will never find him. But he's warned us."

Fiona stopped walking. "What do you mean, *warned* us? He tried to kill us, as well as everyone around us, when I opened the gift!"

"If he truly wanted to kill us, why would he be in the church, sitting alone and wearing sunglasses? Not only do I think he wanted me to see him, but I think he wanted me to see him because it'd tip me off about the gift." He paused, swallowing hard. "The present was the warning. It wasn't meant to go off—he knew I wouldn't let it."

His wife looked at him, her expression cryptic.

"I'm afraid we're not finished with him," Palmer said. "Or that he isn't finished with us."

Fiona took his hand and continued walking down the wide tree-lined sidewalk. "Jake, let's not think about that now and put a damper on our honeymoon."

Palmer pulled her in and kissed her. "Whatever happens, we'll face it together."

EPILOGUE

Sania Reed caught an early flight the next morning from Frankfurt, Germany, to London Heathrow and took a taxi to MI6 headquarters on the Thames. Exhausted and feeling the stress of the past few days, she stopped by the restroom to wash her face and hands and to freshen up.

She reached into her small handbag for her makeup, lipstick, and comb. Within five minutes, she was as ready as she could be. Looking at her reflection in the mirror, she thought, *I look horrible, but I suppose what you see is what you get.*

She took the elevator and stopped at the desk of C's admin. "He's in a right mood today. Seeing you should cheer him up."

The chief was standing at the large window overlooking the Thames. He turned when he heard her. They met and shook hands before sitting at his conference table. "Let's talk about your mission. From what I've heard, it was a demanding and rapidly evolving assignment."

"Nothing ever goes as planned," Reed began. "This mission was proof of that. However messy it may have been, I consider it a success. We brought in two high-value Russian defectors, Sokolov and Volkov. We also sent information regarding a planned attack by the Axis of Evil, although Volkov said it was all a distraction to their move to take control of the Arctic. Navy intel was interrogating him on that issue on the USS *Kearsarge* when I left."

"You said there was a rather high body count."

"The team survived three separate attacks by FSB officers. We, along with the Finnish Utti Jaeger Regiment, killed several FSB officers during some firefights. I killed one, an assassin who was in Finland and about to kill Palmer. We put his body in the border zone so the Russians could find him. We also lost Patrick Howell, a US intelligence officer operating under diplomatic cover at the US Embassy in Moscow. Palmer, Sokolov, and I were wounded. I can go into detail on each one if you'd like."

"That's not necessary. You'll need to file an action report for my eyes only."

"Of course, sir." She paused before adding, "Only two people know that I killed the FSB officer. Neither will ever speak of it."

The chief crossed his arms and leaned back in his chair. "You've done a superb job, Sania, both as the Moscow MI6 station chief and in your performance on this challenging and critically important mission. How's your gunshot wound?"

Reed felt a wave of relief crash over her. "Healing nicely. Palmer told me that the scar would be a badge of honor, earned in service to my country."

The chief smiled. "Have it checked out by our medical staff. Oh, speaking of Mr. Palmer, I met him yesterday."

"Palmer?" Reed said with surprise in her voice. "When did you see him?"

"I attended his wedding to our analyst, Fiona Collins, yesterday afternoon in Sevenoaks Weald. They played critical roles in stopping a nuclear attack in London. Palmer was most complimentary about your performance on this operation. Said you had saved his life, but he didn't provide any details. This gives me pause, however. I'm not certain the Russians know that you were involved or what you did, but we shouldn't risk sending you back to Moscow."

"I have some thoughts on my next assignment," Reed said before he could proceed. "I believe—"

The chief interrupted before she finished her sentence. "I already have a new assignment in mind for you. Take a few days to recover while I sort out the details and get approvals."

Reed left, annoyed that she'd been given no input regarding her next assignment. She was curious about what he had in mind for her and surprised that he had attended Palmer and Fiona's wedding and had spoken with Palmer. Had Palmer said anything to him about her next assignment? Regardless, she had disobeyed the chief's orders and crossed the Russian border into Finland with Sokolov. She had killed a Russian assassin. Given what she'd been through, a few days to recover would only *begin* to take the edge off. She was likely destined for some hellhole where her career would quietly die in obscurity.

She took a taxi to a nearby hotel. Once she checked in, she put the Do Not Disturb tag on the outside doorknob, took a long, hot soaking bath, washed her hair, and crashed onto the bed.

As the chief requested, Sania Reed filed a report on her assignment to assist two American intelligence officers in extracting a high-value defector from Russia and bringing him into Finland and, ultimately, into American custody. She handed it to him the day she returned to work. The chief read it while she was sitting in his office.

"Well done, Reed. Nice report." Before she could respond, he swiveled his chair around and ran the report through the shredder beside his desk.

Reed was taken aback. After spending hours writing, editing, and revising the report, he had shredded it. *What does that mean for my next assignment?*

"I've spoken to our prime minister, as well as to those you'll be working with in your new assignment, to get their input and approval. I apologize for the delay, but the importance of the position necessitated it. As of today, you are the new MI6 liaison in Washington, DC."

—∞—

In a private ceremony at the CIA headquarters in Langley, Virginia, a star was installed on the Memorial Wall. During the ceremony, the CIA director described the stars as "a sacred constellation that inspires us to do more" and presented Howell's family with a marble replica of the star. Patrick Howell's remains were buried with full military honors at Arlington National Cemetery.

—∞—

Dmitry Sokolov recovered from his wounds, was given a new identity, and was placed under protective watch. He made an immediate positive impact on the US's hypersonic missile development program and the missile defense program within the Department of Defense. Within a year, Sokolov got married. He and his wife regularly attended the Washington National Opera at the Kennedy Center Opera House. The first opera they saw was *Aida*.

—∞—

Alexi Volkov was also given a new identity and placed under protective surveillance. He proved to be an invaluable asset for the CIA. Two years after arriving in the US, he was killed by a hit-and-run driver while crossing the street. Police found the vehicle, which had been stolen and wiped clean, but the driver was never located. However, investigators found security footage of two known Russian GRU Unit 29155 operatives arriving and leaving Dulles International Airport. The timing coincided with Volkov's death. Still, they lacked enough evidence to obtain a warrant for their arrest, even though they would never have been able to serve it. When Palmer heard the news, he remembered what Green's father had told her. *Russia never forgets.*

Green returned to the US Embassy in Islamabad and met with General Reynolds. He told her he was proud of her and Palmer's work in getting Sokolov and Volkov out of Russia and obtaining copies of the attack plan and the intel about the Arctic. "As you're aware, I'm leaving soon, too. I've discussed your next assignment with JSOC. Here are your orders." Reynolds handed her an unsealed envelope.

Short and sweet was not Reynold's typical style. *It must be bad news.* She held her orders in her hand. "Time to rip off the Band-Aid." She opened the envelope and read the document, searching for a region or city where she would go. She looked up at Reynolds, her eyes wide. "Paris!"

A couple of days later, Green was heading out the door to her apartment when her phone rang. It was a Pakistani number. On the fifth ring, she answered. "Hello?"

"I'm glad you made it home. I was worried you wouldn't get out of Russia alive."

Green's heartbeat raced as she tried to calm herself. "If it weren't for you, I wouldn't be alive."

There was a long pause before Aaliyah replied, "I wanted to kill you . . . to pay you back for the misery I've suffered since the car crash."

"Why didn't you?"

"When can I see you? I will explain then."

"Is that a good idea?" Green replied.

"I need closure, Alona. Deny it if you like, but you are the American version of me. Where's your next assignment?"

"I don't know yet," Green lied. "I'll find out soon. Have you considered working with me?"

"A double agent? You're not serious," Aaliyah huffed.

"It's the only way, Aaliyah. Otherwise, this is it. We'd make a great team. US-Pakistan relations have improved. We share common counterterrorism interests. Consider the recent US action against Ibrahim Al-Mansour and the Sunni Muslim separatist group Jaysh al-Adl in Khuzdār. That was coordinated with and sanctioned by your government."

"But you're leaving Pakistan, aren't you? Palmer's out and you're being reassigned, right?"

Green noticed the hesitation in her voice. Paris would be a dream assignment, but recruiting Aaliyah would be a victory on its own. "Aaliyah, I love Islamabad. I'll request to stay if you'll work with me."

Green convinced Reynolds and JSOC to allow her to extend her assignment in Islamabad to recruit Aaliyah as a double agent. They agreed. Three months later, Alona Green successfully recruited Aaliyah, also known as Jasmine Abdolahzadeh, as a double agent. Their relationship evolved into a strong working and personal bond over the next year, finally culminating in Green's transfer to a post in Paris.

One day Aaliyah left her a voicemail: "Alona, I need to see you urgently. Call me."

ACKNOWLEDGMENTS

Writing often feels like a lonely endeavor, and at times it is. However, many others contribute in big and small ways to bring a book to its finished form. I am thankful to everyone who has shared their time, insights, and constructive feedback. A beta reader once asked if I would be upset if they criticized something. I replied that I'd be disappointed if they didn't.

I sincerely thank my wife, Mildred, for reading and editing numerous versions of the manuscript as it evolved from a rough draft into the final publisher-ready version, often offering her valuable perspective on the appearance, dress, and dialogue of my female characters. She is truly my editor in chief.

I also appreciate the expert advice and insights I received from Navy Captain Veli-Petteri Valkamo, senior staff officer at Finland's Ministry of Defense, and from a Finnish Army officer, who was one of my beta readers and who has chosen to remain anonymous. Both provided valuable perspectives.

Lastly, I would like to thank my readers, especially those on Page Avenue who frequently see me walking our Maltese, Gracie, for their encouragement and motivation to continue writing.

Special thanks are also extended to Kathy Meis, founder and CEO of Bublish, Shilah LaCoe, Bublish project manager, and their team—especially the outstanding editors and proofreader—for their many valuable contributions to the publication of this book.

Assassin's Mace is a work of fiction, and all characters are fictional. Any resemblance to actual people, living or dead, is purely coincidental. There are two exceptions. The first is Jim DuPont, a friend since childhood in Charlotte, North Carolina, who, along with me, chased down over-the-fence baseballs at the old Charlotte Clark Griffith Park, located across the street from our homes. The second person is John Welsch, who served as a navy rescue swimmer aboard a PT (patrol torpedo) boat in the Pacific during World War II. After the war, he attended Officer Candidate School and was commissioned as a naval officer, retiring from the navy as a lieutenant commander.

AUTHOR'S BIO

Ron McManus is a multiple award-winning author of *Libido's Twist*, *The Drone Enigma*, *The Envelope*, *The Chameleon*, and *Assassin's Mace*. A native of Charlotte, North Carolina, he graduated from the University of North Carolina, where he was also a Naval ROTC midshipman. Commissioned the same day he graduated from UNC, Ron served aboard the USS *San Marcos* (LSD-25) and is a Vietnam combat veteran, having volunteered for a yearlong in country assignment there. Following his military service, he became director of Program Integrity at the North Carolina Medical Peer Review Foundation in Raleigh, where he established the state's first Medicaid fraud and abuse investigation unit.

Ron spent the majority of his professional career in research and development with a British pharmaceutical company, including an expatriate assignment in the United Kingdom. He retired as global vice president of R&D Quality and Compliance. After retirement, he studied creative writing and began attending writing conferences, while crafting a suspense and thriller novel like those he had long enjoyed reading. What began as a retirement goal to write a book, has turned into five books with multiple national and international writing awards.

Ron and his wife, Mildred, reside in Virginia Beach, Virginia, on the shore of the Chesapeake Bay.

For more information on Ron and his books, go to his website and follow him on social media.

Website: ron-mcmanus.com

Email: ronmcmanus@ron-mcmanus.com

Facebook: RonMcManusAuthor

Instagram: @ pbwritervb

www.ingramcontent.com/pod-product-compliance
Lightning Source LLC
Chambersburg PA
CBHW060517160726
47991CB00001B/67